Karin Baine lives in Northe
her husband, two sons and he
notebook collection. Her mot
grandmother's vast collection of books inspired
her love of reading and her dream of becoming
a Mills & Boon author. Now she can tell people
she has a *proper* job! You can follow Karin on X,
@karinbaine1, or visit her website for the latest
news—karinbaine.com.

Louisa Heaton lives on Hayling Island,
Hampshire, with her husband, four children and
a small zoo. She has worked in various roles in
the health industry—most recently four years
as a Community First Responder, answering
999 calls. When not writing Louisa enjoys other
creative pursuits, including reading, quilting and
patchwork—usually instead of the things she
ought to be doing!

Also by Karin Baine

Mills & Boon Medical

An American Doctor in Ireland
Midwife's One-Night Baby Surprise

Mills & Boon True Love

Pregnant Princess at the Altar
Highland Fling with Her Boss

Also by Louisa Heaton

Snowed In with the Children's Doctor
Single Mum's Alaskan Adventure
Finding Forever with the Firefighter

Yorkshire Village Vets miniseries

Bound by Their Pregnancy Surprise

Discover more at millsandboon.co.uk.

FESTIVE FLING WITH THE SURGEON

KARIN BAINE

A MISTLETOE MARRIAGE REUNION

LOUISA HEATON

MILLS & BOON

First published in Great Britain 2024
by Mills & Boon, an imprint of HarperCollins*Publishers* Ltd,
1 London Bridge Street, London, SE1 9GF

www.harpercollins.co.uk

HarperCollins*Publishers* Macken House, 39/40 Mayor Street Upper,
Dublin 1, D01 C9W8, Ireland

Special thanks and acknowledgement are given
to Karin Baine and Louisa Heaton for their contributions
to the Christmas North and South miniseries.

ISBN: 978-0-263-32173-9

10/24

This book contains FSC™ certified paper
and other controlled sources to ensure responsible forest management.

For more information visit www.harpercollins.co.uk/green.

Printed and Bound in the UK using 100% Renewable Electricity
at CPI Group (UK) Ltd, Croydon, CR0 4YY

FESTIVE FLING WITH THE SURGEON

KARIN BAINE

MILLS & BOON

For Tammy & Kieran xx

CHAPTER ONE

IF TAMSIN'S HEART beat any faster she'd soon be the one in need of a transplant. A jest in bad taste perhaps, but surgeons required a dark sense of humour to deal with the life-or-death nature of their work. Literally having the responsibility of another person's life in her hands wasn't something she took for granted, even with all her experience. Especially when it was a ten-year-old girl she'd be operating on. The same age she'd been when she'd first become ill.

She knew all too well the difference a successful medical intervention could make for a child's future when she'd gone on to live a successful and full life. However, the seriousness of potential complications was never far from her mind either. Not when her older sister was still living with the consequences of having donated bone marrow to Tamsin all those years ago when she'd suffered from acute lymphoblastic leukaemia. The very reason she'd gone into medicine in the first place—to give other children the second chance she'd been given. Even if she'd never quite managed to get past the guilt of her sister's ill health as a result.

'Hey, Oliver, I haven't seen you for a while.' She spotted the maxillofacial surgeon in the Great Southern Hospital's foyer and took the opportunity to say hello, whilst distracting herself from any dark thoughts at the same time. On the cusp of performing a kidney transplant was not the time for self-pity.

'Always busy, like yourself, Tamsin. It's good to see you, although it looks as though you won't be hanging around long enough for a catch-up.' He gave a nod towards her buttoned-up coat.

'Yes, sorry. I'm on my way to the Great Northern shortly. Just waiting for the call.'

'Transplant?'

She nodded. 'Ten-year-old patient with established renal failure.'

Oliver gave a sympathetic head-shake. 'At least they're in the best hands with you.'

'Thanks. I hope so.'

'Did you hear Lauren's coming to work here from the Great Northern?'

She had, but hadn't wanted to be indelicate by mentioning his ex-wife. Since he'd brought it up in conversation, she figured he was okay to talk about it. 'How do you feel about that?'

'Lauren is a brilliant reconstructive surgeon. We'll be lucky to have her here in London with us.'

'Very diplomatic.'

'No, really, I'm sure we'll be fine. We'll be working with Willow too, which will be nice.' Their daughter Willow was a doctor at the Great Southern too. Medicine was a real family affair for the Shaws, a difficult concept for

Tamsin to get her head around when she was so used to being on her own.

Her family was back in Northern Ireland, a short plane journey from London but one she didn't make too often these days. Work took all of her focus, keeping her busy enough that she didn't have time to think about anyone except her patients. Which didn't leave room for any sort of personal life, even if she had wanted one.

'Well, I hope things aren't too awkward for you, and maybe we'll get a proper catch-up when I'm back from Edinburgh.' As much as she would love to chat more, her patient came first, and she didn't want to be as much as a second away when they had the donor organ ready to go.

'Definitely. I'll let you go. I see Poppy Evans over there, so I'll go and bend her ear for a while.'

Tamsin waved Oliver off towards the pregnant red-headed neurosurgeon, then hurried up to the roof where the helicopter was soon ready to take her and the vital organ up to Scotland.

She exchanged pleasantries with the pilot before taking her place inside. It was hard not to get overwhelmed by the situation, not only because of the task ahead, but also regarding the journey there. No matter how many times she was rushed around the country for these important operations, she never got used to it. There was nothing natural about flying in one of these contraptions, at the mercy of the person at the controls.

She supposed that was how her patients and their families thought about the transplants, where she was the one in control of their fate. Although these organs often became available due to tragic circumstances, it was her job to make sure something good came of it. Therefore, she was under tremendous pressure to succeed, not only from the expectations of the families involved but also from herself. She already had the guilt from her own surgery and her sister's long-lasting health struggles on her conscience without adding more to her burden.

The modern building and landscaped gardens soon disappeared from sight, giving way to busy motorways and green fields once they were outside London. It seemed no time at all before the Scottish countryside came into view, the rolling hills and beautiful scenery reminding her of Northern Ireland.

As expected, once they landed on the helipad atop the Great Northern Hospital there was a flurry of activity on the cold September afternoon. Time was of the essence and it was as essential for her to be in the operating theatre as the kidney which had been transported from London too.

'The patient is prepped and waiting for you,' someone informed her, in case she wasn't already going as fast as she could.

'Let them know I'll be on my way as soon as possible.' Tamsin didn't know the names of everyone around her, but hoped someone would relay the message.

The team involved in a transplant was huge and impossible to keep track of when there were people from two different hospitals involved. As well as the surgeons performing the transplant, there were the co-ordinator, anaesthetists, nurses and the junior doctors, keen to observe. Ultimate responsibility, though, fell to the surgeons performing the operation. In this case, that was her and the Great Northern's paediatric surgeon, Max Robertson.

Usually, before a transplant she would meet the patient for a chat, as well as run final tests to make sure the patient was suitable for the transplant. It was the norm to have several patients lined up in case the recipient became ill, or some other complication arose.

In this instance, however, Dr Robertson apparently had a close relationship with the patient and had been keen to manage those things himself. It suited her, meaning they could go straight into surgery, which would take several hours. Time was a huge factor in a successful transplant. Especially when they were dealing with a deceased donor.

He was gowned up already when she arrived in the theatre. Though they hadn't worked together before, she knew him by reputation. He was loved by the children he worked with, by all accounts, though some of her colleagues had confided that they thought he was a difficult man to read when they heard she'd be working alongside him. A tall, muscular Scot with black hair and a ruddy complexion, he was certainly a striking figure. And a contrast to her almost snowy white skin and honey-coloured tresses.

'Tamsin O'Neill.' She introduced herself as she walked into the busy theatre.

'Everyone has already made introductions. We all know what we're supposed to be doing. We've just been waiting for you,' he said brusquely, as though she'd been dilly-dallying, and hadn't foregone a last-minute trip to the bathroom in order to get here as soon as possible. Something she hoped she wouldn't come to regret during the long surgery ahead.

'I came from London. With the donor organ,' she reminded him, but bit her tongue to prevent herself from saying anything more which might be construed as unprofessional.

Given what she'd heard from other people who'd worked with him, and their initial interaction when he hadn't even bothered to introduce himself, she figured they weren't going to be best buddies any time soon. Which was okay. They were here to work, and to save a life. This wasn't a social event. As long as he was as good at his job as she'd heard, she'd forgive him his apparent lack of manners.

There was little more conversation after that, leaving no room for her to get to know him any better and figure out if he was as cold as he seemed on first impression or simply feeling stressed. Even at the top of their field, it wasn't unheard of to be overwhelmed by the situation. They had a lot of people relying on them, and others hoping to learn from them.

The only talking now would be instructions given by her or Dr Robertson to the theatre team, or vocal confirmation of what they were doing during the procedure.

'Making incision above the groin.' Tamsin made the first cut.

Contrary to popular belief, the old kidneys weren't removed during a transplant. To create access to the large blood vessels at the back of the abdomen it was necessary to push the bowels aside. They had to connect the renal vein to the iliac vein and the renal artery to the iliac artery with fine sutures, every stitch counting. Often there were multiple arteries and veins to connect. Despite initial impressions, they worked well together.

'I think we can open the clamps now,' she instructed once they'd finished.

'Always a magical moment,' Max commented as blood began to flow through the transplanted kidney, showing some humanity.

She was always relieved at this time too, to see a successful outcome of their delicate work.

'I think we can close her up now,' she said, letting Dr Robertson sew the layers of abdominal wall back up.

By the time they'd finished Tamsin was tired, thirsty and her limbs were aching. Her nerves too were stretched to breaking point. Even if everything went according to plan there was always the risk of complications they hadn't accounted for, and it didn't stop when the patient was wheeled back to the recovery ward. She would have a catheter and IV fitted, and painkillers administered, with kidney function being monitored daily.

There was the high possibility of the organ being rejected, or infection, and aftercare was equally important to the patient's future health. A matter close to her own heart, when her sister's life could've been very different if her medical team had been watching things more closely.

'Good job, everyone.' Once she was as sure as she could be that the patient was stable and they'd done everything they could, she gave the team their dues, though she didn't stick around to try and make small talk with Dr Robertson when there seemed little point.

It was a surprise to find him waiting for her in the corridor after she'd scrubbed out. Even more so to see the man out of his surgical attire and without his mask. He obviously kept in shape, the soft blue cashmere sweater he was wearing clinging to his taut torso. She hadn't been able to see the dimples behind his surgical mask, and she'd got the impression in Theatre he was more of a frowner, but he was smiling at her as he lounged against the wall.

'Sorry,' he said with a sheepish look on his face which did funny things to Tamsin's insides. It was most inconvenient for him to catch her interest in something more than a he's-such-an-insufferable-grouch-I-never-want-to-see-him-again way.

'For...?' It was hard to concentrate when an apologetic alpha male was apparently her type. Not that she'd been aware she even had one when there had been such a big gap between the men in her life.

Her love life was bottom of the list when it came to her priorities. She had her work and her patients to focus on. Besides, it wouldn't have been fair for her to have settled down with a partner and kids and live happily ever after when her sister was never going to have that scenario for herself. All because of the sacrifices she'd made for Tamsin at an age when she could never have understood the consequences, or the impact they would have on the rest of her life.

It was funny how one word could change her opinion

of the man so drastically, and she wondered if that had more to do with his looks. She'd never realised she could be that shallow.

'For being so curt with you in there. I just like to get the job done, you know.'

'I know. Though it's never just a job, is it?'

'Definitely not.' He shook his head with a smile. 'I think I'm more used to being around the kids than adults.'

'Well, I hope you're more patient with them than you are with new colleagues.'

He flinched. 'Sorry. Again. I've known Ashlyn McDonald and her family for quite some time and I just didn't want to let anyone down. I guess I'm more concerned with my patients' welfare than making new friends.'

It was an admirable sentiment, she supposed. Even if she'd been the one on the receiving end of his attitude today.

'I get it. We're under pressure to save lives, and that comes before everything. But remember we're on the same team. And I'm the one who dropped everything at a moment's notice to fly over here and do the transplant. I'd also like to point out that, despite what you thought, I didn't even take time for a comfort break before I joined you.'

'I know, I know. Please forgive me.'

'I'll think about it, Dr Robertson.' She narrowed her eyes at him, unwilling to give in so easily. It wouldn't do any good for him to think he could win her over simply by fluttering his long dark eyelashes at her when they would likely be in consultation over their shared patient for some time to come.

'Please call me Max. Have you eaten? Perhaps dinner would help to smooth those feathers I clearly ruffled.' He was almost like a different person outside of the operating theatre and though she was still a little bruised by their original encounter he seemed to genuinely want to make amends.

He likely had been totally consumed by thoughts of the task ahead at the time and now was able to relax, something she could appreciate. In her time, she'd met some surgeons who were blasé about their work, who no longer seemed to connect the patients lying at their mercy on the operating table with real people who had families and lives outside the hospital depending on the outcome of the surgery. To find someone who understood her work, and the importance of compassion for the patients, was potent.

Perhaps he really didn't have any real friends if he was prepared to hang out with someone he barely knew, or tolerated, up until now. Or, just maybe, he was the kind of man who wasn't averse to hooking up with passing female surgeons, and that was why he was keen to make amends.

A little shiver danced its fingertips along the back of her neck at the prospect. Although she didn't go in for romantic relationships or one-night stands usually, neither had she taken a vow of chastity. Though it would take more than just a pretty face to do something reckless like spend the night with a colleague she'd just met.

'I haven't even checked into my hotel yet, and dinner is usually provided along with accommodation on my travelling expenses.' There had to be some perks when she spent most of her life either travelling to or working in hospitals where her skills were needed most. Although it was rewarding to see her patients get another chance at life, a little pampering after a long day in Theatre was always appreciated.

'Do you need a lift? I have my car here.' He levered himself off the wall, ready to go when she gave the nod. It was her decision whether or not to end things here and now, or see where the night led.

Tamsin wondered if that idea of a well-deserved treat could extend to an evening with a handsome Scot…

Then she remembered she was in Edinburgh to do a job, and that didn't finish when she left the operating theatre. 'I'll probably have to get a taxi. I want to check in on the patient and make sure there's adequate aftercare in place before I leave.'

'Of course. I'll come with you, then we can go get something to eat after.' He started off down the corridor and held the door open so she could walk ahead of him.

It was possible that everyone had Max wrong, and even more possible that she wasn't going to have a bath and an early night like she usually did on these work trips.

'If there are any complications at all, let me know and I can fly straight back over.' Tamsin was talking to the nurse keeping watch over their patient. She'd already gone through all of the test results and observations since being in the recovery ward, making sure everything was going as well as it should after such a big operation.

It was clear she cared for her patients and it was more than just a job to her. She wasn't the hotshot, arrogant blow-in from London that Max had supposed her to be, like some others he'd met in his time. The warm Northern Irish accent had taken him by surprise, as had her interest in their patient's aftercare. Tamsin was obviously someone who cared, and whose duty went beyond the operating theatre. He had a lot of respect for that when the children he worked with meant so much to him too.

With his own childhood consisting of a series of foster homes and adults who'd lied to him, he had a natural distrust of people. He was able to relate to the kids he worked with better. They didn't make promises they couldn't keep or expect any sort of emotional commitment from him. They were the only ones he ever let get close.

He'd slipped up once, imagined he'd had a future with Mairi, who he'd met on his first hospital placement. Only for her to cheat on him, breaking his trust as well as his heart. So he'd kept himself emotionally unavailable when it came to relationships.

Which made his decision to ask Tamsin for dinner tonight all the more out of character. He wasn't a monk by any means, but it wasn't the norm for him to go out with a colleague. Though, strictly speaking, after they left the hospital she was no longer a colleague, when London was her home and place of work.

Perhaps that was why he'd let his defences down a fraction and could admit to himself that he liked her. She was passionate, not only in her work but in defence of herself when he'd been less than courteous with his welcome. Most importantly, she wasn't going to be here tomorrow for him to get caught up in any sort of serious commitment. If she was even thinking about him that way…

For now, it might be nice simply to have some company for dinner. They seemed to have a lot in common and she didn't seem impressed or intimidated by him, like some. He wouldn't have to put a special effort into trying to be someone he wasn't. If she didn't like who he was, or accept his apology, she wouldn't have agreed to dinner in the first place.

'You know I'll be here to follow things up,' he reminded her as she fretted over leaving the hospital.

'I know. I just want to make sure nothing is left to chance. If there are any complications at all…'

'I'll be on it. I care every bit as much as you do, Tamsin,' he said softly. He was equally as conscientious when it came to patient aftercare, but he appreciated her commitment.

She nodded and finally appeared to accept leaving the patient in the hands of the team at the Great Northern. 'I'll just grab my overnight bag and I'll be right with you.'

Max waited whilst she retrieved her things from the locker room, watching the sway of her hips in her tight jeans. There was no question she was beautiful, but there was a lot more to her, and Max almost wished he had more time to get to know her.

He understood her apparent need to have control, wanting to be involved in every step of her patient's care. After a lifetime of being passed around the care system, at the mercy of other people, he too liked to keep a tight rein on what happened in his life these days. Though he knew nothing of Tamsin's background, it was clear they had a similar attitude to life and work.

'Ready?' he asked when she returned, carrying her bag and coat.

She paused to study him for a moment before answering. 'You know, I usually just hole up in a hotel room after one of these. And I never accept a dinner invitation from surgeons I just met. You're privileged.'

With a toss of her hair, she sashayed down the corridor.

'Don't I know it,' he whispered under his breath.

CHAPTER TWO

'I'M AFRAID THE restaurant is closed for the night. Perhaps we could send up some sandwiches or cold salads to your room.' The male receptionist at the hotel desk was very apologetic when they enquired about dinner.

Tamsin had been allocated a nice high-end hotel for her stay, with art deco style mirrors on every wall, monochrome tiled floor and sultry black and gold décor. He would've expected such an establishment to be able to rustle up a couple of hot meals for their residents, and probably would've complained if he'd been on his own. However, it had been a long day, he was with a colleague and he wasn't looking for a confrontation.

Max looked at his watch and frowned. 'I hadn't realised it was that late. I should probably go and let you get settled for the night.'

He got ready to leave. If he was lucky, he might be able to pick up something to eat from the garage on the way home. Although eating a soggy sandwich which had been sitting in the fridge all day, alone in his car, wasn't on a par with dinner in Tamsin's company.

He felt her hand on his arm. 'There's no need to go. Sandwiches will be fine, thank you.'

Tamsin took the keycard for the room and linked her arm through Max's. 'We're tired, we're hungry, and we saved a life today. I think we deserve something to eat.'

Although his stomach was complaining about the lack of food, Max was concerned that going to her hotel room might look as though it was about more than dinner. She was smiling up at him, her eyes twinkling, and he realised he would be okay with that if she was.

'Are you sure?'

She fixed him with a determined stare. 'Yes.'

And, just like that, Max found himself following her to the lift. Once they stepped inside, the mood between them seemed to change. As though there was some unwritten agreement that by accompanying her to her room they were moving into dangerous territory.

It had been a while since he'd been with anyone, and relationships had been few and far between for Max. Trusting didn't come easy for him, and it often caused a rift in the relationship when he couldn't give himself completely to the other person. This would be different though. Tamsin wasn't expecting anything, and if something did happen between them it would be a one-off when she was leaving in the morning.

He reached across her to push the button for the third floor and heard her take in a shaky breath. She was looking at him in a way that suggested she might see him as something other than a colleague. It was more than an ego boost to have a beautiful woman show an interest in him, it was permission. Max's gaze dropped to her parted lips and the hunger inside him was no longer confined to his belly. He dipped his head and captured her mouth with his in a kiss that was as adrenaline-fuelled as their time in the operating theatre.

Perhaps that was what this was—a release for all of that pent-up energy they'd worked up during surgery. It didn't seem to matter what the reason was as they clung together in a passionate embrace. Tamsin slid her arms around his neck and he pulled her closer with one hand around her waist, crushing their bodies and mouths together. He was breathless, his mind buzzing, every part of him revitalised by the taste and feel of her against him.

Unfortunately, the ding of the lift as they reached their floor brought the moment to a close and Max reluctantly ended the kiss.

'I think this is where we get off,' he said with a grin, taking her by the hand and leading her to the room.

'Should I cancel room service?' Tamsin turned to face him before she opened the door, as though she was giving them one last chance to call this off. They both knew now that once they went into that room all pretence was off that this was still about dinner.

His head said to cut and run, but it was being silenced by every other part of his body which desperately wanted to take the next step with Tamsin. For once, he wanted to let go of the fear of getting close to someone and simply enjoy the moment. As long as there were no repercussions or recriminations in the cold light of day.

'It's entirely up to you, Tamsin. We both know what's going to happen if I go into that room with you, but I'm not in the market for anything more than one night.'

'Me neither. But I'm hoping we'll work up an appetite for that room service…' She opened the door with a nudge of her hip, and a clear message for Max that they were on the same page.

He happily followed her in, closing the door behind him. In the confined space, the awareness of what was about to happen zinging between them, the atmosphere was electric, intense, both waiting for the next move to trigger the explosion of chemistry just waiting to happen.

Max couldn't be sure who made the first move, but suddenly they were on each other, picking up where they'd left off in the lift. Mouths mashed together, hands tugging at one another's clothes, lust took over common sense.

He knew they probably shouldn't be doing this, that sleeping with a colleague was probably a mistake, but in that moment he didn't care. For one night he wanted to act on instinct instead of overanalysing everything and everyone. To enjoy himself without worrying that some catastrophe was going to befall him.

When he felt Tamsin's hands on his now bare chest, her lips kissing their way along his neck, there was no way he was going to talk himself out of this. Especially when she was standing before him in nothing but a few scraps of black underwear.

A knock on the door heralded the arrival of their food, and a potential interruption in the evening's much anticipated events.

'Leave it outside,' he barked.

Tamsin giggled close to his ear and the endearing sound only made him want her more.

Blood pounding in his ears, passion throbbing in his veins, Max was lost to his impulses. To the moment. To Tamsin.

Every kiss, every touch, only drove him further away from his usual caution, his partner adding more fuel to the fire inside him when she pulled him towards the bed, and down on top of her. Max was acutely aware of her full breasts pressed enticingly against his chest, and the lacy barrier between their bodies didn't stay there for long. He whipped her bra away so he could better enjoy the feel of her softness in his palms and her nipples harden at the flick of his tongue.

Tamsin squirmed beneath him and he captured her little moan of pleasure with his mouth. She caught him by surprise when she boldly returned his kiss, seeking his tongue with hers. With the knowledge that she was as turned on as he was, Max divested them both of the last of their underwear. With his erection pressed close to her heat, it took all the strength he had to move away and sheath himself with a condom. At least he had one tiny shred of common sense left to make sure he had no reason to regret his actions tonight.

He wanted to take his time, to relish every second of this unexpected tryst when he knew it was unlikely he'd ever see Tamsin again. Indeed, that was the only reason he'd given in to temptation. The idea that this was a meaningless one-night stand gave him permission to let down his usual guard and simply enjoy himself. Without the fear that his partner would let him down in some way, betray his trust, or expect too much from him in return. This was purely about sex. Need and satisfaction. A matter Tamsin reminded him of as she grabbed his backside with both hands and ground herself against his erection. And, well, he wasn't a saint.

He sank into her, drawing a gasp from both of them. It took a moment for him to retrieve a coherent thought, long enough for Tamsin to relax again after that first connection. He hadn't been with anyone for a while and he wondered if it was the same for her, having to get used to sharing her body with someone else again. An act of trust he ironically could only manage with someone he knew he'd never see again.

Max wondered if he'd ever be able to get close to anyone emotionally, or have a meaningful long-term relationship.

Then Tamsin tightened around him, kissed him deeply, and nothing else mattered except tonight.

Tamsin didn't know how they'd ended up here but she was enjoying every moment with Max. Probably because she knew this wouldn't last beyond tonight. She didn't have to worry about anyone getting hurt or expecting more than she was able to give. Work came first. It was the only thing she could commit herself to. That was why this—Max—had been a pleasant surprise. She'd come to Edinburgh to do her job, never expecting to meet anyone, much less spend the night with a fellow surgeon.

However, she'd done what she'd come to do. The transplant so far had been a success, so why shouldn't she have a little fun? This felt like a reward for a job well done, and she wished she treated herself more often. Max was making her feel so good.

Those strong, capable hands she'd seen working in the theatre were now on her body. Kneading her breasts, gripping her hips so he could drive deeper inside her… The rest of her thoughts were obliterated in a burst of bright light exploding behind her eyes as pleasure overwhelmed her senses.

Their bodies rocked together, and for once Tamsin focused on her own satisfaction. She rode that crest of bliss until the wave broke and euphoria completely consumed her. Max followed soon after, echoing her cry of release, and reflecting her subsequent satisfied grin.

It was only when they were lying side by side on the bed, fighting to breathe again, that doubts about what they'd just done began to surface in her mind. Not because she hadn't enjoyed herself, but through the fear that she'd liked it a bit too much. On the rare occasion she did meet someone, she didn't hang around for long once her physical needs had been met. So when he turned as if to cuddle into her she panicked.

The affectionate gesture seemed to her a symbol of emotional attachment, setting off alarm bells that he was expecting more than a purely physical connection from her, not helped by the fact she was tempted to turn into that embrace and keep him there until morning too. That didn't tally with the idea of a one-night stand, or her casual attitude to relationships in general.

Perhaps it was because she knew how important his work and his patients were to him, that he was someone she could relate to, in and out of the bedroom, that had prompted this unwelcome urge to let him stay. Whatever it was, she couldn't afford to indulge the fantasy. It was dangerous territory for someone who rebelled against the very idea of commitment.

Tamsin stretched and forced a yawn. 'That was amazing, but I have to leave early tomorrow.'

Max turned to look at her and the incredulity in his eyes shamed her. 'You want me to go? Now?'

'Yeah. Sorry. I mean, this was never going to have been anything more than just sex. Don't feel bad about it.' She smiled though she was the one dying inside about how this was ending. This way, though, would ensure there was no doubt that it was a one-off, with no room for a repeat performance. No matter what her body was already craving.

'Huh.' Max shook his head and slipped out of bed. 'And I thought I was the one with commitment issues,' he mumbled, pulling on his trousers.

'Sorry. I just don't want things to get awkward, you know.' Something she wasn't managing successfully judging by the changed atmosphere in the room.

'Sure. I get the message. Well, thanks for everything, I guess.' He shrugged on his shirt and, without stopping to fasten the buttons, grabbed his shoes and headed for the door.

Tamsin guessed she'd wounded his male pride by being the one to call it a night and effectively asking him to leave, but it was purely to save herself. The last thing she needed in her life was a long-distance relationship when she had so many other commitments. She threw her head back onto the pillows, feeling a sense of relief when he walked out of the door.

At least until he came back in carrying the food they'd ordered. 'You need to eat. Keep your strength up for your next lifesaving mission.'

He threw her a lopsided smile that made her ache for the man who was thinking about her health even now. For the person she might have had in her life if she wasn't completely devoted to her job and her patients, making up for what it had cost her sister.

CHAPTER THREE

Two months later

'AFTERCARE OF A transplant is just as important, if not more so, as the actual surgery itself. The risk of complications, infection and rejection of the organ are all factors which must be considered in the patient's treatment. The job of a transplant surgeon does not begin and end at the theatre door. It's a commitment which requires patient monitoring long-term. Not a tick list which can be completed in a few follow-up appointments.' Tamsin paused her lecture to take a sip of water. Her mouth was dry, her skin clammy, and every nerve-ending was on high alert.

She'd never expected to be back in the Great Northern so soon after she'd hooked up with Max. It was especially odd seeing the Christmas decorations already up in November, the trees and lights in every department making it feel even more like a different world. However, she hadn't been left much choice in the matter when the transplant surgeon who was supposed to be doing this training talk had pulled out at the last minute due to an unfortunate bout of food poisoning. Usually, she didn't get flustered by public speaking, but she was on the constant lookout for the surgeon she'd thrown out of her hotel room only a matter of weeks ago.

She cringed at the memory. It wasn't her usual style to be so cold, but she'd been afraid of leaving the door open for anything more than a one-night stand and figured that kind of behaviour would make sure it was firmly closed. Now, with the prospect of having to face him again, she was mortified by the way the night had ended.

In hindsight, it hadn't been a great move. Their paths were always going to have crossed at some point, especially when they had a shared patient. It hadn't been easy avoiding him and checking up on the child they'd operated on together. She'd had to go through a third party but, by all accounts, Ashlyn had been responding well, with no complications so far. It meant Tamsin's assistance hadn't been required back here for further treatment, but now her luck had finally run out. She didn't have the benefit of time and distance to fade the memory for either of them.

Unless working in a specialised transplant centre, surgeons like her didn't have the luxury of working solely in their own field. She was often required in general surgery, or called out at a moment's notice for transplants where she was needed. Right now, she was needed to mentor other doctors and assist in general surgery until Christmas at the Great Northern. The best she could hope for was to complete this assignment and get out of Edinburgh before she ran into Max again.

Apart from anything else, she wasn't sure she could deal with the feelings, other than embarrassment, that seeing him would conjure up. It wasn't as though she'd forgotten a single hot moment of their time together. Going back to work, trying to forget that she was a red-blooded woman again to focus on other people's needs, hadn't been easy. Max had awakened something in her. A desire for something more in her life that she knew she couldn't have. Relationships weren't something she had room for, or deserved. Not when her sister had been denied so much because of her.

'Are there any questions?' Tamsin asked to distract herself from her thoughts, before she spiralled too far into the guilt she carried because of the debt she owed her sister. One that could never be repaid, no matter how hard she tried.

Giving bone marrow these days was a relatively safe procedure. However, over twenty years ago, when Emily had donated to save Tamsin's life, things hadn't been so straightforward. Emily had suffered a sacral nerve root injury during bone marrow harvesting, an extremely rare occurrence, which was partially why her ailments following the procedure probably weren't taken seriously enough at the time. Negligence in her aftercare had caused the long-lasting damage. Though their parents had persisted in trying to get medical staff to take their concerns seriously, they'd been dismissed as overprotective, Emily's pain treated as nothing out of the ordinary to be concerned over.

By the time they'd realised painkillers simply weren't enough, over eighteen months later, she had permanently lost some function in her hips and legs, leaving her with little control over her bowels or bladder too, and with little chance of being able to have children.

Now, with the eager faces of junior doctors staring back at her, keen to make a name for themselves, Tamsin wanted to make sure it would never happen to anyone else.

She never had to worry about lack of interest in these lectures when so many newly qualified medics were ambitious about their futures, as yet unjaded by the long hours and underappreciation for their skills. No doubt all fired up by their placements, at some point they'd been intrigued about this field of expertise as she had been, looking at surgery as a puzzle to be solved, never leaving room for boredom or complacency.

'What is the success rate for transplant surgery?' one bespectacled, serious-looking young man enquired. There were some, usually management, who were only interested in figures and statistics where they wouldn't want to associate themselves with any potential failure, but transplant surgery was about more than glory hunting. It was about the patients and the possibility of giving them normal lives. Tamsin would rather take the risk of potentially not succeeding than never trying. In most cases the alternative was a death sentence anyway without intervention, and she did everything she could to ensure a positive outcome for all involved.

'Like any surgery, it comes with risks. More so than most. And it depends on many factors, such as the medical history, age, and which organ is being transplanted. Roughly, a third of organ transplants are lost to organ rejection, but success rates are improving all the time with advancing techniques. A recent study showed that ninety percent of transplant patients live for a year after surgery, and seventy percent live for at least five years following a transplant.' These figures seemed to satisfy the young man, who nodded and jotted down some notes.

'How did you get into the profession? What spurred you on to work in this field?' an equally studious woman asked Tamsin, going beyond the usual qualifications it required to get to this stage in a medical career.

It wasn't something she was usually asked, and she wasn't really prepared for such a personal question. As a result, she didn't have time to concoct a story which didn't hurt so much to recount.

She had no choice but to dig deep and be honest about her motivation. The one consolation she had about opening up about her painful past was that it might inspire at least one person here to follow in her footsteps. Every transplant surgeon meant potential lives saved, and that was what she lived for.

Max ducked his head as he slipped into the room behind the adoring crowd gathered to hear the transplant specialist speak today. He'd hoped to get here sooner but he'd been held up with a patient. Although a surgeon himself, it was always good to hear about someone else's experience, and gain as much knowledge as possible to help with future cases. Being involved with transplant surgery was new to him, but very rewarding. He really had gone on a journey with his ten-year-old patient, one that was never straightforward and would continue for the foreseeable future, forging a more intimate connection, not only with the patient but their family too.

Of course, his new interest in that area might have had something to do with the surgeon he'd worked alongside last time too. Despite her abrupt dismissal that night, he hadn't been able to get her out of his mind since.

It had been an unexpected development between them, but a passionate one. Max couldn't shake off the time they'd spent together as easily as some encounters he'd had in the past. He'd put it down to the fact they'd worked together on a very important, complex surgery. If he was honest, he had hoped that he would at least get to speak to her again when they had a shared patient, but so far Tamsin had kept her distance. She was simply a one-night stand after all and he'd have to get used to that idea, instead of imagining he could hear her voice as he took his seat.

'I suppose my interest started when I was a child…'

Max looked up to discover it hadn't been his imagination after all and Tamsin really was standing at the front of the room speaking to the assembled group. She didn't appear to have noticed him coming in so he sank down in his chair as much as his six-foot frame would allow. It almost felt voyeuristic to watch her, knowing she hadn't spotted him, but it gave him an opportunity to appreciate her beauty without appearing like a creep.

She was in formalwear today, her smart white blouse and navy trouser suit very different to the scrubs she'd been wearing the first time they'd met. His mind drifted then to the last time he'd seen her. Naked. In bed.

Max shifted in his seat, physically and mentally uncomfortable with conjuring that particular image. Tamsin was clearly here in a professional capacity, a replacement for the speaker he'd thought he was coming to listen to. She deserved more respect than him simply ogling her.

Tamsin cleared her throat. 'I had a bone marrow transplant when I was a child. Acute lymphoblastic leukaemia. My older sister was the donor and, unfortunately, her aftercare was somewhat lacking. As a result, I'm afraid to say her quality of life has suffered. She has many ongoing health issues which meant that her selfless act for me, which gave me a second chance at life, cost her her own future.'

Max heard the catch in Tamsin's voice as she spoke of her personal experience, which had obviously had a huge impact on her and her family. He would never have guessed she'd been through so much. Even now she wasn't making a big deal of it, but she would have gone through chemotherapy, along with other serious procedures—not easy for anyone to go through, never mind a child. Though her determination, nor her strength, in getting this far in life in spite of it didn't surprise him. In the short time they'd had together, they were qualities that shone brightly.

The limited information about her background also explained so much about why Tamsin was so passionate about her work and her patients. Clearly, the lack of support and care her sister had received affected how she approached her own work. It must have been extremely difficult living with the knowledge that her sister's plight could have been avoided if proper aftercare had been given by those medical staff involved at the time. Whilst he was glad Tamsin had survived, he felt for the family that they had continued to suffer as a result of possible medical negligence.

He admired her strength in overcoming her own health issues to be where she was today, making such a difference to other patients. Even now, she was setting aside the hurt she clearly still felt at what had happened to her family, to explain her journey as a transplant surgeon, probably in the hope it would inspire someone else to follow in her footsteps.

'How do you avoid becoming too emotionally attached to your patients?' someone in the front row asked.

Tamsin smiled. 'Honestly, if that's something you think is possible then this probably isn't the right road for you to take. Transplant surgery by its very nature is emotional. Patients and families need their doctors and surgeons, and everyone involved, to understand they're more than paperwork. You need empathy and compassion for this job. It doesn't make you a lesser professional if you become attached to people whose lives are literally in your hands. It simply means you're human. And patients need to feel that. They need to know what's happening every step of the way so they can feel comfortable with you—someone who is going to be in their lives for a very long time…'

Max knew the second she spotted him. Her eyes widened, her mouth dropped open and she appeared to lose her train of thought.

'I...er...' She fumbled with the papers in front of her, as though she'd lost her place.

'And are you fully recovered?' someone tentatively asked from the front row.

Max didn't miss the glance she flicked at him before answering, making him feel as if he was intruding, that she didn't want him to hear such personal information. But he was as invested as everyone else in her story.

Tamsin focused her attention back on the people nearest to her and her worried frown transformed into a smile. 'Yes, thank you. Because of my sister, I'm leading a normal, full life.'

Perhaps it was Max's imagination but he could've sworn he saw her flinch when she said that, as though it caused her physical pain to say it. He assumed it was something akin to survivor's guilt, which prevented her from fully enjoying the second chance she'd apparently been given when her sister had suffered as a result of her generosity. Though, from what he gathered, Tamsin had devoted her life to others, not leaving room for a personal life beyond a passionate hook-up in a hotel every now and then.

Even thinking of himself as one of those faceless men she might meet up with when the need took hold left a bitter taste in his mouth. Certainly, she'd treated him as something disposable when they'd parted. Now she was back in Edinburgh he had a million questions, and feelings, he suddenly wanted to work through.

'That's my time up for now, but if anyone has any questions for me I'll stick around for a while.' Tamsin began to pack up her stuff. She didn't look at Max again and he got the impression she'd be gone as soon as possible. If he wanted to speak to her, he'd have to make a move soon.

Unfortunately, as he got up and made his way down the stairs a crowd had already gathered around her. Any conversation he might have with Tamsin needed to be private so he had no other choice but to take a seat near the front of the auditorium and wait his turn.

She kept her focus on those asking her questions, engaged with them whilst studiously ignoring him, though there was a tension in her shoulders which suggested she wasn't totally unaffected by his presence. It gave him some satisfaction to know that she hadn't forgotten their time together, and perhaps wasn't as casual about it as she'd seemed at the time.

For some reason this woman had got under his skin. It wasn't an ego thing, because if he'd been that bruised by her practically shoving him out of the hotel room that night he wouldn't be sitting here now in the hope of getting more time with her.

Eventually, the crowd dwindled until it was just the two of them left and she couldn't ignore his presence any longer.

'Dr Robertson, I hadn't expected to see you here.'

Given her formal use of his name, he suspected she had hoped their paths wouldn't cross. This was her way of getting those boundaries back in place, using their professional relationship as an excuse for some distance from their night together. It was galling at first that it was so easy to dismiss what had happened between them. Another rejection. However, he soon realised that it was probably for the best when he didn't have room in his life for romantic complications anyway.

'Nor I you.' After all, she'd successfully avoided any contact with him since September.

She shrugged as she tucked her papers into her bag, looking as though she was preparing to flee as soon as possible. 'A last-minute replacement.'

That explained her unexpected appearance. Chances were she hadn't wanted to come at all if it meant a possibility of running into him. Then again, perhaps he was thinking too much of himself. He clearly hadn't been a big part of her life, and Tamsin's focus was on her job and her patients. If there was a chance for her to make a difference, he already knew she was the kind of woman who would never say no to the opportunity.

'I see. I thought perhaps you'd adopted another identity in order to avoid me.' He attempted to make a joke to cover the awkwardness which seemed to be engulfing them—a completely different atmosphere from the heated encounter in her hotel room. If anything, it was decidedly cool between them today.

Especially when Tamsin narrowed her eyes at him.

'Work is more important to me than the possibility of running into someone I shared a bed with one time. I'm a professional, Dr Robertson, and what we had is a separate issue. If I'd known you didn't understand that we'd never have got together.'

Ouch. He didn't remember her being so abrupt. Except for her goodbye, of course.

'As it turns out, I'd like to speak to you about our shared patient. I haven't had a chance to update you on progress.' It was partly true. There wasn't anything he couldn't handle on his own, and anything serious would've been relayed to her. In which case, she would have been on the first flight out to deal with things herself, he was sure. However, it would be remiss of him not to get her input while she was here in Edinburgh.

Tamsin abandoned the paperwork which had been holding her attention to look at him. 'Is something wrong? You should have contacted me earlier.'

He suddenly felt bad for making her think there was something serious she should be concerned about, simply because he wanted to spend more time with her.

'Nothing we wouldn't expect at this stage, but you're more experienced in these matters. I just thought perhaps it would be good to have a chat about it, since I haven't managed to get hold of you on the phone.'

Okay, so that was a low blow, and it made her wince.

'I thought things might get a bit awkward between us.'

'I know how to separate my private and professional life.' Although it didn't mean she hadn't been constantly on his mind…

'Sorry. I just didn't want there to be any misunderstanding that we were going to have anything more than one night together.'

Now it was Max's turn to feel as though he'd been gut punched with the reminder.

'I think you made that pretty clear when you threw me out of your hotel room.'

'I am sorry about that. Look, I have to be out of here.' She checked her watch. 'I have a meeting with the board, but if you want to have a chat about our patient I could meet you for dinner or a drink later at the hotel. Strictly business,' Tamsin said with a twinkle.

'Of course. I'll see you about eight?' He should have declined, arranged something on more neutral and public ground, but Max found he couldn't resist her invitation.

'That's great. Same hotel as last time. They do a good salad, by the way, but I'll make sure they're still doing food at that time before you come over.' She gave him a wry smile before she walked away.

The reference to their last night together wasn't lost on Max. In fact, it conjured up all sorts of inappropriate images for someone who'd sworn to keep things strictly professional.

CHAPTER FOUR

'HOW LONG ARE you going to be here?' Max asked as he sawed into his steak, medium rare.

Tamsin had settled for grilled chicken on a bed of Mediterranean-style couscous, something light for her anxious stomach, which had been in turmoil since spotting him in that lecture hall.

She'd known it was always going to be a possibility, an inevitability if she was realistic, that they would cross paths again. Perhaps, subconsciously, that was why she'd agreed to come here. Max Robertson was the first man in a long time who'd really captured her interest beyond one night. Even though she had sent him packing, it didn't mean the memories of being with him had been as easily dismissed.

'Until the New Year. I'm hoping to give some practical lessons as well as spilling my guts about my childhood issues.' She swallowed down her embarrassment with a mouthful of white wine.

The question about her own motivations had thrown her. She'd never expected to share details about her personal experiences as a donor recipient, certainly not in front of Max. Opening up about her personal issues in front of him like that somehow seemed more intimate than their night together. It blurred those emotional boundaries she had set when it came to relationships.

Things were never going to have been straightforward when they had to work together. Relegating Max to the role of a faceless one-night stand was impossible, not least because she found she still wanted to be in his company outside of work. Whatever they had to say to one another could've been done somewhere on hospital grounds at another point in her stay, but she'd used it as an excuse to spend another evening with him. The bigger surprise, given how she'd left things with Max, was that he'd agreed to this.

She'd clearly dented his ego with how they'd parted first time around. He'd made it known he wasn't into serious relationships either, so she couldn't help but wonder why he'd come here tonight. Did he like her too, or did he want to see her squirm again?

'Yes, I was surprised to find out you'd been a recipient yourself. You never said anything.' He stopped eating and held her gaze intently with those deep brown eyes. Tamsin had never felt so seen. It wasn't a comfortable position for her to be in when she'd spent her life trying to avoid anyone seeing past that successful, professional façade to find the scared child within.

'It's not something I generally shout about. But I wanted to be honest with the person who asked the question about why I got involved in transplant surgery. I know the difference it can make to lives, and how important follow-up treatment is. When aftercare isn't sufficient it can ruin the lives of those who made the ultimate sacrifice in donating organs to those who need them, along with their families.'

There was a good reason she didn't talk about her childhood. It filled her with unwanted emotions and memories it was hard to shake off. Guilt, powerlessness, and an urge to curl up into a foetal position and cry. They'd been such difficult times, and still were for her family, that it was easier for her to try to push it all from her mind. When she was working there wasn't time to dwell on those things, and it was easier to pretend none of it had happened than deal with the ongoing trauma stemming from her transplant. Physically, she had moved on, but emotionally she was stunted by it. Which was infinitely better than the hand her sister had been dealt: a lifetime of pain and suffering as a result of the action their parents had forced her to take.

'I'm sure it must've been difficult for all of you at the time.'

That was an understatement. The tears, the sleepless nights, the guilt both she and her parents had taken on their shoulders had weighed heavily. It still did.

'I've tried to turn it into something positive, using my second chance at life to help others, even though there is nothing I can do to improve my sister's lot.' It was a constant source of pain for her that she was helpless when it came to her own family member's quality of life. Perhaps that was why she'd moved so far away from them all, hoping that the distance would somehow ease the guilt.

All it had succeeded in doing was isolating her further from her family.

'There's only so much one person can do, Tamsin. Don't be so hard on yourself.'

Easier said than done in the circumstances.

'Anyway, now you know.' It wasn't something she liked talking about because of the emotions it brought back to the surface. Very few friends and colleagues knew her background, and even fewer of her past partners were aware of her medical history. It was a part of her she was ashamed of, because in giving her life, her sister had lost the quality of hers.

Sharing such personal information left her vulnerable, and she was already feeling off-kilter by the fact that her most recent one-night stand was sitting right in front of her. She didn't need him being sympathetic and understanding about her difficult childhood. That was not in keeping with the nature of a casual one-night stand. Neither was liking the man enough to invite him to another evening together, but here they were…

'You were a sick child, and I'm sure your parents and everyone else only wanted what was best for you. No one was to know that your sister would be negatively impacted long-term by the donation.' His voice was soft, his eyes kind and his words sincere.

It wasn't anything she hadn't told herself before and she wanted to believe it, but that overwhelming burden of guilt wouldn't let her. Tamsin appreciated his support, something she hadn't experienced outside of the workplace for some time, probably because she didn't let anyone get close enough to find out the details of her personal life like this. It was a new territory she wasn't completely happy to enter into.

Tamsin took another sip of her wine and moved the subject away from her painful personal issues. 'So, now you know why I got into transplant surgery. It's only fair you tell me how you got into medicine.'

She saw a dark cloud briefly move across his face, telling her it was a touchy subject for him too. He always seemed so in control it was comforting to see that he was human after all. That he might just have some personal issues of his own.

He took a moment, and a swig of wine, before he answered. 'Why do we all go into it? To help people.'

Tamsin narrowed her eyes at him over the rim of her glass. 'Hmm…not buying it. I mean, yes, that's obviously part of it, but there's always something in the background pushing us towards this profession.'

Plus, she wanted to know that she wasn't the only one driven by a less altruistic motive. A conscience. A desire to make amends. A need to pay back into society. Something she could relate to which made her feel like less of a bad person.

Max gave a half smile. 'I can tell you I went into paediatrics because I genuinely wanted to help children. Does that count?'

'Why children in particular, though?' She kept digging, hoping to find out something more about the man who'd threatened her peace of mind these past weeks. Tamsin wanted to know what it was about him that got under her skin. What made him different to the men she'd walked away from and hadn't given a second thought to.

He took his time masticating the chunky chips he'd popped into his mouth, presumably so he could give her another politician's answer which gave nothing away.

'I guess I relate to them more. I'm a big kid at heart.' His smile this time was genuine, lighting up his whole face as he talked about his young patients.

Certainly, Tamsin had heard from his colleagues how much the children loved him. Perhaps more so than the staff. She'd seen firsthand how frosty he could be when he was focused on his work. It was apparent that, like her, his patients' welfare came first. He wasn't in the profession to make friends, which made their connection all the more remarkable, not least because he'd been willing to talk to her again after the way she'd left things with him the last time she'd been in the city.

'They seem to like you. Though I have to say on our first meet I found you a tad intimidating.'

'Really? It didn't show. And, as I recall, you seemed quite happy with me later on that day.' There was no mistaking what he was referencing as his eyes darkened and his voice dropped to a husky tone only meant for her ears.

That tingling sensation of sexual awareness danced across her skin as she recalled just how happy, how satisfied, she'd been by the end of that night. It wasn't fair of him to use that to change the subject. Especially when she couldn't get it out of her head. It didn't help when he lifted a piece of steak with his fingers and, after eating it, proceeding to suck the grease from his fingers. Those lips, that tongue, had left imprints on her body she hadn't been able to erase. Now she wanted it to be her he was devouring again.

Tamsin cleared her throat, trying to block out the lust that was coursing through every part of her body and threatening to erase all rational thought.

'I don't think there's any disputing that.' Despite her attempt to sound unbothered, she could hear the quiver of excitement as she acknowledged his rightful pride in his performance. 'However, I'm not here about that. You wanted to chat about our patient.'

She fought to regulate her heartbeat as her body apparently had other ideas of what this meeting was about. Max sat back in his chair and she was thankful that he'd given her some breathing room, the spell between them broken again. For now.

'I suppose I just wanted your opinion. Recent tests have shown a drop in Ashlyn's kidney function. A scan yesterday showed a hold-up of urine in the transplanted kidney. I was actually going to contact you about it even if you hadn't turned up here out of the blue.'

'It's not unusual for a narrowing of the ureter to occur and slow the flow of urine. If it's not kidney stones causing it, it'll require further surgery to remove the narrowed area, or to insert a plastic stent to keep it open. Either way, I can look into it, and do the required surgery if needed.'

Tamsin knew he wouldn't have brought it up at all unless he had serious concerns. He was capable enough to take matters into his own hands but she appreciated him consulting her on the matter. She liked to be kept abreast of her patients' progress, especially if there were any complications which might need her attention.

'That's what I thought. I just wasn't sure if it was too soon after the organ transplant to put her through additional physical and emotional stress. She doesn't seem her usual bubbly self, and I'm concerned her mental health is being affected by the setback.' Max voiced his fears and, once he'd finished eating, set his cutlery neatly on the side of his empty plate and drained the last of his wine. Their evening together, or at least the reason for it, was apparently almost at an end.

The thought wasn't as reassuring to Tamsin's equilibrium as it should have been. She'd worried about coming back to Edinburgh and getting reacquainted with someone who was supposed to have been nothing more than a one-night stand. Now she found she was reluctant to send him on his way again.

She'd regretted it last time. Though it was supposed to have been a sign of strength, of confidence that she didn't need him for anything more than sex, these past months had been difficult in an empty bed. She hadn't wanted anyone else to fill it either. Only Max. It had terrified her, but part of her was hoping that being back in Edinburgh with him could somehow get her back on track, to a place where she didn't think of anything except work again.

'No, I think we should act quickly. If you're concerned about her mental health we could get a counsellor for her and the family to make sure they're all dealing with things okay. That's almost as important to patient recovery.'

It wasn't lost on her that in these plans she was referring to 'we' instead of doing everything on her own as usual. She told herself it was nothing more than courtesy when she was on Max's home ground here, but deep down she knew it was because she'd inadvertently become a team with him, a development which had arisen out of circumstance but one she'd stopped resisting. It was almost as if the rules she'd set herself didn't apply whenever she was in Scotland…

Max scowled, and Tamsin's heart sank. For once it appeared as though they weren't on the same wavelength when it came to patient welfare. She'd met a few old school surgeons who didn't believe in 'hippy dippy' talking therapy. Mainly because they hadn't seen the benefits for themselves, or believed that they were the only ones capable of making a difference to people's lives. Tamsin thanked her sister's counsellors, who'd been there to pick her up when she'd been feeling down, every day. Especially when Tamsin hadn't been there for her for some time. It was too difficult to be around her sometimes, when the weight of that responsibility for her sister's condition became all-encompassing. Staying away was the coward's way out, but it seemed easier for both of them for her to remain out of the picture.

Finding out that Max might be one of those naysayers was disappointing, to say the least. He'd struck her as open-minded, someone who would explore any possibilities which could improve his patients' quality of life.

Someone who would take a risk every now and then and hope for the best.

'You don't think we should offer that support?'

'No, it's just…the waiting times are astronomical at the moment and I don't think they could afford to go private. Would we be able to work something out in time?'

The tension Tamsin hadn't realised she was holding in her shoulders eased with the reassurance that Max was the man she'd thought him to be after all. Caring. Responsive to ideas. Not afraid to push for what he wanted.

She began to think, not for the first time, that they were cut from the same cloth. It wouldn't be the first time she'd gone against protocol in pursuit of her goal.

A breath of arousal seemed to warm the back of her neck, sending a familiar tingle down her spine. The last time she'd been in the city she'd gone against common sense to have Max to herself for the night, convincing herself they were both only after one thing, that it would be easy to walk away and forget.

Now, here she was, back at square one, wanting him all over again, and wondering if they were still on the same wavelength.

'I could talk to them. I have some experience in this area, dealing with families of transplant patients, donors and recipients. And, of course, I know firsthand the emotions and mental trauma that recipients experience.'

Tamsin drained her wine, not entirely sure if it was the thought of reliving her own transplant story with the family in order to relate to them was causing sudden anxiety, or the realisation that those feelings she'd acted on with Max hadn't been easily quashed with one night together.

Max smiled. He should have known Tamsin would volunteer to do whatever it took to look after their patient. Including relying on her own, obviously painful, experiences. Another example of how much care she took with everyone in her line of work, going way beyond what was expected of her.

'That would be great, Tamsin. I'll do what I can to be there for them too, but obviously you can relate to the family more than I could ever hope to.'

'I'll do my best.' Tamsin smiled and he had to remind himself that lovely glow wasn't for him, it was about their patient.

He was glad they'd achieved a plan to help the family. Meeting up with her again felt less like a con now that Tamsin was offering to do something to genuinely try and improve the situation. He didn't want her to think he'd been using their patient as an excuse for his own benefit, a reason to see Tamsin again and spend more time with her. It was true he'd experienced a twinge of jealousy that her attention had been taken by her eager-to-learn trainees today, when he'd practically had her all to himself the last time she'd been in the city, but he had genuine concerns on the matter too. Hopefully, ones which they could resolve together.

Professionally, they were a good team, but there had also been moments during the dinner when he'd been sure that chemistry was still simmering away between them. When one move from either party could end up in another frenzied explosion of passion. On its own it wouldn't be a bad thing, but it had the possibility of bringing complications into his life he didn't need. To act on his impulses would be beyond reckless. It would also be worrying for someone who did not give himself easily to others. Yet seeing more of this side of her that wanted to take care of people was lowering his defences bit by bit.

'I take it you'll want to forge ahead whilst you're here, but won't you be taking time off at Christmas to go home to your family?' As much as he liked having her around, he didn't want her to start counselling their patient if she was going to disappear in the middle of treatment. Okay, so he wanted to personally know what her plans were too, before he found himself let down as well.

Experience had taught him not to get too close, too engaged with anyone. Betrayal of his trust had been all too commonplace in his childhood. These days, he preferred to know exactly where he stood. If Tamsin was going to take off back to Northern Ireland in a couple of weeks, he'd rather know now than be unpleasantly surprised if she unexpectedly disappeared from his life. He'd had too much of that growing up, people coming and going with scant regard for his feelings. Though, strictly speaking, his feelings weren't Tamsin's concern, whether or not she was around was bound to have an effect on him.

Except he could see the tension seizing her body, her full lips now tightening into a thin line, and he was regretting asking the question.

'I won't be going home. I'm working over Christmas.'

'Oh?'

Her statement was both intriguing and concerning. For both of them.

It wasn't healthy to be such a workaholic. Even he took time off at Christmas and other big holidays to recharge his batteries. It was a chance also to visit the children at the home where he'd spent a good part of his childhood, and volunteer his services. It was somewhere he was needed, and the only place that felt like home to him.

Tamsin had a family who apparently would have done anything for her, including giving her a second chance at life. He didn't have anyone, partly by choice. Okay, so his family had long since abandoned him, but his single status stayed resolute, especially at Christmas.

It was a dangerous time of year to get carried away by sentiment and romantic fantasy. But he was also aware of how lonely it could be, watching from the outside as everyone else celebrated the season with their loved ones. Tamsin deserved better, especially when she clearly had a family that loved her.

Unless there was more to the story that he wasn't aware of.

He couldn't help but push for more information, intrigued by the notion that he wasn't the only one with family issues.

'Don't you normally go home for Christmas then?'

'They know I'm busy with work and I'd much rather be doing something productive with my time than stuffing my face with turkey and chocolate.'

'There's a lot to be said for indulging every now and

then, but that's totally your choice. Perhaps we'll share a turkey sandwich and a chocolate bar in the canteen on Christmas Day.' He didn't know what had prompted him to suggest they spend more time together, especially on that particular day, only that it seemed pointless for them both to spend the day on their own when they'd likely be in the same place.

'I might hold you to that. I take it you're not going home to family either then?'

Now she was the one pushing for more info, but Max didn't have anything to hide. When it came to family it was straightforward for him. He didn't have one.

'No. I was in foster care from a very young age. Never stayed in one place long enough to call anywhere home, or family. It's just me.' He gave that automatic shrug which came when he shared that information with anyone, that apology he felt he needed to make because it had always been made apparent to him that he'd never been enough for anyone.

That feeling was only made worse by the usual responding head tilt of sympathy and awkward atmosphere. There was none of that with Tamsin.

Instead, she simply said, 'Sometimes that's all you need. It's easier, isn't it, to be on your own than to have to deal with other people's baggage.'

'Exactly.' His smile came from relief that someone finally understood him. Tamsin didn't think him weird for needing to keep people at arm's length to protect himself. Likely because she was doing exactly the same thing herself. Which made the fact that they'd got together in the first place even more out of character. They'd gone against their self-preservation instincts to follow their libidos instead. So far, he didn't think any harm had been done. Would it be tempting fate to see where it led them?

'Anyway, we'll get the ball rolling on further investigation, and I'll make some space in my diary to speak to the family.' Tamsin pushed back her chair and got to her feet, the dinner, and their time together, seemingly at an end.

Max hurriedly signalled for the bill and tapped his card for payment just as she was walking away. A group of drunk men took too much interest in her as they passed her, spinning around to do a double take. A territorial urge, as well as a need to protect her, surged forth and saw him hurrying to catch up with her at the lifts. He slipped an arm around her waist as a young man with a beer in his hand approached her. Once he saw Max he backed off and rejoined his friends.

'Maybe I should see you up to your room.'

She raised an eyebrow.

Max held his hands up, breaking off that contact between them he'd enjoyed. 'I'll keep my hands to myself.'

Once in the lift he stepped aside so there was a noticeable distance between then. A very different scenario from the last time they'd been in this lift together, on their way to her room to explore this chemistry between them. A moment in time he couldn't, and would never want to, change. If anything, he hoped he could get it back some day. The one occasion when he'd thrown caution to the wind and stopped worrying about how much hurt he could be letting himself in for by getting close to someone. And he wanted to do it all over again.

Instead, he settled for escorting Tamsin to her room and making sure she was safe. Away from other lust-fuelled males she didn't need bothering her.

The ding of the doors opening indicated their arrival and he followed her down the corridor to her room. It was the same one she'd stayed in last time.

'I was feeling nostalgic,' she said with a grin when he pointed it out.

So it had been a conscious choice. He wondered if it meant anything more than her wanting to stay somewhere familiar, if their night together had lasted in her memory beyond normal expectations too.

'I guess I'll see you around the hospital then,' he said, feeling awkward now that he would have to leave her again. The last time he'd walked away from this room he'd felt used, and a little embarrassed. He thought he had enough of a grasp on Tamsin's character now to realise that perhaps her actions that night had been an attempt to try and save them both from compounding their mistake. If he'd stayed, if they'd entertained the idea of any relationship, they would have ended up in an even bigger mess. She wasn't the cold, use-'em-and-abuse-'em type she'd tried to portray. But it was clear her sense of self-preservation was as strong as his own. Which, right now, was telling him to leave and not look back.

Something he knew from experience with Tamsin was impossible.

'Thanks for dinner. It was nice to see you again.' Tamsin opened her room door and hovered inside.

Was it him, or was she hesitating in saying goodbye too?

'Well, goodnight, Max.'

Him, apparently.

'Goodnight.' He stood there until the door was closed firmly in his face. Not for the first time.

With a sigh of resignation that this night wasn't going to end the way he'd hoped, Max turned away. Tamsin certainly had a knack for leaving an impression on him. He was still lusting after her even though she'd sent him packing for a second time. It wasn't that he couldn't take no for an answer, more that he thought they could have something amazing. As proven by the last time he'd been in that room with her.

Head down, hands in his pockets, he eventually walked away. Perhaps if she wasn't standing there too with her heart frantically beating, unable to resist this pull of attraction between them, then it wasn't worth pursuing. This only worked when they were both out of their minds with desire, unable to think clearly enough about the consequences of getting together. He didn't want to be the lovesick puppy in this scenario.

But as he walked it occurred to him that whatever did, or didn't, happen tonight would determine their relationship for the duration of Tamsin's stay in Edinburgh. What they had the last time they'd been together was worth fighting a little harder for if it meant he got to be with her again. They both knew the score. Neither was looking for a long-term commitment, and the world hadn't ended because they'd given in to temptation the last time. He'd made enough sacrifices over the years in the pursuit of keeping his heart safe, and he didn't want to give up the opportunity to be with Tamsin again simply because it went against his 'rules'.

He turned and walked back, his hand hovering in mid-air as he pondered whether or not to knock on the door. If he wanted to make the next move, risking further humiliation and awkwardness at work, in the pursuit of his primal impulses.

The door swung open and before he could process what was happening Tamsin launched herself at him in a flurry of kisses. Her lips moulded to his, her arms wrapped around his neck, she all but dragged him into her room. Not that he needed much coaxing. He kicked the door shut behind them, sealing them back into that capsule where nothing mattered except making each other feel good. Something he'd missed in the intervening weeks.

Like the sweet smell of her hair tickling his nose, her soft curves pressed against him and the taste of her on his tongue.

'This was inevitable, wasn't it?' he said, musing out loud.

'Yes,' Tamsin gasped as he grabbed her backside and pulled her flush against his hardening body.

'It's probably not a good idea,' he said in between kisses.

'Probably not.' Though she didn't appear to care as she began stripping off his clothes.

'We can't seem to stay away from one another though. What if we agree to a casual arrangement for the duration of your stay only? The best of both worlds.'

'Sounds good.' She was nibbling on his earlobe now and it was a fight to maintain logical thought.

'So, we can keep on doing this and walk away come the New Year?' He needed the security of having those parameters in place before he could fully let himself go again.

Tamsin stopped her perusal of his body and stepped back, making him regret his insistence of setting those boundaries and killing the mood.

'If it means you'll stop talking, yes.' Her grin, followed by more kissing, told Max she might have let him off the hook.

It was all the confirmation he needed to cast off the shackles of the past which had been holding him back. The last time they'd done this it had felt very much as though things had been on Tamsin's terms. Now it seemed like a more even playing field he didn't have to worry about being tossed unceremoniously from the room once she was done. He'd be going of his own accord, safe in the knowledge they were going to have lots of opportunities over the festive period to do this again.

'You don't want me to talk? I thought some women liked that sort of thing?' he teased her, whispering low in her ear, knowing the effect it had on her. Her knees buckling, goosebumps rippling over her skin and a little gasp emitting from her lips were all things he remembered from their last time together, and he wasn't disappointed.

'Hmm, I'm of the opinion your mouth could be put to better use…'

The growl that came from deep inside his chest spoke of those caveman urges Tamsin appeared to waken in him. He'd never let himself get so wrapped up in thoughts of a woman that he'd brush aside all of his long-held reasons for avoiding commitment for something as basic as sex. Yet that was exactly what Tamsin did to him. All he could hope for now that he was lost to this chemistry was that things between them remained strictly physical. With any luck, a short fling over Christmas would give them both what they needed and they could move on in the New Year without fear of recriminations.

The knowledge that he didn't have to curtail his needs, that they'd gone into this together, eyes wide open, unleashed a part of Max he usually held back. Tamsin was getting more of him than anyone ever had.

He spun her around and took off her jacket. She unbuttoned her blouse and he pushed the silky material down her arms until it fell onto the floor. Max dotted kisses along her shoulders, stopping only when he came to the straps of her underwear, which he quickly unhooked and disposed of, along with the rest of her clothes, to continue his journey free of obstacles.

He pressed himself tight against her rump, his burgeoning erection nestled in the cleft of her buttocks, a place he was content to be until she pushed back against him and his body suddenly craved more. He cupped her breasts in his hands, rolling her nipples in his fingers until the tight peaks were straining for his attention.

'Max…' It was a plea to end her torture, but he wasn't done by a long way.

Tamsin turned in his arms so those tantalising pink tips were in his eyeline, too good to resist. He took one in his mouth and sucked, licked, tugged with his teeth, until Tamsin was grinding against him, seriously testing his limits of restraint. But she was someone who gave so much of herself to others she deserved a little something back.

Once he had her completely naked he moved his way down her body, his hands resting in that dip of her waist and his mouth travelling over her skin. Kneeling before her now, worshipping her with his lips and tongue, he was determined to prove to them both that this was just about making each other feel good, with absolutely no emotions involved other than those feel-good ones experienced from fantastic sex.

He nudged Tamsin's legs apart and dipped his tongue inside her, feeling her buck against him in response. Her hands were in his hair, tugging and pleading for him to help her reach that ultimate release.

He squeezed her backside, plunged deeper, and felt her quiver around him. When her orgasm hit, she buckled against him.

'I guess the earth really moved for you then?' Max grinned as he got back to his feet, proud of himself for having such an effect on her.

'Something like that,' she gasped, then, walking the few shaky steps to the bed, threw herself down on the mattress.

'Glad to have been of service.' Max joined her on the

bed, covering her body with his and kissing her long and deep.

'I knew there was a reason I came back.' She laughed, her body jiggling temptingly against his and reminding him that he had yet to reach complete satisfaction himself.

'I'm honoured you thought I was worth a repeat visit.'

They both knew the real reason Tamsin was back in Edinburgh had nothing to do with him and everything to do with her work, but it was doing his ego good to pretend otherwise for a little while. The notion that someone as amazing as Tamsin, a woman who usually had no time for relationships, came back just to be with him did wonders for his self-esteem. And other parts of him.

'I just wanted to make sure it hadn't been a fluke first time around.' She was teasing him, but he didn't care if that was the real reason she wanted to be with him again when it was obvious there was no fluke involved.

Whatever this was between them, this attraction and passion that made them lose their minds, he was enjoying it. By putting a finite end to it when she moved back to London in the New Year, he was safe.

'I don't think we need to worry about that,' he growled through gritted teeth, Tamsin taking hold of him and reminding him that even her touch was electric.

When she bit her lip he knew he was in trouble. That was confirmed as she began to move her hand up and down, driving him crazy. It was a relief when she took the initiative and rolled him over so he was on his back and she was straddling him. There was literally nowhere else on earth he would rather be.

'I guess not.' Once Max had donned a condom Tamsin slid her moist heat along his length, the slight friction enough to start a raging fire within him.

As though determined to prove the point, Tamsin took control and impaled herself on his throbbing erection, leaving them both groaning the satisfaction the act provided. Their bodies joined together, she rocked her hips, increasing the pleasure and his desire to completely possess her. Max held her in place, hands on her hips, and thrust upward to draw a gasp from her lips, a sound he wanted to hear again and again, hearing her expression of pleasure as good as the feeling of being inside her, chasing his own satisfaction.

Their groans of gratification filling the room grew louder with the increasing pace of their bodies grinding together. Tamsin braced herself against his chest, rocking her hips, head thrown back in ecstasy.

They were both close now, but Max was unrelenting in his pursuit of that final release. He'd never lost himself so completely with another woman and though it concerned him on a level he couldn't access at this point, physically, he'd never felt this good.

Tamsin dug her nails into his skin, her breath coming in quick little pants and her muscles contracting around him again and again until he was fit to burst. Only when she reached her climax did he give himself permission to let go too. He emptied himself into her, so hard and fast it left him dizzy.

'Hmm, maybe talking is overrated,' Max gasped, his

chest heaving as he tried to catch his breath. This was the kind of workout he'd prefer over the gym any day.

Tamsin laughed, collapsing down onto his chest. He swore he could feel her heart pounding against his.

'This is definitely a better way to end the working day than a meal for one and an empty bed.'

'I'm not sure that's much of a compliment, Tamsin.'

'You know what I mean.'

'Yeah.' Unfortunately, he did. It was all very well building his own little world where no one could hurt him by getting too close, but it also meant there was no one to come home to at the end of the day.

She moved beside him and curled up into the crook of his arm. 'I forget sometimes how nice it is just to have someone to cuddle up to. I think I'm always too worried about falling into a relationship I don't want to appreciate the small things.'

'Does that mean I don't have to worry about you kicking me out the door at any second?'

Tamsin buried her face in his chest. 'I'll never live that down, will I? I promise you can stay until you've at least got your breath back.'

'Oh, thanks.' He liked that they could laugh together about their mutual hang-ups when it came to relationships.

'Well, I don't want us to get too comfortable. It wouldn't do for you to fall in love with me or something stupid that would put all of this in jeopardy.'

Max made a vow there and then never to stay the night, because he knew the temptation would always be as great as it was now. There was nothing that appealed more to him than the idea of falling asleep with Tamsin in his arms, waking up beside her and spending the morning making love to her all over again. But she was right—it wouldn't be a good idea to get used to this when she was only his for a matter of weeks. Falling for her was only asking for trouble. It was inviting a kind of hurt he could only blame himself for when he'd known from the start that this could never be long-term.

However, the way she made him lose control made him wonder if he was as powerless to his emotions as he was to the physical need she'd awoken in him.

CHAPTER FIVE

'YOU DON'T MIND if I tag along, do you?' Max asked as he joined the back of Tamsin's training group shadowing her today.

'No, not at all,' she lied, not wanting to make a big deal of his unexpected appearance. First, to avoid raising any suspicions in front of the other doctors, but also because she didn't want him to realise how big an effect he had on her.

If theirs was such a casual arrangement her heart shouldn't flutter every time she saw him, or make her tongue-tied because simply being in her eyeline made her flustered.

She did her best to carry on, but she was hyperaware of his presence. It was impossible not to be when he knew every inch of her intimately. For a couple of weeks now they'd been hooking up after work, sometimes even sneaking the odd kiss in the hospital too. That always made the day go faster. The prospect of being with him, of being free together, was often the only foreplay she needed. It was clear he felt the same way when they barely managed to make it into her room before they were ripping each other's clothes off. On the odd occasion they didn't even manage to strip naked before they gave in to temptation.

It was all very exciting and passionate. That was what worried her. If she wasn't careful, she might start mistaking that for something else. Mostly because there already seemed to be an affection between them she hadn't anticipated. A concern and appreciation for one another that went beyond the idea of an emotionless fling. However, since the alternative was ending things, she promised herself she wouldn't get emotionally invested in Max, or the idea of them as a couple.

'Actually, we're just going to pay a visit to our favourite patient and see how she's doing. One of our organ recipients who has been readmitted due to some post op complications.' She turned to the trainees. 'Dr Robertson assisted me during Ashlyn's kidney transplant so he won't be forced to watch the footage of the surgery like the rest of you.'

That drew a few polite laughs.

'I think I'd still like to see it though,' Max piped up, letting her know she wasn't going to get rid of him easily.

'Of course. Perhaps you'd like to go in and see our patient first to introduce everyone. She knows we're coming but I know you have a close bond with her.'

'I'll go and say hi, before we get to the technical stuff.' Max gave her a grin and left them in the hall to follow him into their patient's room.

'Dr Robertson has a good rapport with all his young patients, something which is very important when working so closely with transplant families. You need their trust when you have their lives, or those of their loved ones, in your hands.'

What Tamsin was telling them wasn't something new to these doctors. It was part of being a medical professional. But having empathy went a long way to building a good relationship with a patient and that was vital in the role of a transplant surgeon.

It was a quality that seemed to come naturally with Max and his young patients and she wondered if that had something to do with his own childhood. Although he didn't go into detail, Tamsin was sure it had been traumatic moving around so much, never having a real home or family to rely on. She'd taken that for granted growing up, and now here she was avoiding her family when Max had never had that security.

For the first time in years, it made her think about everyone she'd left behind in Northern Ireland—if it had been the right thing to do to stay away for so long, or simply just the coward's way out. Even the few calls and visits she used to make had petered out over the years until she had the bare minimum contact on birthdays and special occasions. She'd thought it best not to impose too much on their daily lives when they'd got used to her no longer being in the picture. Although having that space was likely as much about protecting herself, and not having to regularly deal with the guilt she felt around them. Max probably would've done anything for a family and she'd cast hers aside. Once she had some free time, she would ease her conscience by sending some Christmas gifts and checking in with them.

'Why don't you all come in and introduce yourselves?' Max peeked his head around the door and invited the group in. Everyone awkwardly introduced themselves then fell back, leaving Tamsin and Max in the spotlight in the centre of the room.

'Hey, Ashlyn. Good to see you again. How are you feeling?' Tamsin checked her notes, confirming everything Max had told her and the need for further surgery.

'Tired.' Although the little girl had more colour in her cheeks than previously, there were dark circles around her eyes, suggesting fatigue was a major factor.

'I thought a new kidney would give her back her life but she's back to sleeping all day.' The girl's worried mother was at her bedside, as concerned parents always were.

It made her think about her own parents and what it must have been like to watch both of their daughters lying in hospital beds, hoping for the best, fearing the worst. And how torn they would've been, not only making the decision to let one child donate bone marrow to another but also after the transplant, when it became apparent that it had been a success for Tamsin but at a huge cost for Emily. Would they have agreed to it, knowing the outcome? Probably not. In which case, Tamsin wouldn't have the life she had now, able to help other patients get their second chance.

However, she knew from interacting with these families, following their journeys, how difficult the situation must've been for her family. Moving away, abandoning the sibling who'd given her life back must've seemed so selfish, callous. As a family they'd never really talked about what had happened, so she'd never told them of the guilt she harboured. Just as Emily had never been given the opportunity to voice the resentment she must've felt towards Tamsin, but she was sure it was there. She didn't know if it was any easier knowing an organ came from a deceased donor. There was always going to be that level of guilt and heartache associated with the procedure. That was the nature of such lifesaving situations. Perhaps she should start putting as much effort into helping her own family as she did with her patients'.

'These things aren't always straightforward, Mrs McDonald. As would've been explained to you, there can be complications. It doesn't mean Ashlyn won't be up and running about soon, just that it can take some time to get over the fatigue. It's still early days.' Tamsin plastered on a big smile, making it seem to the ten-year-old at least that this wasn't a big deal. She wanted to know more, do more, before worrying her unnecessarily.

She addressed the others to let them know the circumstances they were dealing with at present. 'Ashlyn underwent a kidney transplant in September. She responded well at first, but she's having some issues now. This is why aftercare is so important. The role of transplant surgeon is a commitment to the patient long after the actual surgery. We need to be on call for those little niggles or more complicated obstacles, to do our best to make it a long-term success.'

'What about the pains she's experiencing in her back and abdomen and the constant infections?' Ashlyn's mother naturally wanted definitive answers, and that was part of the reason Tamsin was here.

'The anti-rejection medication Ashlyn is on can lower the immune system, and the prevalent viruses at this time of year can make her more susceptible to them. Although there is some pain to be expected after this type of surgery, we do think there is a blockage in the ureter. We're going to insert a plastic tube to open it, and hopefully that'll make things better for Ashlyn. Dr Robertson and I will be doing the surgery. It's a very straightforward procedure that I've done loads of times, so there's nothing to worry about, okay?' That seemed enough to satisfy Ashlyn and Mrs McDonald, who nodded, trusting everything she told them.

Hers was a privileged position. One that she would never take for granted, and something she wanted to be sure these other potential transplant surgeons were aware of before they qualified. Her presence at the Great Northern was an introduction to the training, telling them what to expect. It would take years of assisting in surgery, tailing transplant patients and the process with their surgeons from beginning to end, before they would be able to go it alone. Before they got that far, she felt it was her duty to instil in them the humanity the job required too. The role wasn't just something which could be learned from textbooks or watching others work, and not everyone was cut out for it.

'Now, does anyone have any questions for me, or Ashlyn?' It was important to include her and her mother and not make them feel as if they were nothing of consequence here with everyone talking over them. Besides, she'd already asked permission prior to this meeting, so she wasn't ambushing anyone.

Hands shot up around the room.

'Will we be able to view the surgery?'

'If Ashlyn and her family are agreeable.' She turned to the people concerned. 'I know it may seem like an imposition, but training more doctors in transplant surgery means we'll be able to help more families in the future.'

'I want to help, Mum,' Ashlyn pleaded to her mother, but Tamsin didn't want to put them on the spot.

'Take some time to think it over. Dr Robertson and I can discuss it with you later.'

'Thanks, Tamsin.' Mrs McDonald's familiarity might have come as a shock to some but Tamsin appreciated that the woman felt comfortable enough to address her on a first name basis.

'Okay, we'll leave you in peace for now.' Tamsin ushered the group back out of the room and dismissed them for the day. They all had other responsibilities in the hospital to get back to.

'I'm not sure that was very helpful to anyone involved.' She voiced her doubts to Max once the others left, worried that the brief interaction wouldn't do anything to stimulate interest in the transplant field.

'It's good to reinforce that idea of a human element. This isn't stuff that can be taught in a class, or learned from a slide show. We both know the importance of good communication with the patients and their families. Nothing takes place without their cooperation, and I think you highlighted that idea of consent, instead of taking all the decisions into our own hands. There is no room for ego when dealing with these families.' Max gave a good pep talk.

Tamsin appreciated his point of view as both attendee at her training and as a surgeon who'd actually taken part in a transplant. He understood the human side of the process, that this wasn't only about the skills of the surgeon in the operating room.

Although the job required a certain amount of confidence, self-belief and authority, there was also a need for basic human compassion, something which Max had in abundance.

'I hope, between us, we can get that point across. Although it is nerve-racking working with an audience. If we do the transplant with the trainees in attendance it will be even more pressure to get things right.'

'You'll be great. You always are.' Max rubbed his hands up and down her arms, the closest they could get to physical intimacy at work without causing a scandal.

She appreciated the reassurance but she was longing for one of those great big bear hugs she'd been accustomed to from him outside working hours, the first thing he did when he saw her at night. It was nice to be wrapped in a warm embrace every now and then without the expectation of more. Only now was she beginning to realise what she'd been missing out on by isolating herself in London, not only from a partner lasting beyond one night but also her family. It had been too long since she'd let anyone else hold her that way. Perhaps that was why she wasn't opposed to Max hugging her. He could give her that physical support she didn't have from her family, at least for a while. Come the New Year, she wasn't going to have Max in her life any more and she'd have to get used to the idea.

'Well, I'm all wrapped up for the day if you're ready to head home?' She caught the last word too late to stop it slipping from her lips. It was too tragic to think of a hotel room as home after a few short weeks, but they'd got into such a routine of leaving the hospital and spending the night together there it had begun to feel that way. All because she had Max there with her.

Alarm bells were ringing but she didn't want to acknowledge them. The idea of going back to being the single traveller alone in her hotel room eating room service wasn't something she was ready to do. She just needed to keep a hold of her senses for another few weeks, not get too lost in this notion of being a couple, and she'd get to enjoy it for a little while longer.

Though the look on Max's face said he hadn't missed her slip of the tongue either, and he didn't look comfortable with the idea of going *home* with her at all. That suggested an intimacy, a familiarity that wasn't supposed to be part of their arrangement.

'I mean we can go out and get dinner. We don't have to go back to the hotel room just yet if you don't want that.' She tried to keep the panic out of her voice that she'd messed things up and did her best to make plans for them to be together in a more casual way.

'Do you mind if we don't?'

Her heart fell into her stomach.

'I'm tired and I just fancy a night in. Maybe a takeaway? If it's a change of scenery you want, you're welcome to come back to my place.'

That instantly propelled her little heart right back to where it was supposed to be. He wasn't blowing her off, and it seemed he was happy just to spend a cosy night in with her. Moving to his place for the duration of the evening made it less of an anonymous affair, when a hotel room kept things more impersonal. Until she'd started to think of it as their home, of course. But if Max was willing to open up something of his personal life to her, she wasn't going to object. Tamsin wanted to know more about the doctor and lover she'd found herself caught up with in Scotland.

She only hoped it was curiosity that killed this particular cat and not heartbreak.

Max watched Tamsin sleep next to him, her arm thrown carelessly across his chest. A sight, and feeling, he'd become accustomed to waking up to. Unlike this crick in his neck, which had come from falling asleep on the sofa. The movie they'd been watching had long since finished and now the TV flashed with too-loud ads for orthopaedic mattresses and kitchen gadgets for people with too much money.

'Tamsin?' He tried to rouse her. They both had work in the morning and they couldn't spend the few hours before then lying squashed up here.

'Mm?' She snuggled closer, making it even harder for him to put an end to the evening.

'It's late. We've both got work in the morning.'

'Okay,' she mumbled, not moving.

Max smiled and brushed the curtain of blonde hair away from her face so he could see her better. She looked so beautiful when she was sleeping, peaceful, without that line of tension which always seemed to mar her forehead at work, when he knew she was worrying about everyone around her.

'Come on, time for bed.' He eased himself up off the sofa, disentangling his limbs from hers.

'Yours?' she asked with a disarming sleepy grin.

'I guess so.' Even though it went against his better judgement, it would be a sin to disturb her too much.

That had been his excuse the first time he'd spent the night with her, going against his vow never to do that. It hadn't seemed like such a big deal at first to simply stay in Tamsin's bed until the morning. Then, the next time it happened he'd reasoned it was safe because they both knew there was a time limit on their relationship. Now it had become commonplace, and he knew they were taking risks they hadn't planned on.

He took Tamsin by the hand and led her upstairs to his room. His sanctuary. The one place he knew he shouldn't. Although he'd had lovers here in the past, everything with Tamsin had taken place at the hospital or the hotel. Neutral territory. This was crossing the line into his personal space.

He supposed he'd done that the moment he'd invited

her back to his place. A spur-of-the-moment decision he'd made when Tamsin had inadvertently referred to the hotel room as 'home'. Their home. Not that coming back to his place now seemed any less risky…

So far, apart from sharing a little of their family history, they hadn't ventured into each other's personal lives. Now, here they were spooning on the couch watching TV like a normal couple. In a relationship.

And he was beginning to wonder why that was such a bad thing. He liked spending time with her, planning their evenings together, and making love to her. It was just the emotional aspect of a relationship which terrified him. That idea of falling for someone who would betray his trust and leave him, like so many had done during his childhood. Like Mairi had done later in his life.

But he was no longer that young boy—he was an adult, and should be able to deal with a breakup if and when it came. He'd survived this far. Certainly, it was inevitable with Tamsin when they had conditions set on this arrangement that meant once she left in the New Year, they were over. He wondered, if like his decision to bring her home and let her stay the night, those boundaries might be stretched according to how they were feeling at the time.

As she'd repeatedly said, her duty to her transplant patients was a long-term commitment, so they'd probably be in each other's lives workwise for some time to come. They wouldn't be able to avoid each other, and he didn't want to.

Fully clothed, Tamsin flopped on top of the bed. 'Do you mind if we just cuddle tonight? I'm wiped out.'

Max spooned in behind her and pulled the folded throw from the end of the bed up over them. 'No problem. Get some rest.'

It was probably for the best that they keep sex off the menu for one night when they were in his house. They could go back to their regularly scheduled casual arrangement in the hotel, where people probably had passionate, meaningless encounters all the time. At least if all they did in his bed was sleep, fully clothed, no touching save for her asleep in his arms, they should be safe from errant emotions slipping in, some subconscious belief that this was going to be anything more than they'd agreed on.

So why did this feel even more intimate than their naked bodies being entwined in a passionate tryst?

Being together in the operating theatre was reminiscent of the first time Tamsin had met Max. Though thankfully there was less tension in the room now they'd come to know each other so…intimately.

At least today she'd been there in time for the introductions and instructions, so everyone knew exactly what their role was during surgery. Ashlyn was under general anaesthetic, and if everything went as well as expected she should be on the recovery ward in a couple of hours.

'We're going to be inserting a plastic stent today to open the ureter to hopefully increase the flow of urine from the transplanted kidney to the bladder. We'll be using a camera to guide us.' Tamsin did a recap as much for herself as for those in attendance, so she was totally focused on the task at hand.

And not the man on the other side of the operating table from her.

Once she'd made the opening to reach the site, she inserted a guidewire into the ureteric opening in the bladder, watching on the screen to ensure correct positioning.

'That looks perfect,' Max confirmed, taking his eyes from the real-time video to lock with hers and she knew he was smiling at her beneath the mask.

Heat infused her cheeks at the praise, more of a reaction to his attention than in regard to her achievement. She had enough confidence in her work not to need his approval, but it was welcome. Sometimes she had to portray a bravado she didn't always feel so those around her were assured all would go to plan. It was nice to have someone to work alongside who could give her an extra boost if she needed it. Maybe not only when it came to work either.

For as long as she could remember she'd done things on her own. Always capable, not needing anyone else…it was almost as though she'd been trying to prove a point. She'd taken enough from her family and she didn't want to rely on anyone else to bail her out again when it had cost so much the last time.

Now she was beginning to realise she didn't have to do everything on her own, and it was nice to have some support every now and then. No one else had been seriously hurt as a result of her letting someone be there for her. At least, not yet.

'Okay. You push the stent over the guidewire, Max.' She got her head back in the game, though she realised she'd used his first name, which wasn't the norm for her. It was a minor slip-up of her usual protocol which no one seemed to take any notice of, but it was a sign to Tamsin that she was getting way too comfortable with a man who wasn't guaranteed to her beyond the end of December.

With a hollow pusher, Max eased the stent over the guidewire she'd already inserted. 'Stent in place,' he confirmed.

'I'm just going to carefully remove the guidewire and leave the stent in situ.' Tamsin watched on the monitor to ensure an accurate placement. Any mistakes here would be hers alone.

The stents were designed with coiled ends to prevent displacement, and were flexible enough to withstand normal body movements. Although it might cause Ashlyn some discomfort at first, it should settle down after a few days.

Once she removed the guidewire, she made sure all surgical instruments were accounted for, and that a drain was in place to take away any fluid which might have built up during surgery.

'I'll finish the sutures.'

'Thank you, Dr Robertson.'

She was happy to let Max finish up, making sure all incisions were closed. He had worked quickly and precisely, in tandem with her thus far. Given the nature of her job, she often worked with different surgeons and she could honestly say she'd never experienced the rapport she had with Max with anyone else before. Not just because they were sleeping together. That could've actually made things more difficult, awkward between them, if anything, since she was the lead surgeon.

A lot of men wouldn't be able to handle that she had seniority, but Max didn't have a problem with it. He was the expert in his field, and they had mutual respect for one another in that capacity. Although they'd clashed at first, she could tell now that had been because they were so alike. They had so much in common, with their work ethic and resistance to commitment when it came to relationships.

That was what made last night so disturbing. It had been sweet, comfortable, and the total opposite of what a no-strings fling should be about. And she'd enjoyed it a little too much. It had been nice to see where Max lived, the neat, tidy home of a man who obviously knew how to take care of himself and his surroundings.

He didn't need her in his life any more than she needed him. Yet they found comfort in one another, that much was obvious. They were both lonely; perhaps that was why the nature of their relationship had gravitated towards more than it was supposed to be. Going 'home' together at the end of their day, or venturing into his bachelor pad were things they'd slipped into. Tamsin knew it was about time she took steps to stop them from falling into something resembling a relationship.

She waited until they were on their own again, after they'd scrubbed out of Theatre and spoken to Ashlyn's family.

'I know we were going to go back to the hotel tonight

for dinner, but do you mind if we postpone it for another night?' Taking a break would make her feel as though she had regained some control over the situation at least.

'Of course. Surgery is always taxing. We can see each other another night, if that's what you want?' There was a hesitation in Max's voice, an uncertainty she knew she'd caused by changing up their ongoing routine. It sounded as though he wasn't ready to end their arrangement yet, but would do so if she requested it. Since their time together would be limited to a few more short weeks, she didn't think it necessary to bring things to a halt. Hopefully, spending one night apart, and a sense that she'd wrestled back some control, would be sufficient to set them back on the right track. The one which would fork into two different directions in the New Year, with no chance of a return.

'Just for tonight,' she reassured him with a smile. 'It will probably do us good to have some time to ourselves for a while. I'm sure you're sick of the sight of me by now.'

'Not at all.' Max risked their usual protocol in public, slipping his arms around her waist to pull her a little closer, but Tamsin didn't object. If they were going to spend the night apart, she wanted to have the feel of him one last time that she might take to her bed instead of the man himself tonight.

'You were so tired last night, and we both fell asleep fully clothed. I think perhaps we both need some rest.' The twinkle in his velvety brown eyes was enough to remind her of the long nights they'd spent together doing much more, wearing a lot less. The instant arousal those images conjured throughout her body was almost sufficient for her to cast her concerns aside and simply enjoy the time they had left together.

Then a cleaner clattered down the corridor with the floor buffing machine, forcing them to spring apart and create a more professional distance. A reminder that this wasn't just about how he made her feel. That was causing the problem here. When she was with him she tended to forget real life, where she had reason to remain on her own, and her career was more important than her sex life.

She needed something to distract her. A trip away from the place where they worked together, the hotel where they usually spent the night in bed, somewhere on her own with no association of Max so she could refocus on the reason she was in Edinburgh in the first place. That certainly wasn't to get involved with someone who had as much baggage as she had.

'A little time out will do us the world of good.' She left him in the corridor to make her own way home for the first time in weeks, feeling a little cast adrift without him. Exactly why she needed to do this. If she got too used to having him there, at work as well as in her bed, when she left him behind to go back to London it was going to feel as though she'd had a limb ripped off. The reason she didn't do relationships in the first place. It would complicate her life, detract from her work, and she didn't think she deserved to have it all—a partner and a career—when her sister had been denied those things because of her.

One night away from Max was such a small concession compared to everything Emily had sacrificed for her. A thought that wouldn't leave her mind until she found herself heading into the city centre instead of back to her room, compelled by the sudden need to show some small appreciation.

When they were kids, she and Emily used to go into Belfast on the bus at Christmas. It was such a special time, going to see Santa at the big department store and marvelling at the window displays. Although Emily was older, she had always been as excited as her little sister about the season. When they were old enough to be allowed to shop on their own, they used to put their money together to buy their parents' gifts on their trip to the city centre. Christmas always reminded her of that time, when they'd been close. Best friends.

Now they hardly spoke.

Before the surgery Emily had been an amazing ballet dancer with hopes of going into full-time training to become professional. They'd gone to watch her Christmas recitals every year as a family. Something else which was stolen from her at too early an age.

After the surgery, Emily hadn't been well enough to walk, never mind dance, and Christmas no longer seemed important in the scheme of things. Nothing had been the same since the transplant. Everything became about Emily's health, and Tamsin's guilt over the situation, their close bond fraying until she'd moved to London and it had snapped altogether.

Christmas reminded her of those joyous times she'd

spent with her sister, but it was also a reminder of everything they'd both lost because of her illness.

Now she wanted to do something for her family in some small way so they knew she was still thinking of them.

The city was dark already, although the bright white Christmas lights strung from every lamppost illuminated the streets. Stepping off the tram, she felt the cold air fill her lungs and she lifted her Aran knit scarf up to cover her mouth and nose.

First stop was the bustling shopping centre offering a variety of shops, along with fluorescent lighting and hopefully some heat. It was tempting to head towards the souvenir shop offering all things tartan and shortbread, and she supposed she could add some traditional Scottish fayre into a care package but she wanted something more personal.

The huge toyshop dominating the ground floor gave her some inspiration. It reminded her that her father used to love painting model aeroplanes. He used to tell her it was his way of destressing as joining the tiny, intricate plastic parts took all his concentration, leaving no room for thoughts about anything else which might have been bothering him. As she recalled, he'd finished a rather large-scale model of an aircraft carrier when she'd been going through her transplant.

She was carried along on a wave of harassed parents shepherding giddy children towards the stacked displays of board games and soft toys inside the open doors. It struck her then that she no longer had any idea what her family members still liked. She'd become so detached she didn't know who they were any more, even though her mother still left voice messages for her—usually asking when she'd make time for a visit home. Then there were the cards and gifts they still sent on special occasions. Even chocolate eggs at Easter.

They tried to keep her included, but that only made her feel worse for wanting that distance. She used work as a constant excuse not to go home, or speak to them. Even social media was a no-go area for her, afraid that she'd be too accessible or, worse, that she'd see evidence of how much Emily had been held back because of her disability.

The thought saddened her that she'd effectively cast her family aside, the way Max's birth family had done with him. The lasting and painful impression that had made on him wasn't something she wanted to be responsible for inflicting on her loved ones when she'd already hurt them so much.

''Scuse me.' A little voice sounded next to her and she looked down to see a girl of about five or six tugging on her coat.

Tamsin pulled down her scarf. 'Hello.'

'I can't find my mummy.' The little blonde scrunched up the front of her blue and white snowflake jumper in her hands, clearly distressed.

To try and put her at ease, Tamsin knelt down beside her. 'Did you come in here with her?'

A teary nod.

She wasn't wearing a coat so Tamsin imagined her mother was likely carrying it and wasn't too far away.

Though a store this size, bustling with stressed shoppers, in the eyes of a five-year-old child must've seemed like an endless, impossible maze to navigate.

'I'm sure she's in here somewhere. Why don't we go and look for her? My name's Tamsin. What's yours?' She didn't want to scare the child any more than she already was, and her time with Max and his patients had shown her about interacting with little ones.

They needed to feel safe instead of being rushed into situations they weren't prepared for. He always took the time to get to know them, to make them comfortable around him before he did any of the medical procedures required of him. Though this was an altogether different scenario, she knew she had to go gently. She didn't spend a great deal of time around children. It was unusual for her to have such young patients as Max and she'd never really thought of herself as maternal. These days her thoughts ventured along all sorts of previously untravelled roads.

'Nell.' Without prompting, Nell took her hand, and Tamsin's heart swelled with the trust she was showing in a stranger. It was something she was sure her mother had warned her against but Tamsin hoped she'd simply come across as a person who clearly posed no danger to the child.

'That's a lovely name. Now, where did you last see your mum?' She stood up, still clutching Nell's hand, and they began to walk along the end of the aisles.

'At the dollies, but I wanted to see the teddies.' Nell

scrubbed a hand across her runny nose and Tamsin rummaged in her pocket for a clean handkerchief.

'Don't worry, sweetheart, I'm sure she's looking for you too.' She could only imagine how frantic Nell's mother would be once she realised her daughter was missing.

Motherhood wasn't something she'd entertained for herself, not only because of the demanding nature of her job. There were plenty of female professionals who managed to have a family along with a successful career. She was sure her self-imposed penance to atone for the suffering she'd put her sister through had something to do with it too. Why should she have a full life with a family and a career when all of those things had been denied to Emily because of her?

One of these days, she might regret not seizing the chance to have those things, by which time it might be too late. Age, circumstance or lack of a partner might mean she didn't have the luxury of choice.

Thoughts turned to Max—someone who'd never had a family but would clearly make a fantastic dad. She wondered if he'd ever considered the possibility or if, like her, he'd been too wounded to even contemplate having children of his own.

'Tamsin?' For a moment she thought she'd imagined his voice, but when she turned around there he was, smiling at her.

He looked so handsome in his brown wool coat, smart grey scarf knotted cravat-like at his throat, a few drops of snow glistening white against his dark hair. Her heart swooned, and she wondered how he'd made it this far without being mobbed by admirers.

'Max! What are you doing here?' When she'd called off their date, she'd almost imagined him sitting alone at home pining for her. Obviously, he had a life outside of their fling, but she hadn't experienced it firsthand until now. It was unsettling, a reminder that once she'd gone back to London he'd continue as he had before her arrival, when she wasn't sure she could ever get back to being the person she'd been pre-fling.

'I…um… I sometimes volunteer at the children's home I grew up in. I like to get them a few Christmas presents so they don't feel completely unloved.'

Of course he did. It said a lot, not only about the kind of man he was to even give them a second thought, but also how sad he must've been in their position at one time. He obviously understood how those children felt to want to prevent them from feeling the same way.

'Do you have a list?' She was teasing, not for one minute expecting him to be that organised, but the slip of paper he produced with a wry smile showed his sincerity.

Some others might have boasted about their charitable work, making it more about them than the people they were helping. Not Max. She'd had to drag the information out of him.

This was a man who cared deeply for children in tough circumstances, a throwback to his own childhood, but nonetheless important. Small gestures like this would mean a great deal to those upset about being in care when they should have been at home with their families. It showed someone was thinking about them.

Her heart ached for the boy Max had been, who hadn't been shown the same consideration. It was a testament to the man he was, to treat others with a compassion that had been missing from his own early life.

'So, who's your friend?' He tucked the list back in his pocket, nodding towards Nell, who was now clamped tightly to her thigh.

'This is Nell. She's lost her mum in here; we're just trying to find her.'

'Ah.' He dropped to his haunches. 'I'm Max, a friend of Tamsin's. Is it okay if I help you to look too?'

'That's really not necessary. You have things to do.' This wasn't how the evening was supposed to go. Yet he looked so good.

Even Nell, who'd been resistant to him at first, appeared to have been won over and was now holding his hand.

'It's fine. I'm sure it'll only take us a few minutes. Then you can advise me on what Santa Claus can get for a nine-year-old and a thirteen-year-old girl because he has no clue.'

He got to his feet and Tamsin couldn't see any way to say no to any of this without seeming rude, or someone who was way out of her comfort zone Christmas shopping with her lover.

The trio began to scour the shop floor, Nell swinging the adults' hands on either side of her, and Tamsin was sure they must've looked like any ordinary family. She glanced at Max, who seemed quite content, and for a moment she fantasised about what it might be like to have this little family for real. To be going home to prepare for Christmas together instead of working at the hospital so she didn't have to admit how lonely she was.

The idea of wrapping presents, decorating a tree and cooking Christmas dinner together seemed fanciful, yet it was the norm for most people. She wondered if Max still yearned for the sort of family Christmas he'd missed out on growing up, or if this was her fantasy alone.

'Nell? I've been looking for you everywhere.' A stressed blonde-haired woman carrying a little pink coat hurried over towards them, eyeing Tamsin and Max somewhat suspiciously.

'See? I told you Mum wouldn't be too far away.' Tamsin immediately let go of the little girl's hand so she could run over to her parent.

'I only turned my back for a few seconds…'

'That's all it takes sometimes. They're escape artists at this age.' Max offered the woman one of his megawatt smiles, which would hopefully go some way to convince Nell's mum they weren't trying to abduct her daughter.

'Do you have kids of your own?' she asked, assuming they were together.

Tamsin's cheeks began to burn, embarrassed that she'd put Max in this situation where someone would mistake them for a real couple. That was what happened when they let their casual arrangement spill over into the outside world. Assumptions and expectations that could never be fulfilled.

Max shook his head. 'No, but I work on the children's ward at the hospital. I know it's hard to keep track of them sometimes.'

'Well, thank you both for looking out for Nell.' The relieved mum took her daughter firmly by the hand and disappeared back into the throng of eager shoppers, leaving Max and Tamsin alone again.

'You didn't tell me what you're doing in here. Other than rescuing lost children and reuniting them with their parents.' Max didn't seem to be in a rush to get away from her and do his own shopping, something which both pleased her and unsettled her.

Since this was supposed to be their time apart she should've fought harder to get away from him, but it was so much nicer having him with her…

'I thought I would do some Christmas shopping for my family. Dad used to love those little model kits. I thought I might send him one, and Emily could never resist a cuddly toy.'

'As we're both here, why don't we do our shopping, then go and get a hot chocolate somewhere together?'

It had all the hallmarks of a romantic night out together, something she should've run a mile from when the whole point of tonight was to put some distance between them, to get a hold of her feelings.

Instead, she found herself saying, 'Sounds lovely.'

CHAPTER SIX

BOTH LADEN WITH shopping bags, purchases complete, it was time for Max to hold up his end of the deal.

'Hot chocolate?' he asked as they approached a café on Princes Street.

'Yes, please. I could do with sitting down. My feet are killing me.' Tamsin slumped against the door, clearly exhausted by their unexpected joint shopping venture.

When he'd come out this evening he'd never expected to see her, only intending to get some much-needed gifts and have something to occupy him. He hadn't wanted to sit at home dwelling on the sudden emptiness not only in the house but in his life when he didn't have Tamsin there to fill his evening.

He understood why she'd suggested a time out for one evening when he too had experienced a moment of *What are we doing?* after spending the night spooning on top of his bed. Yet once they'd reconnected tonight it seemed like the most natural thing in the world to spend it together.

He could've walked away when he spotted her with the little girl in the toyshop, but he'd been drawn over instantly. Her need to help reunite the child with her mother was just another example of her caring nature. Nell had obviously trusted her on sight, and it made him question why he remained so resistant to sharing himself completely with her. If a five-year-old was brave enough to put her faith in a stranger, as a grown man, Max should have the courage to trust the woman he shared a bed with wasn't going to hurt him.

Sharing a hot chocolate seemed an innocuous thing to do in the circumstances.

Except, as he pushed the door open, it became apparent they weren't the only ones who'd had that idea.

'Look at the queue,' Tamsin sighed, weariness evident in her voice as they realised the long wait they'd have to get served and find a seat.

'We can try somewhere else.' He wasn't going to be put off easily when they deserved a treat after their accomplishments tonight. There had been quite a list of children to shop for, and he'd been glad of Tamsin's input when it came to buying appropriate gifts for the older girls. She'd had her own shopping to do, of course, as well.

He was glad she was thinking of her family when she'd told him how strained her relationship with them had become. It would be nice if she was able to get close to them again, for her sake. He knew how it was to be adrift from loved ones, but she still had a chance to reconcile and have the kind of relationship with her parents he could only have dreamed of.

They trudged along the street, bags in hand, walking past more coffee shops filled to capacity with other weary shoppers. Eventually he had to admit defeat.

'Why don't we call it a night?' As he said the words, Max realised he didn't want that. He was still looking forward to sharing a hot drink and a chat as they unwound. He could see too the look of disappointment on Tamsin's face and he didn't want that to be the way they parted, with her feeling let down and him not having fulfilled a promise. He never wanted to be one of those people who said they'd do things and never followed through on their word, because there'd been too many of them in his life.

Tamsin heaved a heavy sigh.

'We could go back to mine. I do have my own fancy machine I'm sure is capable of making you a fabulous hot chocolate. Plus, you can help me wrap these gifts. I might be an expert with a needle and thread, but I've very little practice when it comes to gift-wrapping.' It was only when he said that out loud, and saw the frown of sympathy cross Tamsin's forehead, that he realised how sad that sounded.

Other than Mairi, he'd never really had anyone to buy Christmas presents for, nor received much in return. Even then he supposed he hadn't made a big deal about it, choosing instead to spend his time and money at the children's home. In hindsight, perhaps his closed-off nature had sounded the death knell for their relationship from the start. It was only now he'd begun to open up to Tamsin he was realising how much he'd held back from Mairi. At some point she'd probably given up trying to get close to him, and chosen to find someone else. Though it might have been an idea to finish with him first.

Max's relationships since, both professionally and romantically, had been casual, and didn't need marking with specially chosen gifts. Oh, there was the odd box of chocolates or aftershave from passing acquaintances but, other than the children he bought for at Christmas, there wasn't an extensive list of people to buy for. It only added an extra dilemma to his load. Tamsin had become such a big part of his life lately he felt compelled to get her a special gift this year but, like taking her back to his place, was that crossing a line?

Max realised he didn't care. He wanted to show his appreciation for the time he'd had her in his life, to do something nice for her. It was taxing always being careful not to let his feelings slip out of his grasp, always watching and waiting for what he considered an inevitable betrayal. Tonight, watching other couples and families enjoy the festive atmosphere, just made him crave that normality that everyone took for granted. But he was beginning to realise that idea of settling down and sharing his life with someone was a picture that only ever included Tamsin.

She should have said no. There had been plenty of opportunities to do so. When he'd first turned up at the toyshop, when he'd suggested shopping together, going for a hot chocolate, and again with the offer of another evening at his place. But here she was, in Max's car, pulling up outside his house ready for a cosy night wrapping Christmas presents together.

It hit her then that she hadn't wanted to say no. She wanted this. It was that cursed conscience of hers that wouldn't let her enjoy it for what it was.

'I'll let you unpack in the living room, and I'll make us some hot drinks to warm us up.' He bounced out of the front seat of the car with an enthusiasm she hadn't seen in him before, keen to open the door and get started.

It made her smile to see this boyish side of him, but also made her sad for that young boy who'd clearly never had the sort of Christmas most children took for granted. Despite their physical hardships over the years, Tamsin and her sister had always been guaranteed a plethora of gifts and sweets on the big day. Often in the lead up to Christmas Day they would've been spoiled with parties and trips to visit store Santas for extra presents. It broke her heart to think of this generous, thoughtful man as a neglected boy with very little to celebrate at this time of year. By his own admission, he didn't have many people to buy for, so it stood to reason that he didn't receive much in return either. Not that she supposed he donated gifts to the children in the home for thanks or recognition, never mind expecting anything back in the way of material gifts. It was clear he did it because he didn't want those children to feel as lonely and neglected as he had.

He deserved more—then and now. Since she was going to be here for Christmas, she decided to give him the best one she possibly could. To show him what he could have if he opened his life up to someone other than her, who would stick around for longer than a couple of months. Then perhaps one of them at least would get to have a full, normal life.

The fancy coffee machine was already purring into

life in the kitchen by the time she followed Max into the house.

'Make yourself at home,' he called out as she let herself into the living room.

She was sure the grey suede settee still had the imprint of their bodies from last night, and the remote control for the television was still lying where she'd left it on the coffee table. All signs of her having been here, that falling asleep here hadn't been a dream, any more than it was something she'd been able to forget about.

She shook her head at the fact that, against all promises to herself, she'd ended up back here again tonight. Deciding just to go with events since fate seemed determined they meet up again, she deposited their purchases on the floor. She took off her coat and hung it up in the hallway before coming back to sit cross-legged among the bags and gifts they'd carried in.

'One Max special hot chocolate with cream and marshmallows.' Her host handed her a large mug and joined her down on the floor, clutching his own.

'Do I drink this or eat it?' she asked as he handed her a spoon.

'Both. It's fine. Everyone knows there are no calories in Christmas drinks.'

Whilst Tamsin tried to figure out how to drink it without suffocating, Max seemed to attack his face first, the first sip leaving his nose and chin coated in cream.

'I think you've got a little—' She reached out and wiped the cream off his nose with her fingers.

Max grabbed her hand and sucked it off, his eyes

locked onto hers the whole time. A little shiver of excitement tickled the back of her neck as she watched him, knowing exactly what was on his mind. However, that need to maintain some control wouldn't let her indulge that carnal thought.

She sat back and spooned the cream from her hot chocolate into her mouth so there wouldn't be a repeat incident.

'So, did the home give you this list to buy for, or do you know them all personally?' Tamsin directed him back to the reason she'd agreed to come here before she got too lost in those eyes and naughty thoughts of what they could be doing instead.

'I know most of them now. I volunteer there when I can.' This time he avoided her eye as he spoke, as though he was embarrassed to admit to something so altruistic.

'That's so good of you. I'm sure everyone appreciates it.'

'I'm probably more of a hindrance than a help. The truth is that place feels like home more than anywhere else I've ever been. Probably because I spent so much time there, and I know some of the staff. I suppose the people there are a bit like family to me. It's my way of not only giving something back but I also like to think I'm there as a friend to any of the children if they need me.'

'What kind of things do you do?' This man had such hidden depths it merely highlighted how much of a loving soul he was.

These days doing any good deed seemed more about getting likes and praise on social media by posting video evidence online than genuinely helping someone in need. Max had only disclosed his association because she'd pushed for the information. It made her want to do more and be a better person too. She'd become so wrapped up in work she hadn't made time for anything else in her life. Perhaps it was time she expanded her world beyond the walls of the hospital. It was a chance to do more good and make a difference to the lives of those who weren't as fortunate as others, the way Max was doing.

'Whatever is needed. Sometimes it can be something as simple as helping with washing-up or organising a football match for the kids. On special occasions like Christmas, I help with fundraising for parties or trips out.'

'Like topless car washes?' she couldn't help but tease. Though that backfired when she was now thinking about him covered in soapsuds…

He gave her the side eye. 'Not quite. Sponsored hikes, quiz nights, bake sales…'

'Now that I'd like to see.' Along with rugged Max climbing mountains or dressed in a pair of shorts playing football. In fact, she was beginning to realise she could have inappropriate fantasies about him in any scenario.

Shame moved in that she had reduced this selfless man to a sex object, and she felt compelled to redeem herself. Not only that, she was curious about these people he visited, who might have shown him some degree of affection growing up. And what sort of man he was around them.

She knew efficient Max in the operating theatre, playful Max when he was with his patients and, of course, passionate Max, her lover. Yet she didn't think she'd got to know the real him that he seemed to keep hidden from public view, and it was becoming increasingly important for her to see that side of him. Likely because she knew she was falling for him and wanted to be sure it was because he was the man she thought he was. Even if validating that was going to make it even harder for her to walk away after Christmas.

'Why don't I come with you to give out the gifts?'

'Are you sure? I mean, they always need an extra pair of hands. They'd be grateful to have the help. As would I.' There was that boyish grin again, and she was thankful that she was already sitting down. It did things to every part of her body, making her feel as though she'd been put through a liquidiser.

'I would like to. I don't make enough time for anything outside of work, and since it's important to you I want to help. Besides, I don't want you taking all the credit for these presents.' She made light of her offer to help so he wouldn't realise her ulterior motive.

'Of course. Everyone would love to meet you. Thanks, Tamsin.'

'No problem. Now, you write the tags and I'll start wrapping.' She felt like a fraud accepting any gratitude so set down her hot chocolate and got to work sorting the gifts.

Max lifted an oversized gold-coloured plastic belt. 'This one's for Jay. He's big into his wrestling. I'd like to take him to see it live some day. He's had a bit of a rough start. Parents were alcoholics and couldn't, or wouldn't, look after him.'

'Poor thing. How old is he?'

'Five. Same age as I was when I first went into care.'

A baby.

'It must be scary to be taken away from everything you've ever known at such a young age.' Even just going into hospital at a young age had been traumatic, and she'd had her family around her, supporting her, telling her everything would be all right. Max had no one.

It was easy to see why he related to these children so much and why he wanted to be there for them.

'There's no choice but to try and survive it. Hopefully, he'll have better luck finding a forever family than I did.' The sadness in his voice was heartbreaking and, knowing how painful it was for him to recall those memories, she didn't want to push him for any more information on his childhood.

Especially when he was busying himself sorting the presents and mumbling to himself about who he'd bought what for, making it clear he didn't want to talk about his background any more.

They got a production line going as Max handed her the presents, she wrapped them and he attached the gift tags. All was going well until she was presented with a scooter to try and cover.

'Hmm, this one could be awkward. I should have told you I can only wrap boxes.' Tamsin stood up to try and picture how she was going to tackle it.

'You've done a fantastic job so far. I have faith in you,' Max said with enough sincerity she could've been about to go into lifesaving surgery instead of wrapping a gift.

'Maybe if you hold it in place I can start with the handlebar and work my way down.' She grabbed her roll of tape and some sheets of paper and began taping.

'Hold your finger there,' she said as she wrapped around the footplate.

'That's my finger. You've taped my finger to the scooter.'

'Well, you should've moved it, shouldn't you?'

It was too funny to resist leaving him there taped to a child's scooter, glaring daggers at her.

'I suppose you think this is funny, do you?'

'Just let me get my phone. I need a picture to show the kids.' She turned to grab her handbag to document the occasion and heard the sound of paper ripping behind her.

'Oh, no, you don't.'

Tamsin let out a squeal as strong hands gripped her around the waist and yanked her back. She tumbled onto the sofa with a laughing Max.

'Spoilsport.'

'I can't have you ruining my street cred now, can I?' He had her pinned by the wrists, leaving her immobile beneath him.

Though the moment was light-hearted, now his mouth was only a few millimetres from hers the atmosphere had become decidedly charged.

She could feel his breath on her lips, see the desire in his eyes, feel the hardness of his body flush against hers. That throbbing need between her thighs was pulsing as hard as the blood in her veins. Then his mouth was on hers and her whole body was in flames for him. For his touch.

Despite the passion ignited between them, his kiss was tender, and moreish. It was easy to believe the fairytale when he was kissing her like this. As though time didn't matter and they could do this for ever, forgetting that in a couple of weeks they'd both be back to their single lives again.

Where once her independence had seemed the only way to survive, away from her family and the guilt that plagued her, it was no longer her preferred option. Her quiet, empty hotel room wasn't her safe space any more—it was here in Max's arms.

When he stopped kissing her and pulled away, it was a loss she didn't want to get used to.

'I don't think I can face another night on the sofa. Why don't we go to bed?'

'Are you sure?' She was asking herself the same question. Going to bed with him now, the probability of her staying over, meant relinquishing that last bit of power over her emotions. She was letting how she felt about Max drown out everything her head was telling her.

Max held out his hand. 'We both know that there's no point in fighting against this. I mean, we tried, and we've still ended up here. It's what we both want, isn't it?'

Tamsin looked at the outstretched hand, at the man inviting her to his bed, and thought of the hotel room she could return to instead. Where she would only be lying in bed thinking of where she could've been instead, what she could've been doing, and with whom. Common sense wasn't going to save her, or keep her warm at night. There'd be plenty of time for regret and recriminations once she'd gone back to London.

She took Max's hand, anticipating a night of making love, of feeling wanted, and free from that guilt which plagued her when her mind was quiet. Better than all of that, this was a chance for her to revel in her feelings for Max instead of pretending they didn't exist.

Yes. Yes, she wanted this. A little too much.

'Morning, sleepyhead,' Tamsin's voice greeted Max as he opened his eyes.

She was lying beside him, wrapped only in his towel, her wet hair splayed around her bare shoulders, a more pleasant awakening than an empty bed and the sound of his alarm going off.

'Morning. You're up early.' He stretched and rolled over to kiss her.

'I thought since we're both off today that we could go and deliver these presents. We can drop the ones for my family at the post office on the way there.'

Max was glad she hadn't changed her mind about going with him. The offer had surprised him, but so had everything else that had happened last night. Apart from sleeping together. That had seemed inevitable from the moment he'd spotted her in the toyshop looking after a lost child.

So he'd lost his head again, letting her stay the night, but he couldn't say he regretted it. Not when they'd enjoyed it so much—several times, before they'd passed out from exhaustion. Even now, seeing her almost naked in his bed was awakening his weary body and he couldn't resist reaching out to touch the bare skin of her shoulder, peeling away her towel until she was completely naked again.

This time Tamsin slapped his hand away and pulled the towel back around her. 'I've just had a shower and we have places to be.'

'We could spend all day here instead.'

Tamsin bounced off the bed, clearly not of the same inclination this morning. 'We could, but you have children counting on you and I know you wouldn't want to let them down.'

Max groaned and threw himself back onto the pillow. She was right, his conscience would insist on priority over his libido. 'Can we come back here after? Then we might get to spend what's left of our day off together.'

'Sure. I hope you don't mind, but I used your washer and drier to save me having to go back for clean clothes. They should be done by now. You get ready and maybe we'll grab some breakfast on the way. Okay?' Tamsin gathered his discarded clothes lying around the room and tossed them to him, trying to hurry him along.

'Yes, ma'am.' He saluted her with the hand that wasn't clutching yesterday's shirt.

A pair of jeans landed on his head in response.

Tamsin hoped she was doing the right thing by everyone in accompanying Max to the home. It certainly felt good to be able to do something special for him, and the children. There was a nervous energy about him as they pulled up outside the large stone building. He'd merely picked at the breakfast they'd ordered in a nearby café, whilst she'd finished off most of his avocado toast and her own pancake stack.

'Do they know we're coming?' Tamsin asked as they got out and began to gather the bags of parcels to take inside. She was beginning to regret eating so much as worry set in that she wouldn't pass muster.

Max was bound to be held in high regard here, as he was everywhere, and she wasn't anything more than a visitor. Hopefully, everyone would realise she was here to help, not to gawp at poor abandoned children.

'I phoned ahead and said I'd have a helper this year. Perhaps we should have stopped to get you an elf outfit to validate your position.' Max was grinning, and at least when he was teasing her he wasn't dwelling on anything else.

'Only if you don a red coat and beard.'

'Max, you're here! The children will be so pleased.' A small, bespectacled grey-haired lady rushed out to meet them, putting an end to their jovial banter.

'Lovely to see you again, Isobel.' Max hugged her. Something Tamsin knew he only did with people he felt truly comfortable around.

'This must be Tamsin.' The woman threw her arms around Tamsin and swamped her in her ample bosom.

'Hello,' she mumbled into the stranger's chest.

'Yes. She's a surgeon helping out at the hospital over Christmas,' Max offered.

'I hope you don't mind me tagging along today,' Tamsin said, extracting herself from the suffocating embrace.

'Not at all. Any friend of Max's is a friend of ours. Come in out of the cold. The children are waiting for you.' She ushered Max and Tamsin in through the doors.

Tamsin hadn't any experience of this kind of place, and she'd expected somewhere dark and depressing. Instead, the inside of the building was bright and airy, decorated with artwork obviously done by the children who'd found themselves housed here.

'Max!' They'd barely made it through the doors of the large hall before they were swarmed by small children all vying for her companion's attention.

Clearly, a popular visitor.

'What are you all up to today?' he asked, walking over to the long tables laden with art materials, as little ones clung to his legs.

'We're making Christmas decorations,' Isobel told them, before directing them to leave their gifts under the Christmas tree in the corner of the room.

'Do you want to make some with us?' A little dark-haired boy gazed up at Max with such hope in his eyes that if Max didn't agree, Tamsin knew she would.

'Of course. Why do you think we're here?' Max took a seat at one of the tables and pulled out the one beside him for Tamsin.

As they sat down the children crowded around, keen to show them everything they'd already made and the materials available to them.

'I've made snowflakes!'

'This is my reindeer!'

'There's glue and glitter, and everything!'

The last comment came from the little boy who seemed particularly attached to Max and was visibly excited about the prospect of making some simple decorations.

Tamsin's heart went out to him, and she wondered what circumstances had brought him here. He was so young and innocent, it didn't seem fair that he was in the care system already. Although she supposed it wasn't fair on any of the children that they'd ended up here instead of as part of a loving family.

Again, her thoughts turned to her background and Max's. Everything he'd been denied, and the things she'd taken for granted. These poor kids would've done anything to have had a loving family like hers, and she'd effectively turned her back on them these past three years because she couldn't handle the guilt following her bone marrow transplant. An honest conversation with her sister probably could've helped heal her heart if she'd been brave enough to talk openly with Emily about what had happened.

'Do you want to help me, Jay? What would you like to make?' Max was speaking to the young boy he'd bought the wrestling belt for, and it was clear he had a special bond with him.

Whilst Tamsin found herself as part of a paper chain making line, she watched Max and Jay, heads together in concentration with safety scissors and paper in hand, making snowflakes.

He glanced up and caught her looking at him, his warm

smile proof that he was enjoying himself. It was another indication that he would make a great dad, always making time for play with the little ones who idolised him. It was a shame fatherhood didn't seem to be on his radar when there were little boys like Jay out there crying out for a decent father figure.

'Miss?' Someone was tugging on her dress.

'You can call me Tamsin,' she told the young girl sitting beside her.

The serious-looking child, no more than about eight or nine, leaned in to whisper, 'Can you show me how to make those snowflakes too? I want to make my room look pretty.'

'Of course.' If it wasn't completely inappropriate for a stranger to do so, Tamsin would've scooped the little girl up and given her the biggest, tightest hug she could. It was such a simple request, but there was so much meaning behind it. This child wanted to decorate her living space in an effort to try and make it feel more like her home. It also showed Tamsin what a difference the small things made here, like Max bringing gifts to put under the tree. There probably weren't funds available for sundries like Christmas decorations, which went a long way to making a place feel festive. If Isobel agreed to it, she would purchase a few things for the children herself. A small tree for each of their rooms which they were free to decorate themselves didn't seem like such a high price to pay to put a smile on their faces.

'There are some more scissors and plenty of paper.'

Max pushed some supplies closer and Tamsin took some paper for her new friend.

'Okay, so we fold the paper up into a square like this.' Tamsin demonstrated and waited for the child to follow. 'And you just cut away at the edges, making pretty shapes.' Tamsin snipped a few geometric shapes, then handed the plastic safety scissors over to the little girl.

She was hesitant at first, making a few small incisions. Then she got scissor happy, with bits of white paper flying everywhere as she worked.

'I think that's probably enough. Now we can open our snowflakes and see what pretty designs we've made.'

Tamsin opened hers and Max held his effort next to it, which still managed to look like a folded piece of paper rather than anything creative.

'I think I need more practice.' The disappointed look on his face was adorable.

'Look at mine.' Jay thrust his in front of them, with a more successful geometric design achieved with a few well positioned cuts.

'Mine has a heart in it.' The little girl held up her scrap of paper, which now had a wonky heart shape cut out of the centre. She was thrilled with it.

'Can we put some glitter on them?' Jay's chubby hands were already grabbing for the glue stick and tub of glitter. Luckily, Max intercepted before they were all covered in a layer of silver sparkles.

'You dab the glue on and I'll shake the glitter on so we don't make too big a mess.'

'Do mine too.'

'And mine.' Tamsin copied the excited tone of the kids and held out her snowflake for Max's attention after he'd added glitter to the others.

'I'm sure you could probably manage on your own, Tamsin.'

She fluttered her eyelashes at him. 'But you do it so much better, Max.'

The tight set of his jaw and flare of his nostrils as she teased him told her he was going to get his own back when they were alone.

'We just need some string to hang them up and we're all finished.' Max cut a few lengths of twine, looped through the snowflakes and tied a knot to secure them. 'Ta-da.'

'Aren't these beautiful? We should hang them on our tree.' Isobel clapped and made Tamsin jump in her seat.

They'd been so involved with the children she'd forgotten where they were for a minute. That was the problem with being with Max; he always managed to keep her thoughts so busy with him it left no room in her brain for the ghosts of the past. Then that made her feel even more guilty that she'd been able to forget the debt she owed to Emily. That she didn't deserve one moment of happiness because of the cost to her sister.

Another tug on her dress and her little friend was whispering in her ear again. 'I want to keep mine.'

A small request, but clearly an important one.

'I'm sure that'll be fine if you want to keep yours, sweetheart. We can just put mine and Max's on the tree.'

Tamsin spoke loudly enough for everyone to hear so they would understand what was happening too.

'Do you want to help me put mine on the tree, buddy?' Max and Jay did the honours, leaving Tamsin and Isobel at the table.

'He's great with the children.' Isobel sounded like a proud mother as she watched on.

'The children certainly seem to love him. It's the same at the hospital too. He's a good man.' Praising him came naturally to Tamsin, although she was telling Isobel things she likely already knew.

Isobel sighed. 'It's amazing really, given the start he had in life. He's a great role model for the others here. Unfortunately, a lot of our children who grow up in the care system don't always follow the right path.'

'He certainly must have worked hard to get where he is now.'

'Oh, yes. He was very studious. Something I'll admit isn't always easy here, with so many children in residence. A few can be disruptive, to say the least. So we were thrilled when he was accepted into medical school.'

Tamsin's eyebrows rose at that snippet of information. 'He was here all that time?'

'Yes. Max was here for his last few years in care. Unfortunately, it didn't work out with any of the families he'd been with.'

There was so much heartbreak wrapped up in that one sentence, making it obvious he'd been passed around until he'd come to reside here, a very disruptive, unsettled existence for someone who always went out of his way to try and make his patients feel at ease.

'I didn't realise…'

'He really deserves a family of his own. He always did.' Isobel gave a sad sort of smile that Tamsin felt down to her bones.

Max really did deserve happiness, and if that did include a family then she had nothing to offer him. If she harboured any fantasies about continuing their relationship beyond a fling, it would only be one more obstacle in his way of achieving that fulfilment. Tamsin didn't think she'd ever get over the guilt, the responsibility she felt for her sister's situation, to do something as selfish as start a family of her own.

A buzzing sound reverberated around the room and Max pulled his phone from his pocket. She watched the frown appear on his forehead before he made his way over to her.

'There's an emergency at the hospital. I've got to go.'

'Can I help?' At least in that environment she didn't feel so out of her depth and could do something more practical than cutting up bits of paper.

'I'm sure it will be all hands on deck, so they'll be glad to have you on board. Sorry everyone, but we'll have to go.' Max announced their sudden departure to the group, eliciting a collective groan.

'Sorry you didn't get to stay longer, but we'll see you again soon.' Isobel grabbed him into a hug and the children gathered around them to say goodbye.

'I'll be here to help with Christmas lunch and to open all these presents with you.'

'Yay!'

'Is Tamsin coming back too?'

'Please say yes!'

'Come for Christmas Day!'

The pleas from the children for her to make a return visit were heartwarming and appreciated when she hadn't really done anything to impress them. She presumed she was cool by association as Max's guest, but she'd take it. There weren't many places where she felt this wanted.

'I'm sure I can make some time.' It was the most she could promise when she didn't know how things were going to pan out with Max.

CHAPTER SEVEN

THE THING THAT had struck Max most when they had arrived at the hospital was the quiet. After a mass casualty incident—in this case, a bus colliding with several cars—he might've expected a lot of noise and bustle. By the time he and Tamsin had arrived, however, it seemed that those injured had already been assessed, staff were focused on their jobs and the patients had been given pain relief. Behind that apparent peace though, he knew the adrenaline was pumping and long-term planning for such events had kicked in.

They'd been drafted in to operate on a twelve-year-old boy who'd suffered crush injuries as a result of the crash and the bus he'd been travelling in rolling onto its side after being hit at full speed by another vehicle. Because there were no seatbelts on the bus, most of the passengers had been seriously injured, many suffering from broken bones as a result of the impact and others, like their patient, who'd been trapped in the wreckage afterwards.

'Are you happy for me to take the lead on this one?' he asked Tamsin again before they started. Working in a city hospital, he was often brought in to the emergency department to assist during critical incidents, so he was used to performing this kind of procedure. Plus, he wanted to demonstrate to Tamsin that he had his own area of expertise. He'd been lucky enough to watch, and assist, during her work, and now it was his turn in the spotlight.

Although this should be a straightforward surgery, it was always good to have someone as skilled as Tamsin alongside, one of the few people he was happy to make time for in his life.

'Of course. I know you've got this and you're going to do everything you can to help him get back on his feet.'

He appreciated her belief in him but her comment also served to remind him of the difficulties her sister had faced—it seemed that she would never be able to get back on her feet. It couldn't be easy for Tamsin to be involved in surgeries where the patient's mobility and quality of life would be affected by the outcome. Even more so when she made a positive difference to them, and she couldn't do the same for her sister.

Perhaps that need to help others had prompted her to tell the children she'd come on Christmas Day too. It had surprised him, and though she'd been put on the spot he hoped she would honour the promise, for the children's sake as much as his. He'd already discovered that she'd volunteered to work Christmas Day and it hadn't been forced upon her as she'd suggested. Clearly, it wasn't a day Tamsin expected to enjoy if she would rather work, but at least if they were able to get a few hours with the children at the home she might have some fun.

It wasn't a conventional way of spending Christmas

together, but it would still be nice to have her there with him. He couldn't remember the last time he'd had someone to spend the day with, apart from the children and staff at the home.

The two of them together meant double the impact they could have, including here, with this boy who'd suffered an open pneumothorax, where air had accumulated between the chest wall and lung due to a chest wound caused by trauma. Treating it would be a relatively straightforward procedure which would help the boy breathe easier again.

'We're going to need to insert a chest drain,' he said once he'd cut through the subcutaneous tissue to reach the intercostal muscles. Tamsin assisted him in avoiding the intercostal nerves and vessels so he could angle the drain correctly and suture it securely in place.

'Good job, Dr Robertson.' Tamsin let him take a back seat once he'd finished the intricate work and finished for him, applying a dressing to the wound.

The boy, with his mop of dark hair, reminded Max of Jay at the home—himself at that age too, innocent and vulnerable. None of them deserved what had happened to them—they'd all been victims of circumstance. He was beginning to realise that now.

To keep himself closed off, forgoing the possibility of having any long-term relationship, or even a family of his own, because of all that had happened to him was only hurting him, preventing him from being happy. If, twenty years down the line, Jay told him that he would cut himself off from the world because he was afraid of being hurt, Max would tell him it was an overreaction. That he needed to be brave enough to take a risk and finally break free from the decision his parents had made on his behalf to put him into care in the first place.

Of course, the irony for Max was that whilst he had this revelation, and he was opening up to the idea of a relationship, the woman he wanted one with was walking out of his life soon.

The rest of the patient's treatment would be down to the hospital staff in the relevant department, but he knew they'd both be checking in to make sure everything was okay.

'I think once we're finished here I'll go and see if I'm needed elsewhere.' He was sure the emergency department would be full, not only with the accident victims but also other casualties who would have had an even longer wait with the knock-on effect. The hospital was pulling teams of doctors and surgeons from the local area to treat the wounded but he was sure there would be plenty of work to go around.

'I'll come with you.'

Although he hadn't included her in his plans, Max had expected her to tag along. He was getting used to having her with him, involved in his life here at the hospital and outside.

'Thanks for everything today.' Max handed a hotdog and a plastic cup of mulled wine to Tamsin, then came to join her at one of the picnic tables set up around the Christmas market.

'Glad I could help.' She took a bite of her hotdog, leaving mustard and relish around her mouth.

He was tempted to reach across and kiss it off but she dabbed it away with a paper napkin before he had the chance. Even he would admit it was a romantic setting here in the dark, fairy lights strung everywhere on a frosty night. It wasn't expensive or fancy, but when he'd asked her where she wanted to go for dinner, this was where she'd chosen. After everything she'd helped him with today, he couldn't begrudge her this.

'You were great. Not just at the hospital, but at the care home earlier too. I know the children appreciated it as much as I did.' She continually surprised him, not only with her actions but with how she made him feel. He'd never opened up about that part of his life to anyone, never mind actually let them go there with him. The only thing more surprising than his invitation was the fact that she'd wanted to go.

A lot of people would've shied away from the place, preferring not to acknowledge there were abandoned children with very few looking out for them. Perhaps it was that quality in her, that desire to help, that drew him to her. It was more in his nature to push people away rather than share such personal aspects of his life. Tamsin had been very open to the children, accommodating with her time and patience. In his experience, not all were comfortable around those in care.

During his time in the home he'd witnessed plenty of visitors who'd come merely as a press opportunity, to be seen doing good rather than really wanting to interact, treating the residents with a degree of suspicion and disdain, as though they were guilty of something other than being the victims of circumstance, reinforcing to every one of them the idea that they were unloved and unwanted. It was something he knew many of them still carried with them into adulthood. Including him.

'I enjoyed myself. It's a long time since I did arts and crafts.' Her smile, as ever, lit up her whole beautiful face, as genuine now as when he'd seen her interacting with the little girl this morning.

'Well, you've got a fan club already. They'll be extremely disappointed next time I go in if you're not with me.'

They'd taken to her easily, even though the children were sometimes wary around new faces. Kids usually had good instincts though. He was using that to excuse his uncharacteristic lowering of defences, even if there was still a distance between them, as if Tamsin was holding something back from him. It only ever seemed to vanish when they were in bed together, when nothing else seemed to matter except making each other feel good.

'I'm sure they'll be happy enough with you. You're very popular.'

It wasn't something he'd ever considered himself to be, but he enjoyed being around the children and he supposed they could tell.

'I just know what it's like to be there. Forgotten about.'

'I didn't realise you'd been there as a teenager. I thought it had been a short stint before foster care.'

He supposed he had Isobel to thank for sharing that

information. Not that he had anything to hide, nor was he ashamed of it. He simply tried not to dwell on it too much. It was only when he visited that he was reminded of those days, feeling as though no one cared, and wanting to do his best to prevent others from feeling the same way, even for a little while.

'Unfortunately not. It's not that I was badly treated there, far from it, but it's somewhere you're placed because no one wants you. Not a nice thought.'

Tamsin set down her hotdog.

'I'm sorry if I've put you off your dinner,' he said, his own appetite waning now too, talking about the past.

'No…it's just… I hate to think of you feeling that way.' Her brow was knitted in a display of sympathy Max didn't want to see. Yet he thought it was important she knew his background. He wasn't just an object of pity any more than those children who they'd been with today. There was more to all of them than the people who'd let them down.

He shrugged his shoulders. 'I didn't have much choice in the matter. My parents put me into care at five years old. Any memories I have of them are blurry, and even then I'm not sure if they're real or things I've imagined. It's easy to do that when you're a lonely child. Imagining people. Dreaming of families who'll scoop you up and take you home to live happily ever after.'

'Didn't you see them at all growing up?'

He shook his head. 'There were promises made to come back and get me, but I never saw them again. I don't know what happened to them. I found out later that they were into drugs, and I think they were in and out of prison before I was born. For all I know, they could still be there. As far as I'm concerned, they're not my parents so I've never looked for them.'

Tamsin reached across the table and squeezed his hand. He couldn't believe he was sharing this very personal information with her, especially here, with Christmas shoppers bustling around them and the sound of revellers in the nearby beer tent. But now he'd started unburdening himself he wanted to get it all out. It had been a long time coming for him, sharing his pain with someone. However, seeing her with the children today, free from judgement or prejudice, he knew Tamsin would understand.

'I'm so sorry, Max.'

He could see her tearing up and it nearly broke him too, but he might as well get it all out in the open now and maybe she'd understand why the place meant so much to him.

'I was in a series of temporary foster homes, some better than others. You find out who is in it because they genuinely want to help, and those who are more interested in the funding they get to take on foster kids. In some places the houses were crammed with kids who were no better off there than they were in the home. There were a couple of good families, but they were interim placements so they didn't last long. In the end, no one wanted a teenager, so I came back to the group home. It doesn't do a lot for your confidence when you're passed around like an unwanted package.'

'I don't think it's anything about you personally. I

mean, I don't imagine you were an unruly, uncontrollable child that no one could handle. It just seems to be the way the care system is.'

He gave her a faux scowl. 'What are you saying? That I'm boring?'

Her laugh was welcome in the midst of such a deep conversation. 'No. I picture you as a quiet, thoughtful child, that's all.'

'Boring.'

'No.' She slapped him playfully on the arm. 'What I'm saying is I don't think it was anything personal. Your parents clearly weren't able to cope with the responsibility of having a child. That's not on you. Neither is whatever circumstances led you back to the group home. You're a good man, Max, everyone knows it. And that's completely down to you.'

'I suppose if I hadn't gone into care I might've ended up like my parents.'

'Exactly. Maybe putting you into care was the only good thing they could do for you.'

'Good or bad, I suppose it's shaped me into the man I am now.' He wasn't convinced they'd been that concerned about him, or his future, but Tamsin was helping him to look at things from a different perspective. If he hadn't been abandoned, he might not have pushed himself so hard to be a success and become a surgeon. It was those early experiences which had shaped his desire to help others growing up in similar circumstances.

He'd been abandoned, but perhaps that said more about his parents, or the others who'd failed him in the past, than him. All these years he'd blamed himself, pushed people away in the belief they'd eventually tire of him too and break his heart all over again. Being with Tamsin these past weeks had shown him what it could be like to have someone sharing his life—a partner to confide in, to take spontaneous trips to Christmas markets with, or visit the children at the home with. To have someone he wasn't afraid to be himself around, and let his guard down. It was tiring having to wear the mask of that standoffish, spiky person when he was actually a sensitive man simply afraid of being hurt again.

'The man I happen to like very much.' She squeezed his hand again.

Tamsin was all those things that had apparently been missing in his life, and he knew she liked him. It was just a shame the man he was now still wasn't going to be enough for her. Even she was going to walk out of his life in the end too.

'I think I need another drink.' Max abandoned his half-eaten hotdog on the table and got up.

Tamsin knew he was upset and would've gone after him except she figured he needed some space. Besides, she could do with a time out too from these feelings he'd stirred up inside her.

She already admired him, not only as a surgeon but as a genuinely decent human being who cared deeply for the less fortunate. With everything he'd gone through in his childhood and the way he'd been treated, it made him all the more special.

However, with every facet of Max that she uncovered, Tamsin was getting in deeper and deeper. There was little pretence of a 'casual' fling now when she was getting to know him and the people around him so well. It didn't change the fact that she'd be leaving soon and returning to her own life in London. If she didn't pull back now, it was going to hurt like hell leaving him, and she only had herself to blame.

Her phone buzzed in her pocket, and when she saw her sister's name on the screen her heart sank. It crossed her mind not to even answer it, but her conscience wouldn't let her ignore the fact her sibling was reaching out to her. Something could be wrong at home.

'Hi, Emily.'

'Hi, sis. I just wanted to check in with you and see what you're up to.'

'You know me. Just working away. How are you keeping?'

For two sisters who should've been close, their relationship was clearly strained. It occurred to Tamsin that it was she who'd kept their contact limited to small talk over the years, afraid to dig deeper into Emily's life because she feared hearing the worst. That she'd never got over her dream of being a ballet dancer taken away from her, and hadn't found anything to replace it. It was a shame they'd become strangers to one another in adulthood when the bond they'd had as children had been so strong Emily had donated her own bone marrow to save her sister. Tamsin was beginning to realise what she'd missed over these years, not having that close connection in her life, and how much it must have hurt Emily when she'd distanced herself the way she had. Tamsin should've been there for her and she wondered if it was too late to rectify her mistake.

'I'm good. Mum and Dad are just getting over a bad cold, but hopefully they'll be okay for Christmas.' There was a bit of a pause before she added, 'Will you be coming home this year?'

Tamsin closed her eyes as guilt swamped her at the sound of hope in her sister's voice, almost pleading for her to come and spend some time with them. It was worse now, knowing how much Max longed for a family. Even if she did consider a visit at some point in the future to reconnect with her family, she'd already made her plans for the holidays.

'Sorry, Em. I'm working right through Christmas.'

'Oh.' The disappointment was palpable over the phone, compounding Tamsin's failure as a sister.

'Tamsin, do you want another wine?' Max called from close behind her.

'Who's that? Are you with a man?'

She gave Max a thumbs up but if Tamsin could've shrunk herself into oblivion she would have done. Here she was telling her poor sister she was too busy with work to pay a quick visit home when in reality she was sitting drinking in a Christmas market with her lover.

It felt like rubbing it in her sister's face that she was out here living a full life, whilst she was stuck at home living with their parents because of the generosity she'd displayed when they were younger.

'It's…er… Dr Robertson, a colleague at the Edinburgh hospital I'm working in over Christmas.' It wasn't a lie, even if it played down what had actually been going on between them.

'Sounds busy.'

'We're…um…at the Christmas market. We had a busy shift and just popped out for a bite to eat.' She could hardly say otherwise with the Christmas tunes playing loudly in the background and the noise of the others around them would give it away.

'Ooh, it's not like you to socialise with someone you work with. He must be special.' Emily was teasing her, but Tamsin could feel her cheeks redden and it wasn't from the frosty air. It was because her sister had it spot on. The problem was she didn't want to admit it to herself, never mind anyone else.

'We get on okay. He's the only person I really know here, but I'll be heading back to London in the New Year.' Hopefully, that was enough to throw Emily off the scent of anything more juicy that would make her the subject of gossip at home. She didn't want them to think that was the reason she wasn't going home.

'Maybe you could bring him home with you when you visit?'

Tamsin's heart sank, knowing that in believing she was in a relationship Emily would be reminded again of everything that had been denied to her, and she didn't want that.

'It's not like that, Em.'

Max was heading back to the table and she didn't want

to carry on the conversation with him as a witness when she was bound to upset someone. 'Look, I have to go, but I'll try and get over next year, okay?'

It was the best she could offer for now.

'Okay,' Emily said quietly.

'I've posted some presents home for everyone and hope you all have a lovely Christmas.'

They said their goodbyes, and once she hung up Tamsin huffed out a sigh mixed with relief and frustration.

'Is everything all right?' Max set another mulled wine in front of her and if it hadn't been so hot she would've chugged the whole thing back.

She waved her phone at him. 'My sister, wondering if I'm coming home for Christmas. I had a card from my mum this morning, asking the same thing.'

'You haven't told them you're not going home?'

'I have now. I feel terrible.'

'They obviously want to see you. I'm sure you could find someone to cover you at the hospital if you changed your mind.'

She shook her head. 'It's too short notice. Apart from that, I'm not sure I'm ready to go back. Things are… tricky.'

'I take it you don't get along with them?'

'It's not that… It's totally on me.'

'I'm sure it isn't.'

Tamsin appreciated his support, but he had no idea how awful she felt being around her sister, seeing her struggle and knowing she was the cause of it. Everything was made so much worse by the fact she couldn't do anything to fix it. If it made her a bad person that she couldn't face that, then she had to accept it.

'It's irrelevant anyway. I'm working so I won't be going back. Why don't we take these drinks to go, I'm sure other people need these seats.' She tossed the remainder of her hotdog in the bin and lifted her mulled wine, watching as Max did the same.

'Sorry. I didn't mean to spoil the evening.'

'You didn't. I just don't want to talk about it. I'd rather enjoy the market.' She'd had enough of feeling bad, and she could do that again when she was back alone in London with plenty of time to brood on things. With Max only in her life for a short time, she wanted to continue to play make-believe, pretend the happiness she felt when she was with him was real and could last.

When he took her hand in his she didn't resist and they walked around the stalls sipping their hot drinks, hand in hand like every other couple.

Danger! Danger!

Alarms and flashing lights were going off in her head, but as he put his arm around her waist and pulled her tight in the crowd, Tamsin didn't want to acknowledge them. It was perfect and she didn't want to ruin it.

'Can we stop here? I want to get a few things for the children.' Their romantic meander came to a stop when they reached a stall selling chocolates and fudge and all manner of yummy goodies.

She watched as he loaded up with treats for everyone, knowing it would cost a fortune. 'You've already done so much for them. I'm sure they're not expecting anything else.'

He tapped his card to pay for the purchases, showing no end to his generosity for these children he'd taken so to heart.

'I can't turn up to the Christmas party tomorrow empty-handed. It'll be nice for them to have some treats.'

'You're going back tomorrow?' She knew he was an avid volunteer but she hadn't realised just how regular his visits were.

'I have a clinic in the morning, but I'm going over in the afternoon to help out. I promise I don't make a nuisance of myself. I'm not some sort of sad sack who hangs about the place to make myself feel better. They just need a few more chaperones for this kind of group event to keep an eye on things. There's a disco and party food, and Santa might even make a visit.'

'Sounds like fun. Emily and I missed out on a few Christmas parties with being in and out of the hospital all the time, but I remember going to some when we were younger. I'm sure you'll all have a good time.'

'You're welcome to come. Everyone would love to have you visit again.' He held out the bag of sweets for her to help herself, popping a piece of fudge in his mouth.

Her mouth watered as she eyed the selection. She never had been able to resist anything sweet. That was why she was in a predicament over both offers. Although agreeing to go to the party would mean venturing even deeper into his life, the idea of seeing him with the children again was too hard to turn down. He was in his element when he was with them, relaxed and unguarded. There was always that lingering fear between them about giving too much, but when Max was with the children he didn't hold anything back. She understood that need for him to keep some control when she felt the same way, always worried that by investing too much there would be repercussions. But she was envious of how freely he was able to give of himself with the people at the home. At least if she attended the party she would get to see that side of him again, even if only for a short time.

'I don't have any training tomorrow since it's the weekend.'

'There you go then. Put on your party dress and come with me.' The excitement shining in his eyes was infectious, as was his smile. Tamsin found herself reflecting it.

'If you're going to be wearing yours too, then I definitely won't want to miss it. Count me in.'

'Great. Thank you.' Max kissed her on the lips, warming her from the inside out.

Despite all the promises to herself to the contrary, she wanted to be with Max as more than a casual lover. She wanted to know more about his life, see what made him happy, and be part of it. It was only a kids' Christmas party; it wasn't as though she'd be meeting his family as a prospective suitor.

Then she remembered that this was his family she was ingratiating herself with, getting closer to Max every day. She wouldn't go back on her promise now. All she had to do was remember her sister, the struggles she had and the parties and relationships she'd been denied. Maybe then Tamsin might be able to remember what happened in Edinburgh had to stay in Edinburgh, because it wouldn't be fair to anyone to let it go any further.

CHAPTER EIGHT

'WILL YOU DANCE with me, Max?' One of the younger girls, dressed in a princess costume, was grabbing him by the hand and leading him back onto the floor, where the other children were either dancing or chasing each other around the room.

'Again?' He rolled his eyes at Tamsin, but he dutifully followed his dance partner onto the floor.

Tamsin suspected he secretly loved it. His dance card had been full since their arrival, as had hers. He was twirling the little girl around the floor, her squeals of delight equally as enchanting as her Prince Charming.

Max had given everyone a treat by turning up in a full tuxedo, looking like a movie star. Tamsin had felt underdressed arriving next to him, especially when she had so few clothes with her on this trip. She'd only anticipated needing suitable work clothes or something a bit more formal for the odd dinner out. In the end she'd had to make do with the dress she'd bought for Christmas Day, a red and silver tartan swing dress with a sweetheart neckline.

It had gained Max's approval at least, and he'd greeted her with a wolf whistle when he'd picked her up at the hotel. They'd spent last night together after the market, but he'd gone home early in the morning to change into his swoon suit.

Little Jay sidled up beside her then, looking smart in his blue jeans and button-down shirt. 'This is for you.'

Looking up at her through long dark lashes, he handed her a handmade card decorated with wonky hearts and something resembling a Christmas tree.

'For me? Thank you so much.' She was extremely touched by the effort he'd gone to for her. It was so clear these children had so much love to give, and deserved it in return.

'I made it myself,' he said proudly, his chest puffing up as he spoke.

'You're so good. It's beautiful.' As much as she wanted to gather him up in her arms and hug him, she was still a stranger here, and it wouldn't be appropriate.

She tucked it into her handbag, knowing it would be a treasured reminder of her time here. Jay continued to hover, glancing over at the others now doing the actions to party songs up on the floor.

'Would you like to dance? I don't know the moves. Maybe you could show me?' It occurred to her that Jay was too shy to get up by himself and might need someone to accompany him.

He nodded enthusiastically and took her by the hand. There was quite a crowd on the floor now joining in, but Max stood head and shoulders above all. She watched him and copied his moves, throwing her hands in the air and wiggling her backside to the music. Clearly, this was a well-rehearsed routine here, which brought joy to the adults and children alike. In the midst of the crowd, she locked eyes with Max above the heads of the tiny dancers, sharing a private moment, and a memory she knew they'd both hold dear for ever.

As the music changed to a slower rhythm on a different track, Jay and some of the younger children lost interest and drifted away from the dance floor. Tamsin's heart gave a flutter as she saw Max moving towards her.

'May I have this dance?' he asked with a bow.

'You may.' Tamsin curtseyed as they came together and Max took her in his arms.

It wasn't a particularly romantic song, but they swayed together nonetheless like a couple who'd hooked up at the end of a night out for a slow dance. There were a few sniggers and wolf whistles, but the onlookers soon either got bored or sickened by the display and left them alone.

'Is this inappropriate?' she asked, only half joking.

'They've no interest now the food's out. Besides, it's not as though we're grinding on each other naked. Not yet anyway.'

Tamsin didn't know if it was the promise of doing that with him when they were alone later or his voice whispering in her ear that made her melt against him, but when he let go of her it took a minute to regain her composure.

It was only then she realised the music had stopped altogether. There was a mass scrum going on at the food table for seats as everyone dived on the snacks and fizzy drinks.

'Help yourselves,' Isobel called to them over the racket.

'You're game, letting them have so much sugar,' Max joked, with the children cramming as many sweets as savoury foods onto their plates.

'We've got plenty of party games planned, so I'm hoping they'll burn it all off before the end of the night. And thank you both for all the goodies and decorations you brought. It's very thoughtful. Now, can I ask you another favour and keep an eye here while I pop out for a moment?' Isobel was already backing away towards the door, not leaving them any option.

'Of course. That's what we're here for.' Although it was Max who'd answered on their behalf, they both watched over the children so they didn't eat until they were sick.

'Why don't we keep some of those sweets for later?' Tamsin gently encouraged, handing out some plastic zip bags to the children to make up their own pick and mixes to take away with them.

'Aww, just one more, Tamsin.' Max managed to bag himself a strawberry lace and proceeded to slurp it into his mouth like a strand of spaghetti.

'Only if you promise to eat your dinner later.' Tamsin smacked his hand away before he could reach for another.

'Can we pull the crackers, Max?' one of the children asked, waving one of the crackers they'd brought with them to decorate the table.

'Sure. Save one for me and Tamsin though.'

Soon the air was filled with the sound of bangs and squeals as the children partnered up to compete for the hidden prizes inside. It was Jay who grabbed one and rushed to present it to Max.

'Thanks, mate.' Max's praise made the boy beam before he ran off again to join in with others who were currently engaged in a game of tag around the dance floor.

Max held out the cracker towards Tamsin. 'Fancy a pull?'

Tamsin rolled her eyes at the intentional double entendre and grasped one end of the cracker. It pulled apart with a small bang, but the contents spilled onto the floor. Tamsin was left holding the bigger end of the now empty cracker.

'I think it fell on the floor.' Max got down and began feeling around, eventually presenting her with a pink plastic ring he'd found.

'Woohoo!'

'Are you proposing, Max?'

'Are you and Tamsin getting married?'

The children began to crowd around a now sweating Max, who was kneeling on the floor with a ring.

'No, we…um—' He was struggling for words, and it was excruciating for her too. Mostly because there was a part of her that wished it was real and Max wasn't completely horrified by the idea of actually committing to her like that.

Although an innocent assumption from the children that being together was a possibility, the whole episode was a reminder that the only people they were really hurting with this pretence were themselves.

When they were here, playing happy families with each other and the children around them, they were ignoring the inevitable split which was coming closer every day. Thankfully, before Max had to come up with some terrible lie about their relationship to prevent the children from getting carried away with the idea of wedding bells, actual bells sounded down the corridor. Followed by a, 'Ho-ho-ho.'

The children rushed towards the door, all interest directed towards Santa, now entering the room. An excited murmuring reverberated around the room, the children paying no mind to the obvious fact it was Isobel wearing a too big Santa suit carrying presents.

'Saved by the bell.' A relieved-looking Max got to his feet, and it didn't escape Tamsin's attention that he'd put the ring in his pocket rather than risk giving it to her and her getting the wrong idea.

It shouldn't have bothered her, but it did, an irrational rage building inside her that he didn't want to marry her, even though it was the last thing either of them would ever need in their lives. She'd only known him for a few weeks, for goodness' sake. They lived in different countries. She didn't want a relationship. All reasons why she shouldn't want a real proposal. Yet Max's obvious horror at the thought felt like a rejection she hadn't been prepared for. Probably because she'd believed their connection had become about more than just sex. It had for her. And all the more reason she should rein in her involvement, not only with Max but with the residents here, who were more like his family.

If she'd met him in London, or even in Belfast, she never would've dreamed of getting this involved in his life. Being in Edinburgh, away from her day-to-day life, had made her act as though she was in holiday mode, carefree and able to act without consequence. The trouble was she knew once she went back to her real life there would be a lasting effect when she would have to sever all ties and pretend none of this had happened. For her own sake.

Max had already visibly distanced himself from her, moving over to where the children had congregated, waiting for their turn to see Santa. It wasn't clear if it was embarrassment or a fear that she'd get the wrong idea from the children's teasing which had pushed him away. However, it was probably for the best that they didn't draw any more attention so Tamsin remained where she was, the distance opening up between them beginning to feel like a necessary precaution.

'Quiet down, everyone. We'll call your names one by one to come up and receive your present from Santa. Until then, I want you to sit on the floor, legs crossed, and we'll sing some Christmas songs while we wait.' One of the other staff members called the children to order and managed to get them engaged in some festive singing.

All eyes were trained on Santa, sitting at the front of the room with the sack of presents. Tamsin noted that Max didn't glance back at her once. If he hadn't given her a lift here she would have been tempted to slink out unnoticed, instead of getting herself any further involved.

Santa Isobel called the children one by one until the hall was full of the sound of excited gasps and wrapping paper being torn off.

'Max Robertson.' The last name called brought childish titters from those who'd already received their gifts.

Max seemed as surprised as anyone to be mentioned, but dutifully went to the front of the room.

Santa Isobel patted her lap, encouraging him to rest his backside on her knee, which obviously caused the children to go into fits of laughter. Max played along, making a ridiculous sight perched in his tux on Santa's knee.

'Well, Mr Max, what would you like Santa to bring you this Christmas?' Santa asked in a not very convincing deep voice.

It was only then Max looked at Tamsin, locking eyes with her. 'Nothing. I have everything I need here.'

He hadn't needed to look away for Tamsin to realise that didn't include her. His actions today had already shown her that. It hurt nonetheless.

'Well, you've been a very good boy this year so I think you deserve a present.' Santa Isobel handed him a small package and Max walked away as though he was floating on air.

He clutched it to his chest as if he'd been handed the most precious thing on earth and it was her turn to look away. Seeing his joy at such a small gesture of appreciation and love was a reminder of how much he'd been denied both during his life.

Tamsin didn't want to care, or think that she might be the one who could provide him with that love and stability he obviously needed, because they both knew it wasn't possible.

'Do you want me to come up with you?' Even though spending the night together had become their routine of late, Max wasn't sure if that was what Tamsin wanted this evening. Or if it was a good idea at all.

The drive back to her hotel had been silent, Tamsin preferring to stare out of the window than engage in conversation. He'd put the radio on in the end to interrupt the awkward atmosphere, subjecting them to all the same Christmas songs they'd listened to at the party for the duration of their journey.

It wasn't completely down to her that things had become strained between them. There had been a definitive shift between them after the whole ring debacle. Regardless that the children had most likely been teasing in expecting him to propose, both he and Tamsin had clearly been mortified by the encounter. It had put them in an awkward position, not only because he'd had to struggle to explain why that wasn't a possibility, but it had also made him face the reality of their situation.

He'd convinced himself that once this fling was over they could both go back to their normal single lives as though it had never happened. He was beginning to realise that not only was that getting harder for him to do every day, but he'd also introduced her to other people in his life. Explaining her sudden departure, or the nature of their relationship, to anyone was going to prove challenging later on. He'd made a mistake involving her in his business at the home, letting her venture into a part of his life that he held close to his heart, and with good reason.

Pretending that she'd never been there, winning everyone else over and showing how good they were together, wasn't going to be as easy to forget when there were other witnesses to remind him.

'You should probably come up.' Tamsin unbuckled her seat belt and got out of the car, not waiting for him to follow her into the hotel lobby.

Max got the impression they had 'a talk' coming up, when they'd both have to face up to the fact that they'd gone way beyond any definition of 'casual'. Either they were going to have to end things now or try and figure out how they might continue to have a future together when they lived so far apart. Given how badly she'd reacted to the idea of a proposal, he was certain she was set to call the whole thing off.

'It was really nice of Isobel to get you a gift too,' he commented as they entered the lift together, seeing her clutch the present Santa had given her after Max had received his.

'Yes, I wasn't expecting anything,' Tamsin said politely.

'You've made a big impression in the short time since you've been here.' And not just with the children.

'I guess so.' She looked at the pretty floral notebook and pen she'd received and smiled.

Although it wasn't as personal as the framed photograph he'd received of himself with the children, there was no less thought put into the gift. They'd both been a bit overwhelmed by Isobel's generosity.

'I wasn't expecting them to do that,' he admitted.

'It was lovely of them to think of us both. They clearly

love you, Max.' Tamsin afforded him a half smile as she opened the room door.

'I just like to give something back.' Deep down, he knew it was more than that. They were the only ones who he could relate to, and who really understood him. At least they had been, until Tamsin had come into his life. Very soon he was going to have to get used to the idea that she would no longer be part of his support system.

'It's clearly appreciated. Make yourself at home, I'm just going to freshen up.' She left Max to entertain himself and locked herself in the bathroom.

Max turned the TV on and flicked through the channels, stopping at a music channel playing girl band videos from the nineties. It was a refreshing change from the incessant Christmas tunes which had seemed to blast out from everywhere since November. He didn't usually get into the Christmas spirit as much as everyone around him seemed to, probably because he'd never experienced that cosy family atmosphere in the lead-up to the big day. It always seemed to be a disappointment so he'd learned from an early age not to expect too much.

Although the staff at the home had tried to make it special, it never had quite the same excitement or magic as portrayed in the movies. Nor was there enough money to stretch to the expensive trainers or games consoles that his schoolfriends got on special occasions. Still, today had been fun. Until it hadn't been. Until he'd had a bucket of cold water thrown over him to wake him out of the dream world he'd been living in with Tamsin these past weeks.

He heard the water running in the bathroom and, restless, reached out for the stack of medical books she had by the bedside. As he glanced through them, a card slipped out from between the pages and fell to the floor.

'Merry Christmas to a Wonderful Daughter' was emblazoned above a Christmassy night sky with Santa and his reindeer making their way towards a snow-covered cottage. Not thinking for a second it was something she'd purposely kept hidden, he looked inside to find a note from Tamsin's parents, wishing her a happy Christmas and practically begging her to come home for a visit.

His heart ached to have a family so desperate to have him in their lives and he couldn't understand why Tamsin would want to be anywhere other than with hers. Especially at this time of year.

Tamsin came back into the room, dabbing her face with a towel. 'What's that you've got?'

'The Christmas card from your family. They really want you to go home for a visit.'

'I've already spoken to my sister. I told her I'll try and get back next year.' Tamsin's cavalier attitude towards her family was something he couldn't reconcile himself to when he would've done anything to have parents and a sibling who wanted him.

He especially didn't understand it when Tamsin was so free with her time for everyone else. She devoted herself to her transplant patients long after their surgery, and she'd volunteered at the children's home when she had no reason to. He was sure she could've found time for a short trip home to see her own family if she'd made any attempt to fit them into her schedule, especially when no one was forcing her to work over Christmas.

She took the card off him and tucked it back into the book, out of sight, as though she didn't want to be reminded of them. It spoke of unresolved issues between them, but he couldn't imagine what they were when between the phone call and the card they seemed desperate to see her.

'I would've thought with everything that happened you would've been closer to your family, Tamsin.'

'Yes, well, I'm not. My life is in London now.' She turned her back on him, tidying the night stand he'd deigned to touch.

'Yet you made time to come to Edinburgh. I'm sure you could manage a trip over Christmas just to say hello.'

'Just drop it, Max. I don't want to go back, okay?' When she did look at him, he could see even talking about it was paining her, visibly wincing as he addressed the subject.

Yet she'd been there for him when he'd spoken about his troubles, supported him when he'd visited the home again, and he wanted to be able to do something for her too. Especially if it meant there might be some hope of reconciling with her loved ones.

She was such a private person, so closed-off about her own life, Max thought that maybe she simply needed someone to confide in too.

'One day you might regret not seeing them. You don't want to be left all alone, Tamsin. Trust me.'

'It's easier that way. You have no idea what I live with

every single day. You don't know anything about me, Max, except that I keep you warm at night.'

He flinched with the direct hit. It was true that they'd tried to maintain an emotional distance until now, but he wanted to be there for her if she'd let him.

'So tell me. What is so bad that you can't spare a couple of days to go and see your family over Christmas?'

Tamsin collapsed onto the end of the bed, hands fidgeting in her lap, as though the weight of her secrets had finally got the better of her. 'I can't face Emily.'

'Your sister?'

She nodded.

'But she obviously wants to see you. Why else would she have called and asked you to visit?'

'Emily's not the problem, I am,' Tamsin bit back, angrier than he'd ever seen her, and he knew every bit of that rage was directed at herself, even though he was the one presently on the receiving end of it.

'I'm sure that's not true. If they had a problem with you, they wouldn't want you to come home. At the very least, they must want to work through it.'

She shook her head. 'I have a problem with me. With the guilt that overwhelms me every time I see my sister. Do you know how hard it is to look at Emily, knowing I'm responsible for the pain she's in? She doesn't have a life because she gave it to me.' She pounded on her chest, right above her heart.

'What exactly happened to her?'

He knew Emily had been the one who'd donated her bone marrow to Tamsin, and that she'd been left with life-altering consequences, because he'd sat in on that first training session at the hospital. But he didn't know the details. He was beginning to see how one-sided the relationship had been with regard to their lives outside of their fling. Tamsin had physically been part of his life here, getting to know everyone at the home, yet he knew very little about her before she'd come to Edinburgh.

It was a sign that he was in too deep. He'd let her infiltrate every part of his life, in the full knowledge that she was going to leave. The idea that they'd grown too close was on his part only, and he was going to be the one hurt in the end. Despite his belief to the contrary, apparently, he'd opened his heart to the wrong person at the wrong time. He should've learned his lesson after Mairi.

Tamsin was on her feet again, pacing, and it felt as though she wanted to walk away from him as much as her family. It was inevitable, he supposed, but he wasn't ready for it quite yet.

Eventually she stopped and rested against the table, apparently having finished wrestling with the idea of sharing anything with him. 'She suffered an injury to her sacral nerve and the doctors didn't take her, or my parents, seriously enough when she complained of back pain. Told her it was to be expected. By the time they realised it was more than that, the damage had already been done. She lost a lot of control in the lower half of her body. Emily has gone through hell and hasn't been the same since. She's in constant pain and unable to live any sort of normal life.'

'And you blame yourself?'

'Wouldn't you? She's only like this because she tried to help me. We were only kids and she probably didn't realise the consequences, only that she wanted to make me better. I'm responsible for the way she is and I'm reminded of that every time I see her. So it was easier for me to move away and focus on work. Selfish, I know, but I couldn't do anything for her except be a constant reminder of everything she's been through too. It's better for all of us that I stay away.'

'They probably wouldn't agree if you'd give them a chance and explain how you feel.'

'It's not going to change anything, is it?'

'Look, I understand how guilt and blame can stay with you, no matter how misplaced. You were the one that told me I shouldn't beat myself up about my parents' decision. Or do you think I was somehow at fault for the decisions they made, and what happened as a result?'

'Of course not. It's not the same thing.'

'Yes, it is. It's your skewed perception of what happened. That's what we do when we're kids. We think we're to blame for things beyond our control. It's honesty that's important. I can't have that conversation with my family and resolve those feelings or make amends, but you can.'

'Talking isn't going to fix my sister.'

'No. Nothing is going to do that. But it could help you come to terms with it and stop blaming yourself.'

'Maybe I don't want to do that. Maybe I deserve to be miserable. My conscience certainly won't let me live the life I've denied my sister.'

'Do you really believe that? That your sister thinks you should shut yourself off from the world and spend the rest of your days punishing yourself on her behalf?'

It certainly seemed like a waste of a life to him, something he'd recently opened his own eyes to when he was guilty of doing the same thing. Now he was hoping for more in his life, but if Tamsin really was determined to be a martyr maybe there wasn't any hope for them. He needed a partner who was prepared to be there for him if he was going to open his heart again. Not someone determined to be alone and miserable as punishment for something she had no control over.

It seemed she wasn't the woman he'd believed her to be after all, someone he'd been starting to believe he might be able to share his life with on a longer-term basis. Why else would he have invited her to the home and told her things he'd never told anyone about his life if not because he'd thought she was going to be in it? Only now he realised that he'd never figured in her future plans at all. If a relationship, or any life beyond her guilt, wasn't a possibility then there wasn't any place for him at all.

'It doesn't matter what Emily thinks. It's what I believe that matters. I don't want to talk about it any more, Max.'

That left him almost speechless. 'Why not? I've been honest with you about my life, and shared some deeply personal stuff that I've never told anyone before. Why can't you do the same? You're purposely choosing this solitary existence when I've dug deep and found it within myself to open up to you, Tamsin, because I care about you. I'm sorry, but it just doesn't seem as though you feel the same.'

In fact, it felt as though everything he'd shared with her was being thrown back in his face. That none of it was of any significance to her whatsoever. That she was still only interested in the physical side of a relationship with him and nothing more. He'd gambled with his heart and lost.

'I think you should be honest with your family too,' he continued. 'It's better to say how you feel than have all this unresolved guilt and anger building up inside you. It'll tear you apart, Tamsin, trust me. As for us, I'm going to be honest and say I think we've run our course. We've had an amazing time together, but we've let things get complicated. I think we should end it now. I don't see the point in delaying the inevitable when we're clearly already beginning to rub each other up the wrong way.'

And they clearly had different ideas about what they wanted if she wasn't prepared to even try and make room for him in her life. It was better if he walked away now, rather than believe Christmas was going to be some special time for them. He was going to be on his own, as always.

Max knew he wouldn't be able to bite his tongue over the Christmas holidays either when he knew all that was keeping her from her family was an unwarranted load of guilt weighing on her conscience. Especially when it was clear her sister didn't harbour any ill feeling towards her. Tamsin simply wasn't prepared to let go of her misplaced guilt to embrace those who actually cared about her. She was the one who wasn't living a full life.

It wasn't the way he wanted things to end, and it was likely too late to prevent him from missing everything they'd had together, but he didn't see any choice. Clearly, Tamsin could never let herself feel the same way about him as he did about her.

'Max, you knew going into this that I didn't want anything serious. Why are you spoiling things now when we've had such a good time?' She did care, but it wasn't going to do either of them any good thinking they could have something more than they'd agreed on. He was never going to understand her position with her family because he so desperately wanted one of his own. If they could set their personal baggage aside again, they just might be able to enjoy the few days she had left in Scotland.

'Because things have changed. I feel differently but obviously you don't, so I don't see a future for us. Short-term or otherwise.'

'Look, I'm here for at least another week. Why don't we put all of this behind us and make the most of what time we have left together?' Tamsin was sure if they could just get back to the reason they'd got together in the first place, she could make him forget the shameful reason she couldn't go home.

She wasn't ready for things to end just yet, and she was sure it was simply because family was a touchy subject for Max. Of course he was never going to understand because he'd never really had one of his own, or gone through the things she had. They had a lot of things in common, but when it came to childhood they'd had very different experiences and lasting traumas. It didn't mean she wanted him out of her life.

He made a move towards the door with a steely determination that made her stomach almost leap into her mouth.

'I'm not like you, Tamsin. I can't just forget.'

It was a low blow that left a mark, but she didn't see why her issues with her family had to mean the end of their arrangement. Without Max, her stay in Edinburgh was going to be a very lonely one. Not only that, she wanted to be with him. He'd given her so much of himself, she only wished they could've found some way forward together. But not even Max could alleviate the guilt she felt over her sister, and the different quality of their lives.

'I've promised the children I'd visit on Christmas Day.' It sounded pathetic to her own ears to use them as an excuse to keep her in his life, but she also didn't want to let the others down.

'It's fine. I'll go on my own. They're used to people who don't keep their promises.'

There was a painful look in his eyes that said he wasn't just talking about her, or the children, and it made her sick to her stomach. She knew what he'd been through, those who'd failed him time and again, and hated that she might be one of them.

'Don't punish them, or me, just because you're not

comfortable with how much of your personal life you shared with me. At least let me say hello, or goodbye.' It didn't seem real to her that she might have seen them all for the last time and not known it.

'You don't need to. They're *my* family, Tamsin. You have yours, and they should take precedence. Go and see them over Christmas. I know you weren't forced to work it. You volunteered. Stop hiding.'

Max opened the door and walked away. Tamsin had never felt so seen. Or so alone.

CHAPTER NINE

'DID YOU HEAR about all of that business with Poppy Evans at the Great Southern?' one of the theatre nurses asked, making small talk before surgery.

'No?' Although Tamsin didn't know the neurologist that well, something must've happened for the gossip to have travelled this far from London.

'That's where you're from, isn't it? My daughter works there. It was she who was telling me that apparently there was some mix-up at the fertility clinic and, far from the father being anonymous, it turns out it might be her colleague, Dylan someone...'

'Dylan Harper?' She knew the neurologist in passing. The news must've come as a shock for both of them.

'Yes, that's it. Anyway, looks like they both got an early Christmas present. I hear he's very handsome.'

'Mm.' Tamsin didn't commit herself to further comment. She wasn't one for gossiping. The last thing she wanted was news to spread between the hospitals that she and Max were an item, making things even more uncomfortable at work.

'Are you all sorted for Christmas yourself?'

'Um...not really. I'm not doing much this year.' Even

less than usual, Tamsin mused, happy at least that they'd changed the subject from her colleagues.

Back in London, she might have gone out for drinks or Christmas lunch with colleagues. Here, she had no one. Sometimes that was the way she liked it, but not now, when she'd had Max's company for weeks. Without him, the days, and nights, seemed so much emptier. She didn't even have the visit to the children to look forward to.

'I'm so well organised for a change. All the presents are wrapped and under the tree, food's been bought and the turkey is ordered. I suppose you don't have family here to go to…' The nurse trailed off, clearly aware of this surgeon's circumstances.

'No, but it's okay. I'm working anyway.'

The nurse smiled, seemingly relieved that she hadn't put her foot in it or, worse, felt obliged to offer a place at her Christmas table.

Tamsin had no desire to celebrate the day at all now. She had expected to be at the home with Max, having made some time to help dish out Christmas lunch and watch the children open their presents. That had been denied to her following the argument she'd had with Max last week. Part of her had hoped that once he'd calmed down they might have reconciled for the last few days of her stay, but so far he'd managed to avoid her.

She had to accept that it really was over between them and there was nothing she could do about it. He was never going to understand why she couldn't be around her big sister because he couldn't see past his own mountain of emotional baggage.

'Always busy,' her colleague commented sympathetically before they went into the theatre.

Although the transplant surgery she'd been rushed in for today was to improve the quality of life for this twenty-year-old heart recipient, it was also giving Tamsin a new focus.

It had given her a reason to get up this morning, knowing everyone and everywhere was going to be full of a Christmas spirit she wasn't feeling. The wards in the hospital were festooned with decorations to brighten up the day for everyone who found themselves here, but for her it was merely a reminder that Christmas was just another day for her. There would be no loved ones to open presents with around the tree or share a huge dinner with before vegging out in front of the TV. Even Max had found a family to share the day with. One that didn't include her.

She was working with a different team, no less skilled, but there was something missing. Max.

'Dr O'Neill?' Her fellow surgeon was looking at her expectantly, waiting for her to begin.

'Sorry. I just like to take a moment to collect my thoughts before I start.' It was partly true. She wanted to clear her head of Max-related baggage so she could fully concentrate. Cutting someone open wasn't the time for distractions.

Her colleague gave a nod. 'No problem. When you're ready.'

She was sure he meant, *Get a move on*, but since she was the surgical lead, he had little choice but to respect her process.

Tamsin took a deep breath and set aside her broken heart to give her patient a new one.

'Okay, let's give this woman another chance at life,' she said, wishing it was as easy to do for herself, or her sister.

The heart/lung bypass machine worked to keep the oxygen-rich blood circulating in the patient as they operated. Once Tamsin made the first incision into the chest, she was able to separate the chest bone and open the ribcage to access the diseased heart and remove it. With the donor heart in place, she attached the major blood vessels and waited for it to start beating when the blood flow was restored.

Although this was her area of expertise, it was no less stressful until Tamsin was sure the transplant had been successful thus far. Of course, it was still going to be a long road ahead with biopsies and hospital visits for the organ recipient, but Tamsin had done her part.

'We'll leave those tubes in for a few days to drain away any build-up of blood or fluids.'

Once the patient was moved to Intensive Care, the medical staff there would attach more tubes to administer medicines and fluids, as well as a ventilator to help her breathe. As Tamsin finished up the transplant, knowing that this patient was going to be hopefully afforded a life she wouldn't otherwise have had, she thought of the family waiting outside. Parents and siblings worried that they mightn't get to share another Christmas with their loved one.

She thought of Max, who she'd already lost, and the family she'd pushed away. He was right. If anything ever happened to any of them, she'd never forgive herself for not seeing them one last time, or trying to rebuild their relationship, and she couldn't live with any more guilt.

'Another good job, Doctor,' someone congratulated her.

If only her personal life was as fulfilling as her professional one, Tamsin might believe she was someone of worth, deserving of her sister's gift.

She'd already lost Max through her obstinacy and inability to see things from anyone else's perspective other than her own. It would break her to lose her family too. All for the sake of one visit home to hopefully mend some bridges.

As Tamsin gave one patient another chance at a happy life she prepared to do the same for herself. Or as close as she could get without Max as part of it.

'Tamsin? We thought you weren't coming home.' Her dad swamped her in a hug which immediately made her feel bad she hadn't done this sooner. It had been at least three years since she'd visited.

'Hey, Dad.'

'Sarah, Tamsin's here.' His yell brought her mother rushing to the front door, wiping her hands on her apron.

'We thought you were too busy,' her mother reiterated, grabbing her into another hug.

As embarrassed as she was by the doorstep display of affection, Tamsin realised how much she needed those hugs right now. It felt good to be in someone's arms again, even if those couldn't be Max's arms.

Even thinking about him made her eyes sting with tears, and she knew the relationship had gone far beyond a meaningless fling. She missed him, and some part of this trip back home was about getting away from the hospital and hotel which held so many memories of him.

'Are you going to keep me out here in the freezing cold or are you going to invite me in?' She swallowed down her sorrow and plastered on a smile for her parents' benefit.

'Come in, come in. Oh, look, I've got flour all over your good coat.' Her mother ushered her into the hall and began brushing at Tamsin's coat.

Tamsin sniffed the air, inhaling the scent of cinnamon and ginger. 'Are you baking?'

'It's Christmas Eve Eve. Of course she's baking. There's enough food in there to feed the whole country.' Her father rolled his eyes but they all knew he'd be first to do a taste test regardless of how hot the buns and biscuits were.

It was nice to think that some things hadn't changed in her absence.

'If I'd known you were coming, I would've made the bed up for you.'

'It's fine, Mum. I'll sleep on the sofa. I don't mind.'

'Well, you're not having my bed, sis.' Emily appeared with a huge grin on her face, and the brief moment of happiness Tamsin felt at seeing her was soon quashed when she was faced with the sight of her wheelchair.

'I'll go and make up the spare room now. Emily, you take the biscuits out of the oven as soon as the timer goes off.' Her mother stripped off her apron and handed it to Emily before disappearing upstairs.

'It's good to see you, Em.' Tamsin leaned down to give her a hug. 'I didn't mean to cause any fuss.'

'You know your mum. Any excuse to play Suzy home-maker,' her father grumbled, and now the excitement of her unexpected arrival had passed he went into the living room to reclaim his favourite armchair.

'Home, sweet home.' Emily rolled her eyes, but Tamsin was already glad she'd made the trip.

Guilt and childhood trauma aside, it was nice to have some normality in her life again. Back to the family dynamic of her mother fussing too much, her father pretending not to care about anything and her big sister teasing her. All of them ignoring the wheelchair in the room.

'How are things with you?' she asked Emily as she followed her into the kitchen, which looked like there'd been an explosion in a bakery.

The counter tops were covered in flour and icing sugar. Eggshells were dripping half of their contents onto the floor and batter-covered bowls and spatulas were strewn everywhere.

'Looking forward to getting my own place.' Emily began piling the dirty dishes into the sink and turned the hot water on to wash them.

Tamsin laughed, then realised she was serious. 'You're moving out? But how? Why?'

Emily looked offended by her reaction. 'Yes, because I'm a grown woman and I want some privacy. Not to mention a dishwasher. Dad says there's no point in getting one here as we don't make that much mess, but I beg to differ.'

'Do they know?' Tamsin parked her wheeled travel case and hung her coat on the back of a kitchen chair. This warranted more than a mention in passing.

'Yes, they know. Not that I need permission. Now, enough about me. Are you going to tell me who that was with you the other night, and why you really came home?'

'I just wanted to see everyone—'

'I'm not falling for that. You've hardly bothered in years, and now there's a man on the scene you're suddenly desperate for a visit? I'm not daft, Tamsin. Sit!' Emily pointed towards a chair and Tamsin did as she was told.

'It's not like that…' she protested feebly as Emily came to join her at the table.

It reminded her of when they were teenagers when she was having boy troubles but too ashamed to say anything to Emily, who never got asked out on dates and had more important things like her health to worry about.

'So tell me.'

Tamsin debated whether to lie and pretend she just needed a break from work. However, once she started thinking about Max and the time they'd spent together these past few weeks, she found herself welling up. She'd tried to convince herself that their fling didn't really mean anything, that she could pick up her life from where she'd left it before she'd gone to Edinburgh. Sitting here in the kitchen, facing her sister's concerned face, she no longer had anywhere to hide from her feelings. Apart from anything else, she wanted to share what she was going through with somebody instead of keeping it all bottled up. Since she didn't have any friends or colleagues in Edinburgh, this had to be the next best thing. Even if she was wary of how it might sound to Emily, moaning about her love life when her sister was still here living with their parents, albeit not for much longer.

She heaved out a sigh. 'Max is a paediatric surgeon I was working with in Edinburgh.'

'Hold on. This calls for a cup of tea.' Emily turned her chair around and flicked on the kettle.

'That's who you were with at the market when I called?'

Tamsin nodded, the magical night so embedded in her thoughts that she found it hard to believe it was over. One minute they'd been walking hand in hand enjoying the Christmas sights and sounds of the market, looking forward to spending another night together, the next they'd ended up rowing about her family, which was a moot point now. It all seemed like such a waste when she was back here, trying to sort things out but without Max in her life. She knew that was also down to her inability to open up to him properly, just as she'd failed to do with her family.

Emily finished making the tea and set a large Santa-shaped mug in front of Tamsin.

'It was just supposed to be a casual fling. You know, while I was in the city.'

She could feel her cheeks burning as she confided her dirty little secret. Calling it a fling reduced what they'd had together to such a base level when what they'd had went way beyond purely a sexual relationship. It might have started out that way but, regardless of their promises to keep things purely physical, it was clear now that somewhere along the way emotions had become involved.

Why else would she be sitting here almost in tears, facing up to the fact she wasn't going to see him again? At least, not in any romantic capacity. They might still cross paths professionally now and again, though in some ways it would be worse seeing him and pretending nothing had happened between them when everything in her world had been turned upside down since meeting Max Robertson.

'But...'

'I don't know. We had a row. Things ended. I miss him.'

Emily arched an eyebrow at her. 'I'm going to need more than that to go on.'

Tamsin sipped at her tea. It was strong and sweet, and a poor replacement for what she was missing in her life, but it had to do for now.

'We liked each other, but neither of us wanted anything serious. So, you know...'

'You had a fling?'

'Yes, but it got more complicated than that. We started spending more time together, and he introduced me to everyone in the children's home where he grew up. We bought presents for them, and helped out at the Christmas party.'

The memory of that made her smile, though she tried to blot out the less happy moments of the day, when it became apparent that they couldn't continue with the charade that they had a future together.

Emily tilted her head and watched her with a goofy smile on her face.

'What?' Tamsin demanded, wondering if she was still covered in flour to have her sister staring at her in such a manner.

'You're in love with this Max.'

'What? No. Don't be daft.' Tamsin bristled at the accusation.

'I have never seen you so...unsettled. You never discuss your private life with me, so something has you rattled. As for the trip home, it's obvious you're running from something and my guess is it's your feelings for Max.' Emily sat back in her chair as though she'd just solved the case of the century.

Tamsin was silent as she mulled over the proposition. Leaving Max had always been in the plan, but yes, it hurt so much more than she'd ever imagined. She had no idea how things could ever have worked, based on their emotional as well as their geographical circumstances, but she supposed she had been holding out some hope for the impossible.

Yet how she felt about him could never change her perspective on the idea of a committed relationship even if he wanted any kind of future with her. The way they'd parted left her in no doubt that he thought her a weak-willed coward, not the sort of woman who could ever have tempted him into a commitment.

'It doesn't matter anyway. There's no way we can be together.'

'Surely if he's worth this much upset you might consider transferring to Edinburgh? Especially if you've got work there already?' It all sounded so feasible from the outside, but there was no way of explaining the complications without addressing the very subject Tamsin had been avoiding for so long.

'It's not that simple, Em.'

'Why not? You like him, and I'm assuming he likes you or he wouldn't have introduced you to the other people in his life.'

'I'm sure he did like me, but I've always been careful about not getting too involved with anyone.' He'd told her he cared for her, something she knew had taken a lot for him to admit, but she'd held back from telling him she felt the same. It was easier for her to keep him at arm's length, the way she'd done with her family, rather than deal with those feelings head-on, because she was afraid of what would happen if she did.

'Why?'

It was beginning to get uncomfortable now as she built up to the real reason she'd come back here. Max had made her face up to the fact that this needed to be said, but that didn't mean it wasn't agony saying the words.

'Well, it never seemed fair. On you. I never thought I deserved to settle down and be happy when you're stuck here because of me.'

'What are you talking about? Why do I have anything

to do with the reason you can't be with Max, or anyone else, apparently?'

'If it wasn't for me, if you hadn't donated your bone marrow, and suffered the injury, you wouldn't be in this chair. You'd have a life of your own in London, or anywhere else in the world. Probably with a husband and a couple of kids. How can I go on and live my life as though you didn't sacrifice yours for me?'

Emily was silent, though her scowl grew fiercer by the second. Tamsin's nails were digging into the palms of her hands as she sat, tense and waiting for her sister to tell her she was right and didn't deserve any happiness. That she resented her and had been too afraid to said it aloud all these years.

'Is that what you really think?' The soft question threw Tamsin.

'Well, yes.'

'Is that why you've avoided us for so long?'

She hung her head, embarrassed by her behaviour, knowing she should have been braver and confronted this sooner.

'Yes. Every time I look at you, I hate myself for putting you through this. It's easier to live my life in London, pretending none of it ever happened, than to face you every day. I'm sorry, Emily.'

'You're an idiot.'

'Pardon me?'

'You heard me. You're an idiot.'

'Seems a bit harsh…'

'When have I ever said I blamed you for me being in this thing?' Emily slapped the armrest on her chair.

'But you must. If it wasn't for me—'

'No one could've known what was going to happen. It was just one of those things.'

'You weren't old enough to understand the consequences of a bone marrow transplant. It's not fair that I got another chance at life and yours was taken away from you.'

'Is that how you really see me? As some pathetic creature to be pitied?'

'No, I just—'

'I have a very fulfilling life, thank you very much. You don't need to use me as an excuse not to come home, or to put off having a relationship.'

'I'm sorry. It just didn't seem fair on you. You weren't able to live your dream and become a ballet dancer. That was because of me.'

As Emily railed against the idea that she should take any responsibility for her condition, Tamsin's world began to crumble around her. She was a medical professional, and knew being in a wheelchair wasn't the end of the world, but rational thought wasn't something she was capable of when it came to her family.

For years she'd avoided any close relationships, worked day and night to avoid going home to an empty house, and moved to the mainland away from her family. All to avoid the guilt she thought she deserved. Now it appeared it was all for nothing. She'd sacrificed a lot to punish herself, but the greatest loss had been Max. There was nothing she could do to change that.

'I'm fine, Tamsin. If you'd ever asked me that I would've told you. I adapted. I probably wouldn't ever have made a career out of being a dancer anyway, and I got over that a long time ago. I have a tech job which I can fit around hospital appointments, and I'm about to move into my own house with my boyfriend. I don't need your pity, or your guilt.'

'Wait… You have a boyfriend?' It had never occurred to her that Emily had made a life for herself here when she'd been so caught up in her own guilt.

Emily rolled her eyes. 'Yes, I have a boyfriend. I'm quite a catch, you know. Other people can see beyond this chair, even if you can't.'

'Max was right. I should've had this conversation a long time ago.' She thought of all the time she'd wasted away from her family, with only her overactive conscience for company. It was patronising of her to think her beautiful sister couldn't have any sort of meaningful life simply because of her illness. She'd drastically underestimated her and let her guilt blur her view of Emily, who'd always been so strong, confusing her worst fear with reality.

'Like I said, an idiot.' At least Emily was smiling at her now. Even if it was out of pity.

'I'm sorry for underestimating you, Emily.'

'It's fine. I'm fine. If I had to do it all over again, I would. You're my sister and I love you, Tamsin. But I'm okay. You don't have to worry about me any more. It's time you thought about your own happiness.'

'I think it's too late,' she said with a wobbly smile.

She'd had a few weeks of happiness with Max, but it was over, and she knew she'd never find it again with anyone else.

CHAPTER TEN

'BUT *WHERE* IS TAMSIN?'

'Why isn't she here?'

Max had been bombarded with the same questions since he'd shown up without her at the home.

'For the hundredth time, she's gone home to visit her parents over Christmas. Now, if you don't settle down Santa won't be visiting anyone.' He would've thought they'd have other things on their minds than one missing visitor on Christmas Eve. Obviously, Tamsin had made an impression. And not just on the children.

'But she promised.' Jay pouted, obviously having taken a shine to her too.

'I know, but she decided to go home and be with her family. You still have me though.'

He knew he was a poor substitute and he felt guilty that he was the reason she wasn't here. After all, he'd been the one who'd told her not to come. It was his fault she was breaking a promise to the children, but he couldn't explain to them that it was self-preservation which had prompted his decision. They wouldn't understand, and with a little time even he was struggling to comprehend why he'd done that.

He was missing her so much he would've taken a few promised days with her rather than the prospect of never having her in his life again. She wasn't Mairi. Tamsin hadn't cheated, or lied to him, she'd just been scared to make a change in her life. It was something he'd been guilty of too, so he should've been more understanding, perhaps fought harder for her.

It hadn't been easy walking away from Tamsin, even harder spending these past days without her. He'd found out on the grapevine at work that she'd gone back to Belfast after all, hopefully to sort things out with her family, though it was bittersweet to think so. If only she'd managed to do that before he'd fallen head over heels for her, they might have been able to salvage something of their relationship. By opening up to her family first, she might've found herself able to do the same with him. However, since he hadn't heard anything from her, he had to accept it was over.

At least he had tonight here to take his mind off things. To keep him away from home, where he'd let her enter too far into his life. Although he wasn't sure this place was any better when the kids wouldn't let him forget her either.

'We'll leave some milk and shortbread out for Santa then you'll all have to get to bed.' He did his best to herd the smaller children into the kitchen whilst Isobel and the other staff members were trying to tire out the older children.

'And carrots for the reindeer?' Jay asked.

'And carrots for the reindeer,' Max promised.

This was one tradition at the home he had enjoyed, and still liked to be part of. All the excitement on the night before Christmas Day, waiting on a visit from Santa, though somehow knowing and accepting that the gifts wouldn't be as extravagant as those of school friends.

It made him wonder what it would've been like doing this with children of his own, making preparations on Christmas Eve, reading them a story before putting them to bed, and having a family to share the big day with. In that pipe dream it was Tamsin he pictured with him, opening presents and sharing a glass of wine in front of an open fire. She'd opened his heart to the idea that he could love someone, trust them enough to share his life, and finally have the family he'd always wanted.

Clearly, she hadn't had the same vision or she would've tried harder to be with him.

His phone buzzed in his pocket, and he handed some carrots to Jay out of the fridge before he answered it.

'Hello?'

'Hi. Is this Max Robertson?'

'Yes. Who is this?' He didn't recognise the number or the voice, and wondered who would be calling so late on Christmas Eve.

'My name is Emily. I'm Tamsin's sister.'

'Is everything all right?' His blood froze in his veins at the thought that something might have happened to her. Why else would her family be phoning him?

'It depends on your definition of "all right". It's Christmas Eve and she's miserable.'

'I'm sorry, but I don't understand what that has to do with me.'

It didn't bring him any comfort to discover Tamsin was as unhappy as he was, but she was across the Irish Sea and he didn't know what he was supposed to do about it, or why her sister was phoning him.

'Everything, apparently. Look, I know this is probably pointless since it's so last-minute, and I have no idea how you would even get to Belfast from Edinburgh on Christmas Day. But I want to feel as though I'm doing something for my sister. I'm inviting you for Christmas dinner tomorrow, because I know she wishes you were here with her and she's too stubborn to ask you herself.'

That made him smile. He knew only too well how obstinate Tamsin could be after the way they'd parted. Though apparently she had taken his advice in the end and gone home for a visit. Not that she'd told him so, or reached out in any fashion. He only had her sister's word that she wanted him back in her life at all.

'Thanks, but I think I'd rather hear it from Tamsin herself.' He didn't want to risk trekking all the way over to Belfast, only for her to reject him on the doorstep.

It had taken a lot of courage to let her into his life as far as he had, and he was nursing the wounds left when she couldn't fight for their future. He wasn't prepared to leave himself vulnerable a second time.

'Okay. That's understandable. Sorry to have bothered you, but at least I tried.' Emily hung up on him and Max was left staring at his phone as though he could almost reach out to Tamsin through it.

Emily's call was one tiny ember of hope that Tamsin hadn't gone from his life for ever. He just wasn't sure if it was enough for him to take a chance and risk her rejecting him again.

'Pass the chocolates over.' Emily held out her hand, forcing Tamsin to relinquish her hold on the tub of wrapped sweets she'd been hogging, a typical example of eating her feelings. When she was busy unwrapping sweets and munching on them she had less time to dwell on Max, or the thought of going back to London alone.

'Does anyone want any turkey sandwiches?' her mum asked, in her element all day cooking up a storm.

'No, thanks. I think I'm all turkeyed out.' Tamsin was more inclined towards the sweet stuff now she'd had her fill of turkey and sprouts and everything her mother had piled on her plate at dinnertime, needing that feel-good factor that lasted seconds when the chocolates were in her mouth.

'I'll take a cup of tea,' her father piped up, wakened from his snoring slumber.

'Me too. Can you bring the biscuits in too?'

Emily's request renewed Tamsin's interest.

'I'll take some too.'

Her mother stood and watched her from the doorway with a smile.

'What?' She was beginning to get paranoid by the staring.

'Nothing. I was just thinking how nice it is to have you home and have Christmas together.' Then she turned and walked away, preparing to serve the next course of seasonal overindulgence.

Her mother was right though. It was nice being here. It all felt so normal and festive. The light outside had faded so the colourful glow from the fairy lights on the tree was all the more magical as she sat with her family by the fire. They'd talked a lot of things through last night and she'd promised to visit more often. This morning they'd opened presents together and watched all of the special programmes on TV in the afternoon. It had even snowed, making the perfect Christmas Day.

Yet she was still feeling blue. As though there was something missing.

Max. Max was missing.

She curled up into the foetal position in her chair and pulled her new fleecy pink blanket around her for some sort of comfort.

'Why don't you phone him, Tamsin?'

'Hmm?' She pretended not to hear her sister's question.

'Phone him and tell him how you feel.'

'I don't think that's going to make any difference. He made it clear we were done.' She kept her voice low so as not to wake their father, who'd drifted off into another post dinner nap.

Falling for Max certainly hadn't been the initial plan, and she hadn't realised the extent of her feelings for him until it was too late. When he'd told her he cared for her she should have had the courage to tell him she felt the same way, but there didn't seem any point when she couldn't see a future for them. So caught up in her perceived version of Emily's life, she hadn't believed herself worthy of a relationship with him. Now it had been pointed out to her that in a lot of ways Emily was living a more fulfilling life than her, with a partner and a happy future ahead, Tamsin could see what she'd missed out on. Max had wanted to talk about changing the nature of their relationship, a future together, but she'd dismissed it. Now she had to go back to London and pick up her old life pre-Max. Not something she was looking forward to.

The doorbell rang then, interrupting their cosy afternoon and bringing the outside to their door. Her mother was oblivious in the kitchen, her singing no doubt drowning out the buzzer. Dad was snoring in the corner and Emily made no attempt to move.

'I'll get it,' she muttered, throwing off her blanket and padding to the hall in the knitted slipper boots her mother had gifted her.

When she opened the door, it took her a moment to process what she was seeing.

'Max? What are you doing here?' The breath seemed to whoosh out of her lungs into the frosty air.

It seemed too good to be true to have him standing on the doorstep, wool coat pulled up and scarf tied elegantly around his neck, while the snow fell gently around him in the half light. A dream.

'Emily invited me for Christmas dinner. I know I'm a bit late, but this was the only flight I could get, and taxis are a little hard to come by at this time of the year.' His soft smile did nothing to diminish the ethereal feel of the moment.

'Emily? What are you talking about?' She was beginning to wonder if she was in the midst of some fever dream brought on by excess turkey consumption because none of this was making sense.

'She called me and said you were miserable, and all the children have been asking about you too.'

'So…you're here because other people told you to come?'

He hung his head and took a deep breath. 'No. I'm making a mess of this.'

'Then tell me why you got on a plane and took a taxi to my parents' house on Christmas Day. All of which I assume cost a fortune, so you must have a good reason.'

Her heart was racing now, the adrenaline rush a sign that she couldn't possibly be dreaming any of this. She was wide awake and waiting for an explanation she hoped she was going to like.

Even though she'd been yearning for him, she was afraid to let herself believe he was here for her in case it all ended in disaster again. She didn't want to go all in with him if he was only expecting company into the New Year. It had been too hard to be without him once, and she couldn't bear having to go through a breakup again.

'You,' he said simply, making her melt all over again.

'I thought we were over?'

'I know, but I've had time to think. And miss you. I was in a relationship a long time ago and she cheated on me. Broke my heart and made me determined not to let anyone get that close again. People were always letting me down and abandoning me so I thought being alone was the safest option. Opening up to you about my past, being with you, has made me realise I don't want to be on my own any more. I want to be with you.'

'For how long? Tonight? The New Year?'

'For as long as you'll have me. I don't know how we'll manage it, but I want to try. Otherwise, why would I be standing here in the snow, risking you rejecting me?'

'You must have been pretty sure of yourself to go to all this trouble.'

'No. I just thought you were worth the gamble.'

'I'm so sorry I didn't believe in us, Max. I was frightened to share my life with you and give myself permission to be happy, so I pushed you away. The same way I've been pushing my family away for years. Because I was afraid to face up to the truth.'

Since arriving here and realising how stupid she'd been, she'd longed for this chance to put things right. To have a second chance with Max, and at happiness.

'And now?'

'Talking to Emily has made me see things differently. I have a habit of projecting my fears onto others and being blind to the reality of a situation.'

'You think?' His smile gave her hope that he understood and would find a way to forgive her.

'I know I hurt you. I'm sorry. I thought I was leaving myself vulnerable by opening up, by admitting I had feelings for you. Because I simply couldn't get past the guilt I held over Emily to let myself be happy. I took your advice, though, and talked with my family. Cleared the air, and my conscience. So thank you for that. I'm only sorry I caused you pain in order to get to this point.'

'If I didn't think you were worth it I wouldn't have come here for you, Tamsin. So, tell me… Do I need to remortgage my house and book a taxi back to the airport, or are you going to give me the best Christmas present ever and tell me you want me?'

She could see the uncertainty in his eyes but if he could feel the way her heart was beating for him he'd know he had nothing to worry about.

Tamsin grabbed him by the collar and pulled him closer. 'I want you. I always have.'

When their lips met it felt as though all her Christmases had come at once. This was everything she'd been missing, and she didn't ever want to let Max go.

EPILOGUE

Six months later

'I HOPE YOU have room for all of this because I'm not getting rid of anything. I come from a family of hoarders.' Tamsin carried another box out of the car and dumped it on Max's living room floor. The cardboard towers holding her belongings were getting perilously high and she was beginning to realise how much stuff she'd managed to accumulate in just a few years.

'Don't I know it. Your mother shipped over a lot of your childhood toys in case you wanted them too. I suppose we could use the spare room for storage if you want?' Max followed her in with a box of books and huffed out a laboured breath as he set it down.

Bless him, he'd driven up to London and back to move all of her belongings into his house. Since he had his own furniture, she hadn't needed to bring hers, and had either sold or donated the rest of the contents of her place.

After spending Christmas and New Year together it had become obvious very quickly that they wanted more than a casual fling. Parting had been painful even though she'd already made the decision to transfer to Edinburgh on a permanent basis, and Max had asked her to move in with him. They'd had to make do with commuting in the early days, and since moving to Edinburgh she'd been living out of a suitcase until they'd had enough time off together to get the rest of her things out of storage.

She supposed part of her had been holding back too in case things hadn't worked out, and she was still clutching onto some remnant of her life in London just in case. However, she and Max made a great team at home as well as in the operating theatre. Even though she only needed Max to feel like she was home, it would be nice to have her own things around her again.

'I don't want to waste the space in case, you know… we ever think about expanding…'

Maybe she should have a clear-out. Material things weren't that important to her. Not next to the idea of perhaps having a family. She knew it was a big step to take, more so than moving in together, but it had been on her mind for a while. Now that she was finally moving on with her life, she wanted to embrace everything she'd denied herself, and that included the idea of being a mother.

'It's not something we've talked about…' Max looked uneasy at the subject, and though it was a conversation they needed to have at some point, she didn't need to push it now. Not when they'd both taken a huge step already to get where they were.

'I know. It doesn't matter. Forget I said that.'

'No. It's not that I don't want kids… I just… If we were going to go down that route of having a family together, I'd like to look into the idea of fostering, maybe even adopting. I would like to give a child a loving home if we could but, as you said, we can talk about that some other time.'

'It's Jay, isn't it?' she asked with a smile, Max's request not coming as anything of a surprise to her. They both spent a lot of time over at the home volunteering and had a close bond with the boy.

'How did you know?' The tension eased from his broad shoulders as though, by finally sharing that, a weight had been lifted from him.

'It's obvious and if I'm honest it has crossed my mind too. After the chemo, and the transplant, I don't know if my fertility has been affected. I didn't think I'd ever be in a position to have a family so I never looked into it.'

Perhaps that was part of the reason she'd set the idea of being a parent to one side. That being infertile was something she should just accept was further punishment for what had happened to Emily.

Now, being with Max, and having her sister talk some sense into her, Tamsin was considering the possibility of completing their family with Jay. It was easy to do when she saw Max and him together, and she was very fond of the boy too. She would love to be able to give him a safe, secure home, as well as have that little family of her own she'd believed was too much to ask for.

'We can look into everything and make those decisions together.' Max's face had lit up when she'd told him that adopting was a possibility, as if all of his Christmases had come at once. She knew it would mean a lot to him, not only because it was giving a child the loving home he'd never had, but it would give him the family he'd never had too.

'I mean, it mightn't happen. There'd be a lot of paperwork and red tape to get through, even if they do think we'd make a suitable match for him.'

They had to be realistic and she didn't want them to get their hopes up too much. Certainly, it wouldn't do to tell Jay anything either until they'd looked into everything properly first.

'We're both surgeons, in a stable relationship. I think they'd be lucky to have us.' He moved towards Tamsin with a great big smile on his face and his arms open.

She went willingly into them, letting him hug her close to his chest. Letting her feel that steady, comforting sound of his heart, and knowing a piece of it was hers. 'I'm the lucky one.'

Max kissed the top of her head, then seemed to fumble in his pocket.

'What are you doing?'

'This isn't the way I'd planned on doing this, and I don't want you to think it's only because we're talking about adopting Jay. I love you, I want you in my life for ever. Tamsin, will you marry me?'

He let go of her to produce the pink plastic ring from the cracker at Christmas, a goofy grin on his face that only made her love him more.

As always, she took a moment to process what was happening, assessing the situation before she committed to anything. Though as he'd been so sentimental in keeping the ring, she knew he was in this for keeps. He'd waited until he was sure this was what they both wanted without ever rushing her into it.

Max loved her. He'd opened up his home as well as his heart, and if they were lucky they could be a family. She couldn't think of any reason to say no when she was bursting with happiness.

'Yes, Max, you lovable big eejit, I'll marry you.'

She watched with tear-filled eyes as he switched the plastic for a beautiful diamond ring that sparkled so brightly it was blinding, and slipped it on her finger.

'Who knows? Maybe next Christmas will be a real family affair,' she said, already picturing the scene here together.

'That's all I ever wanted.' Max gathered her back into a hug and Tamsin knew that whatever happened they had a future together. And neither of them had reason to fear it any more.

* * * * *

Look out for the next story in the
Christmas North and South quartet
A Mistletoe Marriage Reunion
by Louisa Heaton

And if you enjoyed this story,
check out these other great reads
from Karin Baine

Midwife's One-Night Baby Surprise
An American Doctor in Ireland
Surgeon Prince's Fake Fiancée

All available now!

A MISTLETOE MARRIAGE REUNION

LOUISA HEATON

MILLS & BOON

For Jamie, who asked!

CHAPTER ONE

AN AIR AMBULANCE helicopter was coming in to land on the roof of the Great Southern Hospital as Dr Lauren Shaw stood before the entrance in the early-morning dark and cold, trying to work up the courage to step inside.

It was impossible from where she stood to feel the downdraught of the whizzing rotor blades that chopped through the air high above, but it felt that way as a chill breeze tried to blow her blonde hair out of its tight pony-tail and she shivered violently, huddling up tighter in her winter coat.

I don't need to be this scared.

It's ridiculous!

I'm a grown-ass woman, for crying out loud!

Oliver wasn't even in the building. Not yet anyway, because Lauren had arrived extra early so she could be ready for anything, figuring that if she were in the hos-pital first she could establish her ground, get a feel for everything, start to make friends, before he arrived and then, when he did, it would feel like equal territory. Or as equal as she could make it, considering he'd been work-ing here since he qualified all those many years ago.

Who am I kidding?

She knew who he was around here. He was a maxillofacial reconstructive *god.* People came from all over the country to be treated by him, and she knew of his successes because she heard all about him from their daughters, Kayley and Willow, whenever they chatted on the phone, or on her occasional visits. Visits that were always perfectly orchestrated to make sure that Lauren never ran into him.

She'd come down from Edinburgh when Kayley had passed her bar exam and qualified as a lawyer. She'd come down when Willow had qualified as a paediatrician, and taken both her daughters out for a celebratory meal. It had always been a struggle to leave them again and get back on the train to Scotland. And now she wouldn't have to. She was here to stay. Though she'd hoped to *not* get a job at the Great Southern but at another London hospital, when the job for a reconstructive surgeon had come up here her colleagues at the Great Northern had encouraged her to go for the role, telling her how good it would be for her career, the professional move she'd been looking for.

And she and Oliver were adults, right? Surely they could be mature about this. Old feelings, old resentments, old *guilts*, could no longer trip them up, right?

Lauren sucked in a breath.

A journey of a thousand miles begins with a single step. I took that step when I applied for this post.

She stepped forward, eyes focused on the fairy lights that were already up in readiness for the festive season, trying to focus on the beauty of them, how they looked like little snowflakes. The reception area was large, with an L-shaped desk and two receptionists sitting behind it. One was on the phone, the other was handing a piece of pink paper over to a couple of guys. The one facing her was an attractive younger man with thick, dark hair. He was laughing and had a broad, beautiful smile and the other was… The other man was…

Lauren's steps slowed. Something about the man looked familiar. The height, the stance. It couldn't be, could it?

His shoulders were just as wide, just as broad, but his frame was trimmer, more streamlined, the love handles she'd once joked with him about, teased him about even though she'd once loved them, were gone. His hair, that had once been dark and devilish, was now peppered with silver and looked distinguished and sexy in a new style and she had no doubt that those gorgeous green eyes of his were exactly the same!

Dr Oliver Shaw was here early.

Her plan to establish her ground had already faltered.

Her position of power was gone.

All she could hope for now was that she would come across as calm and composed and looking as amazing as he did! The years had been kind to Oliver, clearly. And both Kayley and Willow had commented in the last few years how their dad had got into fitness, went to the gym regularly and had even run in marathons the last few years. No doubt due to the influence of Daria, his much younger girlfriend.

Would *he* think that *she* had changed? That the years had been kind to her? She did yoga now and could do a crow pose easily but, unlike Oliver, Lauren had had to deal with the menopause over the last few years and the silver in her blonde hair was hidden with carefully applied highlights, her own love handles caged in by clever undergarments, and the last time she'd run for anything had been when she'd run away from Mike…

You know what? It doesn't matter what I look like. I'm a strong, confident woman and I'm here to do an excellent job and that's what matters. I love who I am and what I look like now. I've grown into this body and it's beautiful and the battle scars tell my story.

It didn't matter what Oliver's opinion of her might be. Because *his* opinion was none of her business!

And so she confidently stepped forward to say hello.

'So you think we can discharge her tomorrow?' asked Dev.

'I don't see why not. She's been on the antibiotics for three days now and hasn't sparked any more fevers, so I'd say we have a handle on her infection. Let's continue to monitor her today, check her stitches tonight and if all looks A-okay then we can send her home.' Dr Oliver Shaw turned to Rebecca on reception. 'Bex, were you able to get hold of that taxi service for me?'

Bex smiled at him, the way she always did, and handed him a piece of pink paper. It had a telephone number on it. 'Sure did.'

'Thanks.' He needed it for his patient. She lived outside of London. She'd come all the way from Canterbury to be seen by him and have her upper jaw realigned and he'd promised he'd find her a decent taxi firm that would get her home again safely without charging her the earth.

His surgery on Stella Malcolm had gone well, but her temperature post-surgery had been fluctuating and they'd discovered that she'd had a urine infection, of all things, that had gone into her kidneys. It had made her quite unwell, to the point that she'd begun to hallucinate, but things had calmed down the last couple of days and she seemed back to normal. He'd stayed all night to make sure she was okay, monitoring her, even though his registrar, Dev, had offered to do so. Besides, he'd known he wouldn't sleep well, knowing that Lauren, his ex-wife, was coming back at some point today. To work here, at Great Southern. It just seemed easier to stay up all night and focus on his patient, rather than stay up all night and think about his ex. A good distraction technique.

The last ten years, the Great Southern Hospital in London had been *his* territory. The Great Northern Hospital, its sister hospital in Scotland, had been Lauren's. When he'd heard she was coming back, had applied for the vacancy of reconstructive surgeon, he'd been shocked. Kayley and Willow had both mentioned that their mum had begun to wish to be closer to them again, but he'd never imagined she would come *here!* He'd thought she'd go to Guys and St Thomas' or someplace like that. He'd never imagined that she would want to walk the same halls as him…

And what about her boyfriend, Mike? Had he come back with her? He was a hotshot reconstructive surgeon, by all accounts. Where was *he* working, because it certainly wasn't here!

Oliver noticed that Dev's attention had been caught by someone behind them and so he turned to look, doing a double take when he realised who it was.

Lauren.

Wow, she looked fine! The years had been more than kind. How could she look better than she had before? It had been ten years since he'd last seen her, walking away from him with her bags packed, struggling to carry them all, because she was so small and there'd almost been nothing to her.

He used to call her 'Baby Bird' affectionately, because her five foot three to his six-foot height had made her seem that way. But now? She'd filled out some, had knockout womanly curves. Her face, once so angular, now had perfect cheekbones and her make-up looked different. Whatever she was doing now really made her light blue eyes stand out. They were almost hypnotising. They were—

'Oliver?'

He was vaguely aware that Dev was trying to talk to him, that his friend and colleague was smiling, puzzled, trying to work out why he—normally so garrulous—had been struck dumb by a hot blonde entering Reception.

She wore heels that accentuated perfect calf muscles. Had she been working out? And now, as she got closer, the fairy lights surrounding the reception desk began to flicker across her face and her eyes gleamed as she stretched out a hand to say hello.

'*Oliver.*'

Speak. You need to speak.

Of course he'd known she was doing all right for herself. Their two daughters had kept him abreast of all their mum's news and he'd been delighted that she had finally been able to throw herself into the career that she'd wanted. But he had to remind himself that she was with Mike now and that today had to be a big change for her too and the last thing she'd need was her ex-husband being struck dumb at the sight of her. She needed him to act normally and in control. To be focused, the way he was when he was in Theatre.

Get a grip.

'Lauren. You're here early.' He somehow managed to dredge up a passable genuine smile and reached out to shake her hand. As soon as he touched her he felt electrocuted, zaps of lightning shooting up his arm that were most troubling. Most disturbing.

Most surprising.

'I wanted to get an early start…you know how it is.'

Her beaming smile when she directed it towards him was awe-inducing in the extreme. It brought everything back. Everything. Why was he reacting this way? Mentally, he tried to get a hold of himself, to find that control he needed if he and Lauren were to carefully navigate this new working relationship. He was a maxillofacial reconstructive surgeon; she was a reconstructive surgeon. They were going to be working together.

'Of course. Lauren, let me introduce you to Dr Dev Singh, one of our highly skilled registrars.'

She shook Dev's hand. 'Pleased to meet you.'

'Pleasure is all mine. I've heard a lot about you.'

'Oh?' She looked at Oliver, but he looked blank because he'd not told anyone anything about her.

'I'm good friends with your daughter Willow. We've worked together on a couple of occasions in Paeds.'

'Ah, yes, I remember her mentioning you. You're the doctor that likes to go rowing, is that right?'

Dev nodded. 'From my Cambridge days.' He smiled.

Oliver stood there, surprised. How had he never heard that Dev liked to row? 'Well…now that introductions are over, should I escort you upstairs? Show you around? Introduce you to everyone?'

Her gaze turned back on him and it was mesmerising. 'Unless there's work that needs doing first? I'm ready to get stuck in.'

Of course. She'd waited long enough to properly focus on her career and he'd played a part in that. Introductions could wait.

'The next patient on my list this morning requires a radial forearm flap for tongue cancer. You could join me on that.'

Lauren nodded. 'I'd love to. Why don't you tell me more about the patient?'

Her smile was bewildering and it hit him in the solar plexus so hard, he almost felt winded.

CHAPTER TWO

'TILLY? THIS IS Dr Lauren Shaw. She's going to be assisting me with your surgery this morning.'

Tilly Garson was a woman of Lauren's age, mid-fifties, who had taken a different route to Lauren and allowed her grey hair to grow through unimpeded. She looked quite stylish with it and was clearly a woman who took care of her appearance. And though Tilly's grey hair suited her perfectly, Lauren wasn't sure she was ready for that just yet.

Tilly looked up at her in surprise. 'Dr *Shaw?* Are you related?'

Lauren smiled politely. She didn't normally like to give out personal details to patients, but she'd never been asked this before, having worked at a completely different hospital to her ex-husband. It had never been an issue. Nor had she ever changed her surname back to her maiden name of Taylor, because she'd wanted to keep the same name as her children. Was this going to be an issue now?

'Er...'

'No. No relation,' said Oliver, jumping in to rescue her.

She turned to look at him, but he didn't meet her gaze. She had not needed rescuing! She would have got an answer out eventually. She'd just needed another millisecond to think of something, some polite way of saying that they were divorced. Was there a way?

But Oliver had got there first and made it quite clear that they were not related. They weren't any more anyway, that was the truth. They just shared a surname. And two children. And a couple of decades of married life.

But nothing now.

And that was good, right? Because he was not hers any more, and though she'd been surprised at her immediate visceral reaction to how he looked—distinguished, sexy, silver fox—his statement made it clear that there was nothing between them *any more.*

Which was perfect, because she didn't want to get involved with Oliver again, except as colleagues who happened to work in the same department. He was senior to her and technically her boss, but that was the only say he would have in her life from this point on. She would prove to him how capable she was. How professional. That was all.

'Tilly, do you have any questions before we go down into Theatre?' Oliver asked.

The patient nodded. 'Yes. I know I said I didn't want to know any of the details before, but I've thought about it and wondered if you might tell me some right now. It's just I figured I could then picture it in my head and visualise good things and send myself some healing thoughts.'

Oliver nodded. 'Of course. Dr Shaw, why don't you explain to the patient what we're doing today?'

He was testing her, checking her knowledge. Every senior doctor did it with subordinates and this was a teaching hospital. Well, she would show him what she was made of.

'Of course. Okay, Tilly, what you're having done today is a radial forearm flap for your tongue cancer. That means we take some tissue from your forearm and use it as a replacement for the tissue we will be removing from your tongue. We use the forearm as it has the terrific advantage of not shrinking when it heals, so that your speech and swallowing will be greatly aided after surgery.'

'Right.'

'We'll use this area here.' Lauren leaned in to indicate the area of forearm near the wrist. 'It tends to be very smooth, doesn't have hair growth and the hole created here on your arm will be covered by a skin graft from either your upper arm or your tummy.'

'Will I be able to use my arm afterwards?'

'It'll be bandaged and held in a special sling for a few days. There will be stitches that will have to come out eventually, and you may feel some tingles or numbness for a few weeks or months because the nerve near the operative site can become bruised, but this should recede with time. Occasionally, it can be permanent, which is a risk, but very rarely does it create pain. Your hand may feel a little weaker to begin with, but we can give you some strengthening exercises and physio and you might notice it feels colder in the winter.'

'That's a lot to take in.'

'It is. If you need more time to decide, we can always postpone your surgery until you feel ready.'

'No. No, I want this done. I want the cancer out.'

Lauren nodded and smiled. 'I understand.'

'Are there any other risks?'

'With surgery there's always the risk of clots, but these are minimal. Maybe two or three percent.'

'And what happens then?'

'Well, if it's a drainage clot, the flap can become filled with old blood and you would have to return to Theatre to have the clot removed.'

'But I'd still have the flap?'

'We'd try to preserve it, but if the flap failed we would have to look for other methods of reconstruction.'

Tilly looked worried. 'It all sounds rather worrying. I wish I'd not asked now. Ignorance is bliss and all of that. I wish my family were here.'

Lauren understood. It was a scary thing to consider.

'We have to tell you the risks, Tilly, but we'd be remiss to not also tell you the *success rate* for tongue flap surgery. You have no lymph node involvement here. It hasn't spread at all and all your scans are clear. The five-year survival rate for localised tongue cancer is in the mid-eighties and it's much less if you don't have it removed. This is your best option for survival and to give you the ability to talk as well as you can afterwards. We know you're scared. But we're here to help you. Let us look after you. You're in good hands and the other Dr Shaw here is the best in the country.'

Tilly looked at Lauren's ex-husband and smiled. 'I know. I looked him up.' She laughed, a little embarrassed.

'I'd look up my surgeon too,' she whispered conspiratorially.

'Okay!' Tilly sucked in a deep breath. 'Let's do this. When am I up?'

'You're at nine o'clock this morning.'

'Okay.'

'We'll send the anaesthetist in to have a quick chat with you, but next time we see you it'll be in Theatre and then Recovery. Okay?'

Tilly nodded.

Lauren gave her hand a quick squeeze. 'See you in Theatre.'

As they walked away from the patient he realised that Lauren was looking at him in expectation. As if she wanted some sort of feedback from him. He stopped to face her.

'Not bad.'

'Not bad?'

'I think you could have been clearer on one or two things, and I wasn't too happy with you suggesting that she could postpone the surgery. I have a full list for a reason.'

She nodded. 'I'm sure you do; you have great renown. But if a patient isn't ready for surgery, mentally, physically or emotionally, then that can have a drastic effect on healing and recovery times. Especially when we're talking about things like implants or donations. If a patient isn't ready to accept the new change, then—'

He held up his hand. 'I understand the science. I wrote a paper on it.'

She nodded, bristling slightly, feeling that this might be the first of many times the pair of them would lock horns. 'I read it. And it was brilliant and that's why I suggested she take a little more time to think about the surgery if she wasn't ready. It's going to be a huge change for her and I don't think she should be rushed into surgery.'

'Tilly Garson is *ready* for surgery. She's been ready

for this surgery ever since she discovered her tongue cancer. Do you know she blamed herself for ignoring the spot on her tongue for three months, because she thought it was an ulcer? That she thought the reason she felt so tired and rundown was because she was stressed, because of her work, and took a sabbatical, even changed her job. That she lost money, not only from work but going on a foreign yoga retreat and on all the home remedies she thought she'd use to try and heal her ulcer, rather than get it checked by a dentist or doctor? She's already fought depression because of that, knowing that because she waited the cancer spread and so she is going to lose a significantly larger portion of her tongue than she would originally have needed if she'd sought help straight away. I know my patient, Lauren, and I know that she is ready. And I resent the implication that I might rush a patient into surgery because it fits *my* schedule, rather than theirs.'

He'd not meant to rail at her, but he couldn't help it. She'd been here minutes and already she was questioning his methods. He knew she wanted to make an impact here, to show what she could do, and he also wanted to see what she could do! But never on this, not on patient care, which he considered himself very conscious of.

Lauren looked subdued. 'I didn't mean to imply anything like that.'

Now he felt bad. The last thing he'd wanted to do was argue with her within half an hour of their meeting. He'd not wanted to argue with her at all! Oliver had wanted nothing more than to show that they were both grown-ups here, having spent a decade apart, and that they were civilised and friendly and adult. And, deep down, he knew she was just trying to show him that she was a well-rounded surgeon, not just someone who wanted to cut all the time but a doctor who considered her patient holistically, who wasn't just there to treat the symptoms, or the cause, but to look at their patient as a whole being and do what was right for them. Her heart was in the right place and there was nothing wrong with Lauren's heart.

'And I didn't mean to give a speech.'

'May I still join you in Theatre?'

'Of course. In fact, I thought I could excise the cancer and you could construct the flap. Show me what you can do. What do you think?'

He was offering her a major part of his surgery, showing her that he trusted her. It was a big gesture, but he also had to see her skills. The last time they'd been in a surgery together she'd only been qualified as a surgeon for a year. He wanted to see how much she'd advanced for himself, even though he'd heard great things about her time at the Great Northern Hospital in Scotland.

He'd just been twitchy because...well...he still couldn't believe the reaction he was having to her presence. He'd thought his feelings for Lauren were consigned to the Finished box. That he'd moved on, built himself a new life. To have her walk in here looking so stunning just reminded him of how he'd felt when they'd first met.

'I'd like that. Thank you.'

He nodded. 'We've time for me to give you a quick tour of theatres and introduce you to the team. And after Tilly we've got a cleft lip and palate surgery to perform on the most perfect four-month-old you have ever seen.'

Her face lit up then. 'I love doing those surgeries. They make such a difference.'

'All of our work makes a difference.'

Lauren smiled. 'I know.' She paused for a moment, looked directly up at him. 'Thank you, Oliver.'

'For what?' He was confused.

She shrugged. 'Just…thank you.'

He didn't know what he was being thanked for. But he did like the way she was looking at him like that. It gave him a warm feeling in his stomach, made his heart thud a little. Made him feel self-deprecating.

'You're welcome, Lauren.'

It felt good to be saying her name out loud again, something he'd not realised he'd missed. Their earlier altercation had passed, it was forgotten. It had simply occurred from the stress of the situation. Of being back together, working together after such a long time apart, establishing positions and roles. Jostling to take their allocated space here. She was beneath him in his department when before, in marriage, they'd been equal. It was always going to be a weird moment. And at least they'd been arguing about patient care, and not about each other.

Hopefully, now, everything else they did with each other would run smoothly.

Lauren had lost count of how many times she'd stood in a scrub room and prepped for a surgery. How many times she had stood at a sink and lathered up with an antimicrobial soap from her fingertips to her elbows, all the while running through the next surgery in her mind as she got her head into the surgical headspace she would need to operate. It was a magical moment. Almost meditative.

But today it felt different, standing next to Oliver as they went through the same procedures to operate together, their first time in Theatre together in over a decade. The last time she'd operated with him, it had been to reposition an upper jaw on a twenty-three-year-old girl and Lauren had only been qualified as a surgeon for a short time. Back then, she'd still been incredibly nervous, grateful for her husband's superior knowledge and skill, knowing he would take the lead and do the majority of the cutting whilst she retracted. But now she would stand by his side as almost his equal. He was still the senior surgeon, but she knew so much more now. She had more experience and was no longer a dewy-eyed novice.

Oliver was going to let her incise and create the forearm flap that would be used to replace the large section of Tilly's tongue being removed for her oral cancer. It was precision work, as a lot of reconstructive surgery was, and she felt thrilled she would be able to show off her skills today.

But she hadn't considered one important thing.

Coming into work this morning for the first time at the Great Southern, she'd assumed that there might be a little awkwardness between her and Oliver. They were divorced, hadn't seen or spoken to each other in ten years—there was bound to be a little tension.

But she'd not expected the sexual tension she'd felt on seeing him that first time. It was as if her body was betraying her...remembering their sex life, how wonderful it had been. Letting her know that he was close by again. She could actually feel a surge in her hormones as her body reawakened being near him. After all this time it was irritating, disruptive to the calm exterior she wanted to present to him.

And it was unexpected. How had he got even more

delicious-looking now that he was in his fifties? His scrubs revealed even more than the suit had this morning when she'd met him in Reception. Back there, he'd worn a fitted, long-sleeved shirt. The scrubs revealed the musculature that now lay beneath—sculpted musculature owed to the hours he clearly spent working out now, something that before, when they'd been married, had been an occasional thing, something he'd fitted in around the many hours he'd spent at work.

Lauren had once resented the hours he'd spent at the gym. He was away so long at the hospital as he built his career while she was at home, a young mother to their two daughters. At the end of each day, she'd been desperate for him to come home to her so she could have some adult conversation, or at least feel like the woman she used to be before motherhood changed her, but he would go to the gym, or occasionally meet up with his friends, and she'd resented that. Especially when he'd told her that he'd gone to the gym because he just needed a little time to himself on occasion.

Well, what about her? When had she ever got time to herself, with two small children crawling all over her every day?

She'd tried to not be resentful, but it was hard. He was working for them, he kept saying. Doing all the hours that he could to earn money, because she wasn't able to work back then. She could have gone part-time, but by the time she'd paid for childcare she'd have been working and exhausting herself for nothing and then her children would have suffered. So she'd stayed home, given all of herself to Kayley and Willow, and hoped that on occasion Oliver would have time for her. She'd missed him whilst they'd been married, had stayed quiet much too long, whilst all the time he'd moved further and further away from them, until they'd become like strangers to each other.

But there was no point in admiring him now. He wasn't single. He was with Daria, his much younger girlfriend, and he must look at her now and see all the lines, all the wrinkles, the grey hair. Lauren couldn't compete—nor did she want to—with a thirty-year-old.

'I remember the last time we did this. Scrubbed in together,' she said.

'Me too.'

'You do?'

He nodded. 'Of course. Jane Cavanaugh. Upper jaw surgery.'

She was surprised yet pleased he remembered the patient and the case.

'I saw her again recently. She'd come into the hospital to visit a relative and we met in the corridor. Asked me if I could recommend a plastic surgeon.'

'Plastic surgeon? What for?'

'She'd begun to very much believe that her realigned jaw was making her nose more prominent and she wanted it reduced and also to have her upper lip plumped up.'

'Why? She's a beautiful girl!'

'She is. But, from what I could discover, our jaw surgery seemed to set off a trail of later surgeries. She'd also had her breasts done and even went to Turkey for butt implants.'

'Wow. That's a lot of surgeries in ten years.'

'Some people get addicted. They see one fault, they

get it fixed and then they just hyperfocus on another part of themselves that they think is wrong.'

'Did she ever get any counselling?'

'I'm not sure. I hope so.'

When they'd finished scrubbing they made their way into Theatre, where nurses helped them into gowns and they put on gloves and went over the list of procedures to ensure they had the correct patient on the table for the correct procedure. Tilly's scans were on a screen and Oliver double-checked these, before going to stand on his side of the table and checking that everything was good on the anaesthetist's end.

He got a thumbs-up from the gas man.

'Okay, we'll make a start.' Oliver proceeded to outline to the theatre staff the procedure they hoped to follow today—that he would operate separately on Tilly's tongue as Lauren worked on the arm to create the flap and collect the skin graft—and once everyone knew who was doing what they began to work.

'Scalpel.'

Tilly's arm was already marked out by Oliver, but Lauren double-checked the markings for herself before she began to cut. The flap needed to be precise and exact if this was to replace a portion of tongue. The flap itself needed to act like the tongue, so that afterwards Tilly would be able to speak as clearly as she could, and so she could eat, so she could swallow. This flap would define her happiness after the surgery. But also, if she did this flap well, then it would show Oliver just how far she had come and where she was destined to go.

Her career had begun many years after his. Her dreams had been put on hold whilst she raised their daughters, and it was her time now. She had lofty goals and wanted to reach the post of consultant, which was possibly within reach in the next couple of years if everything went to plan. And, to do that, she had to show everybody, and not just Oliver, just what kind of surgeon and doctor she was.

She wanted to be exemplary. Extraordinary. She wanted people from around the country, if not from around the globe, to come and seek her out because she was the best—just like they did with Oliver.

'How's it going, Lauren?'

'It's going well. Just working on the blood vessels. What about you?'

'I think I've got clear margins, but Pathology will let me know for sure.' She looked up in time to see him hand a slice of tissue to a nurse. 'Get that to Path, please.' And then he turned back with gauze to dab away any excess bleeding from within the oral cavity before he looked at her. 'Flap looks good. That's excellent.'

'Thank you.' She could see he was smiling at her from behind his mask, crow's feet in the corners of his eyes that had never been there before but now just made him look even more devilishly charming than he ever had.

She felt something stir inside and told herself to concentrate.

It was disconcerting to feel the things for Oliver that she was currently experiencing. Distracting. She'd thought that any feelings she'd ever had for him were dormant after ten years apart, but maybe she ought to have known better. Her relationship with him was over. She'd never expected to awaken anything at seeing him again, yet clearly, her body remembered. And *wanted.* Decades of loving someone could not be so easily erased.

Their sex life had never been a problem. In fact, whenever they'd had a moment—or the energy—to reconnect with one another and they were both actually at home, the sex had always been mind-blowing, frustrations and loneliness being blasted away in moments that felt like ecstasy and reconnecting.

But that reconnection had always been a mirage, a sticking plaster at that point in time to cover the huge cracks that were separating them like an earthquake in a disaster movie. Occasionally they would cling together, choosing to believe that everything was still fine, whilst the world around them crumbled and before too long they were too far apart, unable to reach each other. Eventually, they'd just drifted apart and gone their separate ways.

But, despite all of that, she could still remember, as she stood opposite him now, the way his fingers would feel upon her skin. The trail of his tongue across delicate parts of her. The way they'd enjoyed hours of foreplay, teasing and kissing and tickling and sucking until they finally came together in an explosion of ecstasy that left them both breathless.

I must stop thinking about Oliver's tongue and concentrate on creating a new one for Tilly!

As she transferred the free flap over to Oliver, she watched with a steely focus as he began to attach it to the blood vessels within the mouth. It was delicate, exquisite work and watching Oliver operate was like watching a ballet dancer. He was precision orientated, every move considered, delicate and effortless. But she knew the hours, weeks, months, years of practice that had gone into such work that he could move so purposefully and so expertly and make it look easy. It was a complete and utter turn-on. She was so impressed by his skill and ability.

She needed to focus on her *own* work. So she stopped watching her ex-husband. Stopped thinking about his hands. His fingers.

'Prepping the skin graft.'

'I'd rather you used a skin graft from her stomach. She has good quality tissue there,' Oliver said from behind his mask.

'Of course. No problem.' And he was right. Tilly had good skin there. No stretch marks, no scarring, no blemishing. It was perfect for grafting and didn't take too long to use the dermatome to collect the sample. Lauren concentrated hard as she applied the graft to the site on the arm from where she'd created the free flap and began to attach it into place as a nurse dressed the skin graft site.

When they'd finished, they both stepped away from the table feeling satisfied and happy with the surgery.

'Good job, team. Let's get Tilly to Recovery.'

Lauren followed him back out to the scrub room, where they removed their gloves, gown and mask and dropped them into a bin, before they went back to the sinks to scrub out.

'You did well in there.'

It felt good to hear him validate her. To acknowledge her hard work and her ability. It would have felt good to hear that from any new employer, but to hear it from Oliver in particular felt particularly satisfying.

'Thank you. So did you.'

He laughed good-naturedly. 'Cup of tea before the next one?'

It would have been so easy to say yes. To sit down

and chat with him over a drink, catch up. See what was happening in both their lives. But the cleft lip and palate surgery was next and she hadn't had a chance to sit with the patient and examine them yet and she wanted to do that. Wanted to meet the parents too.

'I'd like to check in with the next patient, if you don't mind. I haven't met them yet and if I'm to assist with you I'd like to do my own assessment and introduce myself to the parents.'

He smiled, nodded, flicked the last of the water from his hands and arms before grabbing the paper towels to dry with. 'Of course. Surgery is scheduled in forty minutes. Theatre one.' He gave her one last nod of acknowledgement before leaving the scrub room.

It was as if all the air in the room left with him and she let out a huge breath she hadn't realised she'd been holding.

Working with her ex-husband was always going to be a strain to begin with, but she could see he would make sure that her skills were spot-on and that he would expect nothing but the best from her.

Well, she would show him that he would have no reason to doubt her ability, and she also hoped to show him that she was so good at her job that he would wonder how he had managed all these years without her there, standing by his side. She had been a good mother. A good wife. But she wanted to be an excellent surgeon.

CHAPTER THREE

OLIVER STOOD AT the window, looking out over the hospital gardens below, trying to remember what they'd looked like when they were in full bloom over the summer. Trying to imagine if Lauren had ever looked out at identical gardens at the Great Northern when she'd lived in Edinburgh. The two linked modern hospitals had designed their gardens to be identical and he'd often wondered if those designs were not just identical in shape and size but also in flower choice and placement. Had Lauren watched the wisteria clamber over the trellises? Had she noticed the bloom of the roses? Had she sat at the Peace bench and marvelled at the wonder of the laburnum as it burst into vibrant yellow?

Now, in mid-November, the garden looked a little less alive. Looked after by a team of hospital volunteers, most of it had died back for winter, withering and darkening, losing foliage and stripping itself bare as it entered the festive season.

He'd once loved the run-up to Christmas, loving nothing more than going Christmas shopping with Lauren, hunting for the perfect gift for both of their families and friends. That first Christmas, when they'd first got together, before the girls had arrived, had been the best.

He remembered walking through Leicester Square with her, hand in hand, as a church choir belted out Christmas tunes beneath fairy lights. He remembered draping an arm around Lauren's shoulder and pulling her in close and kissing her. They'd been so close, it had been so easy to be with one another. And now so much had changed. So much time had passed. The last few Christmases since the girls had moved out and he'd been living alone had felt strange. Empty.

'Olly? You okay?'

Pulled from his reverie, he turned to see who'd spoken. It was Dylan. Dylan Harper, neurosurgeon. They'd worked together on a few cases recently and become friends.

'Hey. Yeah, I'm good. How about you?'

'Great. You seemed miles away.'

'Just thinking.'

'Wife back?'

Oliver smiled. 'Ex-wife.'

Dylan nodded. 'That's right. How's that going?'

'We've just scrubbed in together.'

'Oh, yikes. And how did that go?'

'Not bad, actually. Just feels strange. We used to be so close once and now there's this huge chasm between us. We worked well together. She's got great skills, but…'

'But it was strange?'

Oliver nodded. 'Yeah. And she looked…' He drifted off, not sure he ought to tell the hospital's playboy how good his ex-wife looked. Dylan's reputation preceded him.

'Stunning?'

He smiled. 'Little bit.'

Dylan laughed. 'Maybe she thought the same thing about you. Maybe she's standing at a window somewhere in this hospital thinking about you.'

'I doubt it. She's off with my next patient. We're about to go in and complete a cleft lip surgery.'

'Awesome.' Dylan checked his watch. 'Look, I gotta go, but you must introduce me to the missus some time.'

'Will do. Take care.'

'You too.' Then Dylan was gone, striding away, carefree and confident.

Oliver wished he could be as carefree as Dylan, but he never had been. He'd always felt the weight of responsibility, ever since he'd entered medical school. He and Lauren had met there, they'd had lots of fun in a relatively short time and then she'd found out she was pregnant and they'd got married quickly and suddenly he was a real adult, expected to do real adult things and grow up quickly, from the fun-loving medical student to becoming a husband. *Father.* Not many other junior doctors had a child toddling around when they started their first hospital post. Not many other juniors had a *second* baby on the way within months of starting their job.

Life had moved way too fast. His marriage had moved way too fast and it had been all he could do to try and keep up. To work for his family, to bring in enough income to support them all. He'd done it all for them. The long hours. The time away. The studying. The hard work. The overtime. Extra shifts. And somehow, along the way, he and Lauren had lost one another, become ships that passed in the night, and when they had had time together he'd felt Lauren's frustrations at not being able to pursue the career that she had wanted, and when their girls had moved out she'd left too.

Only now she was back. Qualified. A reconstructive surgeon, hungry to climb the ladder of success, just the way he had. She had sacrificed her career aspirations to ensure she was a good mother. She had held the fort at home for him, to give him a soft place to land when he'd needed. The least he could do was to teach Lauren all that he knew now, so that he could help her climb.

It was only fair.

Glancing at his wristwatch, he saw that it was time to prep for baby Elliot's surgery.

He gave one last look at the garden and couldn't help but think of how it resembled his marriage. It had withered. Died. But there was still potential for life there. Nurtured correctly, it would bloom with the right input.

And he was determined to help Lauren bloom.

Because it was her time to be in the sun now.

The nurses were starting to decorate for Christmas on the children's ward. An artificial tree was being pulled from its box as Lauren went up to them.

'Excuse me, I'm looking for Elliot Kane.'

A nurse with a lanyard decorated in teddy bears pointed to the left. 'Through there, bed six.'

'Thank you. Is Willow around? Dr Shaw?'

'She's in clinic this morning.'

'Oh, okay.'

It would have been nice to have seen Willow at work. Their younger daughter had followed in her parents' footsteps and become a doctor, a paediatrician. Lauren had come down for her graduation ceremony and celebrated with her, but she'd never actually got to see her daughter at work and see what kind of doctor she was. She expected she was an amazing one. It took a special kind of courage to work with sick kids, day in and day out. Sick children could break your heart and get inside your head way more easily than adult patients did. But Willow had always been a strong young woman. Determined. Hard-headed. Kick-ass. As a young girl, she would often find Willow in her bedroom with a makeshift hospital ward—all her toys, dolls and plushies lying in rows that were meant to be beds, with various bits of toilet paper or tissue wrapped around limbs or heads and Willow pretending to be the doctor taking care of them. It had been quite cute and she'd loved listening to her dad's stories of life in the hospital. So it had been no surprise that she'd gone to medical school like them.

Kayley had been different, however. Their eldest had been fascinated with the law and police shows and murder mysteries and she'd studied law and become a lawyer, specialising in criminal law.

The two girls could not be more different, yet when they were together they got on so well, probably because there was only fourteen months between them.

Lauren headed into the ward, located bed six and headed on over.

There was a young couple sitting next to Elliot's bed, trying to get him to play with a carousel that was turning musically above his bed.

'Mr and Mrs Kane, I'm Dr Shaw. I'll be assisting in Elliot's surgery today. How is he doing?' She looked down at the most beautiful baby she had ever seen. Cleft lip babies were beyond special, with the most amazing smiles.

'He's doing great. He has no idea what's about to happen, does he?' Elliot's mum looked to be on the verge of tears and her husband draped his arm around her shoulder.

'He'll be just fine,' he whispered, hugging her close and stroking his wife's arm.

Lauren watched them together, admiring them. She and Oliver had never had to go through this. Had never seen either of their daughters in a hospital, injured or awaiting surgery. They'd been lucky. Just cuts and scrapes, chicken pox, colds. Nothing like this. Nothing where they had to give up their child to strangers, knowing that they were going to be anaesthetised and cut and stitched and repaired. She couldn't imagine how awful it must be.

'We'll take good care of him. The best. Is it all right if I examine him?'

Elliot's mum nodded.

'Hey, Elliot. My name is Lauren and I'm just going to take a look at your handsome face, okay?' she said in a sing-song voice. Elliot might only be a baby and would not understand anything that she was saying, but Lauren had been trained to explain to every patient, no matter how old or how young, who they were and what they needed to do. It was a respect thing. Just because Elliot was a baby, it didn't matter that he couldn't consent on his own. She would still explain what she was doing.

Elliot burbled back at her, a bubble forming on his lips as he tried to blow a raspberry. It was beyond cute and she kept smiling and making soothing noises as she examined his cleft lip. It was a bilateral complete cleft, meaning that there were openings on both sides that extended up into the nostrils. Technically, it was a relatively easy repair and Lauren knew the parents and Elliot would feel the difference as soon as he came out of Recovery. This was one of those great surgeries that was instant, where a surgeon knew for sure that what they were doing would hugely improve a patient's life.

When her examination was complete she gave Elliot a little hug and handed him over to his mum, who took him gratefully and squeezed him tight, knowing that he would be going to surgery soon.

'Do you have any questions before we take him down to Theatre?'

They shook their heads. 'Just look after him, please, like he's your own,' said the mum.

'Of course.' Lauren reached up to stroke Elliot's soft, downy head, before smiling and heading back to the team. It had felt good to take this break away from Oliver. To just breathe and know that the initial discomfort of seeing him again was now over.

It could only get easier from now on, right?

Even though he'd operated with Lauren this morning already, to see her again in the cleft lip surgery simply reminded him that from now on Lauren was going to be around, here in the hospital, working on some of his cases, working on some of her own. He would see her around and about in the halls, the staffroom, the canteen. They might casually bump into one another in the car park. Share a lift. Share frustrations. Losses. Wins. She was back and she was here and she wasn't his any more.

She wouldn't be at home.

That was the weirdest thing, even though they'd been

divorced now for ten years, to have her suddenly back in his life, but knowing that this time she would not be waiting for him at home. It felt strange. Tonight, she would go home to another man. Mike. Who undoubtedly treated her right. She would snuggle on the couch with him. He would put his arm around her. Touch her. Be overfamiliar with her. Sleep with her.

And he'd learned to be okay with that.

He'd learned through Willow and Kayley that their mum was dating another guy, another surgeon, and even though they'd been apart and he was dating too, he'd looked the guy up on the internet. He'd found a picture of Lauren and Mike attending a charity gala and the guy looked like a rock star. Worse still was his impressive resumé, which he'd discovered with a deeper internet search.

He'd told himself to be happy for her. To let her live her life. They were separated now. Divorced. He was no longer allowed an opinion, but he'd still been hurt to imagine that she had replaced him so quickly when he'd believed when they'd first met that they were each other's soulmate. And so he'd thrown himself deeper into work. Then he'd met Daria, and even though she was much younger than him and looking to surge forward in her own career, he'd told himself that what was good for Lauren should also be good for him.

'Tell me the primary function of cleft lip surgery?' he asked her as he began to prepare for the lip repair.

'Function. And aesthetics.'

Her eyes crinkled behind her mask, telling him that she was smiling. He'd always loved her smile. It was warm, welcoming. It made him smile too. Always.

'Function of what?'

'The circular muscles around the mouth, to assist with speech, eating and swallowing.'

'And what are those circular muscles called?' He didn't mean to drill her as he incised the cleft. But this was a teaching hospital and she was here to develop as a reconstructive surgeon and if she was going to be working on his team then he needed to know her knowledge base was strong on the basics, at least. A lot of doctors thought they could skip the basics, but they were there for a reason.

'The orbicularis oris muscle.'

'Good. And what happens after I close the orbicularis oris muscle?'

'It creates a philtral ridge to complete the philtrum.'

She knew her stuff and he gave her an appraising look over the table. She wasn't looking at him but at the operating site, those blue eyes of hers…so warm, so bright. *Beautiful.*

Suddenly aware that he must have paused, Lauren looked up at him.

He looked back down at baby Elliot and asked the theatre nurse for the sutures. 'And what kind of sutures would we use in the repair of a cleft lip?'

'Er…it depends on the area being stitched. A simple interrupted suture on the vermilion edge or a vertical mattress suture on the philtrum.'

'And on the cupid's bow?'

'Tip stitch suture.'

He nodded. She did know her stuff. 'Good.' He passed her the sutures. 'Get to it.'

She smiled at him, the way she had in the good old

days, as if they were sharing a private joke, and she took the sutures from him and began to work.

'More light, please,' she asked the theatre nurse to adjust the large light above them so that she could see better as she now worked.

He watched her carefully, her concentration. The way a small crease formed between her brows. The way her small, delicate hands worked niftily and neatly. She was quick. Purposeful. Knowledgeable. But, most importantly, she was skilled. She wasn't nervous working in front of him. Her hands didn't tremble or shake because he was watching and he couldn't help but admire her for that. He'd had many students work with him in surgeries, or newly registered surgeons, who trembled to work in his presence. But not Lauren.

There'd always been a strength in her. A core of steel. There'd had to be, raising their two daughters alone, putting her career on the backburner so that he could work all the hours he could to provide for them, whilst she'd dealt with everything else. She'd been his rock and his security and he'd simply trusted that she would always be there.

Until she wasn't. And he'd realised, quickly, that he'd taken her for granted. Stopped seeing her. Only realising just what he had lost when she'd packed her bags and moved out.

'I think I'm done.'

He looked down at the neat stitches. She'd done a marvellous repair, just how he would have done it.

'Great job.'

'Thank you.'

'You're welcome.' He smiled back at her, wondering

what kind of surgeon she'd be right now if he'd been the one to stay at home and look after the kids and she'd been the one to work on her career. No doubt she'd be head of her own department by now.

'Let's get Elliot to Recovery, please, Nurse.' He pulled off his gloves and mask and gown, dumping them in the clothing bin before heading into the scrub room to wash down.

Lauren followed him in. 'Thank you for letting me close up. I appreciate that.'

'No problem.'

'I'm glad that we can be adult about all of this and work well together. It's not going to be a problem, is it?'

A problem? No. It was more than that. It was disturbing to have her here again. To be so close. To be so wonderful. Gorgeous. Sexy. A painful reminder of what he'd once had. What he'd lost. It reminded him of his foolishness. Of his mistakes. His pride. His whole body and mind reacted to her being in the room. To being beside him. Opposite him. Close to him. Smelling as wonderful as she did, looking as beautiful as she was. Her skill clear to see, her natural ability now allowed the free rein it had deserved all those years ago. He felt guilty for stopping her from being who she could be.

'Of course not. No problem at all.' He hoped he sounded convincing.

CHAPTER FOUR

THE HOSPITAL CANTEEN was busy, humming with voices and busy people going this way and that. Lauren picked up a tray and chose an egg mayo salad sandwich and a small slice of strawberry cheesecake for her dessert, along with a pot of tea, and then began the tedious task of trying to find a free table.

The canteen was open to both the staff and the public so there was a mix of people and she scanned the faces to see if she could see who she had arranged to meet.

Willow, her daughter. Dr Willow Shaw, a newly qualified paediatrician.

Their youngest daughter had her father's features. Long, dark hair that was silky-smooth and glossy. Green eyes, the same as her father. The only thing she seemed to have inherited from her mother was her small stature and the slight upturn that she had to her nose. Beyond that, she was all Oliver.

Her gaze scanned the crowd and eventually she noticed a raised hand at the back and the smiling face of her daughter.

Lauren beamed and made her way over, edging between diners and visitors until she made it to the table.

She set down her tray and her daughter stood and they gave each other a big hug.

It had been four months since they'd last seen each other in person. Whilst up in Edinburgh, Lauren had tried to video call her daughters at least once a week, which was nice and had made Lauren feel that she wasn't missing out on too much, but it wasn't the same as actually being here. Actually being able to hold them and squeeze them and love them in person.

'Oh, this is nice,' Lauren said, still hugging her daughter tight. Willow smelt lovely, wearing a lightly scented perfume that seemed floral and her hair smelling of coconut. 'I've missed this.'

'Me too.'

They eventually let go, despite Lauren wanting to hold Willow close to her for ever, and sat down opposite one another. It had felt good to hug someone. Since seeing Oliver that morning and feeling such a visceral reaction, her body had needed contact and as she couldn't hug him, hugging her daughter whom she hadn't seen for four months was just as good.

Willow had an iced coffee and looked to be halfway through a jacket potato covered in chilli and cheese.

'That looks good,' she said, feeling a little less optimistic about her sandwich and wishing now that she'd gone for a hot meal.

'It's not bad. You know hospital food.'

'I do.' Lauren wrinkled her nose and laughed. 'So how are you? Settling in to your new job?'

'I'm doing great! Really enjoying it, and my team are fantastic. Lots of friendly faces, which is what you need in Paeds. How about you?' Willow leaned in, almost conspiratorially. 'How did it go with Dad? Have you met up yet?'

Lauren felt a flush of heat suffuse her body at the thought of Oliver, at how well it had gone today. At least to outward appearances. Anybody watching them would never have known of the turmoil she was feeling inside at how she had physically reacted to seeing Oliver again today. Of how all the memories had come flashing back.

'We have, yes. We've even operated together.'

'Ooh! Tell me everything.'

'There's not much to tell. We operated on a tongue cancer patient and created a new flap from her arm and then we worked on a cleft lip baby.'

'Two surgeries?'

Lauren nodded and took a bite of sandwich, not because she was hungry but because it stopped her from saying all the things she was feeling.

Your father looked amazing and I found myself checking him out. You never told me he's turned into a silver fox. I found myself reacting to him, physically. Like I wanted him—actually wanted him! Some remnant of lust or something that my body felt, which clearly hasn't got the message that we're divorced.

'Well, you must have talked about something.'

Lauren nodded, still chewing. 'This and that. Mainly about the patients, but we did seem to get on and we've both agreed that it isn't going to be a problem, us working together.'

'Oh.'

Lauren smiled. 'You sound strangely disappointed. Aren't you happy that your father and I are getting along?'

'Of course I am! I just… I don't know. You haven't seen each other in ten years and have always managed to avoid each other at birthday parties and celebrations—all carefully co-ordinated, no doubt. I just thought there might have been more when you met up with each other again. Do you think he's changed?'

Of course she did. Oliver was more honed. Physically stronger. Sexier. The young puppy fat days had passed and made him leaner and chiselled and deliciously edible-looking!

'A little.'

'Does he know about Mike yet?'

'I haven't told him. Have you?'

'I figured it was your news to share.'

'I'll tell him when the time is right.'

She didn't want Oliver to find out about it and read too much into it. Lauren had made the choice to move back down south to be with her family again. She'd missed Kayley and Willow so, so much. Video calls just weren't cutting it any more and they were all getting so busy, Willow working long hours as a junior doctor and Kayley putting all the hours into her job as a criminal lawyer. There'd been too many times when they'd missed their calls with one another or postponed them, and Lauren had begun to feel as if she was being edged out of their lives and she'd hated that feeling.

She'd wanted to be there with them, close to them if they needed her, and the job at the Great Southern had just happened to open up. It had made perfect sense to her to leap at it, despite the fact that she'd known she would be working with her ex. But their divorce had been quite amicable in the end. They'd both been adult about it, there was no reason why they couldn't work in the same hospital. After all, it was a big place with plenty of room for both of them. And she'd honestly believed that meeting up with Oliver again might be difficult but manageable. It wasn't as if they were dramatic teenagers who'd had a massive falling-out and hated each other. They'd drifted apart over the years, pulled in different directions, and they were proper adults now. In their fifties! Even if sometimes Lauren still felt like she was in her twenties.

She couldn't believe the years had gone by. When she was younger, she remembered celebrating her own mother's fiftieth birthday. She'd wanted a huge celebration and a big fuss made of her and Lauren, aged sixteen at the time, had thought how *old* her mother was!

She didn't feel that way now, realising her own mother had *never* been old at fifty. There'd still been plenty of years left in her. Indeed there still were.

'I guess there's a little part of me that's kind of hopeful about my parents being back in each other's life. That I'll no longer be from a broken home.' Willow grinned and spooned in a mouthful of chilli.

Lauren laughed. 'You're hoping for a grand reunion, are you?' She flushed at the thought, her brain helpfully presenting her with an image of her and Oliver stumbling into an empty linen cupboard as they raked at each other's clothes, kissing madly and having a passionate make-out session in there, like the ones she saw in her favourite hospital drama on television.

'Is that so wrong?' She was still smiling.

'Totally. Your father and I are different people now.'

'Exactly.' Willow pointed at her with her fork. 'You're

both in a place, career-wise, where you've always wanted to be. You don't have the stresses and strains of raising a family any more. Kayley and I are grown up, doing grown-up things. I'm engaged to be married and Kayley already is! We're making our own families now. You and Dad have time to do what you want to do.'

'I'm focused on my career, Wills, that's all. It's my first day and I want to make a good impression, not just on your father but on *everyone.*'

'Doesn't mean you can't have a bit of fun. Hashtag just saying.' Willow smiled.

Lauren smiled back. 'I can have fun *without* your father. Hashtag just saying.' It was their little in-joke with one another. 'Anyway, how is Kayley? I haven't heard from her in a while.' Her oldest daughter had been strangely quiet recently.

Willow shrugged. 'She's a bit down.'

'Because of the baby thing?' Kayley and her husband, Aaron, had been trying to get pregnant since they got married a couple of years ago. There'd been one pregnancy early on, discovered a week or two after they got back from their Caribbean honeymoon, but it had resulted in a miscarriage at six weeks that had devastated them both. Since then, they'd been trying to get pregnant again, to no avail.

'Yeah. She calls me each time her period arrives, usually in tears. It's got to the point where I just don't know what to say to her any more. All my platitudes are empty, you know?' Willow pushed her plate away.

'She calls me too. Didn't they go away on that couples retreat thing? I remember her telling me about it, but I've not heard from them since. She's always busy, it seems. I wonder if she could lessen her stress a little it might help?'

'Maybe. Sometimes I feel she gets a little angry with me when we speak.'

'Why?'

'Because I'm a doctor. And so are you and so is Dad and yet doctors haven't been able to tell her why she can't fall pregnant. Sometimes I get the feeling she blames us.'

'I guess she has to direct her anger and frustrations somewhere. And if that's what she needs then I'll let her do it. Has Oliver spoken to her recently?' Oliver had always been Kayley's favourite. When she was little, if she had a fall and scraped her knee, Lauren would patch her up but it would be Oliver's knee she would clamber on when he finally made it home.

'He hasn't said anything. But maybe he hasn't heard from her either. She has been a little AWOL these last few weeks.'

'Maybe I should ask him?'

The thought of breaching the professional barrier she had with her ex-husband right now was terrifying, though. Because if she suddenly took their relationship from professional to personal, initiated a closer connection than they'd been pretending, then maybe that would be dangerous, considering the unexpected feelings she'd had for him since they'd met again. Because Lauren could not deny the zing she'd felt at seeing and being with him again.

'You could try.' Willow checked the time. 'Wow. How come lunch breaks go so fast?'

'It's a strange anomaly in hospital time. All breaks,

lunch or otherwise, go much faster than shifts. What sort of cases have you got at the moment? Anything interesting?'

'The usual. Nothing exciting or terrifying, which is good. You?'

'I'm sitting in on your dad's clinic this afternoon for an hour or so, just to see how things get processed here and then, excitingly, I get to run the clinic and meet a couple of new patients of my own.'

'Sounds great.' Willow made to stand. 'You must let me know how that goes. And if you hear from Kayley you'll let me know?'

'Of course.' She stood as well to give her daughter another hug. 'We must do this again soon.'

'Absolutely. Now, enjoy your sandwich whilst you can.' Willow kissed her on the cheek, gathered her plate on its tray and headed towards the exit.

Lauren found herself sitting alone and worrying about Kayley. She had been *in absentia* lately and she worried that maybe her daughter was getting so wrapped up in trying for a baby that she was losing herself in the process. It could affect people that way sometimes and she didn't blame them for it. She could recall sitting with Kayley once, a few weeks before her wedding, and the gleam in her eyes when she'd said they would start trying for a baby as soon as the ring was on her finger.

'And it'll probably happen really quickly. I mean, you had no problem, Mum. You just had to sit on the same couch as Dad and you'd get pregnant!'

And they'd both laughed and laughed, because it had seemed true at the time. Lauren had fallen pregnant so quickly, so easily, there was no reason to think that Kayley would have a problem.

And she had fallen pregnant once, after her honeymoon, and Kayley and Aaron had been ecstatic, telling everyone. They'd both been so happy, so proud. And then that phone call, late one evening, from Aaron. Kayley was likely miscarrying, bleeding heavily. A doctor had confirmed it. Kayley had sunk into quite a depression. It had been hard to watch, but slowly, over time, she'd picked up and been ready to try again and the whole family had been hopeful, as Kayley and Aaron were, that it would happen quickly again. And each month had ticked by with disappointment after disappointment, so much so that Kayley had begun to find it difficult to face any of them. She seemed to feel she carried the blame, when that blatantly wasn't true. No one was to blame.

But where was she? *How* was she?

And why had no one heard from her for a while?

Oliver had chosen not to eat in the hospital canteen today for lunch. He'd known that Willow was meeting with her mum there and if he'd arrived at the same time their daughter would have called him over too and expected them to eat lunch together like old times, and he wasn't sure he was ready to do that.

He'd already spent plenty of time with Lauren this morning and he just needed a little breather, a little fresh air, to get his head straight. Reset. Recalibrate. Discover a way he could be with his ex-wife so that he wasn't thinking about her hair, or the way her eyes still shone so bright and so blue that he remembered how dark they would go whenever they were being intimate. Because it was wrong to think of her in that way any more. She wasn't his. They'd divorced. Remembering their more passionate moments whilst standing next to her now was a little off, wasn't it?

And so he'd headed out of the hospital and made it to a local sandwich truck and allowed himself to indulge in a totally unhealthy all-day breakfast sandwich filled with sausage and bacon and egg. He didn't often allow himself a cheat day but he'd not had one for a while, so why not? It had been a stressful day and it still wasn't over. But at least if he could just get through the next few hours, then after that Lauren would be free to do more of her own thing. She had three patients of her own that were coming in later on this afternoon and he'd be able to stop being her teacher for the day.

He was looking forward to that and he had to believe that Lauren was looking forward to it too. She did not want to be chained to her ex-husband's side, right?

'Olly?'

He turned at the voice. 'Daria, hey.'

His relationship with Daria had ended some time ago, but it still felt strange to run into her again. Was this his day for meeting exes?

'Long time, no see.'

'It is. Are you here at the hospital on business or…?' Daria was a drug rep. She'd turned up at his office once to try and sell him on some new skin cream that was supposedly revolutionary in its ability to assist with reducing scarring after surgery and there'd been a bit of a spark between them. At first he'd thought she was just doing a little flirting to make a deal with him on the skin cream, but then she'd asked him out for a drink. He'd accepted and the rest was history.

'Business.'

'Ah. Who are you here to see?'

'I have an appointment with Dr Dylan Harper.'

Oliver smiled. The hospital playboy. Dylan wasn't really a playboy; he just had the reputation for it. He was a good-looking guy. Probably Daria's type?

'Well, I'll let you get to it then. Take care.'

He began to walk away, but then she called after him, 'I heard your wife is back.'

He turned. '*Ex-wife*. And how did you hear about that?'

Daria smiled. 'I have connections. Connections talk and get gossipy when they've had a few drinks in a wine bar.'

He nodded. 'Nothing faster than the hospital grapevine.'

'What's it like, having her back?'

'It's fine.'

She smiled, tilted her head to one side as if she didn't believe him. 'Come on!'

'What?'

'The woman you loved, who you've had two daughters with, is suddenly back in your life after a decade or so. You must have some feelings about it.'

'Well, if I do, they're certainly nothing to do with you. But it's nice to see you looking so well, Daria. Have a nice day.' He raised his coffee cup as a goodbye and strode away from her, determined not to give her any more of his time or attention.

Daria had been great to begin with, but very quickly he had begun to feel like a portal through which she could shop her products. She'd seemed to want to use him to create further contacts and her flirting with other doctors was so off the scale that he'd begun to hear rumours. So it had been easy to end it before it had become something more, not that he could ever have imagined his relatively short time with Daria as anything that could have become serious. She'd not been after that and neither had he. Short flings had not turned out to be his thing. He was a guy who valued commitment and the long-term.

Upon arrival at his clinic he noticed Lauren waiting for him. She hadn't seen him yet, but she stood leaning against the wall worrying at a nail. The action made him smile. He'd forgotten how she used to do that when she was worrying about something. He'd always thought it cute. With a smile on his face, he walked up to her.

'Missed lunch?'

She started and flushed pink, embarrassed at having been caught. 'Oh! Sorry.' She pushed off away from the wall as he unlocked the door with a swipe of his NHS ID card and let them both in. 'And no, I had lunch. I met with Willow.'

'How's she getting on?'

'Good! Good. We had a nice time, though we spent half of it worrying about Kayley. I haven't heard from her in a long time and neither has she. Have *you* heard from her?'

'Er...she rang me about ten days ago, said she was going away with Aaron for a break. Somewhere abroad—Croatia, I think. I would have said if I'd known that you were all worrying about her.'

'So she's fine, then? If she's gone on holiday.'

'I think it was more of a retreat.'

'But you felt that she was fine?'

He shrugged. In all honesty, he'd felt as if there was something she wasn't saying, something she couldn't tell him, and he'd not wanted to push her on it, knowing she would tell him when she was ready. But did he want to keep that tiny nugget from Lauren? He didn't want to hurt her and he already knew she felt it keenly that Kayley was closer to him than she was to her mother.

'I think she just wanted some time alone with her husband. Away from the stresses of home and all her disappointments.'

'Her disappointments? You mean not getting pregnant? The miscarriage?'

'Maybe. I don't know. I did feel like she had something she wasn't saying, so maybe they've gone for a treatment at some spa or special fertility clinic?'

Lauren was pacing. 'But she's got a good head on her shoulders. She wouldn't have gone for some radical treatment abroad without researching it first, would she?'

He could tell that Lauren was getting super stressed by this idea and he reached out to stop her pacing and laid a hand on her arm to calm her, to stop her, without thinking. It was an old habit.

She looked at him in surprise and he let go, his hand pulling away quickly as if he'd just been burned. Her look had said *You're overstepping the mark*. He'd not meant to. It had just happened. Touching her in such a familiar way…it did strange things to his head.

'She's a sensible girl and we have to trust her.'

Lauren was still looking perturbed by his touching her. So much so, he wondered if he ought to apologise for overstepping a boundary, but then she spoke.

'I just wish she'd spoken to me about it.' To stop herself pacing, she sank into the chair opposite his desk, where the patient would sit.

He did the logical thing and went around his desk so

that it lay between them like a large metallic barrier, the perfect wall, creating an expanse from which he could not touch her.

'I know you're worried about her, we all have been. But you've got to allow her to live her life the way she and Aaron decide.'

'I know but… I came all this way to be with my girls and I haven't seen her at all…and now she's gone away? When is she coming back, did she say?'

He shook his head, knowing his answer would disappoint her. He hated seeing her worrying about this. Hated seeing her sad. It simply reminded him of how he'd made her feel in the past and the guilt that had followed and he wanted to make her smile. This was Lauren's time to be happy, not sad.

'I can see you're worrying about all of this but there's not much we can do right now. Instead of you going home and worrying about it, why don't you come out for dinner tonight? We can talk, catch up on family and work and the hospital now that there are three of us that work here.' He smiled, softening the offer, letting her know he wasn't asking her out on a date. It was just family stuff. Adulting stuff. More of a formality, really, than anything else.

She looked at him, surprised, then nodded.

He wasn't sure she'd accept, but when she did he felt inordinately pleased. Good food always made a tense situation better. And if he took her to the right place he might be able to make her smile and forget her worries.

Not that he wasn't worried about Kayley too. It was just that he knew his daughter and he knew that if she had anything to tell them she would.

When she was ready.

CHAPTER FIVE

LAUREN SAT IN clinic with Oliver, trying to focus on the patients that came in through the doors, but she had a lot swirling around her head. That her own clinic would start in a little over an hour and she'd be set free to start establishing herself here. That she was sitting in this room with her ex-husband, who looked delicious, and his rapport with patients was clear to see. The women adored him. The men admired him. He gave them confidence in their surgical choices, he gave brilliant advice on medical matters and they all left with a smile. He was the ultimate professional. He looked good, sounded good. Smelt good.

She thought and worried about Kayley, wondering what was happening with their eldest daughter, and hoped that she was enjoying herself in Croatia with Aaron. Maybe the relaxed time away would do them some good.

She thought about the casual way Oliver had touched her arm when she was pacing and the lightning bolt of awareness that had rocketed through her body. She'd almost gasped. And she thought about the fact that she had accepted an invitation to dinner with him. Dinner! When she'd started this morning she'd not for one minute thought when she entered the hospital doors that she would have accepted an offer from Oliver to join him for dinner that evening. The most she'd hoped for was that they would be civil to one another, for the sake of the patients, their work colleagues and their daughters.

Dinner! It wasn't a date. It never could be—he was with Daria and, besides, they'd been divorced for years, it had been over a long time ago, but there was still a part of her that was thrilled at the idea. Terrified. Nervous. But she calmed herself by telling herself that it was simply a catch-up. It was sensible. Best to get it out of the way. That Daria would be there too, obviously, because she couldn't imagine her being thrilled by her boyfriend going out for dinner with his ex-wife alone, and surely Oliver wouldn't lie to her about where he was going, so it was all going to be above board, right?

She'd watched Oliver advise a patient on a future sinus surgery, a case to realign a lower jaw, advise another patient on the removal of a benign mass that was growing behind their left eye, and then suddenly they were on break and he was turning to her, smiling.

'So do you feel ready to go and do this on your own?'

'Yes, of course.' She felt more than ready. She'd run her own clinics at the Great Northern and she was looking forward to getting her own surgical list here. Oliver had shown her the computer system, how to log notes, but there wasn't anything new to pick up on—the two hospitals used the same system.

'Good. Fancy a coffee before you start?'

She didn't want to get overly familiar with him. They had pretty much spent all day together already and they would be dining out together tonight, so she shook her head. 'I'd like to get set up in my clinic room, if you don't mind?'

'Of course not. You go ahead.' He smiled. 'But we should get together at the end of clinic so you can fill me in on your cases and what's been decided.'

He was her boss, so it seemed reasonable enough.

'Sure thing.'

'You know where to find me.'

'I do.' She gave him one last smile, thanked him and left the room, once again letting out a huge breath of tension that had been building. She headed to her own clinic room next door to his. It was bland, like most clinic rooms, set up with a desk, computer, chair, a set of cupboards containing the medical basics, a weighing scale, a height measure on the wall and an examining couch with a roll of blue paper.

Lauren let out a sigh of satisfaction, feeling as if her proper work was about to begin. So far today, she'd been guided, assessed, observed. Now was her moment to launch from the safety of the nest and fly free. Booting up the computer, she sat down and began to arrange her desk the way she wanted it.

A knock on her door and the lady from Reception came in with a clipboard that listed her patients and their ID numbers, so she could bring up their notes on screen.

'Would you like a hot drink, Dr Shaw?'

'Yes, please, that would be lovely, Shana, thank you.'

Lauren brought up the case notes for her first patient. Callie Mackenzie needed breast reconstruction after a double mastectomy. She'd fought cancer twice now and had been in remission for three years and felt ready to face surgery again after a few difficult procedures. Lauren was looking forward to hopefully making this woman feel better about herself, whether she chose to go through with the procedure or not.

As Shana brought in her tea, her computer system let her know that Callie had arrived. Lauren took a fortifying sip of her hot drink, took one last look around her room and then pressed the button that would notify Callie in the waiting room that it was her time to come in. She stood and waited to greet her first ever patient at the Great Southern.

When she walked in, Lauren was gratified to see a woman not cowed by her past battles but one who emanated happiness, from the bright, broad smile on her face to her elegant way of dress, fashionable pixie cut and expensive perfume that filled the room. Callie shook her hand and said hello, before settling herself down into a chair, with another woman at her side.

'Pleased to meet you. I'm Dr Shaw.'

'Callie. Evie,' Callie introduced her partner.

'Okay, so you're here because I received a letter from your GP, indicating that you're interested in reconstructive breast surgery.'

'Yes, that's right.'

'And you had a double mastectomy just over four years ago?' Lauren double-checked the record.

'Yes. I could have had reconstruction at the time of the mastectomy, but I chose not to. The doctor told me it would be safe, but I just wasn't ready, you know? I'd lived with the idea that my breasts were trying to kill me and I just wanted them gone.'

'I understand.' Lauren smiled. 'But you feel ready now?'

'I do.' Callie reached for Evie's hand. 'I have a new partner in my life. I'm happy and I want to feel like a woman again, make my clothes look better on me. Have greater confidence.'

'Wonderful.' Lauren led her through the options for reconstruction, discussed sizes, expanders, showed her a variety of implants, from saline to silicone or even autologous, using tissue from elsewhere in the body.

'I was a thirty-four B before. I think I'd like to stay around that size. Maybe go up to a C? I'd hate to go too big. I need to think about what will suit my frame.'

'Absolutely.' Lauren examined Callie, to check her old incisions. There'd be no problem with expanding her tissue.

'What about nipples?'

Lauren smiled. There weren't many jobs where people could ask that question out loud and be taken seriously.

'Well, we usually wait until you've healed from the reconstruction before we start to construct a nipple and areola. We create a nipple from skin used in the reconstruction and then, a few months after that, we can either tattoo on an areola or use a skin graft from the groin at the time of the nipple reconstruction to create an areola then.'

'I think I'd like as few procedures as possible. I don't particularly enjoy staying in hospital.'

'So you'd prefer areola and nipple reconstruction at the same time?'

Callie glanced at Evie and they both nodded in agreement.

'All right, that shouldn't be a problem.'

Lauren discussed with them surgical aftercare, timeframes, risk factors to the surgery and any complications that could arise as a result of the procedure, but Callie and Evie seemed happy with everything.

'I can't thank you enough,' said Callie. 'You go through these huge life-changing events and always come out a little changed on the other side. It'll be nice to come into hospital for something positive, rather than negative. I'm rebuilding myself.' She smiled.

'We all need a little rebuilding, I think,' agreed Lauren.

She'd been through a lot of changes herself in life. Having two small children close together. Dropping out of medical school to be a mother. Pressing pause on her career aspirations, watching her husband climb rapidly through the ranks in a career she'd wanted for herself. Divorce. House moves, isolation faraway from family. Starting medical school again and feeling ancient as the oldest in her class and never quite fitting in with everyone else. Being cheated on. Starting again. Having to work under her ex-husband. Worrying about her daughters. At least Kayley and Willow were healthy, right? They'd not had to face the traumas that Callie had. Kayley might be facing tough fertility issues, but she wasn't facing cancer or chemo or radiation or surgery to take away her womb or her breasts.

Maybe I need to stop worrying so much about her. She'll be okay. She has us.

Lauren said goodbye to Callie and Evie and typed up her notes to update the record electronically and then used the voice recorder that would be used to create Callie's letter to her GP.

Her first consult here at the Great Southern was over and now she could move onto the next.

She tried *not* to think that with every patient seen it would bring her closer and closer to her dinner with Oliver.

Oliver wasn't sure how to dress for his meal with Lauren. He didn't want to dress too smartly as he wasn't sure he wanted Lauren to think that he thought that this was a date. Because it wasn't. They were just going to catch up, talk about the girls. About work. About careers. They would talk about how they were both going to navigate this situation they now found themselves in, because he'd never thought for one moment that he would end up as her boss. Well, her senior, anyway. He wasn't head of the department yet, but that was surely only a matter of time.

Phillip Thomson, the current head of department, had already started talking about his retirement coming up in six months' time and the gossip was that Oliver was the front-runner for the post. Even Phillip had told him that he would like Oliver to take over. He'd told him in the same conversation when he'd revealed that he'd interviewed new candidates for the reconstructive surgeon post and offered it to Oliver's ex-wife. That had been one hell of an afternoon!

Oliver stood in front of his wardrobe, trying to decide between a black shirt to go with his black trousers, or whether to go with a white one. Preferring the black, he shrugged that on and began to fasten the cuffs.

He wasn't the man that he'd once been and he couldn't help but remember the first time he'd spotted Lauren at medical school from across a crowded lecture hall. If he remembered correctly, it was a lecture on the peripheral nervous system and Lauren had been concentrating hard, writing notes with a pen that had a fluffy pink ostrich feather on the end that had made him smile, wondering how on earth she could concentrate with that on the end of it. It kept catching his eye, although her long blonde hair had curtained her face until that one moment when she'd tucked her hair behind her ear and he'd been stunned by how beautiful she was.

For the rest of the lecture he'd stolen glances at her and when it was over he'd managed to follow her out, bump into her and ask her what she'd thought of the lecture. When she'd turned those beautiful blue eyes of hers upon him he'd felt winded. And when she'd smiled he'd almost been struck dumb. He'd stuttered an answer to her question in return, laughed, blushed and then bluntly asked her out for a drink. And the rest was history.

He checked his reflection in the mirror and tweaked his hair, which was more silver now than the dark brown locks he used to have. But he cut a decent figure, he thought. He looked after himself these days, had begun filling his spare hours away from the hospital with hours at the gym, or running. He'd done three London Marathons now and was planning his fourth, having caught the running bug. He was leaner, more muscular, and could almost see abs if he sucked in his breath and tensed his stomach muscles!

Oliver checked his watch. He'd promised to meet her outside a pub they both knew, so they could have a drink first and then head on out to find a nice restaurant and grab a bite to eat.

It was time to go and he felt nervous again. As nervous as he had on their first date, when they'd gone to see a movie and then gone dancing afterwards. He'd not been a great dancer, not yet fully confident in his body, and she'd laughed good-naturedly at him, laughter that had lit up her eyes, and she'd pulled him close and they'd shared their first kiss.

He'd liked to tell everyone that he was lost to her at

that first kiss, but that was never quite the whole truth. The moment he'd been lost to her had been the moment she'd tucked her hair behind her ear in that lecture, a moment that he often thought of fondly. He'd been a fool to lose her, but he'd thought he was doing the right thing in working so hard to provide for his rapidly growing family. How many other junior doctors had two young daughters and a wife to provide for? Not many, he'd wager. And he'd lost her for a very long time. It was quite surreal to have her back here, working as a surgeon, following the dream she'd always held close to her heart.

'I'll do it one day, Oliver, just you see. When the girls are older and more settled in school, I'll go back.'

'*Good for you*,' he'd once said—rather patronisingly, he now felt.

But the girls had never got settled in school. Kayley had struggled with dyslexia and Willow with ADHD that she'd masked in bad behaviour. Lauren was always getting called in to speak to headteachers or tutors or pastoral workers and though Kayley's issue had been diagnosed relatively early, everyone had thought that Willow was just acting up because all the focus had been on her older sister.

Of course that had never been the case at all. She'd just struggled to fit in to the strict, ordered timetable of school, forced to learn about subjects in which she had no interest, though she'd excelled in science and especially biology and chemistry.

'*I'm going to be a doctor one day, like Dad*,' she'd said.

His gaze went to a picture he had of the two girls on his bedside table, Willow in her graduation gown, Kayley standing next to her, arm around her shoulders, incredibly proud. His girls had fought so hard to get where they were now, and Lauren had fought for them every step of the way.

He caught a taxi to the pub and waited outside. It was cold and he could see his breath freezing in the air as all around him the street glowed in the lamplight. His teeth chattered a little due to his nerves and he kept stamping his feet so he could keep the feeling in his toes and he was just rubbing his palms together when another taxi pulled up and Lauren stepped out.

It was as if he saw her in slow motion, alighting from the vehicle with all the grace of a royal, her red heels connecting with the ground as she stepped out, revealing her beautiful red dress and the ivory-coloured wrap that she wore about her shoulders. She was laughing at something the driver said and he felt a weird stab of jealousy as Lauren gave him a cash tip and waved him goodbye.

There's no Mike.

Then she turned to face him and smiled and it was as if all was well again as she came towards him, practically gliding, her hair smooth and silken, her eyes smoky and dark.

'Hi. You look great,' he said rather lamely, but he couldn't say all the other things that ran through his mind. Some of them were rather X-rated considering the way that dress hugged her shapely womanly curves and he was too busy trying to calm his runaway heart and his traitorous loins. 'Thought we'd grab a drink first, if that's okay?'

'Perfect.'

Another smile and it was all he could do to step back and hold the pub door open for her, and though the air that whooshed past smelt of hops and beer and cooked food, when *she* walked past him it was all he could do not to let his mouth drop open and have his tongue roll across the floor like a cartoon character.

She smelt *divine.* Floral. Feminine. Dainty, somehow.

His Baby Bird.

Male eyes turned her way when she entered, he noticed as he followed behind and placed his hand on the small of her back as he guided her towards the bar.

The hand said, *She's mine. Back off.*

His brain logically reminded him otherwise.

CHAPTER SIX

'I HAVE TO say I felt quite nervous about coming out here tonight,' Lauren said, gratefully sipping at the white wine before her.

Oliver had chosen a booth for them to sit in, close to the roaring open fire. It was a welcome heat after the cold outside, where the air had begun to freeze and she knew that in the morning there would be a definite frost, a coating of icy white that would sparkle and glisten. The fire warmed her and stopped her legs from trembling. She wore sheer tights with the dress but had wished, after stepping out of her taxi, that she'd worn trousers instead.

But something inside her, getting ready for tonight, had told her to go all out and dress well for this meeting. Out here, away from the hospital, he was no longer her senior. He was just Oliver, her ex-husband, and there was a small, devilish part of her that wanted to dress up and show him what he was missing. Plus, she also knew she couldn't compete with Daria, who was younger, slimmer and who no doubt had less lines on her face and body as she was still just thirty years old. She just wanted to feel good and to that end she'd even put on her best underwear, even though she knew he'd never get to see it. But it made her feel good. Pulling things in, pushing things up, presenting herself in the best light.

Oliver smiled. 'Me too. It's all a bit strange this, really, isn't it?'

Lauren nodded. 'More than strange. Today was how I always imagined our lives would be, both of us working together at a hospital. I just never suspected it would be this way and all these years later. Anyway, how have you been?'

'I'm good. And you?'

'Yes, great. How are things with Daria?' Lauren tried not to sound bitter in any way.

'Fine, I guess. She was here today, actually. To see another doctor, not me.'

Lauren frowned, not understanding. 'And you're both doing okay?'

'I guess so. We're not together any more.'

'Oh.' That was a surprise. He didn't look upset about it. 'What happened?'

He shrugged. 'Just didn't work. It was never ever going to be serious between us. It started as a bit of flirtatious fun and a way for me to blow off steam after a horrendous day and she was there and somehow it became a relationship for a little while.'

'I'm sorry it didn't work out.' But she was re-evaluating her choice to wear the dress now. It had never occurred to her that Oliver was *free* of Daria. Willow hadn't mentioned it. 'The girls never said.'

'They never really liked Daria, to be fair.'

Lauren smiled, recalling some of Willow's phone calls. 'I know.'

'So I never mentioned it when the relationship drifted away.'

'Is there anyone else, then? Someone new?' she teased, as if she were his best friend and not his ex-wife. She wanted to sound as if she was interested in his life, that it was just a fun conversation, but she really wanted to know. If he was with someone, that made being with him much safer. But if he was single, like her…

'No. No one. I'm concentrating on myself and my work right now.'

She nodded and tried to look sage, but inside her heart was thudding. *Oh.*

Oliver was *single*.

Single!

'What about you? How are things going with you and Mike?'

And that was when she realised that he didn't know that she was single either. Should she admit the truth or pretend that everything was fine? Deep down, she knew she couldn't lie to him. She never had and she never would. She'd always been up front about her feelings with him.

'It's over. It fizzled out some time ago.'

He frowned. 'Sorry to hear that. I thought everything was going well?'

'It was for a while. Until I found out he was having an affair.'

'Oh. That must have been awful.'

'I should have known, to be honest. He had quite the

reputation on the hospital grapevine. He was an excellent surgeon but a crappy human being and the only reason the relationship went on as long as it did was because I was so busy with work I didn't notice what was happening right beneath my very nose. I felt quite the fool when I realised, because all of the signs had been there.'

She'd brushed over how incredibly embarrassed she'd felt at the time. Feeling like the whole hospital knew and that they'd all been waiting with bated breath for her to realise that Mike was not only sleeping with a redheaded radiologist, but also a blonde paediatric nurse *and* a student midwife. Clearly, he liked them young, which had never boded well for her, and when she'd asked him about what he'd ever seen in her he'd said something vaguely patronising and misogynistic about how he'd been enamoured with her because of the way she'd looked up to him as her mentor. How she'd wanted to learn from him, the way she'd hero-worshipped him. She'd made him feel good and her giving herself to him had been like the cherry on the cake.

Well, she would never hero-worship anyone again and that was why today had felt so weird, because her new boss, her new mentor, was her ex-husband. A man she had once worshipped and adored. A man she had been intimate with. A man who knew her, probably more than anyone else did! A man who, quite frankly, had known how to give her the perfect orgasm! How could she create that professional distance she needed from him so that she could continue to be the surgeon she wished to be? Their relationship had held her back once before and now that her career was on the rise she would not allow it, or their history together, to press pause on it once again.

'I'm sorry you had to go through that.'

'It was fine and it's over now. In the past.'

Like you and me.

They finished their drinks and then decided to head out to find a restaurant. Oliver said he had one in mind and as they stepped out into the cold November evening Lauren shivered slightly and wished she'd brought her big coat rather than a shoulder wrap.

Oliver noticed and shrugged off his jacket and draped it around her. 'Here.'

'No, it's fine. I don't want *you* to be cold.'

'I'm fine. Honestly.'

The warmth of his jacket around her was very pleasurable and she was most grateful for his kind gesture. It reminded her of the times he'd done it before, saying it was okay because he always felt hot. And he certainly didn't seem to mind, even though when she'd arrived earlier that evening she'd noticed him stamping his feet to keep warm. He wore only a dark shirt up top and, knowing him the way she did, she had to assume he wore no tee shirt underneath.

Maybe all that extra muscle he's grown will keep him warm?

The jacket smelt of Oliver, a familiar scent that scrambled her brain whilst it simultaneously handed her images of being wrapped around him, their bodies entwined, dizzy and breathless after sex. How she'd loved those moments afterwards, just clinging to one another, laughing and snuggling and kissing. Drunk on his scent and with memories swarming all around her, she cleared her throat, trying to ignore the familiar feeling of arousal that was awakening her senses.

'How far is the restaurant?'

'Er...just down here.' Oliver pointed down a side street to a small establishment, lit up with Christmas lights and a sign outside that said Giuseppe's.

He seemed to have no idea at all of the turmoil she was in and the second they stepped inside she slipped off the jacket and passed it back to him, relieved to be breathing in the restaurant aroma of Italian food—lots of rich tomato flavours, aromatic sauces, garlic bread and doughballs.

'Table for two, please.'

The waiter that met them, whose name tag stated his name was Joey, led them to a candlelit table beside the window that flickered with fairy lights. The table had a glass vase in the centre, filled with tiny multicoloured baubles in red, green, gold and silver.

Oliver held out her chair for her so she could sit down. She'd forgotten what a gentleman he was, how he'd always used to do that for her whenever they'd gone out.

'Thank you.'

Joey presented them with a drinks menu and they ordered wine, which was brought to their table in a carafe, and then they began to peruse the menu.

'This looks good. I'm starving,' Lauren said.

'Me too. It's been a long day. A good day,' he added, looking at her over the top of his menu. 'Thought I'd best add that, considering my company.'

She smiled at him. 'I knew what you meant, don't worry. You know, I can't remember the last time I ate out at an Italian restaurant.'

'I can,' Oliver said with a grimace. 'It was before I met Daria and I'd decided that it was time for me to start dating again. I met this lovely woman, Maggie. Blind date, set up by one of my friends at the hospital. She seemed great until we sat down, and then she proceeded to be horrifically demanding to the waiter, and when she didn't get what she wanted she demanded to talk to the restaurant owner. I walked out halfway through her speech about whether the breadsticks were stale or not as I felt so embarrassed.'

'No!'

'I waited for her outside, told her it was probably best we didn't meet up again and wished her all the best for her future.'

Lauren laughed. 'I'm so sorry! I shouldn't laugh, but I know how you feel. I think I probably had my fair share of dating disasters too.'

'What happened to you?'

'Well, there was one guy who kept picking his nose and examining his finds whilst we tried to eat at a friend's barbecue. Then there was Kenny, who kept texting his mum throughout the meal. Oh, and let's not forget Marcus, who told me that he would order for me and then sent my plate back to the kitchen because, and I quote, "You've put way too much food on her plate."'

'Yikes.'

'And I don't even want to go into what happened when I used a dating app. Let's just say some guys ought not to think that sending me pics of their anatomy will somehow get them a date.'

He chuckled. 'Yeah, I've never quite understood that.'

'I hear you. Why can't we just go back to the days when you would send a girl you liked a mix tape? And you'd scrawl your initials in a heart and practise your new surname!' Lauren laughed, then realised she'd done exactly that with Oliver. He'd given her a mix tape. Or, rather, he'd burned a CD of songs for her—songs that he loved and thought she'd like. And she, because they'd been at university, had practised writing Lauren Shaw as a signature, convinced that the name fitted her perfectly, looked perfect with that big, dramatic S shape, and clearly convinced herself that it would be for ever.

It hadn't been. They'd lost ten years.

But maybe they could claw back their friendship, if nothing else?

They ordered their food when Joey returned to the table and Lauren couldn't help but notice how relaxed Oliver was. When they'd been younger, he'd always seemed distant, because his mind was always on other things—work, patients, clinical trials, research. There always seemed to be a million things running through his head. Now he seemed so chilled. It was the relaxed attitude of a man who had got to the place in his life where he wanted to be.

'I envy you.'

Oliver looked up, surprised. Confused. He arched an eyebrow. 'What do you mean?'

'You seem to be in a place where you're happy, career-wise. There's still a way for me to get to where you are.'

'You'll get there.'

'I know, but it will take time.'

'*I* envy *you*.'

Now it was her turn to frown and then laugh in disbelief. 'How come?'

'Because it's all still ahead of you. So much to discover and learn and build.'

'Do you wish you could have done things differently back then?'

He looked at her intently, then smiled. 'I do.'

'Such as?' She wanted to know if he regretted their past. If he regretted his decisions in any way. *Their* decisions.

'I felt that opportunities for us to talk were missed.'

Lauren bristled. 'About?' Because if he was about to start blaming her for something, then she would defend herself.

Oliver sighed. 'We both had dreams, I know we did. But we made the decision that I would work, and I did that. I held up my side of the bargain and I worked hard for us. For all of us. Me. You. The girls. And just as I thought we would have time for one another when the girls were older, that was the moment you decided to leave and walk away. I was hurting. I was lonely. I probably said things that I shouldn't have, and that made it impossible for us to be with one another in the same room, when we could have been if we'd handled it differently.'

'You're saying it's my fault?' she asked, feeling her anger rise. 'What about my feelings, huh? Yes, we agreed you'd work, but that agreement didn't include you spending so much time away from home that I felt like a single mother! You didn't even notice I was hurting! That I felt like I was being left behind so you could become a surgical bigshot. You didn't see me any more because I wasn't a part of that world, so when the chance came for me to take back what was supposed to be mine, I took it! And you can't blame me for that.'

Lauren looked away, at the other diners. They'd kept their voices low but they'd been filled with anger and resentment. How quickly old hurts had resurfaced. How quickly old arguments had returned. It couldn't be this way. She'd moved down here to work. With him. In the same hospital. They had to find a friendlier footing.

She took a steadying sip of wine. Decided to focus on something else. 'Rumour has it that you're about to become the head of the department when Phillip retires.'

He nodded. 'I'm sorry. I didn't mean for us to argue.'

'It doesn't matter.'

'It does.' He also took a fortifying sip of wine, deciding to take advantage of her change in topic of conversation. 'I've heard that rumour too. But don't believe everything you hear on the grapevine.'

'No?'

'It's nice for it to be said, it's nice that everyone agrees that I'm the natural choice, but I like my job right now. I like where I am. My routine. Becoming head of the department would take me away from Theatre. There'd be meetings and admin that I don't particularly enjoy.'

'Then hire people to take care of that for you, whilst you remain in Theatre and treat patients.'

'You think that would be possible within an already strained hospital budget?'

'Maybe.' She shrugged, but she didn't really care. Not about that, anyway.

'I do want to be head of the department. It was all I ever wanted when I first set out as a surgeon. But all that straining to reach something made me such an intense person that I didn't make enough time for anything else. You know that more than anyone.'

He was referring to when they were married, when the girls were small. All the extra hours he'd put in at work.

Overtime. Extra shifts. Working weekends and holidays. How many Christmases did he miss because he kept volunteering to cover the department? It was an old thought that caused her pain.

'The only thing I get intense about now are my visits to the gym, where I have a strict workout routine. Work I want to enjoy. Time off I want to enjoy. Becoming head would mean I'd just spend that time writing reports and worrying about budgets and shift scheduling. I love Phillip. He's a great guy and an even greater surgeon. But he clocks less hours in Theatre than anyone else. He runs one clinic a month. His list is shorter because he's always in meetings. As I've got older and closer to my goal, I've begun to realise that maybe it wouldn't be the best thing for me.'

'Or you could take the role and make it your own. Run it the way you want it to be run. Delegate. Make bold new strides in what a head of department can be.' Now she was trying to be encouraging.

He smiled. 'You always had my back. Even when I didn't have yours.'

She didn't respond because at that moment their food arrived. They'd skipped starters as they always did, preferring to just have mains and desserts, as Lauren could only ever handle two courses. Oliver had chosen a hake, sweetcorn and brown crab orzo, whereas Lauren had chosen a chanterelle gnocchi with spicy sausage. The food smelt delicious and as it was placed in front of her she suddenly became aware of the rest of the restaurant—something that had slid into the background as she'd sat and talked to Oliver.

Music played in the background. Couples sitting at tables all around them were talking and laughing, clinking glasses and raising toasts. Wall sconces lit the room and in one corner a beautiful Christmas tree already stood, reminding her that the festive season was approaching and that this year she'd be able to spend it with her girls without having to worry about catching a train back to Edinburgh.

This was going to be her life now and Oliver was going to be in it again, albeit in a different role to the one he'd always had before. It was a shame that it hadn't worked out for them because she'd always thought of him as the love of her life.

'Do you ever wonder what our lives would have been like if we'd not fallen pregnant so soon after we got together?' she asked. It was something she'd often thought about. The path not taken. What would he think? Would he think she missed him and wanted him back? Because that wasn't true! She missed him—yes, of course she did. She missed that connection. Missed knowing someone one hundred percent. Loving someone one hundred percent. But did she want him back? They were two completely different people now, despite them both being single. And their old hurts still remained, clearly.

He smiled. 'Sometimes I do, actually, yes.'

She smiled back, grateful that he hadn't looked at her curiously, but had simply agreed that he'd often thought the same thing.

'How do you think that would have looked?'

Lauren let out a sigh as she thought and her gaze rested on a couple in the far corner. They were young, about the same age that she and Oliver had been when they'd got together. They were staring at each other, obviously completely in love, loving each other's company, blissfully unaware of anyone else, because no one else mattered.

'I think that we would have had more time for ourselves. I think that I would have finished medical school at the same time as you, started work at the same time as you. Maybe got my career established *before* the babies came along. That maybe we'd have had more time together, even if that was at work.'

He nodded. 'I don't regret the girls, though. They're my greatest achievement, hands down.'

'Mine too.' She was so proud of Kayley and Willow. Of how they'd become adults in their own right. A lawyer. A doctor! They must have done something right together. One final glance at the loving couple in the corner, at the way the guy was staring into his date's eyes, smiling, one hand stretched across the table to hold hers. Funny how talking about the girls could bring them together. But why wouldn't they?

Lauren missed that. Work was great, absolutely. She'd been waiting to start her career for a very long time and she was enjoying it, but she was beginning to miss having someone to come home to. To have someone with whom she could share her day. Someone to hold her in bed at night.

Mike had never been a great cuddler. He'd never been a guy to hang around and linger. They'd meet up, have dinner, or a drink, have sex, and then he'd be getting dressed, checking his watch, apologising for leaving so soon, explaining that he had something on. She'd felt quite lonely in that relationship, worse than when she'd been single. So it had been easy to end it, especially when all the rumours about him had turned out to be true. She refused to be used.

'Do you think Kayley will be okay? If she doesn't get pregnant, I mean? Her and Aaron are such a lovely couple. I'd hate for it to put a strain on them both.' Lauren knew something like that could be damaging for young couples.

'I think she and Aaron both have very sensible heads on their shoulders. They talk. I know they do. Aaron called me once and asked me what he could do to support her, as he knew she was really feeling it each month.'

'He's a good guy, huh?'

'He is. She married a good one.'

Lauren remembered Kayley's wedding. It had been a wonderful day, but a little bit strained for Lauren, knowing that Oliver would be there and that they were a few months free of their decree absolute. It was the first time they'd be seeing each other after splitting up and she wasn't sure how it would go, seeing him again, both of them emotional and proud of their eldest daughter. Would their old bonds of love and attraction lead them back into old habits? Weddings made people wistful. Weddings allowed people to make big mistakes when too much alcohol became involved. Most of all, Lauren had told herself not to get drunk at the feast afterwards and fall into bed with her ex-husband! Because he'd looked so good that day, she'd thought. Dressed in his top hat and tails, smelling wonderful, smiling constantly, proud and happy. They'd had to stand next to each other a lot in photographs, trying to be nice to one another so that the day didn't feel uneasy for Kayley and her new husband, and Lauren felt sure they'd managed it very well.

But there'd been that moment at the bar when she'd fetched drinks for her friends and Oliver had been standing there, cravat removed, top button undone, looking relaxed and gorgeous, and she'd felt a strong urge to drape her arm around him and pull him onto the dance floor and slow dance with him. Hold him close, rest her head upon his chest, feel the pounding of his heart and his hand in hers. Just to pretend, for a little while, at least, that the last couple of years hadn't happened.

But weddings did that to you. Made you maudlin and emotional and full of what-ifs. And she'd known she couldn't be drawn back into her ex-husband's orbit, only for them to fit into old roles of resentment and hurt. It was why she'd avoided him as much as she could after that. Organised family events so she could see the girls on their own, without him being there. It was why being with him was such a risk now.

She must have lost her sparkle for a moment because Oliver leaned in to get her attention. 'Hey. You okay?'

She smiled. 'Just remembering her wedding day.'

'Ah.' He nodded. 'Great day. She looked amazing, didn't she? When I saw her come down the stairs in her wedding dress…' He drifted off, eyes glazed with memory, and she saw briefly the approach of tears, his eyes welling up, and then he gathered himself, sniffed, laughed and took a sip of his drink.

'She did look amazing.' She wanted to reach out then. Take his hand in hers. Squeeze it. So she could show him that she knew how he felt, that she'd been incredibly proud too. That she'd been astounded at the sight of their eldest daughter coming down the stairs, so much so, she had dabbed at her own eyes with a tissue so as not to smudge her wedding make-up.

But she couldn't take his hand. Wouldn't. It was what she'd been afraid of, coming back.

There was a boundary between them now, created by their divorce and estrangement, and she needed to respect that. But it was hard. She knew this man inside out. Knew that he could be emotional and appreciated physicality. His love language was physical touch, as was hers, and so it felt incredibly limiting not to be able to do that.

'Look at us!' He smiled, trying to lessen the tension of the moment. 'Getting all maudlin. That's not what tonight should be about. We should be celebrating!'

She smiled. Nodded. 'We should.'

'You're back. You're doing amazingly. We're all healthy and well. What more could we ask for?'

Plenty, she thought, but did not say.

'We should have fun tonight. Eat this lovely food. Listen to the Christmas music that's playing far too early.' He gestured to the speakers set high above them that were already playing festive songs. 'We should be enjoying each other's company. I want this to be good between us, Lauren. I know we're divorced and we have history, but we should make the effort to enjoy being with each other because we share so much even though we chose to be apart, and there's no reason why we can't do that.'

Lauren smiled, raised her glass. 'Agreed.'

He clinked his glass to hers. 'To a shared future.'

'A shared future.'

They enjoyed a lovely meal at Giuseppe's. After the initial wariness at going out to dinner with his ex-wife, Oliver was glad that they'd both agreed to just enjoy each other's company and the conversation became easy and natural after their little hiccup. He often found he had to remind himself that they were divorced and that they hadn't just gone back in time.

He loved sitting opposite her, sharing a meal. It was nice. More than nice. They'd not often had the time to enjoy each other's company when they'd been married. He'd always been working—overtime shifts, covering when they were short of staff, grindingly hard work, learning as much as he could, as quickly as he could. He'd found a mentor in Phillip and stuck to him and other visiting surgeons to absorb as much information as he was able, so that he could be the best doctor that he could be and all that time Lauren had stayed at home and taken care of their daughters. He'd felt guilty about it. Not being with them. Missing milestones. She'd done an excellent job without him, but in that work grind they had lost opportunities in which they could have been together and he'd missed so much. Family meals. Working during birthday parties. Taking extra shifts at Christmas because of the better pay. Being on call.

Had it all been worth it? Losing his wife, failing at his marriage had hit him hard. It had been so easy to work so hard, knowing that Lauren would always be there if he needed her. And then when she wasn't? When she'd gone and he had no one to come home to? He wondered what it had all been about. He'd so looked forward to the years when they would have time together, but it had never happened. He'd been so focused on their future he'd never noticed the present.

When had he last taken his wife out for a meal? One

of her birthdays? A wedding anniversary? In the restaurant he'd asked her if she could remember.

'Our twelfth wedding anniversary.'

'Really?'

'Yep. We went to that sushi place, where the dishes went around on that conveyor belt thing.'

'That's right! I remember now.'

'And you left halfway through, because you were on call and the hospital messaged you as one of your patients had to go back into surgery.'

'Really?'

He didn't remember that part, but maybe he'd blanked it out because he knew he'd let her down.

As they walked through the square, lit with premature Christmas lights, he marvelled at her strength. She'd put up with so much. No wonder she had finally walked away and claimed back her life for herself.

'Thank you, Lauren.'

'What for?'

'The sacrifices you made when we were married. I'm not sure I fully appreciated what you gave up for me.'

She shook her head. 'I loved my family. I loved being a mum.'

'But you wanted to be a surgeon.'

'Yes. I put up with a lot to hold off on that dream. Most especially from my parents.'

He remembered. Lauren's parents had never had a great relationship with their daughter, but they'd had high hopes for her and had pushed her academically so that she would excel in life. The dark looks he'd received from them as if it was just his fault that she'd got pregnant, not once but twice, would live in his memory for ever.

'How are they?'

'The same.'

'Wondering why you're not head of the hospital yet?'

'Probably wondering why I'm not the Health Secretary yet.' She laughed. 'Whatever I do, it's never enough. I thought they'd be proud of me finally going after my dream and becoming a surgeon, but now all they say is, *Isn't it a bit late for all that now?*'

'Ouch.'

'Yeah.'

They looked across the square. A large Christmas display was going up, Santa on his sledge, led by his flying reindeer, rising up into the sky. Beneath them, a house, complete with a Christmas tree, and outside, a snowman.

'There were so many things I wanted to do with my life, but never got the chance.'

'What else did you want to do?'

She stopped to turn and look at him, consider him. 'That.' She pointed at the display.

He was puzzled. What did she mean? 'What?'

'It's silly but... I always wanted us to build a snowman as a family and yet we never did that. Not in all the years we were together.'

He frowned. 'You did. I've seen pictures of the ones that you and the girls built.'

'Me and the girls, yes. But *you* were never there. You never built a snowman with us. You were never around for snowball fights. You were never there when we would go back inside, all wet and cold, and we'd warm up with hot chocolate and wriggling our toes in front of the fire. We missed you, Oliver. The girls and I, we missed you. A part of us was always missing.'

She sounded so wistful, so hurt. He'd had no idea.

'You never said.'

'Would you have listened? Would you have stayed away from work?'

He thought about it. He would now, that was for sure. But back then? When he was a different Oliver to who he was now?

'No. I would have gone to work. Said we needed the money.'

'We did need the money. But the girls also needed their father. And I needed my husband. Just for those moments. To help us make memories. A lot of our memories don't have you in them. There are almost no photos of you—have you noticed that?'

He felt bad. Guilty. He'd felt bad at the time, but he felt doubly so now. He'd thought he was doing the right thing for his family. It had been drilled into him that fathers provided for their families, no matter what. That you worked. That if you were lucky enough to be offered overtime, then you took it.

'I thought I was doing the right thing.'

'I know. And I appreciated your sacrifice, as you appreciated mine. It just would have been nice, on occasion, to have felt like *we* came first.'

Oliver nodded, knowing he could never make that mistake again. The urge to defend himself was strong but… he knew he was just as much to blame for his marriage breakdown as Lauren was. Her frustrations had often come out as anger and the arguments that they'd had towards the end…

Neither of them had ever dealt with blame in the way that they should have.

'You know, if Kayley ever does get pregnant and you become a grandfather, you'll want to be around. You won't want to miss any of it.'

She was right. He wouldn't. 'Grandfather. That word comes out of nowhere, doesn't it? You can accept yourself as an adult. A husband. A father. But then you hear the word grandfather and it all suddenly sounds so terrifying. Are we really getting that old?'

She laughed. 'Well, you might be.'

He loved her laughter. Her smile.

'Don't speak too soon. Grandma.'

She gave him a playful shove and now it was his time to laugh.

With her. Something that they should have made more time to do, all those years ago.

CHAPTER SEVEN

LAUREN WAS AN hour into her breast reconstruction surgery on Callie Mackenzie when she became aware that Oliver had entered Theatre.

She felt a warm glow grow within her at seeing him once again. Ever since their meal out together a week or so ago they'd been getting along just brilliantly at work and, as ever, she was keen to show him her abilities as a surgeon.

'How's this going?' he asked.

'Yeah, good. Callie was one of my first patients here and keen to have this done urgently and so she chose to go privately. I feel we've come full circle. It will be good to see her going home feeling like everything is back to normal.'

'You're doing body tissue reconstruction?'

'My patient preferred it to an implant.'

He nodded. 'Are you choosing to perform a TRAM or DIEP flap?' A TRAM flap was tissue used from the lower abdomen, specifically from the traverse rectus abdominal muscle, whereas a DIEP flap was tissue used from the deep inferior epigastric perforator. It spared the muscle and had fewer complications than TRAM flaps.

'DIEP.'

'How many have you performed before?'

She looked at him over her mask. 'Three.'

'Solo?'

'Two assisted. One solo.'

'So, this is your second?'

'I suppose.'

'Want help?'

'Don't you have your own patients?'

'Nothing until midday.'

She'd wanted to do this alone, to show that she could do it. She was confident about this and had felt sure that she would stride out of Theatre with a good outcome. She wanted to be able to ring her parents and tell them what she'd done today. Alone. By herself, with no one's help. Hear them say, *Well done.* Plus, she was a surgeon and surgeons could be territorial.

'I'm okay. But you could observe, if you want.' She hoped that he would take that the right way and understand. Surely he'd understand, being a surgeon himself. Or would he take it as a rebuke? She needed him to see, also, that she was capable, not a medical student or junior any more.

'Then I'll observe.'

She sucked in a breath to calm herself as he stood there and watched her perform the surgery. Why did he unnerve her so? She was doing just fine until he came into Theatre and everything was going well.

'BP is dropping,' said the anaesthetist. 'Hanging another unit.'

Callie had bled quite a bit, but she'd got the bleeding under control and hopefully that would assist the blood pressure with the extra unit going in. But the procedure was going well and she'd already had a doctor from Plastics pop his head in to see how she was doing. She felt confident, if only people would leave her alone to get on with it.

'Anything from Kayley yet?' she asked him, to distract him from the intense gaze he was giving to her surgical field.

'No. Nothing. You?'

'No.'

'Willow's not heard anything either. She told me last night.'

'You saw Willow last night?'

'Not for dinner or anything. We just happened to bump into one another as we were leaving the hospital. And I literally mean bumped into one another. She tripped over one of those fake presents under the Christmas tree in Reception.'

Lauren smiled. 'She okay?'

'Yeah, it was just a little trip. She didn't see it because she was texting on her phone.'

'Sounds like Willow.'

He laughed. 'It does. I often wonder if she's been surgically attached to it.'

'We could always perform an amputation.'

She looked up at him and smiled. She liked this Oliver she was seeing these days. He was so different from the intense, driven Oliver she had known in their formative years. That Oliver had always had a frown, had always seemed stressed. This Oliver, this more mature Oliver, seemed much more relaxed. More calm. But she guessed that was what happened when you were confident in your own ability, had been in the same job for years and had reached the top of your tree.

'Suture, please.'

The theatre nurse passed her the suture and needle and she began to close the incision. Lauren was tired, but also not tired. It was a strange thing, theatre. You could stand in there for hours, concentrating, working, saving a life, or rebuilding one, and you could go in there absolutely knackered, but somehow standing there, with a life in your hands, made all those aches and pains disappear. Surgery was a great focus for the mind and body. It was afterwards, when the adrenaline level dropped, that you'd feel it.

'Done. Would you like to take a look?' she asked Oliver, pleased with her work, with the result, with the neatness of her stitches.

Oliver stepped forward to examine her surgery.

She found herself looking at him, holding her breath, as she waited for his praise, and she realised how much she wanted it from him. Just as much as she wanted it from her parents. Praise was something that had always been sadly lacking in her home when she was growing up and so it was something that she always sought out, hungry for it. She hated that in herself sometimes, but she just couldn't help it.

'Looks good.'

That was it? She'd expected ebullient praise, over-the-moon stuff! And all she'd got was, *Looks good.*

She'd have to take it, she guessed. It was better than criticism. And she also had to remember that, as a senior surgeon, it was also Oliver's job to help raise the baby surgeons. Giving them too much praise at the beginning might make them cocky, and a cocky, overconfident surgeon could sometimes be a danger. And she was still a baby, compared to him. He'd been doing this for decades now and she was still in her first five years of being a surgeon.

Your education as a surgeon never stopped. You were always learning. Always being allowed to do more and more complicated surgeries. And with time, knowledge and procedures changed too, as surgery adapted itself with new technologies and assistive machines. The field of surgery was an ever-changing beast and a surgeon had to be prepared to change with it.

She was beaming as she scrubbed out. He could see the pride in her face, the sense of accomplishment, and he was happy for her.

She was glowing, in fact. He'd not seen her this radiant since they'd been at medical school together and they'd sit and chat about their dreams for the future. They'd both dreamed of working in reconstructive surgery, admired the way lives and quality of life could be changed. They'd both wanted to be head of their department. Oliver had dreamed of leading the way by doing surgeries that would be broadcast to other hospitals, so that other surgeons could watch his brand-new pioneering techniques that he would have come up with himself. He'd dreamt of the Shaw Method, not knowing back then what it might be, but hoping that one day it would exist. Lauren had dreamed of being head of a department and lecturing around the world and taking under her wing groups of doctors that she would personally mentor and educate.

They'd sit in the quad at university together and dream

big, laughing and imagining the future together as they ate lunch, or quizzed each other for tests. They were great days. Days that he missed.

But he could see that same glow in her eyes now and he suddenly felt wistful, wishing that Lauren could have had it all back then. That she could have followed her dream at the same time as him. That she could be where he was today, professionally, because maybe they would have stayed together. Maybe there wouldn't be this distance between them, a distance he'd always hated and felt unable to overcome.

But if she'd had her dream then they most probably wouldn't have had Kayley or Willow and he loved his girls more than anything.

Life was strange—difficult—with many winding roads.

If they were together, what would he be doing right now? Kissing her and holding her, congratulating her on a surgery well done? Would they sneak a moment in a linen cupboard on occasion, like some couples in this hospital? Or would they both have been so busy with their respective work that even then they wouldn't have had enough time for one another and would have drifted apart as their careers took off?

Maybe we were always doomed to drift apart?

'I'll let you get on, then,' he said, feeling a little blue.

'Wait, Oliver!' She dried her hands on paper towels and threw them in the bin, then unhooked the safety pin that held her rings from her top. She slid them back onto her fingers. She still wore her wedding ring, he'd noticed. He'd noticed it that night they went out for dinner. 'Are you okay?'

He nodded and forced a smile. 'I am. I'm happy for

you, Lauren. You should call your parents. Tell them what you did today. Tell them that you changed a woman's life.' He gave her a nod, another smile and left the scrub room.

Once upon a time, Lauren had changed *his* life. With her choice of a fluffy purple pen. The way she'd tucked her hair behind her ear in a lecture. The way she'd smiled when he'd asked her out. The day she'd told him she was pregnant.

Everything had changed the day he'd noticed her.

He'd been so determined when he started medical school that he wouldn't let anything distract him from his studies. From his goal. He was the first in his family to go to medical school. The first to go to university at all! He didn't want to screw it up, his one chance to do well. To escape the endless grind of work that his own father had been consumed by.

But he'd been helpless at the sight of her. The way her blonde hair had fallen over her face. The way she'd licked her lips when she was concentrating. He'd been drawn to her like a moth to a flame, telling himself he would only introduce himself, say hi, make a new friend and then walk away.

But it had been impossible to walk away from Lauren. And his biggest mistake was believing that she would find it impossible to walk away from him.

He'd thought that they would be together for ever.

But he'd been wrong.

Through his own mistakes.

She had walked away to pursue the dreams that she'd put on hold for him. For their girls. Now she was working towards her dreams and he was determined he would make her happy.

He would help her excel now.

And he would stand back and watch her star rise. If that meant standing in a darkened corner whilst she stood in the spotlight, tucking her blonde hair behind her ear, whilst the medical world watched her being an amazing, pioneering surgeon, then so be it.

He would watch.

He would help push her.

And he would clap the loudest.

CHAPTER EIGHT

LAUREN WAS ENJOYING a cup of strong coffee on a break when she was beeped. She looked down at her phone and saw she was being paged by Oliver.

Call me ASAP

She wondered what it could be about. Kayley? Willow? A patient?

The last couple of days, there had been speculation in the reconstructive surgery posse that Oliver was planning a huge surgery, something that would put the Great Southern and their department firmly on the map, but no one knew exactly what it was. Nor had she had the chance to talk to him about it, because he'd always been holed up in his office or on video calls and could not be disturbed. It had almost begun to feel as if they were married again, with Oliver being too busy to spend time with her. But that had been okay. She was used to not being with him any more, though since they'd met again at this new job she'd actually been really enjoying his company.

So she dialled the number and he picked up instantly.

'Lauren?'

'Hey. You paged. What's up? Are the girls okay?'

'As far as I know. Whereabouts are you?'

'Er… Level B. Overlooking the gardens, which I have to say are starting to look quite sorry for themselves.'

'Can you come up to my office?'

'Sure. When?'

'Now. There's someone special I'd like you to meet.'

'Oh. Okay.'

For some reason, her stomach turned and she felt oddly concerned that when she got up there Oliver would introduce her to a new romantic interest. The idea of him with someone else was quite disturbing, strangely, now that they were working together. Being in Edinburgh and hearing he was with someone had been easier than seeing it in the flesh. Perhaps he was trying to be respectful to her? To disclose the relationship to her first, before he went public with it with everyone else?

She dumped her coffee, which now left a sour taste in her mouth, in the closest bin and took the stairs, needing to run off some pent-up energy that was now fizzing through her veins with nerves.

As she got to his office she could hear a woman's laughter inside and her heart sank.

Buck up, Lauren. Be happy for him.

She had no idea why she was feeling this way. He wasn't hers any more! But because they were getting on so well with one another lately, the way he'd look at her when he thought she wasn't looking, the way they'd laugh together, she'd kind of figured that…

No, don't be stupid. Nothing is ever going to happen.

Lauren rapped her knuckles on the door and the laughter stopped. She felt sick, knew she needed to gather herself to hear this news. Show that it didn't bother her. She wanted Oliver to be happy. He deserved happiness, of course he did. He was a good guy. A great guy.

'Come in!'

She sucked in a deep breath, squared her shoulders and forced a smile before pushing the door open, and then stopped in her tracks as she realized she'd misjudged the situation completely.

Oliver was sitting behind his desk, smiling, and opposite him were two people, a guy in his mid-forties, holding a blue manila folder that was thick with reports and, beside him, a woman of indeterminate age, who was missing half of her face. Her nose was gone, her cheeks were red with vicious scarring, one corner of her mouth twisted up, exposing her teeth.

'Lauren, come in. Close the door. I'd like to introduce you to Paul Slack. He works with a charity that supports bomb victims and this is Mina Barakzai, our new patient.'

Lauren closed the door quickly. So this wasn't about a new girlfriend—this was about work. She moved forward, shook both Paul's and Mina's hands. 'Nice to meet you.'

'Take a seat, Lauren.' He waited for her to do so. 'Paul and I have been working on and off together over the last few years. When he can, he brings over patients who need extensive maxillofacial or body reconstruction and today we have the wonderful Mina here, who is going to receive a partial face transplant.'

A partial face transplant? Lauren had never seen one of those done, though she'd heard that Oliver had been involved with two before.

'I consult with surgeons in and around the UK and bring together, when we can, a team of surgeons, max fax, reconstructive, plastic, to change an individual's life and we've been consulting on Mina's case for a while. We were never quite sure if it was going to be a go, but now that we have a perfect donor match she's scheduled for surgery next week and I'd like to bring you in on the team.'

Lauren stared at him in shock. She couldn't believe it. A partial face transplant was huge. She couldn't believe that he would value her work like this, bring her in on something that juniors didn't normally get a look in. Usually, they would observe or watch on video as something momentous like this was completed. To actually be in the room…? But she knew she couldn't react with surprise with the patient sitting right next to her. This woman was going to go through an immense change, physically, mentally and emotionally, and she would want to see confidence in her team. So, instead, she pasted a serene smile upon her face.

'That's wonderful. Thank you!'

'I have all of Mina's files and records here and I will go over them with you to bring you up to speed, but what I'd like you to do first is consult with the donor team and the family. It's important you get to know everyone involved.'

Of course. A face transplant couldn't happen without someone donating theirs. Somewhere, a family was hurting, grieving, but generous enough to consent to this. That made them terribly brave and courageous in Lauren's book.

'Absolutely. Just let me know what you need me to do.'

'I've emailed you their details. If you could go over their files before you go to meet with the family?'

'Of course.' She stood again, turned to face Paul and Mina. 'It was a pleasure to meet you.' She shook both their hands again and made for the door, before turning and smiling at Oliver once again before she left. It was a thank you. A sincere thank you. Being involved in a case like this would be momentous, not only for the patients involved, but also for her career.

She couldn't wait to get started. Heading over to one of their consoles, she punched in her access details and brought up the files that Oliver had sent. They were extensive, hundreds of pages long. But she flipped through the files until she reached the donor information. They were here, at this hospital.

Anjuli Maguire was a perfect blood and immunological match for Mina. Aesthetically, she was also a good match for skin colour, tone, gender, ethnicity and even the size of her face matched Mina's. Anjuli had been taken into A&E at another London hospital a few days ago, after being involved in a road traffic accident between a car and an HGV and had suffered irreversible injuries. Her husband, Leo, had consented to the donation after confirming his wife was an organ donor.

Leo and Anjuli had been placed in a side room. Leo sat beside his wife, face pale and blank as he held her hand in his. Anjuli was attached to a ventilator, but had been declared brain dead.

Lauren slipped into the room and stood in respectful silence for a moment, waiting for Leo to notice she was there. He didn't look at her, but began speaking first.

'Is it time?'

'No, Mr Maguire, not yet. I've just come down to introduce myself to you. I'm Dr Shaw. I'll be one of the reconstructive surgeons helping to work on your wife.' She sat down in the plastic chair next to Anjuli's bed and gazed at the donor. She looked serene, at peace. There were no visible marks to her face from the crash. Her records stated that not only had she suffered irreparable damage to her upper spine that would have paralysed Anjuli for life, but she'd also suffered what was called an internal decapitation.

Leo frowned. 'Wasn't the other doctor called Shaw?'

She nodded softly. 'Oliver. Yes. But no relation.' It was just easier to say than to explain. This man did not need to hear the complicated situation they were in. She placed her files down on the cabinet gently. 'Leo, would you mind if I ask you a few questions about your wife?'

He nodded and sighed. 'Sure. But I don't know what else I could tell you that you haven't already tested for. You doctors have taken every conceivable bit of blood or tissue that you've needed for your testing.'

He was probably right.

'Tell me about Anjuli. What kind of woman was she?'

Leo looked at her, surprised. 'You want to *know* her?'

'I do. She's a person and I think it's important and, if you don't mind, with your permission, of course, I'd like to be able to tell the recipient about the kind of woman Anjuli was. Confidentially, obviously.'

He probably thought that, as doctors, they viewed his wife as a piece of meat now, something to be quartered and shared, her organs her only value. But Lauren had never looked at patients like that. Every person was an individual, with a family, a history. With desires and dreams. Loves.

Leo smiled. 'She was wonderful. I couldn't have asked for a better woman to be by my side. Loving. Giving. Generous. She signed up for one of those donor cards as soon as she came to England. She believed in it, you see. She had a nephew, back in Afghanistan, who'd received a bone marrow transplant that saved his life. She wanted to do that for someone.'

'It says in her files that she's also donating other tissues.'

'Her corneas. Her skin. She would have wanted to donate her organs if she could, but they were damaged in the accident.'

'I'm so sorry. I know this must be hard.'

'This bit's easy. It's what she wanted. She would give the shirt off her back. *This*...this isn't the bit that's hard. What's hard is how I treated her. How I took her for granted. I just expected she'd be at home, waiting for me each day, and I'd stopped…' He gulped and wiped at his eyes. 'I'd stopped noticing her. Thought I could carry on every day, without having to make an effort, you know? The day she died, we…we'd argued about it. She told me I made her feel unimportant, like she was a nobody, and that someone at her work was willing to treat her like the queen she ought to be.'

He broke down then and Lauren handed him a tissue from a box to wipe his eyes and waited for him to calm down.

'She stormed out, took the car, and all I could think of was to show her that I wasn't bothered. My pride stopped me from going after her. I thought she'd gone somewhere to sulk, maybe to one of her friends' houses. And then the police turned up at my door. Our last words to each other were spoken in anger and I'm going to have to live with that. So of course she'd do this. It's why I'm letting you do this. Because it's what she wanted, and I never gave her what she wanted.'

'I'm sorry.'

She didn't want to give him any false platitudes, tell him that his wife knew he loved her and that maybe, rather than focusing on those last few moments they'd shared, perhaps he ought to focus on all the good ones. Because that wouldn't help, not really. Humans were curious creatures and she knew that Leo would focus more on those last few hours of his marriage than he would on all the other years when it had been good. Those last few minutes together would colour his memories, taint them. Make him regret. Make him punish himself.

She sat talking with him for some time, learning about the woman that Anjuli was, and he gave her permission to talk to Mina about her, if she ever asked.

Lauren left him to spend his last few hours with her. The machines would keep her body alive until the operation to help Mina. But she couldn't stop thinking about Leo. About how he could only focus on what had gone wrong in his relationship with his wife and couldn't focus at all on any of the good parts. Their falling in love. Their wedding day. Waking up in the morning with her. Cuddling with her during a movie. Sharing a joke. Making a home together.

It made her wonder if she'd done the same thing towards the end of her marriage and afterwards. Why did she never focus on that fresh-faced Oliver who had tracked her down after a lecture and made her blush? The Oliver who had once given her his coat when an unexpected rainstorm had threatened to drench her? The Oliver who had cradled their daughters in his arms, seconds after their births, and gazed at her with such love and adoration and told her she was amazing? He'd been there for her during the two births of their daughters, had hated leaving her home alone to go to work because he'd wanted to hold them in his arms.

She smiled at such memories.

How easy it was to look at the complaints, to focus on the negative, when they'd actually had so much positive stuff too. And this extra time she was getting with him now, learning from him, knowing him in a different way, not as his wife but as a colleague, a friend... She should enjoy it, enjoy her time with him.

Because time was a gift that some people didn't get to have. Accidents happened. Disease happened. HGVs coming out of nowhere happened.

She and Oliver could forge something new now, something different. Maybe even something deeper?

With a renewed mindset she strode towards the ward to do her ward round, feeling positive and excited about life.

CHAPTER NINE

LAUREN WAS JUST finishing for the day when she got paged to the hospital canteen. She frowned as she looked at the details, checking to make sure she was reading them right. *The canteen?*

Her legs ached, her back ached. And she'd been looking forward to going to the swimming pool tonight and getting in a few lengths to stretch out and work out the knots that were forming in her back. Maybe even twenty minutes in the sauna would have been nice.

But, clearly, she was needed, though for the life of her she couldn't think why a reconstructive surgeon might be needed at the canteen, so therefore this had to be a social thing. Oliver? Willow?

Yawning, she covered her mouth and rolled her shoulders, trying to work out the kinks in her muscles as the lift transported her down to the floor she needed. The doors pinged and slid open and then she was striding towards the canteen, thinking about all the delicious food she could eat tonight. Maybe treat herself to a takeaway for a change? She'd not had a good biryani for a while. That might be nice.

She was so busy thinking about food that at first she didn't recognise who she was seeing. It had been a long time since she'd seen them all standing together, but there they were!

'Kayley! Aaron! Oh, my gosh!' Her eldest daughter, Kayley, and her husband, Aaron, were there, with Willow and Oliver. Their whole family together, with the exception of Willow's fiancé. 'What are you doing here? You look amazing. That holiday must have done you so much good!'

She kissed her daughter's soft cheek and gave her a big squeeze, feeling grateful that they had come to see her. It felt so good to feel her in her arms once again. She'd been so worried about Kayley of late, not having had any contact with her, and since her talk with Leo that afternoon she'd been trying to think about her last conversation with her eldest and what they'd said. In fact, it had become a little bit of an obsession as she'd worked that afternoon, thinking of her last words with her daughter. She'd told her she was worried about her and that she could always come and talk to her about anything. Kayley, as usual, had been blue and evasive and she had so much to worry about, with trying for a baby, she'd not wanted Kayley to feel bad.

But now she could put that right. Lauren could put that right with everyone. She wanted her last words with everyone to be kind ones. Words of love. It was important.

'It was amazing. I can't wait to tell you all about it. But Aaron and I have felt so guilty at being AWOL for so long we thought we'd come here and see you all together. We figured it was our best chance to get you all in the same room at the same time!' She laughed.

Lauren laughed too. She was probably right. They were all so busy with their respective jobs and careers that finding a time when they were all available was always going to be difficult.

'Have you come straight from the airport?'

Kayley shook her head. 'No, we came home yesterday. But we were here at the hospital earlier today and figured we'd gather you all together.'

'Here at the hospital?' Something had to be wrong. 'Were you sick whilst you were away?'

'No, not sick. Look, why don't we all sit down? I'd love something to drink.'

'What can I get you?' Aaron asked everyone.

They all ordered hot drinks, with the exception of Kayley, who ordered an orange juice.

They chatted socially for a little while, with Kayley telling them all about how beautiful Croatia was, the coastal towns, the small villages, the architecture. She showed them all photos on her phone.

Lauren thought she looked happy—happier than she'd been in a long, long time—and it was so nice to see. The shadow of infertility had hovered over her daughter's head for far too long. Maybe she'd accepted it. Maybe they'd both come to the conclusion that if it was going to happen, then it would. They just had to relax a bit more about it. Lauren had often heard that once the pressure was off, many couples would go on to conceive naturally and that sometimes it was all the stress and worry that prevented conception.

Whatever it was, it was nice to see. Kayley and Aaron's holiday had certainly done them the world of good.

As Aaron arrived back with the drinks she noticed how happy and relaxed he looked too.

'Croatia sounds wonderful and, by the looks of the pair

of you, maybe we all ought to go there and enjoy the restorative powers of the place,' Lauren joked.

'Maybe!' Kayley laughed.

It had been such a long time since any of them had heard that sound and it gladdened Lauren's heart. She glanced at Oliver and caught him watching her. He was smiling too and, just for a brief moment, she could believe that they were together again. That they were a family again. How many years had it been since they'd all been together like this?

Too long.

And it felt good, so good. She felt in that moment that she could cry with gratitude.

'You mentioned you were at the hospital earlier, Kayley. Is everything okay?'

Kayley glanced at Aaron and reached for his hand. She was beaming. 'Actually, yes, I'm more than okay. We both are.'

'Then why were you here?' asked Oliver.

'Well, we have some news. News that we've both known for some time, actually. I'm…no—*we* are pregnant.'

Lauren gasped, hands covering her mouth in shock. 'Really? Oh, that's wonderful!' Now she did begin to cry tears of happiness as she reached over to throw her arms around Kayley.

Everyone got emotional, even Willow. They'd all been part of Kayley's struggle to get pregnant. They'd all witnessed her depression, her obsession with her monthly cycle—hoping and praying every month that there would be no sign of it. Hoping that each cramp didn't mean the onset of her period but was instead her womb changing because of an embryo. That each time she felt like her breasts were painful or swollen it was because they were changing due to pregnancy. That each time she suddenly felt a craving for a particular food it was because she was carrying a child and not just hungry. They'd all hoped along with her. They'd all dreamed. They'd all lost when they'd wanted to believe in something so much and it had crashed and burned around their ears, and they'd all been stoic and brave as they'd tried to support Kayley and not mention their own sadness.

Kayley pulled out a string of ultrasound photos. 'This is why we were here today.'

Lauren examined a picture, absorbing the details of a clearly shaped baby in the womb. She could see a head, a spine, arms and legs, a little baby curled up, safe and secure. Then she noticed the details. Each scan picture was identified with patient details and measurements of the baby.

'This says the baby is measuring at twelve weeks and three days.'

Kayley smiled. 'Yes, I'm sorry we never told any of you before, but we knew we were pregnant at six weeks. But after the last miscarriage we didn't dare tell anyone. I was so convinced it might happen again, I wanted to wait until after the twelve-week scan, which we had today. Baby's fine. I'm fine. Strong heartbeat. I think we're going to be okay with this one.'

'Oh, Kayley!' Lauren was so happy her tears fell anew as she gazed at the ultrasound of her first grandchild.

Oliver reached out to hold her hand across the table and she was grateful for it. Grateful for his strength. He knew how much they'd both hoped for this one day.

'When's the due date?'

'May twelfth.'

'A May baby. Oh, honey, I'm so happy for you both! We all are!'

'You don't mind that we hid it all from you?'

'Of course not!'

'We just wanted to hold onto it for ourselves, in case of...you know.'

'We do know. And you did absolutely the right thing.'

'We knew we'd be scared in the run-up to the scan, so we booked some time away. We could afford it and thought it would be a good thing to do, and if the baby stuck then it might be our last holiday away as just a twosome.'

'We understand, honey. You don't have to explain yourselves to us.'

'I'm going to be an aunt.' Willow smiled dreamily.

Lauren and Oliver smiled at her.

'Have you thought of any names?'

'We didn't dare. Not until today.'

'You can start planning now.'

'I don't think I'll ever truly relax until he or she is in my arms.'

Lauren laughed. 'And even then you won't, not really. Being a mum means you worry about them constantly. Even when they're fully grown.' She reached up to tuck Kayley's hair behind her ear.

'Thanks, Mum.'

They stayed chatting for a while, then Aaron glanced at his watch. 'We need to get going if we're going to catch my parents and tell them the news too,' he said.

'Oh, my goodness! Of course! We've been hogging you both,' said Lauren. 'Do forgive us, it's just that we've not seen you both for such a while.'

Aaron grinned. 'It's understandable. Don't worry.'

They waved the happy couple away and Lauren sighed as Oliver's arm came around her for a quick squeeze.

'It's great news, isn't it?' she said dreamily, already imagining all the baby clothes she could buy.

'Fabulous news. We should celebrate. This deserves a celebration, a family one. What should we all do?' Oliver glanced at Willow, hoping she'd have some ideas.

'Don't look at me. I've got plans tonight.'

'Oh, anything nice?'

'I'm getting me some culture tonight. I'm off to the theatre to see a musical.' She checked her phone. 'Actually, I've got to dash or I'll be late.' She leaned in, gave them both a peck on the cheek. 'You'll have to wet the baby's head without me!' Willow smiled and headed off.

Oliver turned to her. 'I guess it's just you and me. Unless you're busy too?'

'I'm not busy and I'd love to celebrate the baby with you. We should, actually. Seeing as we're both now going to be grandparents.'

The word settled in her mind.

Grandparents!

It was actually going to happen.

She felt tears of joy threaten again, but she'd shed enough tears.

'Let's do something amazing. Something festive! What do you think? You and I used to love Christmas.'

'Well, we don't have any snow, so we can't build a snowman, but I do know somewhere with ice.'

'I don't want to go to a bar, Oliver.'

'I didn't mean a bar. I meant a rink.'

Their very first date, he'd taken her to an indoor skating rink. It had been vast, echoey and cold and over the scent of the ice was the distinct smell of old sweat from the legions of hockey players that used it for game nights. But they'd been able to dismiss that because they'd been having fun together. Lauren was like a baby deer on ice, much worse than him, but they'd got through it with laughter and fun and it had totally taken away the awkwardness of touching each other, because every time Lauren had threatened to fall over she had grabbed him and held onto him for dear life.

Now, as they bent over to tie on their skates for this beautiful outdoor rink that was situated in Hanover Square, he was reminded of it.

'I hope you're an expert by now,' he joked.

Lauren looked at him with a raised eyebrow. 'Are you kidding me? The last time I went skating was the first time I went skating.'

'You've not done it since?'

'Well, let's see...no. I was too busy raising two children and then becoming a doctor to find time to whizz around on the ice. How about you? Are you about to show off your triple axel?'

'I can do triples in my sleep.'

'Really?'

He laughed. 'No! I haven't been skating either. The

most I've slid around on ice since is when I've done so in my car, and I don't think that's quite the same thing.'

He saw relief on her face that they would both be bad at this and he liked making her feel that way.

Oliver reached out his hand. 'Come on. Let's go show everyone how this is done.'

She took it. 'Show them what, exactly? How to fall on their bum?'

'Maybe not that part.'

'I just want to get out of this without a visit to A&E, okay? Remember, I'm at higher risk for osteoporosis now I've hit menopause.' Her smile was infectious.

'I'll take good care of you.'

'Thank you.'

But then, just before they stepped out onto the ice, he turned and tried to look solemn.

'But if we *do* end up in A&E I'll ask the ambulance crew to take us somewhere other than the Great Southern. I'd hate for our colleagues to show up and take photos of our bruised coccyxes.'

'Very good point.' She laughed, taking his hand as he stepped out onto the ice and held onto the side with his other.

Had ice always been this slippery? He grimaced slightly, trying to look confident for Lauren's sake as she nervously stepped out and instantly began to wobble. One foot went out from under her and she lunged for him, grabbing onto both his arms, laughing.

'Seriously? Oliver, maybe this is a bad idea. I really want to do that face transplant with you, but neither of us is going to be able to do it if we've got broken wrists by the end of this!'

They were both steady again. As long as they didn't try to move.

'If you fall, remember to roll.'

'I don't want to fall.'

'Come on, we can do this!'

Christmas music was playing out over the speakers and in the centre of the rink, protected by barriers, was a ginormous Christmas tree, beautifully decorated with stars and tinsel and baubles and guarded by four Nutcracker soldiers in their finest gold and yellow uniforms. Around the rink were stalls selling all types of food and drink, from roasted chestnuts, which smelled delicious, through to hot chocolates, burgers, loaded fries and even ice cream!

Slowly but surely, both Lauren and Oliver gained their balance. It took a lot of holding onto the side and holding onto each other. A lot of laughing, squealing and shrieking at near falls, but the bit he liked the most was the way that she held onto him. As if she needed him.

Having her this close again, after all those years, did something to his insides that he'd never expected. His body yearned for her, the familiarity of her. He'd loved this woman, had been in love with her, and deep down he would always love her. She was the mother of his children. She was the one who would make him feel good after a difficult day at the hospital. She was the one who would soothe him when he lost a patient after they threw a clot that caused a catastrophic stroke. She was the one who'd held the fort at home, who'd held him in bed, and he missed those soft curves. He missed the way she felt against him, and having her hold onto him like this now made all sorts of thoughts and feelings ricochet around his brain and body.

It was as if he'd travelled back in time and this was their first date again, only this time they *knew* each other. There was no awkwardness. He could just revel in being with her, watching her beautiful smile, hearing her beautiful laughter. He laughed alongside her. How long had it been since he'd felt so carefree, so relaxed, a part of something good?

When Lauren finally got her balance and was able to let go of the side, he tried it too and they skated hesitantly, slowly, holding onto each other's hands, trying to not get bumped by anyone else, and he was so proud of them as they finally began to get their skating legs and could go a little faster.

'Look at us go!' Lauren called.

'We put all these youngsters to shame. Let's show them how it's done!'

And they did, for a little while. If all they were showing was how to skate badly, leaning forward much too far, arms waving wildly at their sides. But they were having fun and they were happy and that was what mattered more than anything else.

But, obviously, pride came before a fall and it wasn't long before one of them—they couldn't agree who afterwards—tried to go too fast and pulled both of them down onto the ice with a thump.

They cackled with laughter, cheeks red, as they tried to help each other up into a standing position again. They weren't near the edge, so had nothing to hold onto except each other, and because they were laughing so much all their strength seemed to have left their legs and they almost found it impossible to stand up without slipping over, again and again. But eventually, somehow, they staggered back to their feet and wobbled to the side to rest and get their breath back and then they pulled themselves along to the side opening of the rink and disembarked, removing their skates, putting normal shoes back on, and then they bought themselves two giant mugs of hot chocolate topped with whipped cream, tiny marshmallows and chocolate flakes.

The drink tasted great and it was the perfect accompaniment, warming them up, giving them back some much-needed energy in the form of refined sugar, and there was something wonderful about sitting next to the rink, sipping at a hot chocolate as Christmas songs played over the speakers and skaters whizzed around on the ice.

'That was such fun, Oliver, thank you,' Lauren said after he'd walked her back to her flat.

They stood outside and he could see the lovely glow of her cheeks in the lamplight from the street. Her eyes gleamed, she looked happy and it made him feel good to know that he had been a part of that. When had they last laughed and enjoyed each other's company like that when they'd been married? Too long ago. They had both allowed work and life to get in the way and they'd been so busy being Mum and Dad that they'd forgotten to be husband and wife.

'It was. We should do it again some time.'

She smiled, nodded. 'We should.'

'Maybe next time we go skating we'll have a little grandbaby. We can get them to push one of those penguin things the other kids were using.'

Another nod.

But then a thought penetrated his head. Here they were, having had fun together, and already he was talking about the next time involving their grandchild. He would spoil any grandkids he had, clearly, he would, but did he have to bring them up right now? He'd just thought about how they'd let their own kids get in the way of them being a couple—would he make the same mistakes with grandkids too? Because, right now, he felt as if they were the old Oliver and Lauren. The ones who were together before they had kids. Shouldn't they enjoy this? Shouldn't he focus all of his attention right now on Lauren?

'Or, you know, we could go there again on our own. That's important too.'

He must have said the right thing because she laughed and smiled, nodded again.

'Maybe we could.'

'I enjoyed being with you tonight.'

'I enjoyed it too.'

He looked at her, wondering if this time when he kissed her goodnight, he should still kiss her on the cheek. Because what he really wanted to do was kiss her on the lips.

'Would you like to come in for a nightcap? I've got a single malt Scotch that I think you'd really like.'

She'd remembered his favourite tipple. And hell, yes! Because he wasn't ready to say goodbye yet.

'That would be great, thanks.'

Lauren got her keys from her bag and unlocked the door and led him up to her flat.

It was smaller than his, but neat and perfect, just like Lauren. She'd filled it with comfy sofas, throws, pillows, soft lighting. There was a floor-to-ceiling bookcase, jam-packed with titles, and he remembered how much she liked to read. How sometimes on a morning before he had work, when he came out of the shower, he would find her reading in bed, glasses on, concentrating deeply as she lost herself in a love story. Lauren adored love stories. In particular, she loved a book that could make her cry. One time he'd found her sobbing as she sat there, turning the last few pages of her book, and he'd cradled her and said, *'Hey, don't read it if it makes you this upset.'*

But she had pushed him away so she could carry on reading and cried, *'No, that's what makes it so good!'*

He'd never quite understood that. Never understood how, after the book was finished, she'd smile and wipe her eyes dry and sniff and sit there looking dazed and say, *'That was amazing.'* He'd never experienced that with a book.

'You've got a nice place.'

'Thanks. I'm still kind of unpacking. Don't look in the spare room—all the boxes are still in there.'

He smiled. When they'd lived together, she'd always had a room, a small storage space, where she'd hidden things, so that if visitors ever came to the house they wouldn't see mess. He used to call it her hiding spot.

Some things didn't change.

'Here you go. It's from a distillery called Bavenny. The guy that owned it brought me a bottle once for looking after his wife in hospital when I was a junior.'

Oliver took the glass and decided to raise a toast. 'To Kayley and Aaron and our first grandchild.'

She smiled and clinked her glass against his. 'Kayley and Aaron and our first grandchild.'

He took a sip and raised his eyebrows in surprise. It

was an amazing Scotch whisky, rich, strong notes flavoured with malt and honey. 'That's good.'

His gaze was caught then by a photo on the wall of Lauren and the two girls. Kayley and Willow were young, maybe three and four years old, and they were on a beach. Lauren sat behind them, holding them close as the wind whipped their hair in all directions. The girls were laughing and it looked like Willow had the remains of an ice cream cone dripping over her fingers.

'I don't remember this.'

'You wouldn't. You weren't there.'

He frowned. 'I wasn't?'

'It was our trip to Cornwall. You didn't go because you had a big case you were prepping for and so the girls and I went alone.'

'That happened a lot, huh?' he asked, already knowing the answer.

Lauren nodded. 'I didn't want the girls to miss out, so we went by ourselves. We were used to it. I found this picture when I was packing up in Edinburgh to come down here. It was in the back of a photo album that I'd forgotten about and I really liked it.'

'Any photos of me in there? All of us together, as a family?'

'One or two. Mostly at your parents' house.'

He nodded. 'I'm sorry that I was absent.'

And he meant it. But he'd been trying to build his career quickly, so that they would be comfortable financially. Having two young babies and a wife to support as a junior doctor had been terrifying, but he'd thought that, with dedication and a little bit of sacrifice, he would earn more money the more shifts he worked. That his skills would improve more quickly than other doctors if he put in the hours and, besides, hospitals had plenty of beds. He could sleep at work and get there early, before anyone else, make connections, study under the best.

'You did what you thought was right for your family.'

'But I never asked you if it was.'

Lauren looked down at the ground. 'I don't want to blame you, Oliver, because you had a great work ethic. You were dedicated, knew you had to make it work for us if I was staying at home and not earning myself. And, you know, maybe I was at fault too. I never showed you how much I felt down at missing out on my career, putting it on hold. I blamed you a lot back then, held resentment tightly to me, like a shield. You made sacrifices too, but I couldn't see that. Time with our girls was so precious and you missed it. But I never once thought about how that must be hurting *you* too. I should never have shut you out so much.'

And in that moment he almost cried. Because she saw him. She realised the pain he'd been in too. He might have been working for them, but he'd also known just how much he was sacrificing by not being there. At the time it had felt like the right decision, but now, seeing how much it still hurt…the repercussions, all these years later…divorced. The sacrifice didn't seem worth it. So what if they'd not had a lot of money? They would have got by. They would have found a way. Lots of people did. Why had he felt so driven to work so hard, and effectively make his wife feel like a single parent?

He would never make such a mistake again, and he knew in his heart that when his first grandchild came along he would not miss out on his or her upbringing. He would be present. He would be a fun grandpa. He would take them out and spend quality time with them, spoil them rotten, because he'd missed his own kids growing up. He wouldn't miss it again.

Oliver put down his tumbler of whisky and reached for Lauren's hand.

Surprised, she set down her own glass and looked up into his eyes. She was so beautiful, even now. If anything, her beauty had grown. The flecks of grey in her hair, the extra laughter lines around her eyes. She looked stunning.

'I want to make a promise to you. To you and the girls and the grandchild to come.'

She smiled, her eyes gleaming.

'I will be present for this. I will not be absent. I will be there for them and for you. Whatever you need of me, I'll be there for you.'

'Oliver, you don't have to—'

'I do. Being with you all at the hospital this evening, sitting at that table in the canteen, felt incredible, all of us together like that, and it made me realise just what I'd missed before. All those times we could have had but I lost, because I put working first. Because I put money first, before my family. Being with you tonight at the rink…that was…so much fun. I couldn't remember being that happy for a long time, and you made me feel that way.'

He couldn't help but notice the way her blue eyes softened, the way her smile widened, the way she caressed his hand in her own. How had he ever allowed himself to lose her? How had he ever been so proud that he had let her walk away?

'I've missed us. I've missed this. And tonight, watching you laugh, seeing your smile, it reminded me of how good we used to be together.'

'Oliver…' She raised his hand to her lips and kissed it. 'I had fun tonight too. Tonight was how it should have been between us. When we first got together, it was fun and surprising. You'd take me places and make me close my eyes and guess where we were. We were spontaneous. We were fun. I've missed that.'

'Do you think we could ever find that again?' he asked, knowing it was a dangerous question, but still thinking intensely about how her lips had felt pressed against his skin a moment ago.

Lauren smiled. 'Well, let's see, shall we?'

And she raised herself on tiptoe and pulled him in close for a kiss. A soft kiss. A loving kiss. A familiar kiss, but, despite its familiarity, it was exciting and strange and his body responded in the only way it could when he was with Lauren and he took her in his arms and decided to forget the world.

CHAPTER TEN

SHE'D WANTED TO kiss him all evening. Something strange had happened at the ice-skating rink. Oliver had gone from being her ex-husband and senior work colleague to someone she wanted to be with. Her feelings for him that she had been keeping contained had spilled over with every fall on the ice, with every time he'd caught her, steadied her, laughed with her. His body had felt so familiar and yet, oh, so different at the same time. She'd felt hard muscle, she'd sensed strength, he smelled delicious, and when they'd both fallen flat on their faces and she'd fallen into his arms and practically landed on top of him...well, she could have kissed him there. On the ice. In the middle of the rink. But the way she'd been feeling then, that kiss would have led to her wanting more, and it would not have been appropriate to do all the things she'd been thinking about doing to Oliver since she'd begun working for him.

He was easy to be around. She'd felt relaxed, happy. The news about becoming grandparents had been wonderful. Knowing that Kayley was actually all right and was finally pregnant had lifted a huge weight off her shoulders that had been there for weeks. There'd been no need to worry. Kayley and Aaron were fine. Willow was doing well, and she and Oliver? Well, she'd wanted to celebrate that. Why not, after all? They'd done something right. They'd raised two beautiful, strong, independent women who were living their own lives and living their own dreams and so was Lauren.

Oliver was the closest person she had to a friend down here now, the one who knew her the most, so of course it was easy to be with him. And as he slowly removed her clothes, as she slowly removed his, she began to feel like the Lauren she'd been when they'd first met. When they'd first slept with one another.

Somehow, they made their way into the bedroom. As much as Lauren liked the idea of their lovemaking being so passionate he could make love to her up against a wall, she also knew that at her age her back and hips would not thank her tomorrow! She knew from experience that she wanted a soft place to fall, a comfortable place to lie, so that she could fully enjoy all the wonderful sensations that Oliver was causing.

Of course he knew how to touch her. He remembered what she liked and so she did not have to teach him or guide him with her soft moans of pleasure. He not only knew where to touch her, but he was also finding new places. Unexpected places. Gentle kisses on the underside of her breasts. A tongue gently flicking at her wrists. And so much more. She lay there, gasping, as his tongue and mouth explored her, as if he was making sure he missed nothing of her, exploring her, re-familiarising himself with her. And all the time she felt his hard body above her, his muscles, his hardness brushing over her, leaving little trails of kisses.

She wanted to close her eyes and just revel in what

Oliver was making her feel, but she also wanted to see him, watch him, enjoy him. Lauren pulled him to her, eager to feel him inside her, but he kept teasing her, brushing her, licking, kissing, the flicks of his tongue hot and tantalising. The small groans of pleasure whenever their lips met, the way he whispered her name…

And then he rolled over, pulled her on top of him, and now she pressed his hands above his head as she decided to play his game. She would tease him, provoke him, explore him with her hands and mouth. His body was rock-hard and a feast for the eyes and she could not believe he was hers. Her tongue trailed his nipples, his abs. She moved lower and teased more, felt him thrust against her in urgency and need, which made her smile and feel her power as she ran her tongue around the tip of him, heard him groan as she took him in her mouth and he clutched at her head, fingers grasping her hair as he thrust towards her again.

She held back, flicked her tongue against him again, before she climbed his body and gave them both what they wanted.

It was the hottest night of her life. Had sex between them ever been this way before? Maybe. But pregnancy and years as an exhausted mother had erased those memories. Perhaps it had always been this great in those early days before the girls had come along. She liked to think that maybe they had been. Or maybe they'd both just learned a thing or two in their years apart. Maybe maturity and satisfaction in their vocations had given them both the ability to just relax now. Maybe before they'd always tried too hard because they were younger and they'd thought they had to be a certain way with one another and it had never had the intimacy that tonight seemed to have.

It was the same, but it was different. Vastly different. Lauren felt more confident, more assured in her power as a sexual being. Plus, there was no risk here of pregnancy. This was fun. Pure fun. Pure lust. Pure need. And there was a freedom in that that she'd never felt before and she was determined to enjoy it to the full.

When she woke the next morning, sated and aching, she had a huge smile on her face. She lay in Oliver's arms and it felt so good. As if she was back where she belonged. Cosy. Snug.

Outside, she could hear the wind blowing, trees thrashing, the gale whistling around her building like a storm was brewing. But for her it felt calm. Peaceful. Right. Oliver was the big spoon and his arms were wrapped around her and she laid her hands upon his and then began stroking his arm as she thought about last night.

Being with Oliver again… She'd never imagined that this might happen between them. She'd thought that maybe they'd moved so far apart in the last decade that it was never even a consideration. She'd thought he was still with Daria! Kayley and Willow hadn't told her anything different, so to find out he was single…

They'd been working well together, getting over the initial discomfort after meeting again, of being his subordinate, worrying over Kayley. But then the good news. The pregnancy. The baby! They were going to be grandparents! A happy day indeed, and that happiness had brought them together again.

The skating at Hanover Square had been hilarious and

bonding and fun. Their walk back to her flat had been quiet, contemplative, intimate. She had felt his protection as they'd walked through the London streets, his reassuring presence by her side, in a way that felt strange, but oddly pleasing. Showing him her flat, the look in his eyes when he'd apologised for being absent. He'd looked so pained and she'd not wanted him to feel that way. All of that was in the past and it had never just been his fault that the marriage failed.

Lauren had made choices too that had contributed to its failure. Giving up her career to be a stay-at-home mother. She'd wanted to do that. Had felt, at the time, that it was the right thing to do. She'd not wanted her children to be raised by nannies and pre-school clubs and after-school clubs, never seeing their mum or their dad because they were always at work, because that was the way she'd been raised. Her father had worked all hours, her mother too. They were consummate professionals, always besuited, always busy, always so focused on paperwork or on the phone, even when they were at home, that Lauren had barely felt noticed, had felt like she was a burden to them. A mistake that they had to make allowances for and work around.

That wasn't how she'd wanted her children to feel. She'd wanted to raise them in a loving family and so she'd prioritised her family over her career. And had continued to prioritise them until the girls had gone off to university, and then she had sat back and wondered what was next for her and what had happened to her marriage.

It wasn't just his fault. She'd never thought about how their situation had affected Oliver. She'd felt pressure to prove to her parents that she was doing well and she'd wanted, desperately, to make them proud of her. Neither of them had been impressed at her staying home and playing mum and housewife. Her mother had often called her and had asked, exasperated, if being just a mother all by itself was fulfilling, that surely she wanted more.

And so she'd gone looking for more, had returned to her initial dream of becoming a surgeon, like Oliver, and she'd pushed for it, and her education, her training, had torn wide open the gap between her and Oliver and it had seemed simpler to just separate. And then divorce.

It had been an incredibly painful decision. She'd never for one moment thought that her marriage would end that way, or in any way, but it had.

And now here she was, right back where she'd begun, and though it ought to feel frightening, or even vaguely embarrassing, to be back in her ex-husband's arms after a night of the most wonderful lovemaking they'd ever experienced, it didn't feel that way at all.

It felt good.

She felt content.

If she were a cat, she'd be purring.

But, like before, Lauren was an early riser. She was always the lark, Oliver the owl. And though she loved being here in his arms, she was also starving and desperate for the loo, reality impinging on her perfect moment! If this were a movie or a book, she thought, she'd get to lie there for a while, maybe even wake Oliver with an arousing touch, or turn to face him and stroke his face, and though she yearned to do all of these things, the siren call of the bathroom proved too much.

Very carefully, she slid out of his arms and grabbed her robe, tying it at the waist. Looking at Oliver briefly, she smiled. He looked good in her bed. Those muscular arms, that broad back, his flat abs…

Bathroom!

She hurried to relieve herself, sighing with release and unable to stop herself from smiling.

In the kitchen, she began making coffee, then remembered that she was absolutely ravenous and opened the fridge. She saw bacon, sausages, eggs. Perfect! She would make a full English cooked breakfast. He used to love those. She had bread too, so she could fry it, or toast it. There was a solitary tomato on its last legs, she could use that too. Pity there were no mushrooms, but in the freezer she found a half empty packet of hash browns.

She hoped she wasn't making too much noise as she pottered about, sipping her coffee, hoping to make a nice breakfast to wake Oliver up with. Maybe they could climb back into bed afterwards, snuggle. She turned the radio on low and quietly sang to some tunes as she cooked and she was so absorbed and so happy in what she was doing—when had she last cooked a meal for someone other than herself?—that she was surprised when Oliver's arms came from around her back and she laughed as he nuzzled into her neck and kissed her.

'Good morning,' he said.

'Good morning.'

Of course she'd worried. Worried about what this morning would look like. It could have been embarrassing. It could have been awkward. She might even have woken up to find Oliver gone, having crept away to do the walk of shame in the middle of the night. But no. He'd stayed in her bed, with her tightly wrapped in his arms, and it had been perfect, but she'd been prepared for the embarrassed excuses, maybe even an apology: *I'm sorry, this should never have happened.*

But she'd hoped that it wouldn't end that way and here he was, snuggling into her, all warm and cosy from her bed, and he seemed to have no regrets about last night, which was good because right now neither did she.

'I hope I didn't wake you,' she said, putting the pan lid over the sausages to stop them from spitting fat everywhere.

He turned her to face him. 'I reached out for you and you weren't there. That woke me.'

She smiled. 'Sorry. I was starving and for some weird reason I'd worked up quite an appetite.'

He kissed her on the lips. Slowly. Pleasurably. Making everything tingle from the tips of her toes to the top of her head.

'Want to work it up even more?'

Lauren laughed. 'I'm in the middle of cooking!'

'Turn it down. Or off. It'll keep for ten minutes.'

'Ten minutes? That long?'

He nibbled on her lip as his hands smoothed over her bottom and pulled her up close against his erection.

'Maybe fifteen.'

How could she resist? She turned in his arms to switch off the cooker—better to be safe than sorry—then giggled as he took her hand and pulled her back to the bedroom, and he showed her exactly how hungry *he* was.

It had been the perfect way to start the morning, back in Lauren's arms, and after they'd finished, they'd squeezed into her tiny shower cubicle and soaped each other up and washed each other down and realised that if they carried on like this then neither of them would make it into work on time!

He'd driven them both in, promising that he would give her a lift home in the evening, but now that he was seeing patients, in between prepping for the surgery on Anjuli, he wondered if taking her home was all he wanted to do.

They'd had such fun together last night at the ice rink and just being able to be with her, spend time with her and enjoy just being them again, had been the most wonderful thing he'd ever experienced. He'd felt like himself again. Like he'd rediscovered the Oliver he used to be, before ambition and needing money to provide for two small daughters and a wife had taken over.

It wasn't about feeling young again, though last night and this morning had made him realise that age really was just a number. In their fifties he and Lauren might be, but they'd stayed up all night, enjoying each other's bodies like two teenagers, and when he'd woken even more hungry for her this morning… Well, he'd certainly scratched that itch too.

'So we started Mina on the immunosuppressive drugs?' Oliver was chairing a meeting with all of the surgeons who would be working on Mina's case of a partial face transplant.

Dr Bartlett nodded. 'Yes.'

'And she's tolerating those?'

'No problems reported. She seems in good spirits. A little anxious, but that's to be expected.'

'And Garrett, you're sure she's okay to go ahead from your perspective?' Dr Garrett Green was a clinical psychologist.

'I'm happy to give my approval. I've spoken to Mina

at length over the last few months. We've generally met once a fortnight to discuss the surgery and what it might feel like to wake up and see a vastly different face in the mirror and she understands all that she might go through, the effect it might have on her mental wellbeing, as well as her physical and emotional health.'

'Good. And the physio team?'

David from the physio team gave a thumbs-up. 'We've gone over the facial and neck exercises that she'll need to do after the surgery and she seems to fully understand the work she'll need to put in, once you guys have done your bit.'

His gaze naturally fell to Lauren, who sat at the back of the room as she was not a primary surgeon on this case. She would only be observing, maybe assisting if she was lucky. The soft smile of encouragement she gave him made him feel great.

'And her family? Her personal support team?'

'Her family is coming over today from Afghanistan. Her mother and an aunt, I believe.'

Oliver nodded. Everything seemed ready. The surgery had got the green light and though he should be nervous, he felt excited. He felt ready. As if he could tackle anything the world threw at him at this point.

'Okay. You all know what to do. Off you go.'

The medical team dispersed, until only Oliver and Lauren were left in the room.

'Impressive,' she said, smiling. 'But then you always were confident in everything that you do.'

'As long as I know that what I'm doing is for the right reasons.'

'Giving this woman a new face…it's mind-blowing.

She must be very strong. I can't imagine not seeing myself when I look in the mirror. Imagine seeing a different face. With freckles or blemishes that you never had before. The donor face has a small beauty spot on the chin, did you know that?'

He nodded. He did know. He'd examined the donor, Anjuli, already. 'And a small scar on the cheek. Barely noticeable.'

'Mina will look at that scar in the years to come and wonder what caused it.'

'Are you okay?'

She nodded. 'I am. You? No regrets?'

He smiled. 'No regrets.'

'Good.'

'You know, I think that you and I should seize the day. Let's not think too hard about us and just enjoy ourselves and do things that are fun. Things that we never got to do before. We should go out tonight, after work.'

She smiled and nodded. 'No regrets and fun? What's not to like about that?'

'I'll meet you in the foyer at six p.m.?'

She glanced around, made sure no one was around to see, before she went up on tiptoe and kissed him on the lips. 'I'll see you there.'

CHAPTER ELEVEN

'HAVE YOU HEARD?'

'Heard what?' Oliver was busy writing up a patient's notes when the charge nurse, John, sat down beside him.

'Your friend Dylan.'

'Dr Harper, you mean?'

He smiled. 'That's the one.'

'I've heard nothing. Why?' He was slightly relieved that the gossip wasn't about himself.

'Well, you know that new neuro, the pregnant one? Size of a house?'

Oliver smiled. 'Is that the medical terminology you use all the time?'

'The one in her third trimester, then?'

He meant Poppy, Dr Poppy Evans. He'd stood behind her once in the queue for food. They'd not talked much, but she seemed nice.

'I do know of her, yes.'

'Apparently, it might be his baby.'

Oliver stopped what he was doing. '*Dylan's* baby? Are you *sure*?'

'It's what I've heard.' The charge nurse leaned in even closer. 'Apparently, she went to a clinic to get pregnant and there was a mix-up with the sperm and they used his sample, rather than the guy's she was meant to use, so he's the baby daddy!'

Oliver frowned, remembering Dylan telling him years ago about donating sperm to help his twin brother and his wife to have a child, and how some of the sperm would be left in the clinic, in case they wanted another child later down the line. So it was possible that this piece of hot hospital gossip could be true.

I wonder how Dylan's feeling about this. Poor guy. What a mix-up.

'We shouldn't pay attention to hospital gossip, John.'

'No, no. Absolutely not.' John made a zipping motion over his lips. 'But…er…you're friends with Dr Harper. Has he said anything about it to you or…'

Oliver raised his eyebrows. 'I thought you weren't going to gossip? Didn't you make it your New Year's resolution at the beginning of this year?'

John laughed. 'Who still sticks to their resolutions by December? Come on, it's end of January, at best.'

Oliver smiled. 'My lips are sealed.'

But no, Dylan hadn't mentioned it, and if it were true he supposed Dylan would need a friend, someone to talk to. Dylan wasn't the type of guy to do commitment. But a baby on the horizon? That must have him feeling some intense emotions. He made a mental note to call him.

'I want my patient in bed two on hourly obs; can you make sure that gets put down in her chart?'

'Sure.'

'And Mr Burton in bed eight has requested extra pain meds. I've written a script for him, but he has quite the addictive history so only give them to him if you feel he is in need.'

'Will do. You're on top of things. Looking snazzy. Got a hot date tonight?'

Oliver smiled. 'If I did, do you think I'd tell you all about it?'

'Oh, God, I hope so!'

Oliver laughed and wished him goodnight and signed out of the computer. He checked his watch. Ten to six. He was finishing on time and he couldn't wait to pick up Lauren and head on out. He had a festive date all planned, determined to give her as much Christmas fun as she could stand, especially since he'd missed out on doing all of this sort of stuff in the past.

Last night with her and this morning had been heaven-sent. Dylan Harper might be about to navigate the early days of fatherhood, but Oliver was an old pro and he knew now how important it was not to let yourself focus only on one thing. Providing for your children and their future was one thing, but maintaining a relationship with your partner and still treating them like a romantic interest was just as important. Both he and Lauren had not done that. He'd devoted himself to being a provider only. She had devoted herself to being a mother. They'd stopped dating one another. They'd stopped seeing each other as lovers. They'd stopped having fun together.

And he was determined, with this second chance, to put that right.

'Where are we going?'

'It's a surprise.'

Oliver was being weirdly secretive as he drove them through the London streets. The car was lovely and warm in contrast to the freezing fog outside, but it made the outdoors look beautiful, all those Christmas lights hazy and blurry. Lauren gazed out at shoppers, laden with bags or clutching hot drinks in takeaway cups, or standing by food stalls and filling their tummies with festive delights. It reminded her of how hungry she was and she wondered if Oliver was taking her out for food. A meal out somewhere would be nice.

'Are we going out to eat?'

'We are, but that's the second place on our agenda.'

'What's the first?'

'This.' Oliver swung into a parking space and she looked out of the window at a vast building that looked like a warehouse, but had a huge sign on the outside that read 'Real Snow!'

She laughed. 'What is this?'

'Believe it or not, it's an indoor ski centre where you can ski or snowboard or even…' he made a drum-roll noise '…it's a place where you can build snowmen.'

'You're kidding!' She felt excitement bubble up through her.

'I am not. I've scheduled us a half hour skiing and half an hour in the snow pit—what do you say?'

Her smile was so broad, she thought it might split her face. 'I say I'm in!' She couldn't quite believe it. Skiing? Snowman-building? That was one of her dreams for sure and she'd told him about it ages ago and he'd remembered! Which meant he cared. He wanted her dreams to come true.

Why could they not have been like this when they were younger? He'd been so good about her decision to put her dreams to one side to focus on the girls and then off he'd gone to follow his own. There had been moments, she could admit, when she'd felt jealous of him. Angry with him. As if her dreams were not as important as his. And sometimes, when he came home from the hospital with stories of everything going on, the patients he'd seen, the surgeries he'd performed, she'd tried her very hardest to smile and be happy for him, when all she'd wanted to do was tap out and swap places and let him stay at home, so she could go out and talk to adults and be a grown-up and perform surgeries.

Only she hadn't. She'd kept that rare anger and jealousy to herself and told no one. Not Oliver, not even her parents. She'd felt ashamed of it, because raising the girls had also been her dream. She'd wanted to be at home for them, she'd wanted them to feel loved, that they weren't a burden, and she felt that she had achieved that. All the same, her dreams had been put on hold. As if they weren't as important as Oliver's. It was silly and illogical because she knew they had discussed it. He had asked her if she was all right with being a stay-at-home mum and she'd told him she was.

But still…she often wondered where she'd be right now, if she'd taken a different path. Would she be like Oliver, heading up a team to perform a partial face transplant? Or still just assisting, feeling lucky if she got to hold a retractor?

Lauren tried to push all of these thoughts aside. Regrets had to stay in the past now. She could do nothing about them and she refused to let them spoil her enjoyment of today. Oliver was giving her one of her dreams—to build a snowman with him—and build a snowman she would!

The ski centre provided snowsuits, boots and skis and,

because neither of them had skied before, they were taken to a baby slope and shown the basic steps before they attempted to ski down a small slope that was only a few metres long. Oliver fell over straight away, which had her rolling around with laughter, and from his place on the floor he grabbed a handful of snow and threw it at her in fun. Lauren helped him to his feet and then it was her turn and it turned out she was quite the natural!

She didn't fall once, but glided slowly and in control down the slope before she could side step back up and come down, over and over again. Eventually, Oliver stopped falling and improved control on his slowing down when he reached the bottom, but before they could feel brave enough about trying the next slope up their lesson was over and they shed themselves of the skis and headed on over to the snow pit.

This was a large expanse filled with snow crystals, where people were building snowmen and having snowball fights, or making snow angels, and everywhere she looked she saw happy, smiling faces as all around them Christmas songs played over the speakers.

She couldn't remember being this happy ever, and to share this moment with Oliver was wonderful, as if it was meant to be, having him by her side. She'd missed him, over the years. The divorce had been the right thing to do at the time and she'd always thought she'd feel an element of freedom by moving to Edinburgh, away from them all, so that she could focus on her education and training, but she'd felt so alone and so far away.

Her weekly video calls with Kayley and Willow had been nice, but it had never been the same as actually seeing them in person. She'd wanted to be like Oliver in those early days together. She'd wanted to be able to come home to tell someone about all the exciting things she'd seen that day, the first time she'd done a new suture technique, the first time she'd led a surgery, but when she came home there was no one to talk to. Her working family had become her only family, and so when Mike had started taking an interest in her…well, it had probably been easier than it should have been to believe he'd actually liked her and wanted something more than just fun and a sexual fling. She should have known better. She should have listened and paid attention to the gossip about him, but she'd felt so lonely, she was desperate for someone to show that they cared. And for a while he'd acted as if he did.

'So how do you want to do this?' Oliver asked.

'Wait, you've never made a snowman?'

'Probably not since I was six. It may be hard for you to believe, but snowman-building is not something I've been practising as much as surgery.'

'Okay. Well, I guess one of us makes a body and the other one makes a head?'

'Which do you want to do?'

'I'll take the head?' She figured it would be quicker and with Oliver being bigger and stronger, he could manhandle the snowman's body.

They got to rolling the snow, pleased with how well it clumped and stuck to itself, so that making the snowman was easy. They rolled and rolled, swiped up armfuls of loose snow and packed it down onto their growing lumps. Lauren spent some time trying to refine hers by smoothing out the roundness of the head, then decided to make a tiny snowball and smooth it onto the snowman's face for a nose. Then Oliver lifted the head onto the body he had made.

'We need eyes and a mouth.'

But they didn't have anything they could use, so Oliver took off his scarf and wrapped it around the snowman's neck and told Lauren they should take a picture before their time ran out. The half hour had passed by way too quickly and he mumbled something about wishing he'd booked an hour in the snow pit.

A friendly fellow snowman-builder offered to take their picture for them and so Lauren found herself standing behind the snowman, hugging Oliver with a big grin on her face, as their photo was taken on Oliver's phone. Looking at the picture afterwards made her smile widen even more.

'Looks great! Will you send me a copy?'

'Sure!'

She glanced at the time. 'What do we do with him? Leave him here? Knock him down?'

'I'd feel sad to do that.'

'Let's leave him here. It's his home, after all.'

They waved goodbye to their snowman and headed back outside into the biting cold and quickly hurried over to Oliver's car to turn on the heater to get warm. As she held her fingers over the warming air vents, she turned to Oliver.

'Thank you for that. I loved it. I appreciate you making one of my dreams come true.'

'Maybe we should come again and bring the girls? Do it as a family?'

She smiled, but they weren't a family. Not any more. Not technically.

'Maybe we should just keep it between us? Don't want the girls getting any ideas about what's going on here.'

'We're just having fun. Nothing to report,' he confirmed.

'Well, they may not see it like that and, besides, Kayley's pregnant. I'm not sure I'd want her to get knocked over or slip over right now.'

'True.'

She didn't want to feel hurt by his comment that they were only having fun and there was nothing to report between them, even though she knew he was right and she had been the one to say that she didn't want the girls getting any wrong ideas. Because the thing was, Lauren was getting ideas. Lauren was dreaming about what might be between them and if she was wrong—which she probably was, as Oliver had said there was nothing to report except fun—she didn't want to be hurt by it.

Plenty of divorced couples got back together for sex, right? It was probably natural and happened a lot more than most people would care to admit to themselves. And though she might secretly dream of what it would feel like to get back together with Oliver, surely there was too much water under the bridge now? They'd changed. They were different. The only reason they were spending this much time together was because…

Well, she wasn't sure, exactly. Comfort played a part. Familiarity, probably. Hidden feelings? Regrets? Attraction was still there for her, very much so! But there was something else, something she didn't want to admit to, and that was maybe, despite their divorce, despite deciding that ending their marriage had been the best thing, there was the sneaking feeling that she still loved him and always would. He was the father of her children and he had been in her life for a very long time, and here they were, back together again, both single, the responsibilities that had once weighed them down were now gone, so why shouldn't they have their fun? Maybe it would be easier this way. Maybe it would be simpler. A fling, no strings attached.

'So, what's next?' she asked.

'Food. I'm starving. Building a snowman takes it out of you.'

'Where do you want to go?'

'I know the perfect place.' Oliver started the engine.

She was happy to be led by him, happy to let him decide where they should go. She trusted him, knew he would find someplace nice, somewhere festive. It was nice to just sit back and relax and let someone else do the organising, the choosing.

As they drove through |London she listened to the Christmas songs on the radio, singing along with Oliver as they drove past businesses and homes all lit up with their trees in the window, their lights outside. She saw girls, all dressed up to the nines, tottering along the road in their high heels and sequined dresses with no coats and remembered the days when she'd done the same and wouldn't have been seen dead wearing a winter coat. Now, she was happy she was snug and warm in her thick puffer jacket, woolly hat and gloves. Glad of the occasional hot flush that ran riot through her body.

At first, she'd hated the signs of menopause, hated that it meant a portion of her life was over now and she was moving into a new phase. But just lately she'd been proud of hitting menopause. It meant she'd reached an age that some people never got the chance to reach. She'd seen too many lives lost much too early during her time working in the hospital and she'd begun to appreciate how precious life was. How every second mattered. Not being able to bear children any more didn't mean she had no purpose in life. Her wrinkles and lines told a story of a life well lived, of a history. And she had two grown daughters and an ex-husband to prove it!

And soon she would be a grandma. A *grandma!* And that was precious and perfect and an amazing gift that she would cherish. A baby to spoil, a grandson or a granddaughter, and she and Oliver would move again into another phase and that was fine. She had no idea what it would be like, but already she had hopes and dreams. She felt optimistic about the future. With Kayley's pregnancy, moving back down here, being with Oliver, it just seemed like everything was moving in the right direction and long might it last!

Oliver pulled to a halt in a side street, bought a ticket to place inside the car so they didn't get fined, and then led her to a stall near the London Eye.

'What's this?'

'The finest turkey Christmas dinner you'll ever taste in your life.'

She raised an eyebrow. 'That's some promise.'

'Try it. You'll see.'

Lauren went and sat on a bench whilst Oliver joined the long queue, and listened to a busker singing *Silent Night* to a backing track of mournful guitar and piano. The singer, a young woman, had a beautiful voice and there was a group of people standing around her, watching and listening, one or two sending their children forward to place coins or notes in her empty guitar case that lay on the floor.

After a few minutes Oliver arrived holding two steaming parcels, proffering one to her.

She gasped in amazement, salivating instantly at the Christmas wrap. It was a large Yorkshire pudding, overflowing with turkey, cranberries, stuffing, mini crispy roast potatoes, baby vegetables and smothered in a thick, aromatic gravy.

'Oh, wow!'

'Wait till you taste it.'

Lauren wanted to savour every mouthful, to delight in every bite. But she was so hungry and the wrap itself was so delicious and she ate it so fast that, before she knew it, she was licking her fingers and making sure she had got every crumb that had fallen into the bottom of the foil wrap that had been keeping it warm on such a cold winter's night.

'You inhaled that,' Oliver said, his eyes smiling.

'I was starving and I've never tasted anything like that in my life, not from a stall. How did you find this place?'

'Confession—I didn't. Willow did and she brought me last year. Knowing your love for Christmas dinner, I figured it would be a hit.'

'Well, it was. Do they finish it off with Christmas pudding, drowning in brandy sauce?'

He laughed. 'I'm not sure. Want me to check?'

'No, I was only joking. I don't think I could eat another bite until New Year's.'

'Want to walk it off for a bit?'

Lauren looked along the river, as far as she could see, lit up with fairy lights. It could have been a photograph, a scene for a Christmas card. Who wouldn't want to stay and linger for a bit?

'Sure.'

It seemed colder along the riverfront, but Lauren didn't mind. She was in a celebratory bubble.

'So…*grandparents*. Are we ready for that, do you think?' she asked him.

'I think so. How about you?'

'I knew it would happen one day. As soon as Kayley and Aaron got married, I knew this part was coming. For a while there, I wondered if it would, what with the miscarriage and then the trying that they did, but yes, I think I'm ready. When is it too early to start buying Baby-gros?' she said, laughing.

'She's made it through the first trimester.'

Lauren nodded. 'So, what you're saying is that I can go baby shopping as soon as I want?'

'Why not?'

She smiled. 'What sort of grandfather do you think you'll be?'

'A cool one, obviously. What about you? I don't see you as one to sit and knit mittens or anything.'

'That's a stereotype!'

He laughed. 'Sorry!'

He gave her a friendly nudge with his elbow and she pushed him back and then they were both laughing and then he was holding her and pulling her close and suddenly she was breathless and staring up into his eyes.

And then they were kissing.

Something happened when she kissed Oliver. The world and its cares melted away. All her worries disappeared and all that mattered was the press of his lips on hers, his body against hers, and all she could think was, *More. More!* As if she wanted to consume him. As if she wanted all of him, her hunger for him insatiable.

Was it because he was available to her now, whereas before she had always had to share him, with the hospital, with his shifts, with his patients and with the girls. She'd never got Oliver one hundred percent to herself when they'd become parents. She'd always felt that part of his mind was elsewhere.

But now? Today? Since they'd been sleeping together again she felt as if he was hers again. One hundred percent hers, no sharing. His focus was totally on her and it was the most intoxicating drug she had ever experienced.

When the kiss broke apart and she was left breathing heavily, desiring more, she pressed her forehead against his and looked deeply into his eyes.

'Let's go home.'

Oliver nodded, his eyes dark with desire, and he took her hand and led her back to his car.

CHAPTER TWELVE

TODAY WAS THE DAY, the partial face transplant, and Lauren and Oliver had got to work extra early. She'd set her alarm for five a.m. and when it had gone off she'd woken with a start in Oliver's arms, reaching over to turn it off.

'Time for work.'

'I don't want to.' Oliver pulled her close. 'I'd rather stay here with you.'

Lauren had laughed as his lips had found her throat and begun to nuzzle. 'You'd rather stay here than perform one of the greatest surgeries a maxillofacial surgeon can do?'

'You're more fun.'

'Am I?'

Oliver could do amazing things with his lips and it was a struggle to not let herself succumb to his ministrations, but eventually he lifted his head and looked her in the eyes.

'Yes.'

'I don't believe you.' She'd laughed again and rolled away from him, out of his arms, and strode naked to her bathrobe, hanging on the back of the bedroom door. 'Come on. Shower.'

He'd sat up, propped on one elbow. 'Together?'

'If you're a good boy.'

He'd grinned and leapt naked from her bed.

The shower had taken a little longer than expected, but they'd got to work on time, as traffic was light. Oliver had headed on up to see Mina and make sure that she was being prepped and was getting her final bloods done, just as a precaution to make sure that her blood count was good and that she wasn't harbouring any infection before her big surgery, whereas Lauren had headed off to ready the donor, Anjuli.

Lauren's surgery would start at the same time as Oliver's, only in different theatres. As she assisted in removing the donor tissue, Oliver would be prepping Mina's face to receive it. It was going to be a long day. A difficult day. An exhausting day. But they were ready for it. So her mind was a little elsewhere as she got in the lift, not noticing who was already in there.

'Er…earth to Mum?'

Lauren looked up. 'Willow! Hello, darling.' She gave her daughter a hug. 'How are you? You're in early.'

'No, I'm still on night shift. I get to go home in an hour,' she said with a yawn.

'Long night?'

'Not too bad. I managed to grab a couple of hours.' Willow was looking at her strangely, eyes bright, looking slightly amused.

Lauren touched her face. 'Do I have toothpaste around my mouth or…?'

'No.'

'Then what is it?'

'Nothing!' Willow tried to look innocent, but she'd never been great at hiding her feelings.

'Come on, what is it?'

Her daughter laughed. 'It's just I heard a rumour, is all.'

'A rumour?'

There were plenty of rumours in a hospital. There always were. Right now, everyone was buzzing with the news about Dylan and Poppy.

'About you and Dad.'

Lauren swallowed, tried not to blush. 'About me and Oliver?' She tried to sound surprised. As if there could be nothing about them that was at all interesting.

Willow leaned in. 'Are you and Dad dating?'

'What?' Lauren tried to look shocked, appalled. 'Whatever makes anyone think that?'

Willow shrugged. 'You've been seen, apparently. Out and about together. And it's been noted that you leave together at night and arrive together in the morning and Dad is sometimes wearing what he wore the day before…'

'Ridiculous! We went out and celebrated *once.* When we got the news about Kayley's baby. That's all!' She tried not to flush with her lie to her daughter, but she didn't want Willow getting any ideas, or getting hopeful that her parents might be getting back together. She didn't want her kids involved. Right now, it was between her and Oliver and they were having fun, as they should have had before, and she didn't need the pressure of her daughter's expectations. Or anyone else's. 'You ought to try telling people to get their facts right.'

'Uh-huh. Then why did I see you come in with Dad this morning? I was on my break, not stalking you, and I saw you come in and you both looked…'

'What? Looked what?'

'Happy. Contented. You smiled at each other with a

smile that said *I've recently seen you naked*,' Willow whispered as the doors to the lift pinged open on the floor Lauren needed.

She flushed with embarrassment and stepped out of the lift. 'You're seeing what you want to see.'

Willow held the lift door open. 'So, you're denying it?'

'Yes.'

'And Dad will say the same if I ask him?'

'Of course.'

'Hmm.' Willow smiled as if she didn't believe her and as the doors closed she heard her shout, 'Methinks thou doth protest too much!'

Lauren stared at the lift doors as they closed and it took their daughter away to another floor. She pulled her phone from her pocket and texted Oliver.

We have a problem.

Oliver was hours into the transplant surgery when the donor team arrived with the replacement facial tissue for Mina. Lauren brought it in and passed it over to his team, who prepped it, rinsing it before it was brought over to him for reattachment.

This was the difficult part. Each blood vessel needed reconnecting. Each nerve. The tissue had been checked for measurements so that it fitted Mina perfectly. It had taken years to find a donor who was the exact match for Mina, not just in blood typing, but in skin colour, size, age. And he and his team could stand here all day doing the reattachment, go through all of this process and still, at the end of the day, Mina's body might reject the tissue.

It was a risk. It was always a huge risk. But Mina had

wanted to go ahead, to take that risk, and if she was willing to undergo it then they were willing to help her and make her feel better about herself every time she looked in a mirror.

But he was ready. They were all ready. They'd practised this. Hours and hours of practice so that the surgery ran smoothly, anticipating all the possible problems mid-surgery, but so far, it was going as well as could be expected. Mina had remained stable, her heart rate and blood pressure staying in normal ranges.

By rights, he should be exhausted, having stood here for so long, concentrating so hard, focused intensely, but he was far from tired. He was ecstatic, thrilled, adrenaline coursing through him with every stitch, with every cut.

He'd not felt that way just before he'd scrubbed. He'd received that text from Lauren that people were gossiping about them in the hospital, and that had thrown him slightly. But he hoped the news about Dylan Harper being the father of Poppy Evans' baby was juicier for everyone and that their relationship would not be as interesting.

Oliver glanced up and met Lauren's eyes. She wasn't at the forefront with the other surgeons. Her part was over now and she could only observe, but he knew exactly where she stood in his theatre. Of course he did. Ever since she'd come back to London, he'd known exactly where she was, sensing her every time. The way she looked back at him was encouraging.

You can do this. You're amazing.

And he smiled behind his mask as a particularly tricky part of the face with the trigeminal nerves came together. He was working with a brilliant plastics team, a world class ear, nose and throat team. His max fax crew and other reconstructive surgeons. There was a lot of training and a lot of egos in the room, but all of that had been pushed aside to focus on giving Mina the best chance of living life with a normal face, and not one ravaged by scars and burns.

As the final few stitches were put into place and he was able to relax, the effect of the adrenaline began to wane and he felt the exhaustion hit as he gazed up at the clock. They'd been there all day. An entire day! And not once had he thought of, or needed, food or water. It was amazing how surgery could make you feel, but he knew he would crash tonight and sleep well. He thought about crawling into bed with Lauren, holding her tight and snuggling into her and falling asleep in her arms.

It would be the perfect end to the perfect day.

They were out Christmas shopping the weekend after Mina's surgery. Lauren loved shopping for presents and this year she was looking forward to it even more, because the presents she bought for people today, she would actually get to see them open. Because this time she lived back home in London, where she belonged, and didn't have to resort to making a video call with her girls and blowing them kisses over a screen and wishing them a Merry Christmas.

Oliver had offered to go with her and she'd happily accepted. She and Oliver used to love Christmas shopping. She recalled that very often he wasn't available to go shopping with her when the girls were young, but there'd been one or two occasions when he had made it and they'd always had the best time.

'Oh, let's go in here!' she said, steering him towards a jewellery shop. Both their girls, Kayley and Willow, wore a charm bracelet, and she wanted to buy them a charm each. It was a tradition that she'd kept up for five years now, ever since they'd both got them. Kayley liked any type of charm, whereas Willow preferred charms that were animals. She'd once joked that her mum would create a zoo on her wrist by the time she'd filled it up.

They perused the cabinets and displays, oohing and aahing over the various charms, and eventually they found a perfect giraffe charm for Willow, and for Kayley, because she was now pregnant, they found one that looked like an old-fashioned pram.

'They're perfect!' she said as the sales girl wrapped it for them and handed them over with a smile.

'Where to next?' Oliver asked.

'Bookshop, of course!'

He laughed. 'Of course.'

No shopping trip was complete without going into a bookshop and they knew that Aaron loved reading spy thrillers and one had recently been released that Lauren had had her eye on for him.

'Do you think we should buy something for the baby?' she asked him as they browsed the shelves looking for it.

He thought for a moment. 'Might be fun to get a little something. But what?'

'Baby-gro?'

'Hmm. I was thinking of something bigger.'

She smiled. 'Like what?'

'The crib.'

'Really? Don't you think Kayley and Aaron would

want to choose that? We have no idea how they're going to decorate the nursery.'

'Actually, Aaron told me that they're hoping to keep it quite neutral and modern.'

'But don't babies prefer bold colours and shapes?'

'I think so.'

'I think that's something we could get by going out with them, so they can give us their opinion. I don't want to step on anyone's toes. Ah, there it is!' Lauren found the book she was looking for and picked it up, turning it to the back to double-check the blurb.

'Then what about something practical, where colour doesn't matter so much? I was thinking the car seat. Safety first and all of that.'

Lauren nodded. 'That's a good idea. It can be quite an expense and it'll be nice to think that a gift we bought them will bring that baby safely home from the hospital. All right, let's do that!'

Oliver grinned. 'We can do a cute little pack of Baby-gros too, though.'

'Motherland next, then?'

He nodded. 'Motherland next.'

They had a whale of a time in Motherland. There were so many cute things that they wanted to buy, so many cute clothes! They bought a car seat, two packs of Baby-gros, some vests, newborn nappies and a mobile to hang over the cot, made of soft, neutral-coloured animals in shades of beige and mushroom and cream. Lauren saw a couple of cute cuddly toys that she wanted to buy and was about to pick up the ones she liked when she became aware of a vibration in her coat pocket. Her phone.

'Oh, hang on.' She delved into her pocket to reach for it, but it stopped ringing by the time she got it out.

Missed call

She clicked on the phone symbol and frowned when she saw the name.

'Everything okay?' Oliver asked.

It was Mike from Edinburgh who'd tried to call her. Why, though? Why would he need to call her? They'd said everything they'd needed to say—they were no longer involved.

Lauren pushed the phone back in her pocket and forced a smile. She would not let Mike ruin this day. This day was perfect. Out Christmas shopping with Oliver again, enjoying this time with him. Walking around the shops, holding his hand, laughing together, shopping for their girls and their future grandchild. This was the kind of family activity she'd missed out on, being so far away in Edinburgh.

'Everything's fine. Cold caller,' she lied, hating that she was lying, but she didn't want Mike's name to ruin this bubble they were in. Their fun bubble.

Because, right now, neither of them had talked about what was happening between them. She'd even denied anything was happening to Willow when she'd heard that gossip on the hospital grapevine. She and Oliver didn't need other people ruining what they had right now and whilst they lived in the moment, whilst they didn't think too hard about what they were doing, then it was simply fun and she'd earned that, after all these years. Lauren was in a place where she was happy and coming back to London had been the right call.

'Okay. Oh, we must pop next door. I want to pick up a new tie for Dev.'

'Your registrar?'

'I buy him a new tie every year and he buys me one. We try to outdo each other with something ridiculous, it's become quite the tradition,' he said, laughing.

She gazed at her ex-husband. He truly had changed with time. He was more relaxed. He was happier than she'd ever seen him. He was secure in who he was now and she loved the way he looked at her, the way he made her feel. She hoped that she made him feel good too.

'Talking of tradition, what do you do for Christmas these days?'

He shrugged. 'Sometimes I've volunteered to work on Christmas Day. No biggie. Being in hospital on Christmas Day is so different to any other day. People are happier, more relaxed, as much as they can be, depending on their situation. The staff are cheerier. We look out for each other more.'

'And when you're not at the hospital, working?'

'I went to Kayley's last year. She did a big lunch for everyone.'

Oh, yes. Lauren remembered now. She'd done a video call with them and she remembered seeing Oliver just out of frame and feeling so incredibly jealous of him being with their girls, whilst she was stuck up in Edinburgh, working.

'And this year?'

'Willow's. She's offered. Are you coming?'

Lauren smiled. 'I am! Apparently, Kayley and Aaron will be there too, so it will be a real family Christmas for us all.'

'That's great.' Oliver looked really happy to hear that she was going to be there.

Was it possible that everything in her life was finally working out? Were the Shaw family about to have the best Christmas they had ever had? They'd all be together. Kayley was pregnant with their first grandchild. Lauren was secure at work and in her career. She and Oliver were finally being how they ought to have been a long time ago.

Her phone beeped. A text message.

She should have turned away. She should have positioned herself so Oliver couldn't see, but she didn't think about it. She had no reason to think about it. She'd not thought there would be anything to hide. But she pulled her phone from her pocket and looked at the screen. It was Mike again.

Call me. Mike x.

She slid her phone back in her pocket as quickly as she could, stomach rolling, unsure as to why Mike would be calling her and wanting her to call him back.

Lauren knew that Oliver had seen her screen, but he was pretending he hadn't. A frown was on his face, a frown he was trying to hide as he sorted through the cuddly toys, trying to find one that he liked.

Clearly, he thought this was none of his business any more.

They were just bed partners right now.

Neither of them had spoken of the future, or had stated what they were, or whether there were any rules.

Maybe she'd misread the whole thing and he wasn't as into her as she was into him.

'I don't know why he's texting me,' she said, needing to explain.

Oliver forced a smile. 'It's fine! None of my business, right?' But he didn't look fine. He looked annoyed. He looked wrong-footed. He looked…angry.

She couldn't believe a simple text could pierce their bubble so easily.

Maybe she and Oliver weren't as strong as she'd thought they were.

CHAPTER THIRTEEN

THIS MIKE GUY probably had a reason to text her, right? Maybe it was something to do with one of her patients back in Edinburgh. Maybe she'd left some stuff at his place.

Maybe he still has feelings for her and wants her to come back.

He'd tried to forget it, tried to ignore the text message, but it had tainted the rest of the Christmas shopping trip for him. Oliver had tried to be normal, to still be his usual relaxed, jovial self, but seeing that guy text Lauren, seeing his name come up on the screen, seeing that message.

Call me. Mike x

He'd put a kiss—what was that all about? He must still harbour feelings for Lauren. He had to. Lauren was great—amazing! Why wouldn't the guy want her back? Perhaps this Mike guy had realised what a mistake he'd made by going after other women and wanted back the one woman he couldn't have. Some guys were like that, wanted what was unavailable. It made them feel safe. Their treacherous little hearts wouldn't be in danger with someone who was unavailable, right?

The question was, did Lauren feel the same way? She'd acted as if she didn't understand why he'd texted, but she'd not been surprised by the text.

And then he remembered. There'd been a call, moments before. She'd said it was a cold call, but her expression had said something else.

Was Mike calling her regularly? Were they talking? Maybe this wasn't even his first contact—maybe they'd been talking all the time she'd been down here in London.

Had Lauren rebounded from Mike and into Oliver's arms? And, like a fool, he'd let her in. He'd told her he was free of Daria—she'd told him she was free of Mike, but she'd only just broken up with him. What if she still had feelings for Mike and she was playing them both?

Oliver groaned. He hated feeling this way, and he hated more than anything realising that he was capable of thinking that Lauren would do that to him. She wasn't that kind of woman, never had been. Why would she be now? She'd not changed. She was decent and caring and loving. She would not play off two guys to keep her options open.

There had to be another explanation. He had to believe that this was about one of her old patients. Perhaps they had a message for her? Or perhaps this Mike had an update he wanted to pass on? They did that when they met patients socially and they asked to be remembered to their surgeon. He had to believe it was that and not some other thing.

Did he have any right to tell Lauren that she must be honest with him? Did he have the right to demand the truth?

Could he be honest with himself and admit that he was jealous? And if he was jealous—which it seemed pretty obvious that he was—then he had to also admit to himself that Lauren had come to mean a huge amount to him again. He'd always love her, but was he in love with her again?

It was an answer he would have to find, or he would drive himself insane.

Kayley looked up from her desk in her office, then laughed. 'What on earth is that?'

'A bauble for your tree.'

'It's a pair of bootees. Baby bootees.'

'Yes, it is. I wanted to get one that said *Baby's first Christmas*, but your dad said that technically it wouldn't be that until next year.'

Kayley came from around her desk, kissed Lauren on the cheek and took the bauble. 'Dad's right.'

'Well, don't tell him that. We don't want to set a precedent.' Lauren laughed and looked about her daughter's office. She'd never been to Kayley's place of work before, but it seemed nice—modern and lively. Kayley had a corner office, with a view of London from the window on her right.

'Where is he? Work?'

Lauren nodded, trying to smile but feeling nervous. She'd come here with an agenda. Kayley was the only one she could ask, the only one she could confide in, because Willow was a doctor and worked at the same place as she and Oliver, so she'd be biased.

'What's up? You look strange.'

'I need to talk to you. I need advice and you're quite analytical and I think that you will be honest with me.'

'Okay. This sounds like it's going to need tea.' She pressed a button on her intercom. 'Sandra, can you bring in a pot of tea for two, please? Oh, and those little biscuits we had yesterday.'

'Cravings?' Lauren asked, trying to lighten the mood.

'Yes. Incredibly so. Baby seems to want all the junk food. Biscuits, sweets, cakes, chocolate, you name it—if it's going to raise my cholesterol, baby wants it.'

Lauren smiled as she continued to look around the room. A neat little cactus in a pot. A framed picture of Kayley and Aaron in Croatia. A bookshelf full of law texts. A filing cabinet. A computer.

'Sit down, Mum. You're making me feel anxious.'

'Oh. Sorry.' She slid into a seat opposite her daughter's desk and began to twiddle her thumbs.

'So...what is it?'

'Don't you want to wait for the tea and biscuits?'

'No, I want you to tell me why you've crossed half of London in your lunch break to come and see me. Oh, God, is Dad sick?' She leaned forward, a panicked look on her face.

'No, no! Lord, no! Nothing like that. No, I just want your considered opinion on something. On a choice.'

'A choice?'

There was a slight knock at the door and then in came Sandra with a tray. She laid it on the table and disappeared again, closing the door behind her.

'What choice, Mum?'

'On whether I should stay here or go back to Edinburgh.'

Kayley stared. And blinked.

* * *

Mina was doing very well, healing nicely, with no infection and no sign of rejection. Oliver had been staying at the hospital to watch her and his other patients around the clock, ever since his shopping trip with Lauren. Keeping busy kept his mind off all the visions he had of Lauren being touched by another man.

He knew he was being irrational and illogical and that all he needed to do to clear this up was to talk to Lauren, but he was so afraid of what he was going to hear that he didn't. He kept their conversations when she rang him fun and light and upbeat. He tried to make it clear that he had no claim on her, no expectations.

They'd even had one night at the cinema to see a film, but he'd not been able to concentrate on it at all. When they'd got back outside in the falling snow, Lauren had started talking about a particular scene in the film and he'd had no earthly idea what she was going on about. And then, when she'd snuggled into him for warmth, he'd closed his eyes in rapture, wondering if this was the last time he'd get to hold her like this. And if it was, then he needed to truly appreciate it and remember every moment. He couldn't believe he was about to lose the love of his life to that lowlife rapscallion who had already cheated on her.

He was just on his way to Theatre to operate on a patient when Lauren caught up with him in the corridor. 'Hey, are you free? Can we talk?'

His stomach plummeted. She wanted to talk? This couldn't be good. 'I'm on my way to a surgery.'

'The rhinoplasty on the Treacher Collins patient?'

Treacher Collins was a rare genetic disorder that could

affect the way a patient's face developed. It could affect ears, cheekbones, eyes and the jaw, causing many problems, both physically and sometimes socially.

He nodded.

'So you'll be done in about two to three hours?'

'Yes, but then I've got other patients and—'

'I really need to talk to you, Oliver. It's important.'

He sighed and checked the time. He might be done by one o'clock. 'I suppose I could meet you in the canteen. About one?'

'One o'clock? You're sure?'

Wow. She really wanted to peg him into a time. Must be serious.

I don't want serious. I don't want the serious conversation where you tell me you're going back to that creep.

'If the surgery overruns, I'll get a message to you.'

'Thank you.'

He walked away then, not trusting himself to stay and say anything else.

Was she really going to walk away from them all again?

Lauren sat with a coffee in front of her, but it had been cooling for a while.

Oliver was late. Maybe his surgery had overrun. But he'd told her he would get a message to her and she'd not received anything so…

Things hadn't been quite right since Mike had got back in touch. She'd sensed a change in him and knew that he'd seen the text arrive and who it was from and though he'd pretended to be the same, he wasn't. There'd been a distance between them and perhaps that was his way of preparing himself for her to leave.

But she wasn't going to do that. She couldn't, could she? Her life was here now. She wanted to be here. Kayley was going to have her first child in a few months and work was great here. She liked the hospital, she liked the staff and she loved being back with Oliver.

Only...she couldn't help but linger over Mike's suggestion about her going back. It would be an amazing opportunity and would really put her name as a reconstructive surgeon on the map. She wanted to be the best. She wanted to be like Oliver and have people come from all over to be operated on by her.

She'd spoken to the girls, but now she wanted to talk to Oliver. Get it out in the open. Let him know what had been said and what she'd decided. Or thought she'd decided.

What if you're doing the wrong thing?

In the distance, she saw Oliver enter the canteen and she sat up straighter and raised a hand to grab his attention. He headed on over to her, his expression impassive, almost stony, as he slid into the seat opposite.

Where was his jolly Christmas mood of only a few days ago? Where was the happy, laughing Oliver who'd kept dragging her back into bed every time she'd got up to try and get dressed?

'I don't have long,' he said.

'Nor me. But I thought we ought to talk.'

'If you're leaving us, then just say it.'

Us. Not me.

'Mike called. As you *know.* He wanted me to get in touch because he had an offer for me.'

'Oh? What kind of offer?'

'There's an opportunity for me to return to Edinburgh and work with Mike and his team on bringing over a group of people from India that have suffered burns and bodily disfigurements. It's going to be a big promo thing for the Great Northern and it's going to be a yearly programme. He wants a good team around him and he's asked me to join him on a permanent basis. Better pay. Better hours. So, yeah. They want me to go back.'

She watched him mull over this news, his expression getting stonier, his frown deepening.

'And are you going to go?'

'It's a great opportunity for me. It would be a step up in my career, look great on my CV. And I'd be doing important work on people who need it and can't receive the treatment they need where they are.' She wanted him to see that she understood what a career opportunity this was for her.

'I see.'

'Only I've needed to think about it, obviously. I didn't want to make a knee-jerk reaction, especially as I've really settled here and begun to know everyone.'

He nodded.

'And then there's you and the girls. The baby. I want to be here for that, but what if I don't get an opportunity like this again? I mean, is the Great Southern about to have a programme like this?'

'Not that I know of.'

'Exactly. I'm torn.'

'But you said you've settled here. You said you came back to be with family, that you felt alone up north. Why would you want to go back to that?'

'Because it's not just about feelings, is it? I have a chance here at becoming a great surgeon.'

'You are a great surgeon. You took part in a partial face transplant just weeks into your time here. Without you, that donor tissue wouldn't have been as perfect as it was. And you want to be here! You want to be here for all of us. For Willow. Kayley. Me. The *baby.* We're all getting used to having you back again and it's been wonderful.'

'Thank you. I appreciate that. But if I stay, will I *regret* prioritising my family over my career again if I don't take it? Because I did that once, remember? I let you go on ahead and chase your dreams and I stayed behind to be a mum. I raised my babies, I put my career on hold for decades, because I put them first. Yet I'm just getting started with my career again and I want to be the best, Oliver, the very best! If I let this opportunity go, I may just regret it.'

Oliver shook his head, anger crossing his face as he stood up, clearly fuming. 'And is that all?'

'What do you mean?'

'You're sure all this talk about going back is just a career opportunity?'

'I don't understand.'

'This Mike…this hotshot reconstructive guy who, I might remind you, has not proven reliable or loyal to you in the past, suddenly wants you back? As just a surgeon?'

'What are you implying?' She did not like what he was suggesting. Was he trying to imply that Mike wanted her back for other reasons? 'You think he wants to add me back into his harem, is that it? You think I'd go back for that?'

'I don't know what to think!' Oliver's voice was raised now, everyone looking at them, then pretending not to.

'Oliver!'

He leaned in, angry. 'You said you were settling here. You said you were happy here. You said you were looking forward to being back with your family and how you were going to spoil that new grandchild we're about to have. And what have *we* been doing, huh? Just messing around? Just having fun? Was I *convenient* to you? Were you using me until you got a better offer?'

She stared at him in shock. 'No! Of course not! I can't believe you're acting this way. Kayley and Willow both think that this would be a good chance for me to further my career—'

'*The girls?* You've spoken to them already about this? Before talking to me?'

Never before had she seen him this angry. Not even when they'd decided on divorcing. But now he seemed apoplectic with rage as he stormed away and she was left alone, on the verge of tears, staring after his retreating form.

Lauren sank back into her seat and dabbed at her eyes with a napkin, trying not to lock gazes with anyone else in the canteen. Her heart was thudding painfully in her chest. From embarrassment, from shame, from anger and from grief.

She'd not meant to hurt him. She'd not thought he would get this upset. She'd honestly believed that he would sit and listen to her and calmly go over her options with her.

Maybe they'd not been having fun, after all.

Maybe it had been so much more than that.

CHAPTER FOURTEEN

OLIVER KNEW HE had no right to be angry with Lauren but he couldn't explain how he felt, not even to himself. Feeling that he was the last to find out, when he was the one who stood to lose the most if she left him again.

It was now a week before Christmas and he'd hoped so much to have a Christmas to remember, with Lauren back by his side. He'd pictured it. It would have been perfect. Waking up in her bed, going over to Willow's and helping cook dinner together, pulling crackers, telling stupid jokes, being together as a family and then at bedtime, holding her close and telling her that she was the best Christmas present he could ever receive.

She was back and their relationship had seemed better than it ever was.

Had. Past tense.

Of course he could see why she might consider going back to Edinburgh. It was an amazing career opportunity for her. It was the sort of programme he wished the Great Southern was doing too, something he'd leap at for the lives they could change, for the people they could make better and improve their quality of life. Of course she should consider it and of course she was right. She had put her family before her career once before and her time was now. He was where he was today because of her career sacrifice to stay at home and raise their girls and give them the lives that they deserved.

Had he ever truly thanked her for that? Had he ever gone out of his way to make her feel special and appreciated? Or had he been working so hard, grafting every single day, sacrificing holidays and birthdays and yes, Christmases, that he'd just taken her sacrifice for granted?

Was he going to make her stay and hold her back again?

He hated himself for making her feel that way, that he was putting this pressure on her. But if he took that pressure off, if he saw her, apologised, then he'd lose her again, lose what they had, and he wasn't sure he could be the orchestrator of that either.

'Damn it!' His stitch slipped and he had to retie it before going onto the next. He was doing a lower eyelid reconstruction on a patient who had lost a large part of tissue there, due to a basal cell carcinoma, having taken some skin from the forearm to replace it.

'You okay?' Dev, his registrar, looked at him over his facemask.

No. No, he wasn't okay. He couldn't think straight and this patient had been through enough and needed someone who was truly focused on the task at hand.

'Just a lot on my mind. Do you want to finish for me? I'll stay and observe.'

'You're sure? Thanks, boss.'

He stood and watched Dev attach the new flap of skin, making sure they reconstructed the tissue near the tear ducts accurately, so that there wouldn't be so much swelling there afterwards that might block them. They didn't want to get an infection in there. Dev worked well. He was a good registrar and had picked up a lot of good habits from watching Oliver at work.

'You're a family man, Dev.'

Dev raised an eyebrow. 'Er, yeah, I've got a big family.'

'They'd miss you if you weren't around at Christmas, right?'

'Of course!'

'But if you'd been offered an unmissable career opportunity and it meant you had to leave totally—move house, uproot everything—would they mind?'

'They'd miss me, but I think they'd understand. Why? Are you about to offer me something?'

Oliver shook his head. 'Just thinking about something, is all.'

'Are you leaving us? I'm not sure I'd be happy about losing my mentor.'

'Not me either.'

'Ah.'

'*Ah?* What does *ah* mean?'

'It's Lauren, isn't it?'

He sighed. Was he so obvious? But he nodded.

'And you guys are close again? I try not to listen to gossip, but even I've seen how happy you've been this last month or so with her here.'

'Her ex contacted her about this job offer back in Edinburgh and she's considering it.'

'Right. Gotcha.' Dev tied off the last stitch and dabbed at the area with a pad. 'Well, you know what they say?'

'What's that?'

'If you love someone, set them free.'

'That's an idiotic saying! Why would you let them go?'

'So you love her, then?'

Oliver stared at Dev. He'd only meant to share the hypothetical and yet here he was, being asked out loud by a colleague if he was back in love with his ex-wife!

'Sorry. Not my business. Forget I asked anything.'

'I do love her, I always have, and she sacrificed her career for me once before. Can I really ask her to do that again?'

'Can I speak candidly?'

'Of course.'

'If you stop her from going then she may resent you for the rest of her life and that will eventually break up anything you share right now.'

'I'm not sure we share anything right now.'

'You're wrong. You're both hurting and you both need to talk to one another.'

'But every time I look at her, I just want to pull her close and never let her go.'

Dev nodded. 'Then you, my friend, are in a quandary.'

'Thanks.'

His registrar pulled off his gown and gloves. 'For what it's worth, I think you two are great and, selfishly, I hope she stays because since she's been back you've let me do more procedures than I've ever got to do before!' He winked as he headed into the scrub room.

Oliver smiled and pulled off his own gown and gloves and mask. As he scrubbed, he became aware of his mobile phone ringing again and again. It would have to wait. Whoever it was would have to wait. When he picked up his phone, he saw that Lauren had tried to call him three separate times.

What did she want? To tell him that she'd made a decision? That she was leaving because her ex-husband had behaved terribly?

He was in no rush to hear that. So he silenced his phone and went to check on a patient.

CHAPTER FIFTEEN

WHERE WAS HE? Why wasn't he answering his phone?

Lauren thrust her phone back into her pocket as the taxi driver pulled up in front of the hospital and she found a note to pay him with. She wasn't even aware of what kind of note she thrust at him and told him to keep the change as she leapt from the vehicle and ran towards A&E.

She'd been sitting at home, staring at the wall, mulling over her decision to stay or to go, when the phone had rung and Willow, distraught on the other end, had informed her that Kayley and Aaron had been involved in a road traffic accident, a bad one, and all that she knew was that her sister and Aaron had been rushed to A&E.

She'd not been to A&E here before, so she wasn't aware of the layout as her gaze scanned the reception area, looking for the desk. There was a queue of people standing, waiting to be seen, the guy at the front holding a bloodied tea towel up against the side of his head.

It would take ages to ask, to stand there and queue and politely take her turn, and she couldn't bear to do that, so she rushed past them all, through the packed waiting room of the walking wounded and into Minors, looking for the sign that said Majors. Or Resus.

A nurse came out of a cubicle, sliding the curtain behind her closed, and noticed the distraught look on Lauren's face. 'Are you okay?'

'I'm looking for my daughter, Kayley Smith. She was brought in by ambulance with her husband, Aaron. They've been in a car accident.'

'All right, come with me. I'll take you to the family room whilst I go and find out what's happening, okay?'

Lauren nodded, even though she didn't want to be in a family room. She wanted to be by her daughter's side, holding her hand, telling her everything would be all right, whilst she fired questions at the doctors treating her.

But when the nurse opened the family room door she saw Willow inside, crying.

'Willow!' She rushed into her younger daughter's arms. 'Oh, my love.' She held Willow tightly, desperate to ask her if she knew any more, but staying silent because she knew how much her daughter needed to be held right now, rather than questioned.

Eventually, they broke apart and settled down onto the sofa. 'Tell me what you know.'

'A doctor has just been in. She's sustained a head injury and she's unconscious.'

A head injury? Lauren's heart sank. That could be anything, from minor to major. It could just be concussion, or shock, or low blood pressure. But, equally, it could also be a fractured skull, or a brain bleed, or worse.

'And she's bleeding. She could be losing the baby!'

'Oh, my God!' Lauren pulled Willow close, not willing to think about that. After all that Kayley and Aaron had been through, trying to get pregnant, if she woke and found out she'd lost that precious baby…

If she even wakes up at all.

Lauren wanted to throw up. She felt so helpless.

'Is your father here yet?'

Willow shook her head. 'I called you and you said you'd call him.'

'He's not picking up. I think he might be avoiding my calls—we've had a little falling-out.' She felt embarrassed to say it. Their argument seemed so insignificant in the light of the news about her daughter and son-in-law. 'Can you try him?'

Willow nodded.

'What have they said about Aaron?'

'Minor injuries. Cuts and scrapes. He's being stitched up.'

She nodded, listening as Willow called her dad.

He picked up and in the quiet of the room she heard him say, 'Hi, pumpkin!'

Oliver said nothing else she could hear as Willow told him the news and then ended the call.

Willow looked pale and shocked as she glanced at her mum with her tear-stained face and said quietly, 'He's on his way.'

They sat around Kayley's bed in a dread silence, each of them shocked by the visage of their loved one lying in a bed in a now medically induced coma.

Oliver stood by the foot of the bed, whereas Aaron and Lauren sat either side, each of them holding one of Kayley's hands.

'It was a drunk driver,' Aaron said. 'On his way to a work Christmas party, the police said.'

Oliver closed his eyes in dismay. Too many people still thought that they were safe to drive when they'd been drinking and threw all the rules out of the window, just because it was Christmas. They always thought they were sober enough to drive. They always thought they'd get away with it.

'Was he, or she, hurt?'

'Minor injuries. Why do bad people always seem to get away with things like this, whereas good people, lovely people, my beautiful, pregnant wife, have to suffer for *their* bad choices?'

Aaron was angry, but so was Oliver. They all were. That things like this were still allowed to happen… For a long time, with the advent of electric cars, Oliver had often said that cars shouldn't be able to start unless the driver took a breath test that was somehow registered by the vehicle. Surely the technology existed.

He'd said it to Willow earlier, and she'd agreed, but said, *'People would just get their friends to breathe into the breathalyser for them.'*

Perhaps she was right.

'I'm going to get a coffee. Or what passes for coffee in this place. Can I get anyone anything?' Aaron asked.

They'd been sitting by Kayley's bedside for well over twenty-four hours.

'I'll come with you,' Willow said. 'I need to stretch my legs.'

Aaron stood, turned to Oliver. 'You'll call if anything changes?'

'Of course.' He gave Aaron a hug and squeezed him

tight, knowing how he must feel to see his pregnant wife lying unconscious in a hospital bed, with tubes and on a ventilator. If that had ever been Lauren… He sat opposite her now after Aaron and Willow left and took his daughter's hand. It was warm but unresponsive and he felt tears prick at the backs of his eyes.

'I'm sorry, Oliver.' Lauren spoke, looking across at him.

He met her gaze, heart breaking. 'I'm sorry too. All our issues seem stupid in comparison to this, so… I'm sorry I reacted badly. That I got angry, that I shouted at you in public. That was wrong of me and you should take that job, the one in Edinburgh. When this is all over and Kayley's better, you should go. Fly. Be brilliant in Edinburgh. I'll be so proud of you.'

Lauren's gaze softened. 'Thank you. But I need to say sorry too. I should never have sprung the news about the job on you like that. I should have told you first. I never thought about how it might hurt you.'

'Call Mike. Accept the job. We're a family and families support one another.' He lifted his daughter's hand and kissed the back of it. 'Family is what matters and you give family what they need, and you need this. I should never have tried to hold you back.'

Lauren smiled at him. A soft smile. An appreciative smile. One of gratitude and thanks. 'I'm still deciding. And what with this now…'

'She'll get through this. Kayley's strong. So's the baby. We'll all be okay if you decide to go.'

He couldn't quite believe he was saying it, but maybe Dev was right. If you loved someone you had to let them go, and he loved Lauren. Deeply. Intensely. And he would rather see her walk away, knowing that she loved him for it, than she stayed and hated or resented him instead.

Poppy Evans had given birth to a baby girl. It was Christmas Eve and Lauren and Oliver were shaking Dylan's hand, congratulating him, glad for him.

'Her name's Belle and she's beautiful.'

'We're so happy for you, Dylan,' Oliver said.

'I forgot to ask. Any news on Kayley? And the baby?'

'The baby's fine, but they're going to try and wake Kayley today. The swelling in her brain has gone down, her intercranial pressure has normalised. They think it's the right time.'

'Let me know how it goes.' Dylan gave them both a quick hug. 'Gotta go. Take care, guys, and all the best.'

'Thanks.'

'Thank you.' Lauren and Oliver headed towards Kayley's room. She'd been put on a neurological ward and they had to get the lift to that floor, but they were both nervous about the outcome of the day. Would Kayley have any deficits? The neuro team didn't think so, but the brain was a mysterious organ still and no doctor could one hundred percent say whether she would be totally fine or not.

'Everything's going to be fine. Everything's going to go well,' Oliver muttered.

'We don't know that,' she said evenly, not wanting to get her hopes up.

'We have to believe that it will. It's Christmas. Good things happen at Christmas.'

'It's only Christmas Eve.'

'Christmas Eve and it's snowing outside. When

has it last snowed at Christmas? I tell you, it's a time for miracles.'

As they walked down the corridor towards their daughter's room they saw Willow come out of it, crying, dabbing at her eyes and nose with a handkerchief.

'Willow! What's happened?' They rushed towards her and she couldn't speak, just pointed at Kayley's room.

Lauren rushed forward, bursting through the door to see her daughter lying in bed, eyes open, smiling and squeezing the hand of Aaron, who was crying happy tears. 'Kayley!'

They were all crying, all emotional, happily reassuring her that her baby was safe and doing well. She'd bled from her cervix, which had torn slightly in the accident, but the baby's heartbeat was strong and healthy.

'What do you remember of that night?' Lauren asked.

'Not much, thankfully.' Kayley smiled. 'The last thing I remember is Willow telling me that you guys were secretly getting it on.'

Lauren laughed and glanced, red-faced, at Oliver.

'I hope it's true. I hope you're together.' Kayley dozed off then—which was normal, the nurse who'd come into the room at their frantic button-pushing said.

Lauren found herself watching Oliver as they sat around Kayley's bed. Her family were going to be all right. They were all going to be all right. They'd got their Christmas miracle, but was there room for one more? One more miracle that would get her out of this terrible decision she'd been left with?

There was an uncertain future ahead of her and she

needed to decide soon. Mike had been calling, anxious for her decision.

But she knew she needed to talk to Oliver.

CHAPTER SIXTEEN

'I THOUGHT I'D find you here.'

Snow was falling heavily on Hanover Square, delighting the ice-skaters whizzing around on the ice to festive music.

It seemed an age since they'd been here. In reality, it hadn't been that long and yet so much had happened in the meantime.

Oliver turned around and smiled at her. 'I was just thinking.'

'About?' She joined him at the rail and watched the skaters.

'About whether that triple axel was a pipe dream.'

He turned to her and she laughed, expecting something more serious to come out of his mouth. Once again, he had surprised her. Just like he'd surprised her at Kayley's bedside when he'd asked her to meet him here.

'Maybe if you practice?' she suggested, feeling the nerves in her tummy swell as she thought of what she had to ask him. Of what she wanted to say with all of her heart.

'I don't think so. Getting on the ice will only ever remind me of you.'

She looked at him then. Turned fully. Hesitated. The

words were there, waiting to be said, but, once said, she would never be able to take them back. They'd be out there and she'd either be devastated or overjoyed. She truly did not know which.

'Oliver...can we talk?'

'Sure.' He led them away from the rink and over to a snow-covered bench. Behind them rose a giant Christmas tree that glinted and twinkled with lights as Oliver cleared the bench of snow so they could sit down. 'Though I'm not sure I'm ready for whatever you have to say.'

She smiled sadly. Nervously. 'Nor me.'

'Just say it.'

'Do it fast?'

'Rip off that plaster.'

Lauren liked the analogy. Sometimes it was best to do things quickly when you were afraid.

'I've been thinking a lot just lately and I've decided that I'm *not* going to take the job in Edinburgh.'

Oliver let out a breath, as if he'd been punched in the gut. 'You're not?'

'No.'

Why did he look so glum? She thought he'd be overjoyed. It made her faith waver.

'It's my fault, isn't it? I've forced you into staying. Ignore me, Lauren. I'll be okay. You should go if it's what you want.'

'But it's not what *I* want,' she implored. 'I want something else.'

He frowned. 'What is it? Anything. I'll give it to you, if it's within my power.'

She sucked in a breath, those nerves making her feel sick. 'I'm not the same person I was before, Oliver. I'm older. Wiser?' She laughed. 'I have my career here. It can be built here. My family is here. *You're* here.'

He reached for her gloved hands.

'I want to stay with those that I love, and that includes you. I'm in love with you, I've always been in love with you, but I need you to be honest with me right now and you need to tell me if you don't want to try again. But I do. I think we could work now if we make a solid attempt at it. And I mean more than the sex. More than the ice-skating and the skiing and the dinners and the snowman-making. I want to wake up with you every day. Go to sleep with you every night. I want us to be exclusive and I want you to be mine again. But even if you don't want *me*… I'm staying, so you'll just have to get used to seeing me around the place.'

She gave a nervous laugh then, unable to read his face. She used to be able to read him like a book but, like her, he'd changed. Time had done that to both of them.

He lifted her hands to his lips and kissed them. 'You're sure? You're saying all of this because you mean it? Because I'd hate to hold you back. I don't want you to resent me, not again.'

'This is my decision and only my decision. I have nothing to prove to anyone. I'm already a good reconstructive surgeon. This is a good programme and I can learn from the best here, but that's only a small consideration. The majority of my decision is because my heart is here. With Willow, with Kayley, with that baby yet to be born, but mostly it's here because of you. I love you, Oliver Shaw, and if you love me too then maybe one day we can come back and you could try that triple axel.'

He laughed, his head thrown back, exposing his throat,

and then pulled her towards him for a kiss. When they broke apart, breathless and giddy, he looked deeply into her eyes. 'I love you, Lauren Shaw. Will you go out with me?'

Lauren nodded, smiling widely. 'I will. For ever and ever.'

And he kissed her again.

EPILOGUE

Two years later

'PRESENT TIME!'

Oliver called for them all to gather in the living area of the large London flat that he and Lauren had bought together. They'd been able to afford something really nice, spacious and modern and close enough to the hospital so that commuting hadn't become a chore.

Lauren sat by the Christmas tree with Kayley at her side and grandson Zachary being bounced up and down on her knee, giggling with glee. Aaron sat opposite, next to Willow's fiancé, and Willow herself sat cross-legged on the floor.

'Finally, Dad! Come on, old man!' Willow joked, pushing out the pouffe for him to sit on, so they could all be in a nice little circle.

He began to distribute the gifts—pyjama sets, fluffy socks, make-up for the girls, tickets to see shows in the West End, which Kayley and Willow were thrilled with. Aaron got a football kit of his favourite team and Oliver received some books he'd had on his wish list, with some chocolates and a fine bottle of single malt Scotch.

'There is one last present that I didn't put under the

tree, that I wanted to give Lauren in front of everyone,' he said, smiling, feeling nervous, though he was pretty sure what she was going to say.

Their relationship over the last two years had been nothing short of wonderful, but they'd both agreed to not rush into marriage again. Not whilst Lauren was still occasionally going up to Edinburgh by train to consult—a situation that Oliver had encouraged her to do. Why not have everything, the best of both worlds? This way, Lauren got more exposure, more experience plus everything that she wanted here at home, and though he missed her when she'd disappear for a day or two, he always looked forward to her coming back.

Absence certainly made their hearts grow fonder.

But now all that was over he felt the time was right and he'd been thinking about this for a while. He'd consulted with the girls, got their opinions on a stone and shape, carat and cut, and now was the time.

Oliver got down on one knee and pulled a small ring box from his pocket.

Lauren gasped, hands covering her mouth.

'Lauren...you are my world, my everything, and you have made me the happiest man in existence ever since you arrived in my life. I love you so much, Baby Bird, and will you do me the honour of becoming my wife? Again.'

He proffered the box, opening it to reveal a perfect platinum diamond engagement ring.

'Oh, my goodness! Yes! Of course, yes!'

He stood with her and slid it onto her finger, kissing her and hugging her as everyone got to their feet to congratulate them.

Lauren examined the ring on her finger. 'It's beautiful! It's perfect!' She looked up at him. 'As are you.'

'Get a room!' Willow catcalled, making them all laugh.

He couldn't quite believe he was engaged to be married to her once again. But this time he knew with absolute certainty that they'd get it right.

Because time and life had given them both a second chance.

* * * * *

Look out for the next story in the
Christmas North and South quartet
Melting Dr Grumpy's Frozen Heart
by Scarlet Wilson

And if you enjoyed this story,
check out these other great reads
from Louisa Heaton

Finding Forever with the Firefighter
Single Mum's Alaskan Adventure
Bound by Their Pregnancy Surprise

All available now!

MILLS & BOON®

Coming next month

MELTING DR GRUMPY'S FROZEN HEART
Scarlet Wilson

This guy didn't know her background. He didn't know why she was here.

For Skye, cancer research was personal. But she didn't know his background, or what had made him do years of training and decide that oncology was the place he wanted to work. She wasn't here to make an enemy. But from the expression on his face, she was doubting she was making a friend.

She decided to push in another direction. 'You know,' she said breezily, 'I am a huge Christmas fan. You'll learn that over the next few weeks. My favourite movie is The Grinch. I'd hate for people to start calling you that.'

The edges of his mouth hinted upwards and he gave a sigh, as his eyebrows raised. The expression had the hint of a cheeky teenager about it. 'My nickname is Dr Grumpy, and yes, I know that,' he replied in that delicious thick Irish accent.

'And mine is Miss Sunshine,' she replied, holding her hand out to his.

Jay Bannerman didn't even hide the groan that came out his mouth as he shook her hand. 'This is going to be a disaster, isn't it?'

For a second – at least in Skye's head – things froze. She was captured by the man sitting in front of her. Now she'd stopped focusing on everything else she realised just how handsome he was. Discounting the fact that every time he spoke that lilting accent sent a whole host of vibrations down her spine, even if he hadn't opened his mouth, and she'd seen him in a bar, this guy was hot.

Skye didn't mix business with pleasure. She'd never been interested in dating her colleagues.

But at least he was semi-smiling now, and she would take that.

Continue reading

MELTING DR GRUMPY'S FROZEN HEART
Scarlet Wilson

Available next month
millsandboon.co.uk